P9-CSW-288

Queen Victoria's Book of Spells

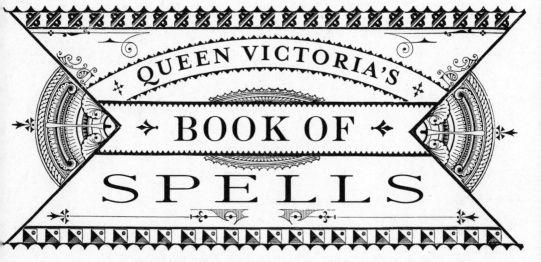

QUEEN VICTORIA'S
BOOK OF
SPELLS

AN ANTHOLOGY *of* GASLAMP FANTASY

Edited by
ELLEN DATLOW
and
TERRI WINDLING

A TOM DOHERTY ASSOCIATES BOOK
NEW YORK

This is a work of fiction. All of the characters, organizations, and events portrayed in these stories are either products of the authors' imaginations or are used fictitiously.

QUEEN VICTORIA'S BOOK OF SPELLS

Edited by Liz Gorinsky

Design by Heather Saunders

A Tor Book
Published by Tom Doherty Associates, LLC
175 Fifth Avenue
New York, NY 10010

www.tor-forge.com

Tor® is a registered trademark of Tom Doherty Associates, LLC.

Library of Congress Cataloging-in-Publication Data

    Queen Victoria's book of spells / edited by Ellen Datlow and Terri Windling.
       p. cm.
    "A Tom Doherty Associates book."
    ISBN 978-0-7653-3226-4 (hardcover)
    ISBN 978-0-7653-3227-1 (trade paperback)
    ISBN 978-1-4299-6091-5 (e-book)
    1. Steampunk fiction, American.   I. Datlow, Ellen editor of compilation.
  II. Windling, Terri editor of compilation.
  PS648.S86Q84 2013
  813'.0876608—dc23

                              2012042624

Tor books may be purchased for educational, business, or promotional use. For information on bulk purchases, please contact Macmillan Corporate and Premium Sales Department at 1-800-221-7945 extension 5442 or write specialmarkets@macmillan.com.

First Edition: March 2013

Printed in the United States of America

0 9 8 7 6 5 4 3 2 1

Copyright Acknowledgments

To the Faery Godmothers of Chagford:
Carol Amos, Elizabeth-Jane Baldry, Hazel Brown,
Wendy Froud, and Marja Lee

Acknowledgments

Many thanks are due to Merrilee Heifetz and Liz Gorinsky. We have long dreamed of creating an anthology like this one, and their help was instrumental in turning that dream into reality.

Contents

PREFACE

by ELLEN DATLOW and TERRI WINDLING

Welcome to *Queen Victoria's Book of Spells*, a book of all-new tales of Gaslamp Fantasy, or stories set in a magical version of nineteenth-century England. Gaslamp tales can take place at any time during the 1800s, from the Regency years early in the century to Queen Victoria's long reign (1837–1901). The stories may occasionally stray into the Edwardian era, but the genre ends with World War I. Although commonly set in England itself, such tales may also unfold in other locations, including Britain's former colonies—especially those where British culture has been, or remains, a dominant force.

Steampunk fiction, which blends nineteenth-century settings with science fiction elements, receives a great deal of popular attention these days, yet it is only one form of the diverse range of fiction that falls under the Gaslamp Fantasy label. You'll also find historical fantasy, dark fantasy with a deliciously gothic bent, romantic tales, detective tales, and "fantasies of manners": magical fiction that owes more to Jane Austen, William Thackeray, and Anthony Trollope than to C. S. Lewis and J. R. R. Tolkien.

Popular works of Gaslamp Fantasy can be found on both the Adult and Young Adult shelves, including *Homunculus* by James P. Blaylock, *A Great and Terrible Beauty* by Libba Bray, *Jonathan Strange & Mr Norrell* by Susanna Clarke, *Mortal Love* by Elizabeth Hand, *The Anubis Gates* by Tim Powers, *The Prestige* by Christopher Priest, *Tooth and Claw* by Jo

Walton, and *Sorcery & Cecelia* by Patricia Wrede and Caroline Stevermer . . . as well as A. S. Byatt's mainstream novel *Possession*, which has more than a little magic around the edges. A longer list of books in this vein is in the back of this book.

Since many excellent Steampunk anthologies already exist, our purpose in creating *Queen Victoria's Book of Spells* was to explore and celebrate the broader genre of Gaslamp Fantasy, encouraging the authors herein to approach our nineteenth-century theme in a wide variety of ways. Some of our writers were inspired by classic nineteenth-century texts; others by historical personages, including Queen Victoria herself, in youth and in old age; still others by diverse aspects of nineteenth-century culture ranging from theatre, science, and politics to fairy lore and spiritualism.

Why, it might be asked, are so many of us in the fantasy field so fascinated by the nineteenth century? Perhaps because the culture of the period was awash in fantasy. As Terri will discuss in more depth in the introduction immediately following this, at no other time and place in Anglo-American history were magical stories so widely read by the general public, or elements of the supernatural so prized. Bestselling works of fantasy literature were published for readers of all ages, "fairy art" hung on the walls of respectable galleries, and a passion for supernatural romance swept through the theatre, ballet, and opera worlds from the 1830s onward. Throughout the nineteenth century, the industrial revolution created enormous societal upheaval, disrupting old rural ways of life and transforming the British countryside in a manner both astonishing and distressing. Fantasy provided both escape from the social pressures caused by rapid urbanization, and a means to address these issues through the metaphoric language of myth and symbolism.

Today, as our own technological revolution causes sweeping societal change and upheaval, many of us turn to fantasy for the same reasons: to escape the modern world. And, perhaps, to understand it just a little bit better when we return.

INTRODUCTION

Fantasy, Magic, and Fairyland in Nineteenth-Century England

by TERRI WINDLING

As the English-theater historian Michael Booth stated in *Victorian Spectacular Theatre, 1850–1910*, "The acceptance and rapid growth of fairyland as a fit subject matter for literature, painting, and the stage from the 1820s to the 1840s and its survival until at least the First World War is one of the most remarkable phenomena of 19th-century culture." In the following pages, I'd like to look a little closer at this fascinating historical phenomena, which bubbles just under the surface of the magical tales gathered in this volume.

The first thing to note about the surge of interest in fairies and fairy tales in nineteenth-century England is that adult interest in these subjects developed late in comparison to continental Europe. Fairy stories for adult readers had been popularized by Italian intellectuals in the sixteenth century, the French avant-garde in the seventeenth century, and the German Romantics in the eighteenth century, but it took until the nineteenth century for the trend to finally catch on in England. The British Isles have always boasted a wonderfully rich oral folklore tradition and are steeped in myth cycles both Arthurian and Celtic; furthermore, English literature rests on works by writers unafraid to dip into this well of magic: Sir Thomas Malory, Geoffrey Chaucer, Edmund Spenser, Christopher Marlowe, and William Shakespeare among them. So why did it take so long for fairy-tale arts to blossom across the Channel?

The answer is religion. British society was governed by Puritan social codes after the Revolution of 1688. Certain art forms were made illegal, while others were effectively discouraged by the culture, fantastical arts among them. English literature of the seventeenth and eighteenth centuries was expected to be serious, rational, Protestant, and deeply moral, while the magical tales of Great Britain's folk heritage were deemed to be crude, perverse, frivolous, lower-class, and uncomfortably pagan. Magic did not entirely disappear from literature: Alexander Pope's *Rape of the Lock* and Jonathan Swift's *Gulliver's Travels* were both popular eighteenth-century texts . . . yet these were satires, poking fun at the conventions of folk and fairy tales; the magic in them was rationalized as allegory and distanced by humour.

Not until the end of the eighteenth century did fantasy, rooted in the folklore tradition, once again begin to cast a spell of enchantment through the works of the English Romantic poets, and mystical artists such as Henry Fuseli and the poet/painter William Blake. Early in the nineteenth century, magical tales and poems by the German Romantics (Johann Wolfgang von Goethe, Johann Ludvig Tieck, Novalis, etc.) were translated and published in English magazines—including "Undine," an enormously popular story by Baron de la Motte Fouqué about a water nymph's love for a mortal knight, which inspired a host of subsequent stories, paintings, and dramatic productions. At the same time, Sir Walter Scott and other antiquarians were busy collecting folk tales and ballads from all across the British Isles, preserving old country lore in a nation that was rapidly urbanizing. Two groundbreaking volumes by Thomas Keightley (*Fairy Mythology*) and Thomas Crofton Croker (*Fairy Legends and Traditions of the South of Ireland*) proved popular among antiquarian scholars and creative artists alike, kicking off an explosion of folklore collections by the Reverend Sabine Baring-Gould, Anna Eliza Bray, Joseph Jacobs, and many others. The word *folklore* itself was coined by the English antiquarian William Thoms in 1846.

Two nineteenth-century continental imports brought magical tales to an even wider audience: *German Popular Stories* by the Brothers Grimm (first published in England in 1823) and *The Fairy Tales of Hans Christian Andersen* (first published in 1846). These popular collections helped make fairy tales, and fantasy in general, more acceptable to Victorian readers . . . for although both books are darker in tone than the simplified Disney fairy tales of today, they were not as dark, sensual, or disturbing as fairy and folk tales from the oral tradition. The Brothers Grimm revised the folk tales they collected to reflect their own Protestant values, and Andersen's Danish fairy tales were unabashedly Christian. Subsequently English fairy-tale books continued this moralizing trend, taming the complexity and moral ambiguity of older fairy stories by turning their heroines into passive, modest, dutiful Victorian girls and their heroes into square-jawed fellows rewarded for their Christian virtues.

Throughout English history we find that when the untamed side of human nature is at its most repressed in polite society, it tends to erupt and express itself in obsessive and subversive forms. Thus, while we generally think of Victorian culture as rigid, pious, and strictly divided into hierarchies of class and gender—all of which is true—it was also a society obsessed by sex (there were more brothels in Victorian London than at any other time in its history); awash in alcohol and narcotics; and rife with subversive political ideas such as socialism and feminism, both of which would dramatically change British culture in the century to come. While respectable Victorian society was as straitlaced as it could possibly be, among young artists and other rebels the nineteenth century was the heyday of British bohemianism, as exemplified by the colorful lives of painters such as Dante Gabriel Rossetti, writers such as Oscar Wilde, aesthetes such as Lady Ottoline Morrell, and culminating in the notorious wine-and-women life of "gypsy painter" Augustus John. When we look at these twin cultural movements—strict morality and wild bohemianism—it is easier to understand another odd aspect of Victorian life, which was a widespread interest in psychic phenomena and the occult.

Spiritualism flourished in all classes of society, right up to the royal court, with "mediums" enabling contact with the spirits of the dead. The fad was started in 1848 in America by the Fox sisters, who claimed to communicate with the dear departed through mysterious knocks upon a table. They took this talent on tour, and other mediums followed suit, bringing American-style Spiritualism to England in 1852. Soon "table-tapping" parties were all the rage, especially among idle, upper-class ladies and the recently bereaved. Spiritualist societies sponsored lecture tours, opened reading rooms, and published newspapers, while mediums developed huge followings.

As the nineteenth century progressed, ghosts, goblins, sylphs, fairies, and other supernatural creatures not only visited parlors rich and poor through séances and Ouija boards, they also populated all areas of visual, literary, and performance art. In fine art, Shakespeare's fairies were reimagined with the aid of newly published folklore texts, inspiring paintings crowded with sprites in detailed natural settings. Richard Dadd, Richard Doyle, Francis Danby, Joseph Noël Paton, John Anster Fitzgerald, Daniel Maclise, Thomas Heatherly, and Eleanor Fortescue-Brickdale were just a few of the artists who created an entire genre of "Victorian fairy art"—a genre that was not marginalized, as fantasy art tends to be today, but was found in prestigious galleries and at Royal Academy exhibitions. These were paintings for adults, not children, and they had subversive qualities. Fitzgerald's fairy imagery, for instance, was often dark and hallucinatory, full of references to opium pipes and medicines. (Opium derivatives, such as laudanum, called "the aspirin of the nineteenth century," were available without prescription in England until 1868 and commonly used for insomnia, headaches, and the pains of menstruation. It may not be an accident that England's twin obsessions with fairies and Spiritualism occurred during the same years when casual opium use was widespread.)*

The fairy fad among Victorian adults must also be viewed in light of the rapid changes wrought by the industrial revolution, as Britain moved from its rural past to its mechanized future. With factories and suburban blight destroying huge tracts of English countryside, fairy paintings and stories were rich in nostalgia for a vanishing way of life. In particular, the art of the Pre-Raphaelite Brotherhood and their followers (Dante Gabriel Rossetti, William Morris, Sir Edward Burne-Jones, John William Waterhouse, Evelyn De Morgan, etc.), which was often based on romance, legend, and myth, promoted a dreamy medievalism and the aesthetics of hand craftsmanship to counter the ugly new world created by modern forms of mass production. ("For every locomotive they build," vowed Edward Burne-Jones, "I shall paint another angel.") The Arts and Crafts movement, which grew out of Pre-Raphaelitism, embraced folklore to such a degree that by the end of the nineteenth century, fairies and other magical creatures were commonly found in middle-class homes in every form of decorative arts: wallpaper, draperies, ceramics, stained glass, metalwork, etc. At

---

* Many fairy paintings were distinctly salacious, such as Paton's huge canvases of luscious fairy maidens in various states of undress. At a time when public expression of sexuality was severely repressed, when medical "experts" proclaimed that respectable women were incapable of sexual pleasure, artists both male and female discovered that sensual scenes were acceptable as long as all their nubile maidens sported gossamer fairy wings.

the dawn of the twentieth century, many lavish new fairy-tale volumes were produced, illustrated by the likes of Arthur Rackham, Edmund Dulac, Kay Nielsen, Jessie M. King, Warwick Goble, Eleanor Vere Boyle, and the Robinson brothers. Not until 1915, however, did the most famous fairy picture of the Victorian/Edwardian age appear in exhibition in London: *The Piper of Dreams* by the English-Italian artist Estella Canziani. Canziani, the daughter of fairy painter Louisa Starr, grew up among the Pre-Raphaelites and studied at the Royal Academy; her work drew on her interest in Italian folklore and peasant traditions. *The Piper of Dreams,* a wistful picture of a country boy surrounded by fairies, was published as a print by the Medici Society and became a runaway bestseller . . . a print as ubiquitous in England then as Monet's water lilies are now. This gentle, forgotten fairy picture was a favourite among English soldiers in the trenches of World War I.

In the pre-television, pre-cinema world of the Victorians, theater, ballet, and opera had greater importance as forms of entertainment than they do today, as well as a greater influence on the visual and literary arts. In the 1830s, the new Romantic ballet (influenced by Romantic art and literature) thrilled large audiences in London with productions that dramatized tales of love between mortals and spirits. Aided by innovations in "point work" (dancing on the points of one's toes) and improvements in theaters' gas-lighting techniques, a sumptuous vision of fairyland was created in hit productions such as *La Sylphide,* the tragic story of a mortal man in love with an elfin maid. In theater, fairy plays were staged with stunningly elaborate special effects, each new production striving to be even more spectacular than the last. Fairy music was another popular phenomenon, much of it imported from Germany. Favourites included Weber's fairy opera *Oberon*, Hoffman's *Ondine* (based on Fouqué's "Undine"), Wagner's *The Fairies,* and Mendelssohn's overture for *A Midsummer Night's Dream.* Fairy music for the harp was composed and performed by charismatic musicians as popular then as pop stars are today; young women swooned and followed their favourite harpists from concert to concert. Magical music and dance reached its height at the end of the nineteenth century in the works of Tchaikovsky, the brilliant Russian composer who took London—and, indeed, all of Europe—by storm with his fantastical ballets: *Swan Lake, The Sleeping Beauty,* and *The Nutcracker.*

⚜

Magical music, dance, drama, and art . . . these things all fused together to create an enchanted atmosphere, inspiring the writers of books that are now considered classics of the fantasy field. Some of these works were written for adults, such as the "imaginary world" novels of William Morris (*The Well at the World's End*), the adult fairy tales of Anne Thackeray Ritchie (*Bluebeard's Keys, and Other Stories*), and the adventure novels of H. Rider Haggard (*She*), as well as the Arthurian poetry of William Morris (*The Defence of Guenevere*) and Alfred, Lord Tennyson (*Idylls of the King*). But one of the major shifts we see in magical literature from the mid-nineteenth century onward is that more and more of it was published in books intended primarily for children.

This shift occurred for two major reasons, despite the fact that adult fascination with fantasy and magic had rarely been so high. First, the Victorians romanticized the idea of childhood to a degree never before seen; earlier, childhood had not been viewed as something quite so separate from adult life. Children, according to this earlier view, came into the world in sin and had to be quickly, strictly civilized into God-fearing members of society. By Victorian times, children had come to be seen as inherently innocent—and childhood was thus a special golden age before the burdens of adulthood.* Just as the "innocence" of the countryside was vanishing due to the industrial revolution, the golden innocence of childhood was doomed to vanish as a child matured. This theme runs through many great works of Victorian fantasy, in which magic is accessible only to children and lost on the threshold of adulthood. From Lewis Carroll's Alice books to J. M. Barrie's *Peter Pan*, Victorian writers grieved that their young, wise heroes would one day grow up.**

The second reason that Victorian publishers produced so many new volumes for children was due to the growth of an English middle class that was both literate and wealthy. There was money to be made by ex-

---

* Our modern notion of childhood as a sheltered time for play and exploration is rooted in these Victorian ideals, although in the nineteenth century they held true only for the upper classes. Most Victorian children still labored long hours in fields and factories, as Charles Dickens portrayed in his fiction, and as he experienced in his own childhood.

** This ideal had a darker side, however, in that some prominent Victorians were a little too interested in children. Lewis Carroll may or may not have been a closet pedophile, but he certainly had an uncomfortable interest in photographing scantily clad little girls; while the great Victorian art critic John Ruskin famously fell in love with an eight-year-old child and constantly pestered the illustrator Kate Greenaway to send him drawings of unclothed "girlies." Kate declined.

ploiting the Victorian love affair with childhood; publishers had found a market, and they needed product with which to fill it. Children's fiction in the previous century had been diabolically dreary, consisting primarily of pious, tedious books full of moral instruction. By the nineteenth century, some educators were still decrying the evils of "immoral" fairy stories, but once the Grimms and Andersen collections proved so popular, English publishers jumped on the fairy-tale bandwagon in increasing numbers. Cheap story material was available to them by plundering the fairy tales of other lands, simplifying them for young readers, then further revising the stories to conform to Victorian gender roles and moral standards. A lot of these fairy-tale volumes, marred by heavy-handed alterations, make abysmal reading today, but some retain enough of the magic of their source material to stand the test of time, such as the famous series edited by Andrew Lang (*The Blue Fairy Book*, *The Green Fairy Book*, *The Red Fairy Book*, etc.).

In addition to retelling traditional fairy tales, the Victorians also created original stories by using the tropes of folklore in innovative ways. From the middle of the century onward, some of the best writers of nineteenth-century England turned their hand to fantasy: John Ruskin (*The King of the Golden River*), Charlotte Yonge (*The History of Tom Thumb*), Christina Rossetti (*Goblin Market*), Charles Kingsley (*The Water-Babies*), Lewis Carroll (*Alice's Adventures in Wonderland*), Jean Ingelow (*Mopsa the Fairy*), Edward Lear (*Nonsense Songs*), George Macdonald (*The Princess and the Goblin*), Mary Louisa Molesworth (*The Tapestry Room*), Mary de Morgan (*The Necklace of Princess Fiorimonde*), Juliana Horatia Ewing (*Old-Fashioned Fairy Tales*), Oscar Wilde (*The Happy Prince and Other Tales*), Ford Madox Ford (*The Queen Who Flew*), Laurence Housman (*House of Joy*), Evelyn Sharp (*The Other Side of the Sun*), Rudyard Kipling (*Puck of Pook's Hill*), J. M. Barrie (*Peter Pan in Kensington Garden*), Edith Nesbit (*The Enchanted Castle*), and Kenneth Grahame (*The Wind in the Willows*).

Chances are that unless you've done more reading than most in the field of Victorian literature, you're probably more familiar with the men on the list above than the women (with the exception of Christina Rossetti and E. Nesbit). As I prepared this introduction, a number of well-read friends asked me if there were *any* female fantasy writers in nineteenth-century England, and the answer is, yes, indeed, there were—writers so popular and financially successful in their day that as a group they incited the envy and approbation of many male colleagues. George Gissing's novel

New Grub Street, for example, published in 1891, paints a vicious portrait of an outspoken woman writer, vain and utterly talentless, who is lionized for her children's fiction while the lives of "real" literary artists fall into ruin all around her.

So if these women were so successful, why are the books by the men above still known and loved by children today while most of those by women are read only by feminist scholars? It's not just gender bias, but also because the tales by nineteenth-century women can make for distinctly uncomfortable reading. Down through the centuries, fairy tales have often been used as a way of speaking in symbolic language about topics at odds with the dominant culture. For Victorian women, it was the totality of their lives at odds with the culture they lived in, hemmed in by nineteenth-century ideals of femininity, duty, and motherhood. Over and over again beneath the surface of magical stories by Victorian women one finds rebellion and *anger*. This is addressed by folklorists Nina Auerbach and U. C. Knoepflmacher in their insightful book *Forbidden Journeys: Fairy Tales and Fantasies by Victorian Women Writers*:

> The most moving Victorian children's books are steeped in longing for unreachable lives. Lewis Carroll, George Macdonald, and J. M. Barrie envied the children they could not be; out of this envy came their painful children's classics. Most Victorian women envied adults rather than children. Whether they were wives and mothers or teachers and governesses, respectable women's lives had as their primary object child care. British law made the link between women and children indelible by denying women independent legal representation. As Frances Power Cobbe pointed out in a witty essay, "Criminals, Idiots, Women, and Minors" were identical in the eyes of the law. In theory, at any rate, women lived the condition Carroll, Macdonald, and Barrie longed for.

Yet in the years when the children's book industry was still new (and before Sigmund Freud and Carl Jung taught us to look at the subtext of fiction more closely), Victorian women had a freedom of expression that was all too rare. As long as their tales conformed outwardly to the conventions of popular children's fiction, they were able to populate their tales with extremely subversive characters and creatures, such as clever, hot-tempered, female fairies, and irascible, intractable heroines.

It was not, however, just the women of England who used the writing of magical tales as a form of social critique, nor were they the only writers who challenged Victorian gender assumptions. As Jack Zipes points out in the introduction to his excellent collection *Victorian Fairy Tales:*

> There is a strong feminine, if not feminist, influence in the writing of both male and female writers. In contrast to the Kunstmärchen tradition in Germany and folklore in general, which were stamped by patriarchal concerns, British writers created strong women characters and place great emphasis on the fusion of female and male qualities and equality between men and women.

Zipes cites George Macdonald's work as an example of Victorian fantasy literature in which boys and girls alike develop qualities of intelligence, courage, and compassion—for magic, in Macdonald's tales, "is nothing else but the realization of the divine creative powers one possesses within oneself."

In *Victorian Fairy Tales,* Zipes divides the magical fiction published from 1860 onward into two groups: the conventional and the utopian. Although a few good writers worked in the conventional mode, such as Jean Ingelow and Mary Louisa Molesworth, on the whole these were forgettable books full of twinkly fairies with butterfly wings and good little boys and girls who caused no disturbance to the status quo. Utopian fantasies, on the other hand, demonstrated (in Zipes's words) "a profound belief in the power of the imagination as a potent force" to change English society, and they were being written by some of the finest writers of the day. Macdonald, Carroll, de Morgan, Ewing, Wilde, Housman, Kipling, Barrie, Nesbit (in her later works), and others created extraordinary tales that were archly critical of Victorian life, promoting the possibility of a better society. The prevalence of fantasy in this mode is explained, as discussed earlier, by looking at the culture that produced it—a society in the grip of great upheaval due to rapid industrialization. Fairies flittered across London stages and nested in bucolic scenes on gallery walls. But outside, the city streets were a long, long way from never-never land, crowded with beggars, cripples, prostitutes (many of them children), and homeless, desperate men and women displaced by the new economy.

While the upper classes charmed themselves with fairy books and dancing nymphs and clapped to bring Tinker Bell back to life, among the lower classes (where the fairy faith still existed in living memory), fairies were seldom viewed as the sweet, little moth-winged creatures of Victorian children's stories; they were still the tricky, capricious, dangerous beings of the oral folk tradition. Throughout the nineteenth century, British newspapers still reported cases of fairy sightings, curses, and abductions. The most famous occurred in 1895 and riveted readers across the nation. This was the murder of Bridget Cleary, a handsome young woman in Ireland who was killed by her husband, family, and neighbours because they thought she was a fairy changeling.

The facts are these: Bridget, a twenty-six-year-old dressmaker, and her husband, Michael, a cooper, lived in a comfortable cottage near her family home in southern Ireland. Bridget fell sick with an undiagnosed illness (it may have been simple pneumonia); within a few days she was feverish, raving, and (according to her husband) no longer looked like herself. When regular medicine did not help, the family called in a "fairy doctor"— for the cottage was located close to a fairy hill, which was deemed bad luck. The fairy doctor stated that the ill woman was actually a fairy changeling and said the real Bridget had been abducted, taken under the hill by the fairies as a consort or a slave. The doctor devised several ordeals designed to make the changeling reveal itself. Bridget was tied to the bed, forced to swallow potions, sprinkled with holy water and urine, swung over the hearth fire, and eventually burned to death by her increasingly desperate husband. Convinced it was a fairy he and Bridget's family and neighbours had killed and buried, Michael then went to the fairy fort to wait for the "real" Bridget to ride out seated on a milk-white horse. Instead, Bridget's disappearance was noted, the body found, the crime brought to life, and Michael and nine others charged and prosecuted for murder.

Although the most flamboyant, this was far from the only case of changeling murder in the Victorian press, although usually the changelings were children, born with physical deformities or struck by sudden illness that caused the child to waste away. A less gruesome but equally famous case unfolded in Yorkshire in 1917, when Elsie Wright, sixteen years old, and Frances Griffith, her ten-year-old cousin, contrived to take photographs of fairies in their garden at Cottingley. Three years later, Elsie's mother attended a Spiritualist lecture by a friend of the prominent

Theosophist Edward Gardner, which led to the photographs being sent to Gardner, and then on to Sir Arthur Conan Doyle (creator of Sherlock Holmes, and son of the fairy painter Charles Doyle).

Although the photographs are rather unconvincing by today's standards (the fairies look one-dimensional, sporting the clothes and bobbed hairstyles of the day), professionals at the time could find no evidence of photographic doctoring. The pictures, championed by Doyle, caused an absolute sensation and brought the fairy craze well into the twentieth century. Only when Elsie and Frances were old ladies (in the 1980s) did they admit that the Cottingley fairies were actually paper cutouts held in place by hatpins. Yet their final deathbed statements on the subject were more ambiguous, implying that the fairies, and one of the photos, may have been real after all.

In her fascinating book *Strange and Secret Peoples: Fairies and Victorian Consciousness*, Carole G. Silver suggests that the Cottingley photos, despite briefly reviving interest in fairies and fairy communication, were actually one of the factors that marked the end of the fairy-art era. "Ironically," she says, "the photographs, the ostensible proof of the actual existence of the fairies, deprived the elfin people of their grandeur and their stature. The theories that Gardner [and other Spiritualists] formulated to explain the fairies' nature and function reduced them to the intelligence level of household pets and the size of insects." In addition to this, the popularity that the fairies had enjoyed throughout the nineteenth century was enough to ensure that they would be branded old-fashioned by generations to come, particularly those whose "innocence" was trampled on by two World Wars.

Various scholars give different dates for the end of England's Golden Age of Fantasy Art, Literature, and Drama—just as folklore postulates different dates for "the flitting of the fairies," which is when, supposedly, the Fair Folk left British shores forever. In 1890, Fiona Macleod wrote that "the Gentle People have no longer a life [in] common with our own. They have gone beyond the grey hills. They dwell in far islands perhaps where the rains of Heaven and the foam of the sea guard their fading secrecies." In his famous poem "Blow, Bugle, Blow," Alfred, Lord Tennyson wrote that even the echoes of elfin bugles were "dying, dying, dying."

And yet, of course, the fairies never die. Despite these waves of departure and farewell, the green hills of the British Isles are still thickly populated by elfin tribes, who seem to be thoroughly enjoying their present revival in popular culture.

When one compares the many social issues common to both the industrial revolution of the nineteenth century and today's new technological revolution (a changing economy, disappearing countryside, conflicting ideas about gender and class), it is no surprise that fairies and fantasy have made such a strong comeback. As Silver notes, "to believe or half-believe in fairies was, by the turn of the century, an expression of revolt against complex urbanized society, so tightly conscious of its manners and morals. Moreover, such a faith was a response to the conflict between society's demand for respectability and conformity and the forces of demonic energy that lie beneath the surface of human nature. Conservatives and radicals alike could find in such belief a cogent criticism of the age."

She was talking about the dawn of the twentieth century, but her words could apply to the dawn of the twenty-first century as well. Magic is thriving once again—in fantasy books and mythic arts, in folk music, in film, in online journals, and in numerous other contemporary art forms. The horns of Elfland still blow, for a whole new generation.

Listen close, and you will hear them.

Queen Victoria's Book of Spells

QUEEN VICTORIA'S BOOK OF SPELLS

I'm in Windsor Castle.

To be exact, I'm in the Round Tower, in the Reading Room of the Royal Archives. It's raining outside—not an astonishing occurrence, given English springs. My feet are wet and will undoubtedly stay wet because the Royal Archives are like a meat locker. The Royal Archivist has an electric fire under her desk and still looks cold.

On the table in front of me lies a stout folio volume, bound in red calf, with *Queen Victoria's Book of Spells* stamped on the cover in gold. Beside it lies a pair of acid-free, white, cotton gloves. As soon as I put them on, I will have begun what my sponsor, Sir Reginald Jolley, calls the Victoria Project.

It's a real plum. Reggie has told me so, numerous times. "There are wizards all over England," he says, "with bloodlines going back generations, dying to get their hands on Victoria's spell book. You should be grateful."

And I might be. If I were a Victorianist. If the project were actually mine.

Slowly, I pull the clownish gloves over my hands and rest my cold fingers lightly on the cover. Through the thin cotton I feel a faint prickling, like a mild electrical charge. My excitement rises, as it does when I discover a new *oratio obscura*.

An *oratio obscura* (the phrase means "hidden word") is a spell that obscures text. It's like a code in that it can be used to hide sensitive information from prying eyes. There are three basic *orationes obscurae*, which, with their respective aperients (revealers), are familiar to any bright schoolchild with access to a spell book. People with more important secrets to hide typically craft their own, personalized variations, giving out the aperients (if at all) on a need-to-know basis. It's possible to create a new aperient for a custom *oratio obscura*, but not easy. They're hard to detect, hard to analyse, hard to unravel.

I'm lucky. I have a talent for it.

I can't take credit for it, really—it's genetic. Both my parents are preternaturally good at finding things. Mom finds tumours in cancer patients. Dad finds oil deposits. I find encoded texts.

I open the book.

The text of Victoria's first diary entry hides nothing but the creamy linen paper it covers. It has been quoted often. But it's different seeing it in the fourteen-year-old princess's own hand:

JUNE 7, 1833

<u>Today</u> is my first lesson in <u>magic</u>. My tutor is Sir Thomas Basingstoke, of the <u>Royal College of Wizards</u>. He is a Professor of <u>Practical Magic</u>. Mamma says a <u>lesser</u> wizard would be sufficient to teach a <u>neophyte</u> her first spells, but <u>he</u> says it is an <u>honour</u> to teach the future <u>Queen of England</u>. He has given me this <u>book</u> for the <u>spells</u> I learn and the <u>theory</u> behind them, as well as any <u>exercises</u> he may give me to <u>strengthen</u> my <u>self-discipline</u>.

The lesson was <u>very odd</u>. He began by asking me to knock a <u>spillikin</u> from a table without touching it, which I did. And he asked me about my <u>dreams</u> and whether I was prone to <u>sleepwalking</u>. Mamma answered that I was not.

Next week we will begin to study magic in <u>earnest</u>, with a spell to <u>light a candle</u>.

I remember lighting my first candle. It was in seventh grade. The spell was in the book of basic spells I'd stolen from my mother's study. It worked the first time I tried it, although I almost set the house on fire. My parents sent me to the Westaway Magic Academy in Amherst. I did well enough to earn a free ride to Harvard, where I majored in thaumaturgy.

I discovered my sensitivity to text junior year at Harvard. I was home for Thanksgiving break, hanging out in Dad's study, when I felt something odd in a letter on my father's desk. It was a business letter, about oil rights, as I recall, from an associate of Dad's, and it burned my fingers. On the off chance this might mean something, I ran a decoding spell over the letter. It was from the business associate, all right, but it was a love letter. A torrid love letter, which made it clear that Dad had been living a double life for years.

That night, when Dad came home, I was waiting for him. Mom heard us arguing, came in to see what the fuss was about, and—well, the cat was out of the bag. It wasn't pretty. Mom and Dad divorced. Dad moved to Amsterdam to be with his lover. I applied to the Master of Thaumaturgy program at York University, which led to my current Junior Research Fellowship in the History of Magic at John Dee College at Cambridge University, under the direction of Sir Reginald Jolley, BT, MT, D'Thau.

Reggie is a jerk. The grants he gets for his fellows are generally more useful to him than they are to the fellows. My current project is a prime example.

Up until recently, Queen Victoria's spell book caused everybody to assume that Victoria's magical education was limited to the candle-lighting and silk-sorting taught to all young women of noble blood. It is little more than a commonplace book of spells and potions copied down from other sources, of interest mostly to biographers and scholars of women's studies. Then Prince Philip, the only royal with a degree in Scientific Magic, ran his newly invented thaumatograph over it and discovered that the T-readings were off-the-charts high.

This fluttered the dovecotes of every Department of Thaumaturgical Study all over England. It is a tribute to Reggie's wheeling-and-dealing skills, as well as the purity of his pedigree (his father is the Earl of Avon), that the grant should come to John Dee. Not to mention the fact that he had a canary to check out the magical mines for him.

That would be me.

Which is why I'm stuck here in the Royal Archives, reading a teenager's exercise book. A royal teenager, granted, but I don't care about that.

Victoria had one two-hour magic lesson a week. With summers off for grand tours through England with her mother and her household, that works out to between thirty and forty entries a year, at a page or more a lesson. In order to get a feel for her personal *oratio obscura*, the way her mind works, the kind of spells she knew how to cast, I have to read them all. In order.

June 22, 1833
(A Receipt for a Potion Against Carriage Sickness.)

Today's lesson was to be summoning a <u>breeze</u>, which is the first lesson in the <u>Mastery of Air</u>. However, as Mamma is planning another tour, I begged Sir T to teach me some small cantrip or spell against carriage sickness, from which I suffer <u>extremely</u>. He gave me the receipt I have writ down above. It is my <u>first potion</u>, and I am <u>eager</u> to try it.

Eager to make a mess, I suspect. I know I was, at that age—although my messes were more likely to explode than to settle the stomach.

My hands are so cold they ache. I cast a very small warming spell. The Royal Archivist shakes her head warningly. I flash her my most charming smile. She does not seem to be charmed. Her eyes are slightly exophthalmic, very good for glaring.

Noon brings me to the end of 1833 and my endurance simultaneously. I find a pub, eat, and warm up. Then it's back to the Royal Icehouse for more schoolgirl exercises. I'm glad to see Victoria's potion seems to have relieved her motion sickness, although it didn't do a thing for the backaches brought on by hours in a jolting carriage. Improved carriage springs—and the smoother roads they ran on—were mechanical breakthroughs, not magical ones. And mechanics, like science, was a skill of the working classes. Magic, in those days, was the sole prerogative of the nobility.

Reggie frequently bemoans (humorously, of course) the passage of the Alchemical Act of 1914, opening the study of English magic to foreigners and commoners. He seems to think that my American blood somehow makes me more foreign than if Mom were French or German. But what he really minds is my father, who may be as English as five o'clock tea, but is also descended from a long line of engineers and fabricators, as black-blooded (the idiom refers to coal) as Reggie is blue-blooded (the idiom refers to haemophilia).

The afternoon wears on. I'm cold and irritated and so impatient to reach the first *oratio obscura*, I almost miss the telltale tingle, like a cell phone vibrating deep in a briefcase. It's pretty faint, but then my hands are freezing. I huff on my fingers, rub them together like a safecracker, and check again. Yep. There it is.

My heart rate goes up. I close my eyes and search for the threads of the spell. It's a variant of the oldest of the basic *orationes obscurae*—simple, elegant, clearly not the work of a girl who has been studying magic for less than a year. Bit by bit, I feel my way into it, and text relaxes under my hands like a Victorian lady released from her corset, revealing the second text that lurks beneath it.

JANUARY 4, 1834
(Text hidden under a Spell for Finding Lost Objects)
Today Sir T (who has a nose like a parrot's beak and smells most pungently of bay rum) taught me a very special spell. Its purpose is to keep anything I write hidden from all eyes save my own. I said I should never wish to write anything Mamma or dear Lehzen might not read. He said he did not doubt that, but that I might well change my mind as I grew older.

The spell is extremely advanced. I am a little anxious lest my casting be clumsy. Were Mamma to discover that I have tried to keep secrets, I shall be writing in my Book of Good Behaviour for hours.

Later: TRIUMPH! Both Sir T and Lehzen have read over my opening words without so much as a conscious look. Lehzen, of course, cannot penetrate the flimsiest illusion. But Sir T is a powerful Wizard—much more powerful than Mamma, who cannot levitate a teacup without slopping its contents into the saucer. In any case, as he did not react to my uncivil (though accurate) description of his nose, I am confident he could not read it!

I like my magic lessons extremely. I only wish I had one every day.

No sooner have I read the entry—the true entry—than the spell snaps back over it.

In the Reading Room of the Royal Archive, it's not the done thing to cheer or even cry "Eureka!" The Archivist would certainly object, might even turf me out, permission from the Royal College of Wizards notwithstanding. I restrict myself to beaming goofily down at the page.

"Dr Ransome?"

I look up. The Archivist is hovering at my elbow, looking stern.

"Yes?"

"The Reading Room closes at five thirty, Dr Ransome."

"Oh, yes, of course. Listen, I've just found something interesting, I wonder if I might—"

"The book will still be here in the morning."

Her round face is stern. I remind myself that it never pays to alienate the support staff. On my way out, I humbly request a table near an outlet for my computer, then retreat to the nearest pub for a celebratory pint.

The Windsor Knot is not my first choice for a watering hole. It's a Victorian theme park of a pub, all horse brasses and tartan carpeting and men in Savile Row suits. But it's near the archive and they brew their own beer. I take my hoppy bitter to a table in a back corner and try to sort out my emotions.

I should be pleased. I *am* pleased. My first day of work, and already I've cracked Victoria's code. From now on, it's just a matter of finding the coded entries and transcribing them. Easy. Mechanical. Boring. Victoria as a girl is rather charming, but I can't forget that she grew up to be the Widow of Windsor, prim, pious, pigheaded, perennially unamused. After all the research I've done on her for this project, I'm forced to admit that she was a better ruler than her grandfather or either of her uncles, but that's hardly a ringing endorsement, given that George III was barking mad, George IV a libertine, and William IV a royal wastrel. And I profoundly disapprove of her support of the Crimean War and her expansionist policies and her championship of the Alien Magic Act of 1862.

You'd think she would have known better, given her ghastly childhood.

From the moment her father, the Duke of Kent, died, when Victoria was eight months old, to the moment she became queen of England at eighteen, her mother and Sir John Conroy, her mother's treasurer and secretary, oversaw every aspect of her life. They developed something they called the Kensington System, after the palace King George IV had given them to live in, designed to keep the young princess safe from infection, accident, and making her own decisions.

Victoria was never to be alone. She spent her days with her governess, the Baroness Lehzen, and her nights in her mother's room. She could not go up or down the stairs without someone holding her hand. She had to record her transgressions in a Book of Good Behaviour and each day's events in a journal. Every word she wrote was read and approved by her mother.

Except, apparently, these.

Limited magical education, my sweet aunt Sally. Clearly, there was more to Our Dear Queen than even the most revisionist historians have imagined. Reggie is going to be delighted. I just wish I didn't feel quite so much like a trained pig, hunting for truffles.

The next morning is clear and brisk. The Reading Room is cold as a tomb. The Royal Archivist, looking like a tiny Michelin Man in a puffy down vest, is up on a ladder with a clipboard. She descends when she sees me and shows me to a table by a narrow window. Icy drafts seep under the wooden frame, but there's a grounded double outlet in easy reach. I wrap my muffler around my neck, set up my computer, and get to work.

At first, Victoria is sparing in her use of the *oratio obscura*. In early July, she encodes a quarrel with her mother; two weeks later, a small trick played on Conroy's daughter Victoria. Then comes something Reggie will love.

SEPTEMBER 12, 1834
(Text hidden under A Receipt for Sorting Embroidery Silks)
C particularly horrid today. I am astonished that Mamma allows herself to be ruled by such a monster. I have heard the Duke of Wellington say that they are lovers, presuming, perhaps that I would not understand his meaning. Well, I do understand, and I think that he is wrong. Primus, I have often heard Mamma remark upon the foulness of C's breath, which does not sound lover-like; Secundus, Mamma retires to bed with me, even when C sleeps at Kensington; Tertius, C is Irish and baseborn and Mamma is a Princess and very proud.

If it weren't for the fact that Sir John Conroy was, by all accounts, vain, controlling, and cruel, I might have some sympathy for him. I've had my own difficulties infiltrating the sacred company of English wizards. Admittedly, I'm also hampered by my politics, which have inspired Reggie to call me a Communist. He has also, at different times, called me a boor (for coming to work in jeans), and an uncultured, bourgeois Yank (pretty much constantly). If I weren't a kind of magical sniffer-dog as well, he'd have found a way to get rid of me by now. As it is, I'm useful. And John Dee College does have the most prestigious Department of Thaumaturgy in the country.

As I turn the page, I wonder just what Victoria understood about lovers and how she came by her information. Frustratingly, she doesn't say.

Days pass. Outside, it's either raining or about to rain—or, occasionally, to sleet: in other words, a typical English spring. The Archivist huddles over her electric fire; I take to wearing thermal underwear. I'm becoming a regular at the Windsor Knot.

Page by hidden page, I watch Victoria learn the basic principles of Elemental Magic. In early 1835, she begins using a new *oratio obscura*. It's simpler than the old one, but it takes me much longer to find my way into it. When I do, I find that she has invented it herself. She uses it to complain about her mother and fantasise about what she'd do to Sir John, if Sir Thomas would only consent to teach her some curses. She's surprisingly inventive, and more than once the Archivist is forced to request that I refrain from laughing.

July 3, 1835
(Text hidden under A Spell to Make Dolls Dance)
Today, I asked Sir T if I might not learn a spell that would allow Dash to walk upon his <u>hind legs</u> and <u>speak sensibly</u>. Sir T looked grave. "There is a cost to such spells, Your Highness," he said. "A dog's legs and back are not designed by <u>Nature</u> to bear him upright, nor his mind for human discourse. He would pay a price of <u>pain</u>, <u>confusion</u>, and possible <u>madness</u>."

When I heard this, I caught my <u>dearest</u> Dashie in my arms and promised, sobbing, that I would <u>never</u>, <u>never</u> cause him as much as a <u>moment's</u> pain. When I was calm again, Sir T taught me a spell to animate my <u>dolls</u>, which amused me extremely. Lehzen, however, finds their wooden capers so <u>distasteful</u> I am determined <u>never</u> to cast it when she is present.

Most wizards wouldn't think twice about turning a spaniel into a miniature courtier, if they knew the spell. Power is heady stuff. I know. Once you've had a little, you want more. I've never met a wizard who didn't have control issues. Look at Reggie. After all, what is magic but the exercise of control over the essentially uncontrollable: nature, physics, logic, free will? A wizard who doesn't, on some level, want to abuse the power magic gives him (or her) isn't a very good wizard.

Victoria, apparently, was a very good wizard. With a conscience, which is a lot rarer. And nobody's wooden dancing doll.

JULY 10, 1835

(Text hidden under a passage on Spells of Influence and Coercion, from
On Political Magic, *by Viscount Mortimer)*

I have been wondering whether C might not have cast a <u>Spell of Co-ercion</u> on Mamma. There is something about the way she <u>never, ever</u> disagrees with him, even when he is <u>wrong</u>. As he himself could not <u>be</u> a wizard, he must have <u>hired</u> a wizard to cast it—a <u>Foreign</u> wizard, for I <u>will not</u> believe an <u>English wizard</u> would so <u>debase</u> himself. I cannot but <u>wonder</u> why he has not had one cast upon <u>me</u>.

I have heard that my Uncle King, when he was Regent, used spells of coercion upon <u>respectable</u> ladies to make them fall in love with him. I find this <u>extremely</u> shocking. I would <u>never</u>, upon <u>any provocation whatsoever</u>, use such a spell. It is <u>wrong</u> to tamper with the free will of <u>any human soul</u>.

I've been wondering myself when Victoria would work out that particular equation. She's bright, but not terribly imaginative. Also a terrible snob. I note, without surprise, that she is incapable of believing that a base-born Irishman would be able to enchant a royal duchess. Commoners don't learn magic. Therefore, commoners can't learn magic. QED.

A year of dealing with Reggie has persuaded me that, the law and all evidence to the contrary, deep down, he believes the same thing. Which is probably why he felt free to cast a coercion spell on me.

It was not long after I'd turned down a flattering offer of an off-campus fling. Not because he's a man, mind you—I've never seen the point of limiting myself to one gender when it comes to lovers. I do, however, limit myself to people I actually fancy. Which is what I told Reggie, with perhaps more force than diplomacy. The episode was unpleasant, but I thought the subject closed.

Until I found myself in Reggie's office, unbuttoning my shirt and wondering how I'd failed to notice before how utterly hot he was. If he'd just sat still, I'd probably have been another notch on his bedpost before I knew what was happening. Because he couldn't wait to get his hands on me, because he stood up, leering and eager, the spell broke.

I left his office even more abruptly than I'd entered, went to the loo, and was sick. Then I washed my face in cold water and got back to work.

Of course I thought about turning him in, but what would that have gotten me? Humiliated, unemployed, with a cloud over my head that would make employment at a first-class institution all but impossible.

It has crossed my mind that this project is Reggie's idea of a fitting punishment for escaping his clutches. If I don't turn up anything useful, so sad, too bad, not all scholars can make the grade, and I'm out on my ear, scrambling for a job teaching survey courses. If I do, he gets lots of lovely data for his next book.

AUGUST 15, 1835

<u>Hateful</u> touring. <u>Hateful, hateful</u> carriages and crowds and having to smile when my head aches and Mamma <u>refusing</u> to believe that I feel unwell, even when I am <u>fainting</u> from weariness. Yet even this <u>endless</u> travel is preferable to Kensington, with C insisting I appoint him my private secretary when I am queen and Mamma <u>insisting</u> that I dismiss <u>dearest</u> Lehzen.

I refused. Lehzen is the <u>only</u> person in the whole of England who loves me for myself alone. And I would rather have an <u>adder</u> or a <u>rat</u> for my secretary than C. He has turned Mamma into a <u>mindless automaton</u>, who smiles when he threatens me and agrees that I am stupid, childish, undutiful, <u>unfit</u> to be Queen. With Lehzen's help, I stand my ground, but I do not scruple to confess that I <u>fear</u> John Conroy as much as I <u>loathe</u> him.

I think about the Duchess of Kent smiling and nodding while Conroy does his methodical best to break her daughter's spirit. It's not exactly news—there are accounts in all the standard biographies of the lengths Conroy went to try to make himself de facto king of England. But seeing it in her own hand makes it more real, more immediate.

The next entry, written during Victoria's convalescence from a bad case of typhoid in September of 1835, is even more infuriating.

NOVEMBER 15, 1835

(Text hidden under a Spell to Change the Colour of Silk Ribbons)

I <u>hate</u> Sir John Conroy. I know this is a <u>sin</u>. But so is it a sin to <u>persecute</u> the <u>sick</u>. While I lay ill almost to the point of <u>death</u>, he read me a letter he had prepared in which I declared myself too young to be Queen and appointed Mamma my Regent and himself my Private Secretary and Personal Treasurer until I am <u>twenty-five years of</u>

age! Then he thrust a pen between my fingers and commanded me to sign it.

I held firm in my refusal, despite his bullying and Mamma's tears and recriminations. My anger strengthened me wonderfully, while Lehzen, with her kind looks, reminded me that I need only endure a little while longer, until my 18th birthday frees me from the threat of a regency.

Sometimes, I hate Mamma hardly less than C. Surely a mother's duty is to comfort and protect her child, not stand by while a monster savages her. I try to remind myself that she is unable to help herself. Still, it is hard to forgive her.

Poor kid, I think. Poor isolated, beleaguered, abused kid. Who, I remind myself, will be crowned queen of England before she turns nineteen. Who will banish Conroy back into obscurity, move Mamma's apartments as far from her own as the endless corridors of Buckingham Palace will allow, marry the love of her life, and live happily—if not ever after, at least for the next twenty years.

Still. She didn't know that when she wrote in her Book of Spells.

I'm lucky. My parents are proud of me. "You're like me," Mom says. "Total dedication to your career!" "Ruthless," Dad says. "A scholar has to be ruthless to get ahead."

I would be delighted to be ruthless. All I need is an opportunity.

The Archivist is beside me. I get the impression she's been there for a while. "Last call," she says.

May 13, 1836

We are over-run with princes!! In March, there was Prince Augustus of Saxe-Coburg-Kohary and his brother Ferdinand; in April, the Princes of Orange. Augustus is good looking and quite clever, although not so handsome as Ferdinand, who is worldly and dances beautifully and kissed my cheek very near my lips. I love him extremely, but he is to marry the Queen of Portugal. The Oranges will not do. In fact, I wonder at anyone thinking that they might. They look like frogs, they dance like frogs, and their hands are damp, even through their gloves.

Uncle Leopold makes no secret of intending me to marry his nephew. He writes so frequently of Dear Albert's beauty, purity, cleverness, and kindness, that I am quite sick of the subject. I shall do my duty, however, and <u>strive</u> to like him—better than the <u>Orange frogs</u>, in any case. I do hope he <u>dances</u>, because there is to be a <u>ball</u> for my 17ᵗʰ birthday, and I intend to be as <u>dissipated</u> as possible.

Reggie's more like a bull than a frog, although he does have damp hands. The thought of him getting the inside scoop on Victoria and Albert's love story is more than a little distasteful. Maybe I won't tell him about it. Maybe I'll just throw in the towel altogether and get a job on a freighter. There's lots of time to read at sea.

May 30, 1836

What can Uncle Leopold be <u>thinking</u>? Albert is <u>impossible</u>. I suppose he is good-looking enough, or will be when he grows out of his spots and into his whiskers. His <u>eyes</u> are quite beautiful. But he is <u>stiff</u> and <u>brusque</u>, <u>blushes</u> when I speak, <u>looks grave</u> when I am merry, turns faint after <u>two dances</u>, and retires at <u>eight</u>. I would a thousand times rather marry his elder brother Ernest, who is <u>much</u> handsomer and more <u>charming</u>—though Uncle Leopold warns me that Ernest is <u>very</u> like my Uncle King, and likely to prove a <u>sad husband</u>.

In truth, I do not wish to marry <u>at all</u>. Yet it seems I will be compelled to do so. Lord Melbourne believes it <u>unnatural</u> for a woman to reign <u>alone</u>, and indeed, I have recently made some <u>very serious</u> errors of judgment that have cost me dearly. Albert is <u>steady</u> and thoughtful as I am not. And I have so <u>few</u> other choices. I have written Uncle Leopold what he wishes to hear and have promised Albert that I will answer any <u>letters</u> he may please to write me. But I am very <u>unhappy</u>. What is the use of being <u>Queen</u> when I may not please <u>myself</u>?

That doesn't sound much like the romance of the century. I wonder what happened. I wonder if she's going to write about it.

I've been here nearly two weeks. The Archivist has relented to the extent of giving me my own electric fire. My greatest disappointment is that Victoria would rather rant about how much she hates Conroy, her mother, and her life than talk about Albert, who she hardly mentions.

On May 26, 1837, she celebrates achieving her majority by inventing a new and more sophisticated *oratio obscura*, which takes me a full day to unravel. "My BIRTHDAY celebration was <u>one in the eye</u> for Mamma and C," she writes, "who were hard-put to pay me the most <u>commonplace</u> compliments of the day." She was now an adult, legally able to rule England in her own right. Unfortunately, it did not make her life significantly easier.

June 15, 1837
(Text hidden under A Spell for Prolonging the Life of Cut Flowers)
Word comes from Windsor that Uncle William is almost certainly on the point of death. Mamma and C have <u>redoubled</u> their efforts to <u>bully</u> me into signing away my <u>rightful</u> authority. I am <u>very</u>, <u>very</u> weary. When I am <u>Queen</u>, I shall be able to <u>speak my mind</u> without <u>fear</u>. Or will I? Is it possible that my <u>crown</u> will prove but another, heavier <u>chain</u> upon my soul? My life here in Kensington is <u>insupportable</u>. Will my life in Buckingham Palace be <u>less</u> so? I do not know, I cannot tell, and I am <u>very afraid</u>.

I comfort myself with the certainty that I shall, at last, have a <u>room</u> of <u>my own</u> and need not show my <u>journal</u> to <u>anyone</u> if I do not wish to. I shall no longer be forced to <u>hide</u> my <u>true thoughts</u> in my Book of Spells. And yet I find I cannot contemplate abandoning it, any more than I can abandon <u>Dash</u> or <u>Lehzen</u> or my <u>dolls</u>.

This book holds the <u>heart</u> of a princess. Surely it may hold the heart of a <u>QUEEN</u>.

Victoria was young, so very young. Smarter than she thought she was, arrogant and insecure, with a strong sense of duty and a trusting nature scabbed over by repeated betrayals. I haven't changed my opinion about hereditary monarchs, but nobody can say Victoria didn't try to be a good one.

The next entry is dated October 11, 1839.

I check to see if pages have been torn out. They haven't. Apparently, Victoria overstated her devotion to her spell book, if not to her spaniel or her governess. It's interesting, though, that she should return to it the day after Albert comes to visit her for the second time.

(Text hidden under A Spell to Settle a Nervous Stomach)
I cannot <u>think</u> what is wrong with me. When I am with HIM, I feel quite <u>clumsy</u>. When by chance HIS hand brushes mine, my heart <u>pounds</u> so I am almost <u>suffocated</u>. Last night, I was visited by <u>dreams</u>

that confused me <u>extremely</u>, and yet, upon waking, I longed to dream again. He is <u>very</u> beautiful, with his eyes like limpid pools and his mouth so grave and sweet, and his strong, broad shoulders. I <u>love</u> him so <u>extremely</u> that it quite <u>frightens</u> me.

But what if <u>HE</u> does not love <u>me</u>? He is so calm, so <u>moderate</u>! And I am so passionate, so <u>headstrong</u>! I yearn to <u>kiss</u> him, to feel his arms around my body, but dare not. He <u>says</u> he loves me, but I fear lest the <u>violence</u> of <u>my</u> love <u>frighten</u> and <u>disgust</u> him.

I know he will be a good and conformable husband to me, for he is very <u>dutiful</u>. Is it wrong of me to desire his <u>love</u> as well? I am Queen of England, but it will mean <u>nothing</u> if I cannot be Queen of <u>AL-BERT'S</u> heart.

At this point, I am much less surprised by Victoria's passion than she is. She's always had it in her—all her heavy underlines, her violent hates and her no less violent enthusiasms, her sensual delight in music and dancing and food, indicate that she's more like her Uncle King George IV than she knows. And yet there's something there that's more than lust, something that reads very much like real love.

I've never felt like that. Oh, I have had affairs, but love scares me. Mom and Dad loved each other, and they made each other miserable. Dad couldn't bear being tied down; Mom couldn't bear secrets and silences. The battleground of their marriage has left me with a fear of commitment and a perfect horror of manipulation and power games.

Victoria, who had even more pressing reasons to fear love than I do, clearly overcame them. Knowing the story has a happy ending, at least for her, I give an indulgent chuckle and turn the page.

October 13 is a short entry, hidden under a simple spell to keep domestic animals off the furniture: "He <u>must</u> love me. He <u>shall</u> love me. My plans are laid. I will go <u>tonight</u>."

And then, nothing.

Well, nothing I can read, anyway. When I touch the entry dated October 15, I can feel the resonance of the *oratio obscura* clear to my teeth. But the obscuring knot is denser and more complex than anything I've ever seen before. I can't even tell which spell it's based on.

My first reaction is pure, unadulterated fury. Things were going along so smoothly—Victoria would come up with a new variation on her familiar theme, I'd unravel it. We were growing more sophisticated together. Why would she spring something like this on me?

In the back of my mind, my internalized Reggie Jolley chuckles nastily, "Because you're a muck-common Yankee with ideas above your station and Victoria was queen of England, that's why."

"Shut up, Reggie," I mutter.

The Archivist looks up from her work, startled. "Sorry? Did you say something?"

"I'm going to lunch."

At the Windsor Knot, I order a pint of bitter and a packet of crisps. I don't usually drink at lunch, but this is an emergency.

Oddly enough, I'm not mad at Victoria, who was just preserving her privacy, and effectively, too. If I've learned nothing else in the past two weeks, I've learned that she was a first-rate practical wizard.

Well, I'm not a bad practical wizard myself. And the thoroughness with which she's locked this entry has got to mean that the mysterious plans mentioned on October 13 are startling indeed.

I *must* decode this entry. I *will* decode this entry.

I go back to the Royal Archives, exchange nods with the Archivist, and set to work.

Day after chill, dreary day, I commune with Victoria's spell, analysing, tweaking, picking at its component threads. Lunch is a sandwich in the cloakroom. Sleep is a luxury I can't afford. I've never seen a working like this before: seven separately structured spells, cast at intervals, woven into an all-but-impenetrable barrier. I haven't had so much fun since I unravelled my first personalized *oratio obscura*.

Sunday night, after I hang up after talking to Dad, my cell phone rings. It's Reggie.

There's no use ignoring it. I'm going to have to talk to him sooner or later.

"Hello, Reggie."

"Ransome," he says, all hearty bonhomie. "How's it coming?"

"Fine."

"Why haven't you checked in? It's been a fortnight."

"I've been busy. There's a lot of material to get through."

"Good," he says. "I look forward to your getting a preliminary report. Shall we say Tuesday?"

"Are you still there?" I say. "Sorry. I seem to have lost you."

After that, I leave my mobile off.

It takes me seven solid days to untangle the spell. By the time I come up with an aperient that looks as if it should work, I'm almost too tired to cast it. But I can't possibly wait until tomorrow to find out if it works. I suck back a cup of tarry tea in the staff canteen, come back upstairs, and cast the spell before I can lose my nerve.

The long, dull treatise on the permissible uses of magic in diplomacy falls away, revealing a heavily underlined scrawl.

Victoria always underlines a great deal when she's upset.

OCTOBER 15, 1839

I am <u>inexpressibly</u> weary. Today, I have broken the <u>law</u>. I have betrayed <u>everything dear</u>, <u>dear</u> Lehzen and <u>dear</u> Sir T have taught me. Though I value truth extremely, I have lied and lied.

The first lie was a <u>small</u> one: I informed Lord Melbourne I desired to learn about the <u>poorer boroughs</u> of London. He said that only <u>very low</u> folk lived there, and I told him, quite in <u>Mamma's</u> own manner, that I hoped I was <u>their</u> Queen as well. Which is not <u>precisely</u> a lie, for I <u>do</u> concern myself with the welfare of even the <u>most wretched</u> of my subjects, among whom the cunning folk of <u>Greymalkin Lane</u> and its environs must certainly be numbered.

I <u>blush</u> to remember the lies I told so that I might go to London. Suffice it to say that by 1/2 after 11, I was in a common <u>hansom</u>, disguised in a plain cloak. <u>Alone</u>, although for once I did not wish to be, for I possess no <u>friend</u>—not even Lehzen—I would trust not to betray me. Trust, no less than Truth, is a <u>luxury a Queen</u> cannot often <u>afford</u>.

Greymalkin Lane is a <u>horrid</u> place, <u>narrow</u> and <u>foul</u>, haunted with <u>shadows</u> that cough and spit and jeer. Having seen it with my own eyes, I shall never again be able to read Mr Dickens's <u>Witch Lane</u> with pleasure—although it did teach me the sign I must look for: a <u>card</u>, marked with a <u>heart</u> and a <u>dagger</u>.

After <u>much</u> anxious searching, I saw such a card, stuck up in a window. The name on the card was "Madame Rusalka."

The lady who answered my ring was as foreign as her *nom de <u>magie</u>*, with high, flat cheeks and a bright shawl embroidered with flowers. She led me into a small, shabby parlour, and once I had made her understand what I sought, left me, returning with a <u>phial</u> made of polished stone. "I sell this only because I am <u>poor</u>," she said in strangely accented English. "Please to remember, should you <u>regret</u> what you do." Struck by the <u>intensity</u> of her manner, I wept and assured her that I <u>would</u> remember. Then I begged her to fetch me a hansom (for I was still <u>sadly distressed</u>) and reached Buckingham Palace just before dawn.

The cost of the philtre was <u>30 shillings</u>.

Today, I am <u>extremely</u> weary. When I am rested, I shall return to Windsor and <u>take tea</u> with my <u>dearest</u> Albert. Then I shall ask him to <u>marry me</u>.

[The page ends with a note, dated ten years later:] <u>I have devised a sevenfold oratio obscura. Heaven grant it will keep my words safe from all eyes but mine.</u>

The spell snaps shut as I reach the last line. If it weren't for the cold sweat prickling my armpits and the pounding in my ears, I'd think I'd fallen asleep and dreamed it. But I didn't. Victoria, twenty years old, popularly supposed to be sheltered, truthful, and as emotionally naïve as her spaniel, had slipped Prince Albert a love Mickey.

Reggie's going to bust his buttons over this. He might even decide to let bygones be bygones and let me get back to my beloved Elizabethans.

It's great material, after all. The articles will write themselves: "Queen Victoria's Secret Journals: A Study in Domestic Tyranny"; "The Sevenfold *Oratio Obscura:* Queen Victoria's Superspell."

Only one more entry left in the Book of Spells, also locked sevenfold. It's dated May 20, 1841, some six months after the birth of the princess royal. The covering text is a receipt for an ointment to soothe teething pains.

I have come to realise that I have made a <u>TERRIBLE MISTAKE</u>. <u>Whoever</u> or <u>whatever</u> Albert might have been without my intervention, I will <u>never know</u>. Dearly as I love him, I see him <u>very</u> seldom, for it is only when I am <u>not</u> present that he can be his own <u>dear self</u>. In my presence, he becomes the creature of <u>Madame Rusalka's spell</u>, without a thought in his head but how he may <u>please</u> me. What a <u>fool</u> I was to think I would <u>like</u> a husband who always <u>agreed</u> with me. The reality is <u>terrifying</u>. And how can I <u>trust</u> a love that springs

I try to turn the page, but there's nothing to turn. I've reached the end of the book.

"Damn!"

"Shhhh," the Archivist hisses.

I look around the Reading Room. She and I are alone. "Why are you bloody shushing me?" I demand. "I'm the only person bloody here."

Her round face flushes. "I am here as well, and I am not accustomed to being sworn at."

I get a grip on my temper. None of this is her fault. In fact, she's been helpful, hunting up magic texts for me to consult. "Sorry. I've had a bit of a shock. The Book of Spells breaks off in the middle of a very interesting sentence. Is there another volume?"

"There was," she says primly. "At least, we think there must have been. But either Princess Beatrice burned it with the rest of Victoria's original journals, or it's been misplaced somewhere. I'm sorry."

I shut my teeth against all the things I'd like to say, but shouldn't. After a long pause, I settle for, "Oh. Oh, dear."

She looks amused. "Quite. I do, however, seem to remember a folder that no one's sure where to file. It has some loose sheets in it, written in the queen's hand. Would you be interested in seeing it?"

Hope springs, painful and shaky, in my heart. "I very well might."

A long half hour later, she drops an acid-free file folder in front of me, hesitates, then goes back to her desk.

Hands shaking, I go through the papers carefully. The one that sears my fingers is, of course, on the bottom, by which time I'm so exhausted that I can hardly cast the aperient.

from <u>Magic</u> and not from the <u>Heart</u>? I <u>cannot</u> bear it. I cannot bear myself. I have deliberately <u>enslaved</u> Albert—I, who strove so <u>passionately</u> against Conroy's attempts to enslave me. Truly, I am <u>well punished</u>. For in <u>forcing</u> my darling to love me, I have not only robbed <u>him</u> of <u>himself</u>, but <u>myself</u> of his <u>unbiased</u> advice. Reading his <u>dear</u> letters, written in the years of our separation, I am struck anew with his <u>wisdom</u>, his <u>deep knowledge</u> of history. All, all <u>lost</u> to me, through my own <u>great folly</u>!

I have resolved to make what <u>reparation</u> I may. First, I will bend <u>all my energies</u> to the discovery of a spell or potion to counteract Madame Rusalka's <u>cursed</u> brew. I will give my darling <u>responsibilities</u> in which I have no part. I shall encourage him to voice his <u>true opinions</u>, and <u>defer</u> to him, as a good wife <u>ought</u>, subduing my own <u>unhappy</u> nature. It is my <u>greatest fear</u> that, left <u>unchecked</u>, I shall grow to be a Monster <u>of self-regard</u>, like Conroy—without <u>compassion</u>, without <u>humility</u>, without <u>grace</u>.

Should I succeed in breaking the chains with which I have imprisoned my <u>darling</u>, I may again find some measure of <u>happiness</u> in the company of one who will always be as an Angel to me.

As I read, my excitement gives way to nausea.

It's like uncovering Dad's letter all over again, only worse. Much worse. That only blew up three private lives. This is going to cause a complete re-evaluation of Victoria and her reign. These entries add a whole new dimension to Victoria's character and throw every biography of her into instant obsolescence. She's going to be called a slut, a hypocrite, the biggest fraud to dishonour the English throne since Charles II.

I have to tell Reggie. I can't tell Reggie.

He'll call a press conference, give Lady Antonia Fraser a run for her money. He'll publish articles and books, go on TV. He'll take poor Victoria's dirty laundry and wave it around in public, pointing out the significance of each ugly stain.

And if I don't tell him? Well, I won't perish, though my academic career is likely to. Reggie will find some way of cutting my fellowship short that makes it impossible for me to get another one. On the other hand, I'll never wake up in the middle of the night worrying that I was turning into Reggie. And I won't feel as if I were nineteen again, watching my mother cry because I couldn't keep my nose out of other people's business. I might even feel as if, this time, I've done the decent thing.

Over the three weeks it has taken me to read, decode, and transcribe Victoria's Book of Spells, I've grown fond of her. Not because I identify with her—good Lord, no. I'm not sentimental over animals, and Italian opera bores me almost as much as politics and paperwork. And not because I feel sorry for her, either. I haven't lost sight of the fact that she was pig-headed, self-righteous, arrogant, and made a number of very bad decisions, the consequences of which England is still suffering. But she did try to be good, she really did. God knows she didn't succeed, but at least she tried. And when she failed, she tried to fix it.

I bury my head in my hands. After a moment, I hear footsteps, feel a featherlight touch on my shoulder. "I say, are you all right?"

I give what I mean to be a sardonic laugh. It comes out as more of a sob. "No. I'm not all right."

"Did you not find what you were looking for?"

I sit up and look at the Royal Archivist. Her face is a plump oval, her nose long and straight, her brows narrow and knitted with concern. "No, I found the missing page—and thank you, by the way, for remembering that file. It's just—" I shrug helplessly.

She bites her lip. "Look here. It's nearly five, and you look like you could use a drink. Come to the pub and I'll tell you nasty stories about Reggie."

"You know *Reggie*?"

"My brother knew him at Harrow. He calls him the Jolly Roger."

I snort.

She grins like a mischievous schoolgirl. "Come on then."

Her name, oddly enough, is Victoria. The Honourable Victoria Pendennis. She's a specialist in restorative magic and stasis spells. She's also a thoroughly nice woman. I tell her everything.

When I've finished, she goes to get another round. When she comes back with my pint and her single malt, she says, "The situation is not as dire as you think it is, you know."

"Isn't it?"

"No. There's no reason not to give Reggie the early entries. They're new material and they're genuinely useful."

I shake my head. "Reggie's never going to believe there's nothing hidden under the last two entries. They're too obviously placeholders."

"Tell him you can't make them out, then. He'll get to feel superior, and you'll have a chance to work on something more to your taste. You can always go back and publish them later, if you change your mind."

"Why would I do that?"

Victoria smiles. It's a slightly wistful smile, but that could just be the way her mouth is shaped—a true Cupid's bow, with a full lower lip. "Because you'll realise that sooner or later, somebody's going to publish them. And it should be someone who really loves and understands her."

I have no answer to that, so we finish our drinks in silence. As we leave the pub, I ask Victoria if she's hungry. She says she is and asks if I like curry. I say I do.

It's one of those April nights that feels more like late May. Even though it's half past seven, the sky is still light. Victoria tucks her hand into my arm as we walk past a drift of daffodils blooming in an iron-fenced square. I unzip my leather jacket. Spring is really here.

About "Queen Victoria's Book of Spells"

The Victorians have always fascinated me. There's something about their combination of extreme formality and extreme reck-lessness, their generosity and greed, their curiosity and close-mindedness, their creativity and their conformity, and their pure, raw (often misguided) energy that I love. And there was no one, no one who embodied all the good and evil in Victorian culture, society, and politics like Victoria herself. In old age, she calcified into an almost Dickensian caricature, controlling, insensitive, and insular. But as a young girl, she was brave and strong and curious—and cruelly isolated. I wanted to write about that girl. And magic, of course, because I've been playing with the idea of a Britain ruled by a Council of Wizards ever since I wrote "The Parwat Ruby" in 1999. And scholarship, because I've always been conflicted about Victoria's daughter Princess Beatrice's decision to burn her mother's diaries after she'd copied out the parts she judged fit for publication. Victoria had so little privacy in her life, it feels as if she ought to be able to retain the little she could carve out for herself. And yet, and yet.

JEFFREY FORD

The Fairy Enterprise

Once upon a time, prior to the mastication of mill gears, the clang and hellfire of factories, before smog and black snow, fairies grew up naturally from out of the earth, out of the bodies of the dead, and found life again in one of the four elements. They gambolled invisibly but oft enough appeared as lovely women or tiny men or a demon come to lead you astray.

Their boons and curses were a thread of magic in our lives. It was just the old world's way of showing us its dreams. But fairies can't survive on soot and fetid water. Cold iron is murder to them. Manufacture drove them away, to the desolate places, where, eventually, the miasma of commerce found them and cast its deadly spell.

From the street to the palace, the fall of the Fairy Realm was roundly lamented, all the while industry spread like the cholera. Where others saw an unavoidable tragedy, though, and looked away, Mr Hollis Lackland Bennett, a man of a peculiar nature and vast capital, saw opportunity. It came to him on a carriage ride one mid-December night. The wind was frigid and the driving, black snow gave the streets a grimly festive appearance.

When leaving the industrialists' soirée at Thrashner's mansion, Bennett gave orders to his shivering driver, Jib, who held the carriage door. "Take the long way home, old man, I need a rest." It was said of Bennett that his mind was steady as the movement of a watch but one whose gears were greased to speed ahead of the thoughts of others. He found it diffi-cult to sleep at night. Only while the wheels of the carriage turned, pull-ing him ever forward, was he content to lay aside his ambition for a few hours. Sleep for Bennett was utter darkness, he never dreamed.

Wrapped in a bearskin throw, he leaned into the corner of the carriage and closed his eyes. For a few moments he was aware of the sounds of the wheels on cobblestones, Jib's chattering teeth, the murmur of the wind, the hard snow pelting the window he leaned upon . . . and then he wasn't. Sometime later, he woke suddenly and sat forward. Rubbing his eyes, he ducked his head to look out the window and immediately realized they were passing Milner's Bakery. Then he noticed, only for a flashing instant, a tiny white figure of a man, no bigger than a finger, ice-skating horizon-tally across the place's windowpane, leaving a gleaming streak in his wake.

Before Bennett could register his amazement, the scene was out of sight, the carriage moving on. He banged three times on the ceiling with his walk-ing stick, a signal to Jib to now head directly home. Bennett's mind was sprinting forward toward the assumption that the strange sight was merely an optical illusion caused by the snow blowing through the light of the streetlamp until somewhere in its course it tripped and fell into a memory.

He was in his childhood bed, the counterpane pulled up to his chin. The elm outside the open window rustled, and a soft breeze blew in to gut-ter the candle flame. His mother sat back in the rocker, and like every night, when she returned late from the mill, she told him stories. If he woke early enough before dawn, he might find her gaunt figure, like a ghost in the moonlight, asleep in the chair. The gleaming creature he'd seen on the baker's window was like something from one of her tales.

The memory of his mother faded into a memory from the gathering earlier that evening, at Thrashner's. Binsel, the butler, freshened every one's brandy, and the conversation turned to predictions of the next devel-opment in the bounding evolution of industry. Cottard spoke of electric-ity and the experiments of Edison. Dodin resurrected the spectre of Malthus before suggesting that a factory-like approach to thinning the herds of the poor might catch on with the moneyed set. The economic theories of Mills and Carey made the rounds until Thrashner laughed aloud. "Bollocks to all that rubbish," he said. "It's simple. Ask yourselves, 'What is it people want?' People with money, that is."

The vision of the fairy, the two odd memories, seeped and mingled together behind Bennett's eyes. Perspiration on his moustache, a prickling of his scalp, were definite signs forecasting a brainstorm. His mind sped to meet it. When the carriage finally came to a halt outside Whitethorn Hall, he looked up to see the sun shining. Jib had driven in circles all night through the storm. Upon disembarking the carriage, Bennett discovered his man frozen solid, icicles hanging from the eyes and nostrils, the ends of the hair. It was the horses who had eventually brought them home. He petted their snouts and, taking a last look at Jib, whispered, "A pity, old boy," then went in to warm up.

After a nap, a bit of lamb stew, and a bath, Bennett, wearing his yellow silk lounging attire, settled down at the desk in his study with a pot of tea by his side. He lifted his pen and began to jot down the plans for his new factory. He worked all afternoon and was only disturbed once, by his butler, Jennings, who approached to inform him that Jib could not be buried, the ground was frozen.

"Put him in one of those old whiskey barrels, sprinkle some kerosene on him, and torch the blighter," said Bennett impatiently. In a second, he was back to work.

Jennings cleared his throat and timidly asked, "And what, sir, should we tell his family?"

"Good question," said the master of the house, and looked out the window. "Send them three farthings and my condolences." The pen went back to the paper.

He was finished work for the day, sitting by the window, with a glass of port and his pipe. Through the twilight, he could make out Jennings and son, rolling a barrel into the courtyard. This was set upright on the snow-covered walk. Next they passed his view carrying the pale Jib, stiffened in the posture of the driver's box. Bennett heard a terrible crack as they shoved the corpse into the barrel. Then Jennings's boy had the kerosene and Jennings had the matches.

A moment later, Bennett was outside, in only his slippers and billowing yellow silk, waving his walking stick and directing the immolation of Jib. "Don't be cheap with the kerosene, boy," said the master. For the lad's trouble, he slapped him across the backs of his thighs with the stick. "Three matches at once, you dolt," Bennett yelled at Jennings. The butler threw the lit matches and there was a sudden puff of flame. A few minutes later, Jib began smouldering. "Good Lord, he smells like the queen's own turd," cried Bennett.

"Quite," said Jennings, whose son nodded.

More cans of kerosene were called for, and when Jennings threw the matches this time, there was a great whoosh of flame reaching eight feet into the night. It quickly settled down to merely a steady fire, and the three of them moved closer to it for warmth. They each stared into the burning barrel at where Jib's left leg jutted up. The ankle turned black, the old shoe melted. Suddenly there was a great pop, and Bennett jumped back a step.

"That'd be the head popping. Right, Pa?" said the boy.

"For certain," said Jennings. "Now watch for the libban." He and his son stood leaning forward in anticipation.

"What are we looking for?" asked Bennett.

"A certain spark that always flies up when the skull cracks in the heat. The libban. The other sparks die out just above you, but this one stays lit, no matter how high or far it goes. As long as you can see it, it burns. From the soft core of the nut," said Jennings, and knocked twice on his forehead with his knuckle.

"There now!" said the boy, and pointed up.

Bennett cocked back his head and caught sight of the so-called libban. He watched for a long while as the winter wind carried it high away over the dark silhouette of treetops.

"Like a soul?" he asked, still staring into the distance.

"Like a seed," said Jennings.

"From a will-o'-the-wisp," said Jennings's son as if reciting.

The master wondered just how many bodies the boy had seen burned.

For the remainder of the winter and well into spring, Bennett applied himself as a student of the vanished Fairy Realm. He spent a small fortune on books, most of them ancient, their yellowed pages crumbling to dust once read and turned. The gears of his mind became tarred with fairy lore and the mechanism slowed to a crawl. He was struck by long bouts of lassitude and imagination. These creatures that were the object of his scrutiny were elusive, and understanding came to him only in glimpses. He persevered, though, through long hours, pots of tea and pipes, and eventually reached a point where his natural disdain for the fanciful turned to admiration and respect.

The natural settings of the tales and histories he consumed made him long for a journey to the forest. So, in the early days of May, he set out in the carriage—his new driver, the Jennings boy—and headed south, away from the city, toward a small village, Ilferin, on the edge of the wild.

Enormous stones stood in a meadow nearby. A steady stream of fairy sightings had poured forth from the place, down through the ages.

They found lodging at the Inn of the Green Dog, Bennett renting out the entire second floor of rooms, young Jennings getting a tattered blanket and a half bushel of hay in a corner of the stable. Mr Yallerin, the owner of the establishment, was delighted to have Mr Bennett and Mr Bennett's money staying beneath his roof. Over a welcoming glass of spirits on the front porch, the industrialist asked his host where he might find someone who could speak to the local fairy lore. Yallerin rubbed his bald pate, drew on his pipe, and said, "We call her the crone, just for a laugh, of course. They say she's over a hundred. Lives out past the meadow in an ancient stone cottage next to the stream."

"And you," said Bennett, "have you seen the good folk in your years here?"

"As a scamp, I saw them once," said the innkeeper. "My grandpa was laid out for burial in the sitting room of our house. His box, lid off, rested atop two sawhorses next to the hearth. I woke in the middle of the night from a frightener in which the old man called to me. I crawled out of bed, lit a candle, and crept out to where he lay. I didn't want to, but I did hold the candle high to see one last time his death expression. Shock, sir, shock and zero to the bone when I discovered a half dozen tiny, violet men with pointed heads perched upon his forehead, cheekbones, and chin, using long-handled spades to dig out his eyeballs. Only for a moment before the candle blew out, and then I fell through the dark."

"His eyes?" asked Bennett, and he took a small notebook and pencil from his jacket.

"The next morning, I found myself in bed. When I went out into the sitting room, the lid was on the box and my ma and pa were crying."

"Did they explain?"

"I knew not to speak of it."

"What did it mean, their taking his eyes?"

"Mr Bennett, even a brilliant gentleman such as yourself can never know the ways of the fairies. They seem to us crazy as a mad woman's poo."

The industrialist jotted down *mad woman's poo*.

The next morning, after a hardy breakfast of bacon and potatoes for the master and a dry biscuit and a hunk of cold fat for his driver, the two set out on foot. The sun was warm, the sky was blue, and a breeze was coming out of the forest, carrying the scent of blooming life. Bennett had had a suit of clothes made for this very occasion—a jacket and trousers, a shirt and vest—all the same colour of grass. He swung his walking stick and whistled. The boy ran to keep up with him.

They set out across the meadow. At the centre of the rings of silent sentinels, there stood a thin, ten-foot-high, pointed stone, like a crooked finger, accusing the sky. Here Bennett stopped and put his arms around the crude obelisk. Young Jennings watched as his employer touched his lips against the hard rock. When he was finished, he wiped his mouth and told the boy to do as he had done. The lad stood wide-eyed, unable to move. Bennett employed the stick. "Kiss it good," he commanded. "Hug it tight."

When the boy completed his duty, his master inquired, "So, did you feel the enchantment?"

"I don't know, sir."

"You're a chip off your father's blockhead," said Bennett.

"I should hope so, sir."

Across the meadow, at the tree line, they found a path that led in amid the Wych elms and ashes. Sunlight dappled the forest floor as the leaves rustled. Bennett breathed deeply, taking in the heady green fizz of nature. Before long, they came upon a brook, and the sound of the water moving swiftly over the rocks reminded him of his mother's voice when, with eyes closed, she'd continue to murmur her tales from the other side of sleep.

At the brook they turned west as instructed by Mr Yallerin of the Green Dog, and before long, they came upon a small clearing inhabited by a trio of deer. "Be gone, demons," said Bennett, and swung his stick over his head. The gentle creatures fled, clearing a pathway to the stone cottage. Smoke issued from the chimney, a grumbled song from the open window. Just before reaching the steps to the door of the place, the industrialist put his hand on the boy's shoulder and stayed him. "Take this," Bennett said, a silver derringer in his hand. "It's loaded. Remain outside here and keep an eye. If I call for help, you must rush to my assistance. Should the necessity arise, you'll be ready to shoot?"

The boy took the gun and put it in his coat pocket. "Yes."

"There's hope for you, Jennings," said Bennett, and took the steps. He knocked. There was movement inside, then the door slowly opened. A squat, old woman with white hair and large forearms appeared. Her simple grey dress was much mended, her kindly smile was a grimace. "You're the gentleman about the fairies," she said in a gruff voice. "I had word you were coming."

The hair on her pointed chin was disconcertingly long, and it took Bennett a moment to focus. "From whom?"

She turned slowly and retreated back into the place. He followed her inside and shut the door behind him. There was a large room at the front of the cottage, and they settled down at a table by its window. A steaming pot of tea, cups, and saucers awaited them. She lit her clay pipe and moved it to the side of her mouth. "Name, sir," she said, squinting at him.

"Hollis Lackland Bennett."

"Tima Loorie." She nodded.

"I heard it said in the village that you're over a hundred."

"Are you a gullible man, Mr Bennett?"

"Not usually."

"Then there's no reason to begin now. Give me your hand," she demanded.

He reluctantly offered it to her.

She squeezed his wrist with a powerful grip and turned it so his palm was facing her. "I see you're a self-made man," she said. "Come from the salt and now a king of factories. Wealthy. When you sleep, unbeknown to yourself, you call out in the dark. Always the same word."

"Progress?" He smiled.

She shook her head. "You're not to know."

"All right then," said Bennett. "Tell me something else. I want you to tell me where fairies come from."

"They come from wherever they are."

"No. What is the process by which they're created? Do you understand?"

"I might."

"I intend to manufacture fairies. I want to make the household fairies, the ones that help with chores and play mischievous fun on their adopted families. There's a need for them in the city. Playthings for the wealthy, helpmates for the poor."

"A fairy's a living thing," she said. "These aren't brass hinges we're discussing."

"I've done my research. I know they won't thrive in an environment of iron and smoke. My plan is for an organic process, beginning with the libban."

Tima Loorie laughed loud, flashing her one tooth. "You're barmy, Mr Bennett. A fairy factory?"

"I'm also wealthy enough to make you wealthy as well. I've brought a substantial amount of capital with me, and it is now locked away in the safe at the Green Dog."

"How much of the filthy soft have you brought?" She poured him a cup of tea.

"Two hundred pounds, if you have the answer I'm looking for," he said and took a sip.

"Drink up and I'll take you to a fairy circle. It'll be easier to explain."

He finished his tea and they left the cottage. As they moved into the trees, the boy followed them. Tima turned to Bennett and said, "The boy can't go."

"Jennings, there, is my protection."

"From a hundred-year-old woman?"

"Go back and guard the cottage," he said to the boy.

Tima was none too fast on her feet, but she inched ever deeper into the forest. It seemed that the dial of the day moved with the speed of Bennett's mind, passing them. It seemed they went far but walked little. As they strode through morning and afternoon, she spoke intermittently, dispensing fairy knowledge. He jotted it all down in his notebook.

"The fairies you spoke of—household fairies, hobs, goblins—they're of the earth, a mix of dirt and the freed crux of a corpse's being. This seed sprouts into the fruiting body. Like here," she said and pointed at the ground.

Bennett looked away from his notes. It was late afternoon and the forest was filling with shadow. They stood on a particularly shaded by-way, beneath a giant oak. He followed Tima's direction and looked down to see a circle of strange mushrooms growing out of the forest floor. They were pale like a toad's belly with brown spots, and their heads were large, fleshy globes. He watched as Tima bent over and picked one of them. She handed it to him. "Glasfearballas, they're called." He took it from her.

"A fairy factory," she said.

In the dim light of the path, it appeared to him that something was moving inside the globe of the mushroom. He brought it closer for a better look, and with a whisper, it suddenly burst open, spewing a black powder at his face. In an instant, he lost his balance and dropped to his knees, coughing. When he blinked to clear his eyes, he went blind. "Help me," he managed to choke out .

"There is no money in the safe at the Green Dog, is there?" he heard her say. "Be honest or I'll let you die."

He shook his head and began to drool uncontrollably.

"For that, you shall have your wish."

Bennett managed one more strangled "Help," and a moment after there was a loud bang. His sight returned at once and he found himself sitting at the table in Tima Loorie's cottage. It was late morning. The door was open and the boy stood in the entrance holding the derringer aimed forward. A trail of smoke issued from the short barrel of the gun.

"How did I get back here?" Bennett said to Jennings.

"You never left, sir. A few minutes went by and you called for help. I come through the door, sir, and this rabbit I shot come running at me."

"A rabbit?" said Bennett. He stood and moved around from behind the table to see the boy's kill. A large, grey rabbit lay on the floor with a trickle of blood coming from its blasted face. "Where's the crone?"

"She must have gone out the back," said Jennings.

"She put something in the tea, no doubt, the hag." Bennett reached for his jacket pocket and retrieved his notebook. Opening it, he frantically flipped through the pages and found he'd recorded every word Tima Loorie had spoken on their journey through the dream day. He snapped shut the book. "I've got it," he said. "Well done," said the boy. By that afternoon, they were in the carriage, heading back toward the city.

A fter his journey to the wild, the master of Whitethorn secreted himself away for months, only to emerge in late August for a business meeting with Thrashner. Bennett had the collateral for the factory, but he needed Thrashner's powerful connections both political and local to make its construction move at the rapid pace he desired. The meeting took place on the gruff, old industrialist's veranda, beneath the summer stars. Bennett arrived promptly at seven. The night was stifling save for an occasional breeze rolling through the back gardens.

"All right, Bennett," said Thrashner when both men were seated, "you know I don't like a lot of dither. Cut through and let's get to the meat of it."

"I aim to construct a new type of factory, and I need you to help me grease the palm of government so I don't get tripped up by deeds and inspections. My plan would also benefit from the availability of some of your private work crews."

"Not impossible, by any means," said Thrashner. "But what are you making and what's in it for me?"

"What I'll be making is fairies."

"Did you say fairies?"

"You asked the question at the industrialist's soirée, months ago, 'What do people want?' I've determined they want fairies."

"I'm not a good man for a joke, Bennett. I'd have thought you'd known that by now."

"No joke. I've studied the process. It starts with fresh corpses."

"Bennett, are you having some sort of episode of hysterics? You look pale."

"Fresh corpses, not left to lie past the dawn following their moment of demise. We need the heads."

Thrashner's eyes widened. He smoothed his moustache. "Corpses! Where does one acquire corpses for manufacture?"

"Believe me, sir, deals can be made with the morgues, etc. Out of a sense of morality, so that all's on the up-and-up, we'd only use those without close kin. The lonely dead."

"So your factory will run on the remains of the lonely dead?"

"No, we will burn their heads to release the libban, which we will gather through a vacuum sitting at the vaulted ceiling of the libban silo."

"Libban?" asked Thrashner.

"The soul or seed of the dead. A kernel of life that flies off once the head pops open in a fire."

"I believe I may have heard the term."

"Of course you have," said Bennett. "The libban are gathered up at the top of the silo and then pushed through a tube into a chamber where they are blasted with the powdered dirt of the earth. This mix of spirit and dust is then spewed out across the fruiting vats of the factory, wherein will grow large, globe-headed mushrooms. When they succeed to a certain plumpness, these fungi will burst and fairies will be born."

"You've gone round the bend, Bennet. You're completely off your chump."

"We use the dirt because we're making hobs and goblins, brownies, household fairies that help with chores. It's not that people need fairies, Thrashner, it's that they want them."

"Even if you could make them, how do you intend to sell them?" The old man laughed at himself for not having thrown Bennett out.

"When they burst forth from the mushrooms, they're invisible—the natural fairy state. Then comes my secret technique of gathering them up and capturing them individually in coloured glass balls. These are sold to the public, and they are instructed to take them home and smash them on the kitchen floor, which will release the hobs into their homes."

Thrashner leaned across the table that separated them. He facetiously whispered, "What is the secret?"

Bennett also leaned in. "The secret is, there are no fairies."

"You mean you're selling humbug?" Thrashner smiled from ear to ear.

Bennett nodded. "That's why the process must be both gruesome and a tad mysterious. The better the show on that end, the more empty glass balls we can sell to the hopeful."

"A moment ago, I was certain you were mad, but now I'm certain you're a genius."

"We'll need a good artist. The advertisements will be important. Once we fill every house with a hob, we'll start turning out sylphs. I've envisioned a demon that I'm sure will catch on with those who consider themselves naughty. The sceptics, of course, will scowl, but I predict it will be all the rage.

"The factory will cost money, as will the fruiting vats and the mushrooms. I thought we'd make the latter out of rubber and paint them. Have two or three automated ones that burst and spew black powder on cue. We'll give tours of the factory once a week and charge a few coins. A hoax the customer will long to have perpetrated upon him."

"The appearance of industry and yet the manufacture of nothing," said Thrashner, closing his eyes in delight.

By the time Bennett left Thrashner's veranda, he had the old man's agreement of political and labor support but also a promise of cash for a share in the enterprise. After a year of work, Bennett's scheme was beginning to take shape. He felt so good, he gave an order to the Jennings lad to troll the city streets for a pretty, young dolly-mop for hire. "Be courteous, boy," Bennett reminded the driver. "We must respect how these women have turned themselves into factories."

Down by the waterfront, the carriage slowed to a crawl. Bennett slid back the glass of the window and leaned out. Up ahead a few feet, standing to the side of the cobblestone lane beneath a dim gas lamp, was a young woman with her blond hair in barley curls. He quickly checked the condition of her clothing, which let him know how long she'd been on the street plying her trade. When he decided he could live with their degree of shabbiness, he said, "Young miss, would you like a ride?"

"Where will you take me?" she asked.

He noticed she was wearing boots without socks, and this put him off, but her face was lovely. "I'm inviting you to my mansion to drink champagne and to celebrate."

"A party?"

"Of course," said Bennett and did his best to smile. "Come now."

She nodded and stepped toward the carriage. Jennings held the horses still for her to get in. As the girl was getting situated on the bench next to Bennett, he banged on the ceiling of the cab five times to indicate to the driver to go as fast as possible. "What's your name, miss?" Bennett said. The horses lurched forward and threw the passengers together. Gas lamps seemed to fly past the windows, and the racket of the wheels on the stones was hellish.

"My name is Tima Loorie."

"What?" Bennett put his hand behind his ear to hear her better.

She pulled him to her and brought her face close to his as if expecting a kiss. Bennett acquiesced and opened his mouth in preparation. He waited for her lips to touch his, then she spit directly into his mouth. He was paralysed with astonishment, and before he could utter a groan, he felt the thing slide down his throat with the heft of an oyster, tasting of bile and rot.

"Tima Loorie," she shouted.

This time he heard her and lunged, brandishing the stick, but with one graceful move she opened the carriage door and leaped out. Bennett managed to close the door and bang on the ceiling once for Jennings to stop. When the horses came to a halt, he called up to the boy, "Head slowly back the way we've come. The fool girl jumped out. We need to find her."

"Yes, sir."

"And, Jennings, have you got the derringer?"

"In my pocket and loaded."

They drove slowly back along the streets they'd galloped through but saw no one. Eventually, Bennett had to satisfy himself with the idea that the carriage was moving so fast that she'd no doubt broken her neck in the fall. He finally signalled for Jennings to head back to Whitethorn. The moment he got into his study, he downed three quick glasses of whiskey in hopes it might kill the witch's scurvy spit he could feel swimming in his stomach. That night he needed no further driving in the carriage to sleep. He fell into utter darkness, fully clothed, in the chair by the window.

He woke late the next morning, unusual for him, yet still felt exhausted. Using a hand mirror, he gazed upon the dark circles surrounding his eyes, his pale complexion. His gut was in a turmoil, and every time he thought back to the spit, he grew nauseous. He went to his bedchamber and got beneath the counterpane, pulling it up to his chin. Farting and shivering, he closed his eyes and tried to sleep, but the phrase "fruiting body" repeated in his thoughts in the voice of Tima Loorie. At noon, the elder Jennings came in to deliver a message that had just been brought by Thrashner's man, Binsel.

> *My good Bennett,*
> *I've been up and at work early today on the Fairy enterprise. Drinks at my place this afternoon at 3:00 with Lord Smith. He'll take our money in the long run, but he'll want us to grovel a bit in his presence. We can't do anything without him on board. I've invited a few others so as not to make the scene too awkward.*
>
> > *Your Partner in Manufacture,*
> > *Thrashner*

Bennett needed both Jennings and Jennings to pull him out of bed and get him into his formal attire. He said little but belched profusely, and the father and son, one on each arm, led him to the carriage. In the fresh air, he felt a bit better and managed to get into his seat by himself.

"Shall I accompany you?" asked the elder Jennings.

"Don't be a fool. The boy will take me."

Only moments after pulling away from Whitethorn, Bennett grew worse, with waves of nausea and difficulty breathing through his nose. He pulled out a handkerchief and blew. For a moment, it felt as if he were bleeding, and he looked into the folded handkerchief to check. What he found there wasn't the red stain he'd feared, but a tiny green man, struggling to be free. The creature scurried across the expanse of material and then leaped to Bennett's knee. He felt the thing land and brought his fist down, but too late. It had already hopped into the shadows below. For over a quarter mile, Bennett stamped his feet around the floor hoping to crush the thing he'd convinced himself was an insect.

The affair at Thrashner's was crowded with important people, who no doubt sensed palm greasing in the offing. Bennett struggled from room to room, meeting the highwaymen of the aristocracy. The most difficult thing for him was smiling. His guts were twisting like a pinwheel, and the sweat was pouring off him. Before he'd yet run into Thrashner, Bensil handed him a brandy and introduced him to Lord and Lady Smith.

Bennett knew he needed to rise to the occasion, so he stretched his smile another agonizing jot and took a sip of his drink to seem debonair. "A pleasure to meet you both," he said. The brandy set fire to his insides.

"Likewise," said Lord Smith, a stately man whose eyes barely opened. "Lady Smith and I would like you to do us a courtesy, if you would. To the gathering today my dear lady has brought a new dish she has invented. She's a culinary expert, of course, you know. In the French tradition. She'd like you to have a taste and give her your unmitigated opinion."

Bennett looked to Lady Smith and bowed slightly, for the first time noticing the platter she held in her arms. The aroma struck him, and he felt the saliva coursing to the corners of his mouth. He knew he dared not look, but he did. Slices of grey meat in what appeared a dishwater sauce. Breathing deeply, he managed to regain a modicum of composure.

"Orange goose," she said. Her outfit, to Bennett, made her look like some kind of circus performer. The sparkle of her diamonds prevented him from seeing any more of her. She stabbed a slice of goose with a long, thin silver fork and held it up to his mouth.

Lord Smith looked on, smiling. Thrashner suddenly appeared behind the lord and gave a quick hand motion and a wink to convey the message *Eat it and like it*. Bennett closed his eyes and opened his mouth. He couldn't help a slight gag when it touched his tongue. Slowly he chewed it as it seemed every guest looked on. The goose was tough as gristle. It became evident during that eternity of chewing that he'd need a visit to the crapper posthaste. Through clenched teeth, he announced, "Delicious," then excused himself for a moment.

He could have thrashed Thrashner with his stick, he was so angry with him. "No wonder Lord Smith's smile had no sign of pleasure," he grumbled, scuttling down a long hallway. One thing he could say for his business partner, though, he had the state of the art in toilets. Bennett locked the door, hung up his jacket, undid his trousers, and settled onto the bowl. He was breathing heavily and his heart was racing. At times the dizziness swirled toward a blackout and then pulled back. He leaned forward and strained to free the beast. Trickles of sweat fell from his forehead. As they tumbled through the air, they became tiny blue women, who landed in a crouch on his bare knees and then sprang away onto the floor.

He cried and his tears became fairies that he brushed away into flight. A belch became a will-o'-the-wisp, glowing as it issued from the cave of his open mouth. He felt them crawling from his ears, down his cheeks to his shoulders. Then turmoil below, and a riotous gang of goblins clawed their way out of his quivering hindquarters with a cumulative birth shriek. He heard them laughing and swimming in the water beneath him.

Jennings was sitting on the driver's box when Bennett appeared from behind a hedge. One quick glance and the boy leaped down and caught his tipping employer by the sleeve of his jacket.

"What's wrong, sir? You look horrible."

"I shat a populace."

"Yes, sir."

"Get me home, lad."

As soon as Jennings managed to get him in the carriage and start on the way, Bennett felt their pointy heads poking up through the pores of his skin, like a living, writhing beard. He whimpered as they bored and poured out of him from every conceivable egress. It was as if his body were turning inside out, and the agony of it was mythic. He beat himself all over and clawed at his own face. Then he felt the spades dig in at the corners of his eyes and the light failed.

Back at Whitethorn, when young Jennings opened the door of the carriage, he saw no fairies, though during the ride Bennett had manufactured thousands. A strong, sulphurous breeze blew out of the box, and behind it sat the master's corpse, desiccated, full of holes, the sockets empty. The boy ran to the house to get his father.

It's said that Bennett's fairies spread out around the city and multiplied. They weren't the good ones that he'd intended to produce but were ones who thrived in soot and took energy from iron. They found homes in all of the myriad factories and worked their enchantment to cause accidents, sabotage machinery, create explosions, set fires, and generally gum up the works. They were responsible for more than one industrialist, of his own volition, leaping into a smokestack.

As for Bennett, Jennings and his son found an old whiskey barrel and rolled it into the courtyard. They didn't spare the kerosene. When the elder threw the three matches, a pillar of fire shot up into the night. Eventually the flames settled down and the skull popped. Jennings retired just passed midnight, but the boy sat alone by the barrel and waited for the libban until the dawn revealed a smoking heap of ashes and bones.

About "The Fairy Enterprise"

"The Fairy Enterprise" is an attempt to combine two of the most iconic phenomena of nineteenth-century Great Britain—the industrial revolution and the fairy. I pictured those big, old gear-work machines stamping out identical pieces, and then my mind wandered to what a factory that makes fairies might look like. That Bennett comes up with a product that is nothing but hype is reminiscent of the great huckster P. T. Barnum, whose autobiography sold more copies than the Bible at certain times in the nineteenth century.

Also, I thought that products that were nothing but a promise and a lot of advertising were not so different from many of the items in hot demand at stores and on the Internet today. These items can only be purchased by a class of people who were created by the type of work that large-scale manufacture gave rise to. And so the cycle continues.

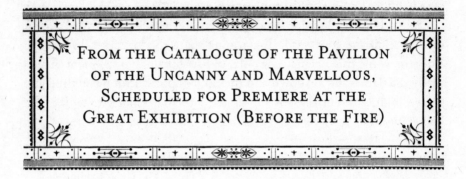

FROM THE CATALOGUE OF THE PAVILION
OF THE UNCANNY AND MARVELLOUS,
SCHEDULED FOR PREMIERE AT THE
GREAT EXHIBITION (BEFORE THE FIRE)

> It may be called a bazaar or a fair, but it is such a bazaar or fair as
> Eastern genii might have created. It seems as if only magic could
> have gathered this mass of wealth from all the ends of the earth—as
> if none but supernatural hands could have arranged it this, with
> such a blaze and contrast of colours and marvellous power of effect.
> **—from Charlotte Brontë's letters, 1851**

London's Great Exhibition more than lived up to its name, providing nearly 100,000 exhibits' worth of spectacle, at a price the public could afford, from an Empire that had by then reached heretofore unimaginable levels of expansion and technological advancement.

It also stands as a confluence of two of the era's strangest bedfellows: its passion for intellectualism, and its unquenchable thirst for spectacle. It was an era that idolized the gentleman scientist even as it queued for the grotesque and the fraudulent.

Perhaps the most obvious marriage of these two attitudes was in the visibility of non-Western cultures (most under the banner of the voracious Empire), whose displays of "exotic" offerings provided the trappings of science with the thrill of the fair.

By then, the Crown had more spoils than could be displayed at once, and many of the items offered to the Exhibition were never displayed. Many of these pieces exist today in the Victoria and Albert Museum (a watered-down replica of the colony-maker's might).

Among the Exhibition's many achievements (the most lasting of which were the ephemeral successes of public perception), it was a triumph of finance. The only true material losses to the Crown during the Exhibition were China's decision not to participate (solved by buying out an importer's inventory and leaving the public unaware of the slight), and the fire that consumed the Pavilion of the Uncanny and Marvellous.

Even with these losses, however, the Exhibition turned enough profit to finance construction of the Victoria and Albert Museum itself.

—Sarah Powers, "Opiate of the Masses: The Great Exhibition and
Its Legacy in England," *Journal of Victorian Studies*, 1984

BY AUTHORITY OF THE ROYAL COMMISSION
OFFICIAL CATALOGUE
Of
THE PAVILION OF THE UNCANNY AND MARVELLOUS
Presented as a Special Attraction at the
GREAT EXHIBITION
Of the works of
INDUSTRY OF ALL NATIONS
1851

"[ ] therefore as a stranger give it welcome.
[ ] are more things in heaven and earth, Horatio,
[ ]an are dreamt of in your philosophy."

[ ] ONDON:
[   ] Brothers, Printers

—handwritten cover craft of the catalogue, Victoria and
Albert Museum Archives (fire damage in brackets)

---

14 JANUARY 1851
Have hired two young ladies at the suggestion of the Commission—
Mary Hammond, Rose Smith—to assist in compilation of the

Catalg–s [sic]. Miss Smith shows promise—meticulous in her work—
but Miss Hammond—can only recommend penmanship and punctu-
ality. Still—in this city one must take such as can be found.

—from the diaries of Alfred York, Undersecretary to the Commission

———

The Biddenden Maids [Germany]—Pair of "Siam-ese" conjoined twins fas-
tened from the shoulder through the torso by supernatural means. Several
surgeries have been attempted, but none has yet severed them. Taken from
a pagan mother and christened Eve and Mary, the Maids remain wards of
the German state and appear in this exhibition with the greatest caution,
as their heritage and the spell that binds them suggests the influence of
witchcraft. As such, the Biddenden Maids should not be viewed by any
ladies in a delicate state, or the very young.

The Scythian [Greece]—Authentic mermaid specimen, a scientific discovery of a most unusual kind. After many hoaxes and fabrications, the
true mermaid is presented after due scrutiny of scientific minds. With the
head and torso of an ill-favoured woman and a lower half of slimy scales,
this mermaid is thought to be a direct descendent of the line feared by the
ancient Greeks. It is of vicious nature, and ruthless in its attempts to escape captivity; this hunting trophy is a gift from Greece to Her Majesty's
exhibition. Though displayed in silhouette and intact to the general public, as a medical lesson the mermaid is bisected laterally to allow examination of its singular anatomy. Academic viewings may be arranged at the
Exhibition Committee's offices.

———

Walter Goodall, a London artist, was hired by the commission to paint
watercolours of Exhibition highlights. Designed to be "snapshots" of the
event, they were actually painted before the opening, as some of the exhibits
he depicts were unfinished—the howdah in the India Pavilion, for example,
was painted *sans* the taxidermy elephant on which it would be displayed.

Many of these watercolours were made available as lithographs in *Rec-
ollections of the Great Exhibition;* though not all survived, the extant watercolours give a fascinating glimpse into the Exhibition itself.

—introductory card from "Impressions of the Great Exhibition,"
Victoria and Albert Museum

March 27, 1851

My Dear Ed,

Since the Commission asked me to paint these watercolours, I have chanced to see some of the workings of such an endeavour, and how each thing is decided. Never again shall I make complaint about the processes of the Royal Academy—very unfortunate, as that was my favourite pastime.

In the offices there are a vast number of very busy persons cataloguing the contents for this Pavilion and that one, making sure each piece of rope is accounted for. You would not believe the quantities of rope that will be on display in Hyde Park this summer. Thankfully I am tasked with painting their more majestic offerings. The howdah made for Her Majesty is truly a wonder.

The Pavilion of the Uncanny and Marvellous, which I understand has half a dozen or so live elements that must be present, is to be painted last. There is a Miss Hammond assigned to assist me—I feel quite the professor—though she seems solemn as a nun whenever the Pavilion is mentioned. Suspect it must be grim stuff. Let us pray it is not a display of insects—my least favourite of God's creatures.

Give my love to Mother.

Your Very Affectionate Brother,
Walter

Some of the most telling developments of the Exhibition were those that changed *in situ* to reflect the difference between the initial grand design and the eventual compromise that formed the Exhibition itself. The most famous of these is the arched atrium in the centre of the Exhibition hall that is now considered to be an architectural focal point, but was in fact added as an afterthought to preserve the large trees around which the Exhibition itself was built. There were several such obstacles that had to be overcome for the Exhibition to be successfully staged.

The Pavilion of the Uncanny and Marvellous, which was to stand alongside the scientific displays in the British Wing, and can still be seen in Paxton's initial sketches, was not present when the doors were opened to the final exhibition, and would have provided an interesting barometer to the limits of public interest.

The Exhibition as a whole had several draws (such as the Austrian perfume fountain which guests could sample *gratis*) that gave attendees a sense of being treated to something unique. Conversely, this Pavilion would have charged an extra shilling admittance.

The Committee's archives record this price differential as an attempt to underwrite "the many expenditures and dangers undertaken to provide the Crown with the exhibits to be displayed," though one wonders if, surrounded by so many other marvels, there would have been much appeal to part with another shilling.

Whatever the attractions might have been, the plan was moot; the fire (mere weeks before the Exhibition was scheduled to open) erased the planned displays, and no attempt was made by the Exhibition's organisers to provide an official inventory of what had been lost.

Perhaps this is due to the fact that, prior to the Exhibition's opening, it came under widespread scrutiny, and was primed in public opinion to be a disastrous expenditure; in this atmosphere, an entire Pavilion going up in smoke would have been an opportunity no newspaperman could have resisted. (It is likely that those who saw it were paid for their silence, perhaps with a reminder how close the Exhibition was to the Queen's heart, and the duty of a good subject to keep his counsel.)

—**from "Opiate of the Masses"**

---

2 APRIL 1851

Work on the Catalg-s [sic] shall take remainder of the spring. HRH the Prince has requested early inventory of British wing—to examine number and kind of machinery on display. Suspect French display at fault. Miss Smith seems equal to the task—excellent notes from all quarters.

Miss Hammond taking dictation from the Secretary for the Uncanny and Marvellous as exhibits arrive and are classified—she seems soured of it all but her penmanship second to none. Will postpone presentation to HRH until satisfied—this is the Crown.

—**from the diaries of Alfred York**

Osiris [Egypt]—From the heart of this desert country comes a beautiful deaf-mute, given the name Osiris by his people, whose seizures were regarded by those of his own tribe to be communion with the ancient gods. English doctors have determined his seizures are of a medical nature, though Osiris provides an excellent opportunity to study the connection between nature and the supernatural that may have been eliminated forever from more advanced minds, and experimentation continues to determine if there is, indeed, some spiritual force at work. Osiris has been put under the care of a physician familiar with the very latest in electric current treatment, and his seizures are examined by spectrograph as they occur throughout his hours of display, each day of the week from eleven o'clock in the morning until four o'clock in the afternoon.

On the Bonny Sweet Hills of Kilkenny [Ireland]—A tableau of the Fey, taxidermied in the finest style. Exclusive to the Exhibition, the fairy folk have never before been seen outside the Isle that is their native land. Eight examples of this species have been carefully preserved as they were found down to the smallest detail, dressed in Classical costume, and set in a garden scene that recreates some of Ireland's most beautiful flora. This rare prey has been procured at great risk for the wonder and enjoyment of Her Majesty's subjects.

You will behold there A MONUMENT OF NATIONAL GREATNESS. Britain, viewed in her insular situation and her geographical dimensions, is amongst the least of all the nations of the earth. Her own immediate territories of England, Scotland, and Ireland, are, comparatively speaking, of very limited extent.

What are we in relation to France, Austria, Russia, or America? A mere speck in the bosom of the ocean deep; yet the sea is our strong rampart, our chosen element, and our undisputed empire; and great indeed is Britain, by the confession of every tongue.

—**from "Sermons on the Great Exhibition," the Reverend George Clayton, York St. Chapel, Walworth, 1851**

---

10 April 1851

My Dear Ed,
The Committee would not be pleased to know I am writing this. I hope you shall handle this letter accordingly once you have read it.

I have seen some of the Pavilion of the Uncanny and Marvellous. It is troubling in a way I dare not say—if India has refrained from displaying living things at their exhibit, surely England might, but this is even worse. There is grotesquery here that does no credit to the Crown.

When I told Miss Hammond, she seemed pleased in the way a gravekeeper is pleased, and said, "Would that others felt the same as you about what's happening here, sir," and I find myself agreeing. There really is no wonder she looks so sepulchral.

She has an odd face—I did not think her very pretty when I met her first, but now I am thinking I should like to sketch her. You might, too, if you liked women as much as you like birds.

Give my love to Mother.

Your Very Affectionate Brother,
Walter

———

The Martyr-Bird (Gallicolumba sanctus) [Italy]—This rare specimen, a species properly identified only in this year of Her Majesty's reign, was previously dismissed as Papist sentimentality, before it was examined this year by faculty at Oxford and determined to be an authentic phenomenon. The Martyr-Bird is immortal; no attempt to end its life has been successful, nor any mark remains save a single red wound on its chest, which bleeds when it is injured. Demonstration killings and resurrections are enacted on Saturdays at one o'clock in the afternoon.

Salome [Ottoman Empire]—A harem prisoner of the savage Sultan until her rescue by British troops, Salome is a descendant of the succubae of legend, and was scheduled to be put to death for her ruthless seduction of men. Her beauty is beyond imagining, but those who look upon her risk being the victims of a most powerful and relentless lust; while she was good only for the gallows according to Ottoman law, the Sultan himself still murdered six Englishmen during her liberation, helpless under her spell. Though robbed of much of her power outside the lands of her people, Salome is still presented veiled and shackled, and behind a guarded partition past which ladies and children shall expressly not be admitted, to preserve their moral character.

The Dressing Table [India]—This display is the original dressing table of Lady Penelope Howard, who, during her husband's time as an envoy of the Crown in India, became an expert in native remedies and poisons. Her demise is assumed to have been a casualty of her hidden and occult passions. Transported here and recreated in situ, the dressing table contains dozens of unusual vials, talismans, and other artefacts whose purposes are, in some cases, still unknown. Visitors should be most careful not to touch any part of this display.

———————

18 April 1851

Mr York,

Yesterday, as I followed Mr Pentney through the final preparations for the Pavilion of the Uncanny and Marvellous displays, I noticed Eve and Mary—perhaps known to you as the Biddenden Maids—taking a glass vial from Lady Howard's dressing table as they were guided to their places beside the Martyr-Bird for the sketches that Mr Goodall is making.

When they saw me watching them, they gave me such looks as I shall never forget, but I only nodded as I would to a fellow on the street. I said nothing of it to Mr Pentney. For this I am not sorry.

I know from cataloguing its arrival that the vial they took smells of camphor. I suspected then what they intended. When I returned to the offices, I gathered the draft of the Pavilion's catalogue and all its other papers, and waited until darkness to leave the building with them in hand. I stole your satchel in which to carry them. I ask forgiveness.

When I arrived back at the Pavilion, as if by assignation, the sisters were there also. The Martyr-Bird sat in one of the old trees—even in the dark I could never mistake that bird for any other—and I believe I saw behind the partition that the woman who must have been Salome stood beside the man who has been named Osiris, and knew that whatever means the sisters had used to escape from their captivity, they had done the same to free their fellows.

Without looking at me, the sisters passed their hands over the camphor and murmured strange words. A violet flame sprung up, and they flung the vial inside, where it caught on all objects that had the supernatural in them, and left the rest untouched.

You are not a man of imagination, but if I could explain to you the terror of a scentless fire, the sight of all those things vanishing into smoke, disappearing into the night—!

But I will go on. Osiris and Salome soon vanished into the park. The flames inside the Pavilion rose quickly, and I threw the papers into the fire, where they were at once consumed, and within moments it was as though the Pavilion itself had never existed. For this I am not sorry.

The sisters and I said nothing to one another, as I speak no German and they no English, but we watched the flames together until they seemed satisfied and departed, I know not where. The Martyr-Bird flew after them, and then the Park was as quiet as if nothing had occurred.

I came here to write this letter. I have before made my feelings about this Pavilion clear, so you will not be surprised I am sure that I would be so eager to rid England of this low display, but I do not want the sisters to be accused of taking anything that was not theirs. I alone burnt the Catalogue, this is my sworn confession.

I have no plans to take flight. I remain at my lodgings. You may send the police, if you choose. I know the Crown might find me guilty of a crime, though you and I shall know differently.

Please take this as my notice to resign from my post, and I wish you great success in the Exhibit.

With best wishes, and most sincerely,
Mary Hammond

-----

18 April 1851

My Dear Ed,
Last night I got an unusual visit from Miss Hammond, who had some news about recent developments to the Pavilion. Despite her certainty that nothing shall be said about it in the papers, I still think it best I say nothing here. One never knows, these days.

Have disposed of some of my sketches for the Exhibition watercolours. Suggest you do the same with some of our correspondence—you know which.

When will you be in London next? You should meet Miss Hammond—a singular young lady.

Yours, etc.,
Walter

19 APRIL 1851

An incident with fire has consumed the Pavilion of the Uncanny and Marvellous. No loss to the Exhibit or the Crown. Some setbacks in the Catalogue—work continues. Dismissed Miss Hammond.

—**from the diaries of Alfred York**

The effect the Great Exhibition had on Britain cannot be precisely quantified, but neither can it be overstated. Its attractions spurred an industrial and cultural rivalry with other nations that was unheard of until that time (and which, many of those involved admitted later, had been largely the point of the Exhibition all along).

However, the estimated six million visitors were in themselves a force to be reckoned with; they brought tourism (both from within the United Kingdom and without) to an all-time high, which in turn had far-reaching consequences for London's economy.

Savvy businesspeople took advantage of the crowds for tertiary displays of their own, hoping to siphon some of the wealth that was pouring into the Crystal Palace. While the Pavilion of the Uncanny and Marvellous was a casualty of circumstance in this respect, entrepreneurs outside the Commission's purview were still scrambling to make a good showing. A savvy few did.

In particular, John Gould's remarkable stuffed-hummingbird exhibit at the Zoological Gardens in Regent's Park attracted more than 75,000 visitors. The display included several rare breeds and brought the colourful birds squarely into the public's scope of interest; they would continue to have a strong presence in fashion and design for the next century.

—**from "Opiate of the Masses"**

Alexander, on the shore of the Indian Ocean, sighed that he had no more worlds to conquer; the triumvirate of the Crystal Palace appear to be very differently situated. Having overrun the globe, and gathered its spoils within a glass case, they do not fold their arms and sit down contented. They wish to be useful in turning to the best account the opportunities thus created.

—*Guardian* **newspaper, May 7, 1851**

That majestic palace of iron and glass! A while ago, its pillars were coarse rude particles, clotted together in some deep recess of the earth, and its transparent plates were sandy masses, without beauty or coherence. How a little fire and a little art have changed them! . . . Oh, 'tis indeed wonderful, how God gives man skill to make an inheritance of all things!

—from "The World's Great Assembly," *English Monthly Tract Society*, London, J. F. Shaw, 1851

About "From the Catalogue of the Pavilion of the Uncanny and Marvellous, Scheduled for Premiere at the Great Exhibition (Before the Fire)"

Though the Pavilion of the Uncanny and Marvellous is fictional, it's probably not through any lack of trying on the part of the Victorians.

The comparatively rapid development of the natural sciences and a boom in occult pastimes among the upper and middle classes led to the popularity of séances, ghost photography, and quasi-scientific sideshows, of which the Pavilion of the Uncanny and Marvellous would have been welcome. And for a setting, nothing was more natural than the Great Exhibition, which arose in tandem with the swelling of patriotic sentiment accompanying the reign of Queen Victoria, which was, at its best, a myopic view of globalization that put British sentiments before all, and at its worst, xenophobia.

The Great Exhibition (a notable precursor to both the modern museum and the modern shopping mall) was designed as a celebration of industry, but it was also a ready platform for displays of the "exotic," and a handy pat on the back for anyone who wanted to feel that the British Isles was at the apex of the cultural ladder. The public reaction to the Exhibition was enthusiastic (the extensive catalogue of its wonders was one of the bestselling books of 1851); for some, it was a nearly religious event that demonstrated how Providence had smiled on England.

The Pavilion of the Uncanny and Marvellous is an imaginary missing chapter from this fraught and fascinating event. Some of the narrative excerpts in this story are fictional; others are real historical documents from the most pivotal cultural event of Victoria's reign.

THE MEMORY BOOK

Laura Anne presented herself at the door of her new employer on Monday morning, while London was still awash in mist. From the bottom of the steps, her younger brother, Peter, who had escorted her, waited until the maid opened the door and said, "Oh. I shall fetch Mrs Finch." He lifted one hand in a kind of half wave—he was really a tiresome boy—then skipped off.

Mrs Finch was a short, buxom woman, with her hair pulled severely back. Her Monday-morning washing dress, Laura Anne noted, was plain and damp in places. And unflattering. Not because the cut was so obviously from a few years before, since that was to be expected, but because even when new it would likely not have been flattering. Mama was not nearly so favoured by nature in her figure as Mrs. Finch and yet she was ever so much smarter. Laura Anne knew that even in her mourning (black bombazine from Black Peter Robinson's on Regent Street and cut in the latest continental manner, which served admirably to accentuate her tiny waist) she far outshone dowdy Mrs Finch. Mrs Finch flicked her eye up and down Laura Anne and apparently knew so as well.

The dining room, where Laura Anne had been engaged to be the Finches' governess, was as she remembered it. Mrs Finch sat at a cunning little desk, and Laura Anne stood demurely. "You are very young, and without a character," Mrs Finch said. Laura Anne did not feel this was quite fair. She had a character, that is, a character reference, from her pastor, but of course she could not have one from a former employer because she had never been employed and would not be now if it were not for the death of her dear papa. "But given your circumstance, we felt it a Christian service to give you this opportunity," Mrs Finch continued.

Mrs Finch had the children called for introductions. The nurse brought them down, dressed in their best. William, five, looked sleepy. Elizabeth, seven, hid her face in the nurse's skirts and would not look at Laura Anne. The nurse, a tall, awkward woman with a hatchet of a chin and narrow eyes, had obviously been crying. Now that the children were old enough for a governess, she would be leaving. "Nurse will show you the arrangements," Mrs Finch said.

From down the stairs, Laura Anne caught the whiff of boiling laundry. At least as governess she would be spared the ordeal of laundry day.

The second floor had three bedrooms. The nurse, the children, and Laura Anne trooped past the bedrooms on the floor and then climbed the narrow stairs to the third floor. At the top of the house were the nursery and the nurse's room, the latter stripped bare now, only a lone carpet valise sitting in the middle of the floor. The nursery was whitewashed and had a high fireguard in front of the fire, bars on the windows, and a table in the centre, covered in a bright red-and-white oilcloth so it could be washed down. On one wall was an eye of God, watching them all. They no sooner got to the nursery then the nurse dropped to her knees and hugged both children. The little girl, Elizabeth, immediately began to cry, a high, keening *eh-ehh-ehh* that put Laura Anne's teeth on edge. William was set off by his sister and sobbed, too. Elizabeth was going to need correction, Laura Anne thought.

Laura Anne didn't quite know what to do with herself, faced with this extraordinary performance. The nurse sobbed out something about how the children liked their tea, and some other generalities about their preferences. By the by, she kissed them both, called them her ducklings, her angels, her own dear loves. Then she stood up and said, "This is your new governess, Miss Huntley. Be lambs and be good for her and remember your prayers." She went to her room and got her valise.

Elizabeth let out a high screech and ran after her, throwing herself against the woman's skirts in a most theatrical manner. William, of course, copied. There was more sobbing.

The maid came up the stairs, the front of her dress soaked. "Miss Huntley," she said.

"Yes?" Laura Anne said.

"The mistress sent me up special to say that the carrying on up here won't do and to get the little 'uns under control." The maid delivered this without rancour and turned and clumped down the stairs again.

The nurse heard and soothed the children, quieting them. She sat them at the table and got them scrap pieces of paper and crayons. "William is a right proper artist," she told Laura Anne mournfully.

"I'm a right proper artist, too, aren't I?" Elizabeth said.

"You've got a nice eye, and that's an ornament on a young lady," the nurse said.

She had a common way of speaking that Elizabeth adopted easily; proof, Laura Ann reflected, that it was good that she was leaving. After more sighs, the nurse and her valise clumped down the stairs.

Laura Anne sat down and watched the children colour for a while. William was drawing a house, she thought. Or a square face. It was difficult to determine. Elizabeth explained she was drawing an angel. Laura Anne was grateful that Elizabeth had told her because she was not sure she would have known otherwise.

Elizabeth handed her drawing to Laura Anne, who pronounced it "very nice."

"What do we do now?" Elizabeth asked.

Laura Anne had no idea.

By the time Peter met Laura Anne to walk her home, she had a horrible headache. She had determined that the thing to do was to teach the children the capitals of Europe, but William had proven impossible. Elizabeth was not much better, but at least she managed Paris and Madrid. Then Laura Anne had read to them from the Bible while they fidgeted and William whined. Finally, she had taken them for a walk, which wore her out much more than it wore them out. She was certain she had a natural way with children, but these children were heathenish little creatures who had obviously been spoiled by that awful nurse.

She waited for Peter to ask how her day had been. Peter walked along the other side of the sidewalk, now and again giving her a sidelong glance.

"How was school today?" she asked, to prompt him to ask about her day, but he just said, "Fine," and sulked along as usual.

At home she went to her room and got down her regular scrapbooks, not the special one, just the ones anyone could see. Everyone knew she was quite mad about scrapbooks. She dug around until she found a scrap sheet of butterfly fairies, little, sweet cherub faces with wings like stained glass. She cut out a fairy—it didn't look like Elizabeth at all—the hair was the wrong colour, black and curly—and centred it on the page. Underneath she wrote *My first day of teaching*. She needed a quote, and Tennyson was always good. She found a quote about knowledge in the book of quotations and copied it out:

> Who loves not Knowledge? Who shall rail
> Against her beauty? May she mix
> With men and prosper! Who shall fix
> Her pillars? Let her work prevail.

Her sister, Jane, was twelve and the youngest and shared a room with her, and of course it was at this moment that Jane chose to come in and sit on her bed. "We're having a cold joint tonight."

Laura Anne said without looking up, "We always have a cold dinner on Monday." Because it was laundry day of course, and their mother and Sarah, the maid, were too busy to cook.

"What are the people like?" Jane asked.

"What people?" Laura Anne said. She got out her paste pot and carefully applied paste to the back of the butterfly fairy.

"The people you work for? Are they above our station? Are they rich?"

"Of course they are above our station. They have a governess."

Jane sighed. "Is their house beautiful? Do they have a couch and four?"

"No," Laura Anne said. "They are a bit vulgar, I think. And they don't have a couch and four. They have a terrace house, like us."

"Like our house?"

"Bigger. Five bedrooms. Jane, go downstairs and help our mother. I'm busy."

"You're just doing your scrapbook."

Without looking up, Laura Anne said, "You know what will happen if you don't do as I say."

Jane got still a moment, then got up and quietly went out. It was not good to cross Laura Anne. Laura Anne listened until she was sure Jane had gone downstairs, then she pulled out her own, her special, scrapbook, her memory book. She stroked the deeply embossed, rich red leather cover. It was her favourite scrapbook and she kept it hidden so no one could ever look at it. It fell open to a page she had done a few months ago. It was a tracing of a photograph of her father on tracing paper—she had stolen the photograph from her parents' room. It had been taken years ago, long before she'd been born, but it was the only photograph of him they had had, at least until he had taken sick and died. (Then her mother had had a photographer in to take a photograph of him, deceased, but seated in the drawing room, one hand on a book, looking a little stiff and with one side of his face still droopy, but if one didn't think about it, it could almost be as if he had fallen asleep there.)

Laura Anne had traced it carefully and drawn many curlicues around it, and as she was quite good at curlicues, she fancied it had turned out well, perhaps her best drawing ever. She remembered how angry she was when she drew it and how her anger had come out in the ink, careful curlicues of anger, all around him. Then she had stuck a sewing needle, over, under, over, through the head of the drawing.

Now she did not like to think about it.

She flipped to a new page now and chose a butterfly fairy that had fair hair and blue eyes like Elizabeth. She pasted it down and put an old piece of flannel over it in case the pages stuck together, although she was careful with her paste and that almost never happened. Then she closed the scrapbook, her red memory book, and was about to hide it back up in the top of the wardrobe, making a note as she did so that Jane was getting tall enough she might see it. Laura Anne thought she would have to find a new hiding place soon. Then she had a bolt of inspiration and took the book down and opened it. She inked out the little butterfly fairy's eyes so that they were two black pits. She admired the effect for a moment. Underneath it she wrote *Elizabeth Finch* and the date. Then she closed it and hid it.

Mrs Finch had a brother who was four years younger than she, although he was still an ancient twenty-two. Coming down from the nursery one evening, Laura Anne met him as he arrived for dinner. He was handing his umbrella and hat to the maid. The Finches appeared to entertain unfashionably early, serving dinner at five as if they were someone's grandparents. At Laura Anne's, when Papa was alive they had never eaten before six, and when they entertained, it was usually seven o'clock when dinner was served. Now, it was true, things were at sixes and sevens. Mama had let things slip terribly since Papa died and often took to her bed, leaving the house in a state of total disarray.

"Good afternoon, Miss Huntley," Mrs Finch said. "This is my brother, Anson Risewell. Anson, Miss Huntley is the new governess."

Anson Risewell nodded graciously and murmured his pleasure.

Mrs Finch asked, "How does William do?"

Laura Anne lied, "I think he is taking to geography most admirably, ma'am."

"And how is Elizabeth this day?"

Laura Anne looked serious and troubled. "It is difficult, of course. She loses so many days to her headaches that it is often one step forward and two steps back."

"We have recently started her on Dr J. Collis Browne's Chlorodyne when she has an attack," Mrs Finch explained to her brother. "There has been a tremendous improvement."

Laura Anne thought so, as well. When dosed, little Elizabeth was placid, her pupils so large they turned her blue eyes dark. It was not the result that Laura Anne had anticipated, but the butterfly-fairy image had not really looked very much like Elizabeth.

Anson Risewell pursed his lips. "A difficult trial for you, Louise," he said to his sister. He had fair hair and dark brown eyes. It was, Laura Anne thought, a striking combination. And he had a wonderful, ticklish-looking blond moustache, a dashing thing. His sister was drawn of much the same cloth, but what looked fleshy and common on her gave him an athletic robustness that Laura Anne found quite attractive.

As Laura Anne was collecting her rainwear, she overheard Anson Risewell say, "So things are working out?"

"Certainly until William goes to school," Mrs Finch said.

"Of course."

Mrs Finch sighed. "I can't be expected to take care of them without a nurse, what do I know about children?"

Laura Anne rather agreed.

"But when William goes to school, I think I will teach Elizabeth myself."

Anson Risewell nodded. "Excellent. Miss Huntley seems quite charming but"—he leaned a little closer to Mrs Finch to say quietly—"she seems very young."

Laura Anne was furious, and her brother Peter was late, which left her standing on the street waiting. He rounded the corner, running and panting. She slapped him. "How dare you keep me standing here like some common woman," she snapped.

Startled, he burst into tears. "But the omnibus kept stopping and stopping! I ran the whole last six blocks!"

"Just because father said you were the favourite, don't think it was true," Laura Anne hissed at him.

He blanched and was silent all the way home.

She began to watch for Anson Risewell. He did not come over often, of course. A gentleman such as himself certainly had much more interesting things to do than to eat dinner with his dull sister and her dull husband (a drab, little man who Laura Anne rarely saw, although she sometimes heard him come upstairs and vanish into his study on the second floor).

Near the end of the summer, the air thickened and the Finches decided the only escape was a holiday to Brighton. It was decided that this would be good for Elizabeth, as well. They booked three rooms at the Royal Albion Hotel—not as exclusive as the Grand Hotel, but on the King's Road overlooking the promenade and very respectable. Laura Anne was to accompany them and share a room with the two children. Anson would meet them there as well.

The preparations for a week away were immense. William was overexcited, prone to running around the nursery screeching, and Elizabeth developed a headache so severe she could keep no food down, nor could she swallow Dr J. Collis Browne's Chlorodyne. Laura Anne cleaned up after her, since the maid was overwhelmed with airing and sorting and packing. It was a perfectly dreadful week, and not even the season. The Finches never seemed to quite manage to do things the right way. Laura Anne had quickly realized that she had been hired as a sort of pretension, and that they were not people of means sufficient to hire a governess. Which was why all the business about her not having a character and them hiring her out of Christian charity was claptrap. They had hired her because her inexperience made her cheap. And now they were going to Brighton when the only people there would day-trippers and desperate sorts.

But Laura Anne had never been to Brighton. And it would be a chance to see more of Anson.

The train trip was a horror. Elizabeth was still sick, and William would not settle and be quiet, no matter what Laura Anne did. Mr Finch sat in the corner, parked behind his newspapers and invisible. Mrs Finch said, "Miss Huntley, please control William!" several times. It was all Laura Anne could do to keep from bursting out that he was a horrid and spoiled child when she got him and whose fault was that?

But when Mrs Finch rebuked Laura Anne the third time, Anson Risewell said, "Oh, Louise, you know how boys are."

Mrs Finch said sharply, "I certainly do not."

"I was just as difficult," Anson Risewell said. "William, come here." Anson lifted the boy on his lap and pointed out the window. "You see, we're outside of London now. You've never been outside of London, have you?"

The boy stared out the window, thoughtful. "Where are we?" he asked. "Are we in Madrid?"

Everyone laughed.

"What makes you think that?" Anson asked.

"Madrid is the capital of Spain," William said, as if this explained everything.

"Yes," Anson said. "Very smart! Did Miss Huntley teach you that?"

To Laura Anne's astonishment, William went on to list a half dozen European capitals, Athens, Greece; Rome, Italy; Vienna and Budapest, Austria-Hungary; Berne, Switzerland; and triumphantly, London. He was an obstinate little thing usually, unable to remember anything she taught him. But now Anson beamed at her. "Capital, little man!" he said, but she knew it was really a compliment to her and her heart lifted.

They made the transit from the train station to the hotel in a flurry of luggage and porters.

The air smelled of sea, and everything was so clean after the soot and fog of London. Even Elizabeth seemed revived, although she said that the sun hurt her eyes. The hotel rooms were clean, bright, and airy, and as it was not the season, they had been able to get them overlooking the ocean. The ocean was entrancing. Anson declared they should go down to the promenade immediately.

"We are all in need of a rest after the journey," Mrs Finch said.

To Laura Anne's surprise, Mr Finch said, "Louise, we have come all this way, it seems foolish not to take a turn on the promenade."

Elizabeth began to cry. "My head hurts," she whimpered.

Laura Anne could feel Anson's eyes upon her and the child. She felt a rush of fury. Now she would be forced to sit in this room with two children while everyone else enjoyed Brighton. But she smiled and sat down and gathered Elizabeth to her, pretending to be unaware of the observers to her performance. "It's all right," she said. "You and I will stay here and you can rest your little head and breath the clean air. I'm sure that by the end of the week you'll be right as rain."

Elizabeth was startled into immobility by Laura Anne's unaccustomed embrace. Really, it was the wrong way to treat the child, giving in to her whims. But men were stupid about child rearing.

Anson said, "I have a wonderful idea, Lizzie dear. Why don't we get you a pushchair. That way you won't have to do a thing and I will push your carriage up and down the promenade and you can be a princess."

Elizabeth wavered.

Mrs Finch looked worried. "She's really overstimulated, Anson."

"Nonsense," Anson said. "Nothing will be better for her than good sea air. Put colour in her cheeks." He was looking a little irritable.

So they all trooped down. Anson procured a big, wheeled wicker chair and deposited Elizabeth in it and started down the promenade. The sea crashed and there were seagulls everywhere, just like in pictures. But pictures did not give a sense of how the ocean just went on and on until it disappeared. In pictures there was something cozy about the ocean. Laura Anne felt uneasy. Resolutely she set her eyes on all the promenaders, dressed in summer linens. She felt a little shabby in her mourning bombazine, but as she was still in second mourning, all she had been able to do was add linen cuffs and a collar to her two dresses.

She had liked the theatricality of mourning, but seeing all the women in jaunty dresses this day, she was sick of it. She wanted a nice hat. She wanted to be noticed. No one noticed girls in mourning.

The promenade was crowded. There was a minstrel band including a negro with a banjo and checkered pants. Men and women thronged the beach, many of the women carrying black umbrellas against the sun. Boys stood on the rocky beach or waded in the water, their shoes and socks discarded, their pants rolled up exposing their white legs. There was a man with a monkey that capered and turned somersaults. Elizabeth clapped.

A man in a bowler and coat stood next to a cart with a sign that said BEACH PHOTOGRAPHS WHILE YOU WAIT, 6D.

"Mr Risewell," Laura Anne said, "you must get your photograph."

Every one turned to her, startled.

"It would mean so much to the children," she said. "They so adore you and to have a little memento of this occasion."

For a moment she thought she had been too bold, even for Anson. But a man's vanity could always be counted on, and even as the Finches frowned, he laughed. "Lizzie? Would you like my photograph?"

Elizabeth nodded solemnly.

Mrs Finch said, "Oh, Anson, don't be foolish."

"It's a lovely sentiment," said the photographer, a short, common-looking fellow with sideburns that stood away from his face.

Once Anson had decided, there was nothing to be done. The photographer prepared the plate, asking them how long they had been at Brighton. William was intensely curious, whispering to Laura Anne, "What is he doing?"

"Making a tintype of Mr Risewell," Laura Anne said.

After a moment, William whispered, "What is he doing now?" The man was sliding the plate into the camera.

"It's all part of making the tintype," Laura Anne said.

William gazed at the tintypes on display. "Can I have a tintype?"

"You will have one of your uncle, to keep. But you must share it with your sister."

"No," William whined. "I mean one of me."

"They're sixpence." She frowned at him. "Now be quiet."

Anson posed and the photographer whisked the cap off the lens. Everything hung still, expectant, and then the photographer covered the lens. "There you go," he said, "and if you'll just wait a minute's time, we'll have this ready for you."

But it was more than just a minute as the man busied himself at the cart, the tintype hidden as he swished it around in some liquid.

"What's he doing now?" William whispered.

Mrs Finch glared.

Laura Anne told herself it didn't matter.

The tintype was finally produced. It was fine, if a bit dark. Even Mrs Finch had to admire it. Anson held it out. "I don't know, Miss Huntley. Maybe I should keep the thing."

"I want to see it, please!" William said.

Anson laughed. "So you shall." He handed it to William.

"May I see it?" Elizabeth asked.

"Certainly, princess," Anson said. "Just let your brother have his turn."

The tintype had caught Anson's expression well, Laura Anne thought. It would do nicely.

The week in Brighton was a mixed success. Elizabeth was terribly sick for the first three days, but then the sea air seemed to work its improvements upon her, for which Laura Anne was grateful since she had spent those three days in the hotel room with the little girl while the rest enjoyed the pleasures of the promenade and the piers.

Near the end of the trip, the unthinkable happened.

Their little party was gathered in the lobby, deciding on tea, when Anson spied newcomers and happily hailed them. They were an older couple, genial and well dressed. The woman wore a dark red dress with a bustle, much in contrast to Mrs Finch's old-fashioned crinoline skirt. But it was the daughter accompanying them that drew all eyes. She wore a dress of emerald-green-and-white shot silk, artfully trimmed in black velvet ribbon. Mrs Finch murmured, "Surely that is from Worth."

Anson strode across the lobby to meet them and brought them back. Once close, the girl was a mild-faced thing, not quite so pretty as her elaborate couture, Laura Anne thought. "Mr and Mrs Gower, Annabelle, may I present my sister, Louise Finch, and her husband, George Finch." Anson beamed. "I believe I am able to announce that I have offered Annabelle a proposal of marriage, which she has been so kind as to accept."

Laura Anne felt the shock to her nerves, vibrating through her. For a moment everything in the lobby drew far away and she saw dancing specks of white. It was so impossibly warm, and she heard nothing of what was around her. But then her vision cleared. Anson was beaming at the girl and everyone else was looking on, except William, who had started off across the lobby toward one of the potted palms. He was unhealthily fascinated with them.

Laura Anne caught up with him, scolded him in a whisper, and brought him back. "So we shall meet you for dinner then," Mrs Gower said. "At eight."

"I do so look forward to it," Mrs Finch said.

"Until then," Anson said to Annabelle.

The Finches strolled out to the promenade. "Are they connected to the Leveson-Gowers?" Mrs Finch asked.

"Yes, I believe Mr Gower is a distant cousin of the Duke of Souther-land," Anson said lightly, as though this were a bit of trivia.

"What does Father say?" Mrs Finch breathed.

Anson laughed. "He said they'll do, even if they are Scots."

Everyone laughed, even William, who had no idea what he was laugh-ing at. Only Elizabeth and Laura Anne did not laugh.

They came home on Saturday because Mrs Finch preferred service at her own church and thought perhaps it was not quite right to travel on Sunday. Mrs Finch was punctilious in her relationship with Our Lord. Mr Finch, to Laura Anne's surprise, did not go to church. She did not quite understand Mr Finch, who seemed to be such a nothing but who on closer examination was prone to unexpected actions and statements. But this was the first time she had ever spent even the smallest amount of time in his presence.

She was so delighted to be home she could have cried. She was ex-hausted from dealing with Elizabeth and William and still quite disturbed by all that had happened in Brighton. Jane came running down the hall when Laura Anne got in. "You're home!" Jane said. "What was it like?"

"It was very nice and very healthy and I brought you a postcard." Laura Anne dug out the postcard—tucked next it was the tintype of An-son, which she left in her bag. The postcard was a scene of the promenade and the beach, with the West Pier off in the distance. Jane tucked her skirts behind and sat down on the stairs to admire the card.

From the drawing room, Laura Anne's mother called her.

Mother looked sallow and tired. She was seated at her desk with her writing slope. Her hair was not carefully done and her dress was stained. She so did not take care of herself these days. She had been so tiresome since Papa had died. It was all very well to mourn, but there were stan-dards, and even Mrs Finch, who had none of Mother's old style, looked better.

Propped on the writing slope was Laura Anne's own, her special, memory book. She was speechless.

"The maid found it," her mother said. "I am only grateful that Jane did not."

"You should not meddle with that," Laura Anne finally managed.

Her mother opened the book, paged through it, the images of family flickering past, Papa with the needle through his head, Elizabeth as a butterfly fairy with blackened eyes. She paged back to the image of Papa.

"Why him?" she asked. When Laura Ann didn't answer. "Why not me? He always doted on you. He didn't see—" She sighed. "It would have been so much better if it had been me. As it was, you might as well have stuck that needle through my heart."

She closed the book and handed it to Laura Anne, then looked down at the desk, lost in thought. It was as if she had forgotten Laura Anne was there.

Why had she stuck the needle in Papa instead of her mother? She didn't like to think about these things, it made her thoughts skitterish and disturbed. But she and her mother had not always gotten along. Papa had understood that Laura Anne needed special things, had snuck her toast with marmalade when most people thought it was wicked to give it to children. Papa had teased and cajoled and called her pet names.

Peter had recited his poem from school and Papa had said, "My favourite boy! There is nothing closer to a father's heart than his son."

Laura Anne had said without thinking, "But I'm your favourite!"

"Laura Anne," her father replied, "don't be foolish." He meant it.

"Because you never betrayed me," Laura Anne whispered.

Her mother's head jerked up and they met each other eye to eye. Her mother's eyes were wild, red-rimmed. "You were such an angel when you were a baby," she said. Her voice ground with despair.

Everything felt hollow for a moment and Laura Anne thought she would cry. She wanted to throw herself on her mother and cry and cry. But her mother would not comfort her. Fury surged through Laura Anne, red and then white, burning out the tears. She could feel the colours chasing on her face. Her mother was watching her.

"If something happened to me," her mother said evenly, "I should not care for myself, but I would feel saddest I think for you, for it would be on you that would fall the burden of this house, and of raising Peter and Jane. There is not so much money, and if you did not work, we would have to let the maid go. It is," she said deliberately, "perhaps the one thing that keeps me going on, that your dear papa loved his children so, and I must take care of them as best I can."

Laura Anne fled upstairs and flung herself across her bed, her memory book clutched to her.

She had to escape this house. She could not stay here. And she did not want to be a governess all her life. With a character from Mrs Finch she could get a good position in a more prosperous house, but she would always be invisible. No one had introduced her to the Gowers. She had been taken to Brighton as a servant, and Mrs Finch was already tiring of her, she could tell.

She had a plan, it was a good thing. The poor little Miss Gower would never know what had happened.

At the door to the bedroom, Jane said, "Laura Anne—"

"Get out," Laura Anne hissed.

Jane looked at her and fled.

Laura Anne took out the tintype of Anson Risewell. She dug out scraps of cloth, black wool, and made a little coat for him to wear and a top hat. She made buttons out of little knots of thread, quite cunning. Then she dug out a square of red cotton and folded it and cut out a heart. She opened the heart and carefully wrote *Laura Anne* on the heart. She was buzzing, buzzing the way she had the night she drew the tracing of her father, and the tintype was even better, she knew. She felt powerful. She glued the heart to Anson's chest and then covered it in the coat, so that the tintype was "dressed." She added the top hat.

She pasted it in the memory book. It was stiff and she would have to be careful. She would have to hide the memory book again, this time where no one would find it. She would. She would think about that in a moment.

But first, she surveyed the result.

Anson Risewell at the beach, wearing a coat and hat glued on, and underneath it, the barely visible lump of the heart. Underneath the tintype she wrote *Mine*.

Anson was rather drunk, although it was just after three in the afternoon. He turned when Laura Anne came into the drawing room and his face registered delight, a flicker of something, perhaps dismay, and then again the flood of delight. "Sweetheart," he said.

It was almost two years from the day she had pasted the tintype in her memory book. The day she had decided she had to get out of her house. Breaking off an engagement takes a little time, then there is the new engagement period and the picking out of a house—a bigger house than the Finches'. (How was Laura Anne to have known that Louise, her dear sister-in-law, had married down. For love.) There were the furnishings to pick out.

The house had turned out well, Laura Anne thought. This room in particular, with its red trimmed in black. And she had her own Morning Room.

Anson had not turned out as she expected. "We are going out tonight," she reminded him.

He looked chagrined. "A little spirits, it's nothing."

She let him see her displeasure.

Again, his face was a curious mixture, dismay, and then a crack of something smothered breaking out, disgust and maybe even a bit of fear? But it all disappeared again under his embarrassment.

Still, she could barely look at him now. Such a disappointment he had turned out to be. She had thought he would be fun, he had been so bluff and hardy in the first days of their engagement. Now he looked as if he was going to fat.

"Oh," she said, "photos have come." They were carte de visite photographs, pages of eight the size of visiting cards. There was a page of Anson in the coat and hat he had worn on their wedding day, and a page of her in her wedding dress and veil. Eight little Ansons, eight little Laura Annes. Except the Laura Anne page was missing one. She had already cut it out.

Anson glanced at them. "Very nice, sweet."

"I like photographs," she said. "Remember when I asked you to have the tintype taken for Elizabeth and William?"

He frowned.

"At Brighton," she prompted.

"Oh, yes," he said, although she was fairly certain that he did not. "What became of that?"

"The children lost it, I do not doubt. Louise lets her children run like heathens."

Anson did not like it when Laura Anne criticized his sister, but he did not like to disagree with her, either. He busied himself topping off his glass of claret.

She was growing tired of Anson. She had not expected to be so lonely when she was married. But there had been a lot of fuss and discomfort when Anson had broken off the engagement with Miss Gower. Many people had preferred to blame her. Mostly, Anson was not good company. But he drank quite a bit these days, and things happened to people who drank. They fell down stairs or stepped in front of carriages.

She had taken care of her loneliness.

Just now, she had pasted a wedding picture of herself in the memory book. She had covered her wedding dress with an actual piece of watered silk cut from the hem of the actual dress. Underneath it, on the belly, was pasted a picture of a tiny baby.

An angelic, tiny baby. Not like Louise Finch's children at all. Hers. Her very own.

About "The Memory Book"

I don't usually write historical fiction. It's a lot of work, for one thing. For another, one of the pleasures of writing science fiction is that the world can act as a kind of lens—the things that are different about it are the things that cause the character to act, to change. Those differences can emphasize theme or just be really fun. Historical fiction is full of differences, too, but the writer doesn't get to pick them. But I heard that Ellen and Terri were looking for Victorian stories, my mercenary heart beat faster, and I decided to try it.

I loved the research. Who knew that reading could count as "work"? I am particularly indebted to *Inside the Victorian Home: A Portrait of Domestic Life in Victorian England,* by Judith Flanders.

This story was workshopped at the Rio Hondo workshop in Taos, New Mexico. The workshop is at nine thousand feet and we were all a little oxygen deprived. There I learned that I had committed one of the most rookie errors of writing historical fiction. I so loved my research that I inflicted it on my readers. The workshop gently suggested that I cut several hundred words of explanation of Victorian housekeeping (particularly the rigors of wash day). Wash day was pretty awful, and if you read *Inside the Victorian Home,* you will come to appreciate washing machines as you never did before.

The story was pleasure to write. And I'm grateful to Ellen and Terri for actually giving it a home when it was finished.

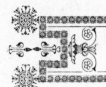

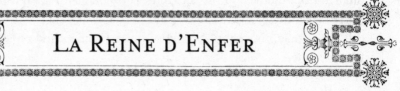

LA REINE D'ENFER

Once, I said to Davey, *I saw the Devil plain.*

  Go on, Davey said. *Save it for your fine gentleman.*

  I did. A raven landed in the chimney pots and looked straight at me, eyes all bloody red, and big as a dog, on my honour.

  Honour's not in you, Pearlie.

Davey named me that, Pearlie, for my fair hair and pale skin; the muvver used to say I was from the white side of the blanket. Davey had his own way of talking, and he taught me to talk it as well, that is, the kind of elocution that gets a fellow somewheres in this world. The way the gentlemen like for you to talk, to pretend that what you do with them is a lark for both of you, a jolly wolly roly-poly while they're dosing you with the Remedy and sodding themselves off. *Do you relish the scent of juniper?* one of them asked me once, and I hadn't no idea what to say. Later I asked Davey, and he laughed: *Juniper is that gin smell, Pearlie. Allardyce's Remedy is just gin, with a little wormwood and a pinch of mercury for the clap.*

  I loathe gin, I said, and Davey laughed again, for he was the one taught me what that meant: *Not just* hate *it,* he said, *hate it with your belly and your teeth, that's* loathe.

  I loathe the Remedy, too, it works half as well as using nothing at all. Half the boys round here stink of it noon and night, and the girls, too, and half of *them* are fat as tadpoles, all swagged up with the next round of baby boys and girls. I am so perishing glad that I am not a girl. . . . Davey says the only thing the girls have that we haven't is that a gentleman might grow so fishy-dotty that he will loop her to St. Paul's, which means to get matrimonial, and take her off the streets for good. Blinkers, that we call so because he's got a tic could blind you if you watch it too long, Blinkers says that where he used to Maryann it, up by Crispin's and the arboretum, was a corner girl so pretty and so fine that the second gentleman who had her wed her: *You should of seen her sausage curls,* says Blinkers, *all ribbons and such.* And *she could sing!*

Sing what?

Anything! It's how she met the gentleman. She was chirpin' at the arbo, by the gates outside, and the gentleman said, "Why, it must be a pretty bird." By this part in the story Blinkers would be blinking so quick-like it was hilarity to watch. Davey said that Blinkers must have been sweet on the little crimper himself, why he was so well versed in her whole story: *And what was it that she sang for the gentleman, Blinkers? Can you sing it for us now?*

Stop it, Paulo would say, Paolo the dark boy who sometimes plays that he is Italian or a Spaniard, even though his name's not Paulo any more than mine is Pearlie, he comes from Crippleton. *Stop it, it's not his fault that he—*

Saint Paulo, shut your hole. Go on, Blinkers, give us a song.

And then Blinkers would sing and we would laugh fit to split, always the same tune, "The Nightingale's Nest," tra-la-la, by the end he would be crying and Paulo would throw down his cap and say, *See what you done? Why you got to be so bleeding dark-hearted?*

Shut your hole, Paulo. I knew that crimp, she had a jaw like a slop jar from suckin'. Anyway Pearlie can sing, too, can't you, Pearlie?

Which was not particular true, but what I *can* do, and Davey taught me even better, is say verse. Just like one of them parrots the sailors bring home from India, say it to me once and I know it and can give it back to you perfect anytime.

It was how Davey took me up, in the beginning, in the tavern where I was slinging pots, my muvver's friend's tavern, though she was no friend to anyone and for certain not to me. Davey saw me, then heard me, then said me strings of nonsense, gammon and spinach, to test what I could do. Then he took me off and bought me a new pair of breeches and taught me the names of gentlemen, read them squinting off a paper he paid for from one of the hotel slaveys: *Mister P. Atherton, Esquire. Doctor Arthur*

Wells. Oh, here's a one, here's a lord, Lord Kilmarry! John Adderley Walsington,
Earl of Kilmarry. Got that, Pearlie?

John Adderley Walsington, Earl of Kill Mary. Later I found out it was all
the one word, but that's the beauty of it, you don't need to know what
you're saying for the thing to work. And then he would take me round to
places where those gents were known and have me declaim, he'd call it,
drop a name or two like I knew the gentleman truly personal. And in that
way we would get things, lagers and such, or Trinidad tobacco, Davey was
a regular fiend for the weed. Once I got a pair of fancy braces, the nicest
things I have, silver-blue with a gilty kind of sewing up the sides; they are
flash, those braces, I won't put them on against a soiled shirt. There was a
hat went with them but Davey took it, which made me grim, since it was
my declaiming that bought it and he has three hats already and I have
naught but this old cap that I wouldn't use for a piss cup, all it's good for is
keeping off the rain and not even that.

Why can't I have that topper? I asked Davey. *It goes lovely with the*
braces—

Because I said so.

It's mine from the declaiming, ain't it?

And you're mine, Pearlie, so the hat's mine and your pretty face is mine and
whatever you declaim is mine, too, got it? Got it?—smacking me all the
while with the flat of his hand, and smiling, his choppers all brown. . . .
I thought I'd run away that night, hunkered beside the eaves at Freddy's
alehouse, cursing him from under that stupid cap. Me who makes all
the lucre, more than any of his others, me who gets him his fancies and
tobacco—sitting there chastised, with my lips all swollen! I got no nibbles
that night, the gentlemen don't like you so much if you're marred, unless
it's them who does it—one time a gentleman wanted to burn me, put a
hot pin to me in the shape of a Frenchy fleur-de-lis. I got myself away, but
it was too near a thing. Which was why I went back to Davey: a fellow
needs someone to keep the streets off, with the coin or the power or both,
it's no good to be alone. But I was still that miffed that I said I couldn't
declaim for the day, my mouth was still too sore—

Pearlie, now, don't be like that!

It's not me who made it so, is it?

—and took myself instead to the tea shop and then down to the panto,
where they was putting on *The Crying Ape,* a fellow trussed up in feathers
like an outlandish African chased by another fellow in a bear suit who

was the Ape. The stage was that small that half the time the Ape chased the African and half the other way round, but they did it slick and got the crowd laughing. I kept myself to the shadows where I could scout the gentlemen, for it was my thinking that maybe I'd pick up a quick larker and buy myself a hat for secret spite.

But instead *he* picked *me*, that gentleman who said to call him Edmund: Mr Edmund Chute, fresh of the countryside, of the schoolroom and the library and the books. I watched him come in and step all round the playing space, gazing and nodding at the curtains and the crowds, clapping for the African and Ape—until he saw me in the shadows, until I let him see me watching, too. And then it was closer, closer, closer still, but not like most gentlemen do, like I'm a sweet in a shop window or a piece of meat to chew, but as if he'd never seen the like of me before, which I could tell he hadn't. Mr Edmund Chute, fresh of the countryside.

Finally he stepped into the shadows, he stepped right up to me, and *Did that fierce Ape get after you, young fella?* he asked, joking like but kindly, too, like he would offer help if I should need it. *Or perhaps it was fighting? There are laws here against street brawling, you know.*

I put my head to one side, angled into the light to make my hair shine even whiter, like a halo; I sucked in my lower lip and smiled. Not a flash suit but a nice one, and he didn't smell of juniper, just Pears soap and coffee and clean sweat; his eyes were clear and brown as a spaniel's. I put my hand on his arm.

I don't bother so much, I said, *about the law.*

It was the first time I ever ate sauced quail, almost the whole bird!— and prawns in blue butter, and little rum cakes and quantities of boiled coffee, it gave me the headache so I had to chase it down with ruby port. *I'm glad the port pleases,* said Edmund Chute, *I'm not much for spirits myself. Coffee is my vice!* "Black as the devil, hot as hell, pure as an angel, sweet as love." *As the theatre is my mistress.*

Mistress? I looked around his rooms for a girl's duds or furbelows, I couldn't see what he meant. But he went on talking, to say he was a kind of teacher of the drama, who left his scholars and schoolhouse, his muvver and old da and younger sister—*It was a leap of faith, truly*—to come all the way to the City and put on plays, be what he felt called to be, what he called an *impresario;* I didn't know that word, but there was some Maryann in it for sure. He told me of his time in the City, what he'd seen, *all the magic of the theatre!*—by then he was in shirtsleeves, and braces not so nice as mine; it was late, Davey would be hopping when I got back, for missing another night's work. Be fucked to Davey. *I mean, you see, to court the muse, brew strong wine for strong hearts! We construct such a play now, myself and my company, about love, and terror, and damnation:* La Reine d'Enfer, *a beautiful lady makes her way to hell, to free her lyre-playing husband. . . . Did you know, Pearlie, that in Shakespeare's day, all the female parts were played by boys?*

If he's such a liar, I said, *maybe he belongs in hell,* but I said it saucy so he could see it was meant for clowning. *Don't you want your play to tell the truth?*

He tried clowning back: *Why, I thought you said you didn't bother much about the law—?* But he swallowed hard when he said it, like Adam with the apple stuck in his throat. So I turned down the gas, all a-flicker like the panto, shadowy and pretty, and *I know some Shakespeare,* I said, and sat on the arm of his chair to give him the bit of *Romeo and Juliet,* my mouth right up against his ear. *Soft, what light from yonder window breaks? It is the east'n Juliet is the sun.*

Arise, fair sun, he said; he touched my hair, his hand was trembling, just a little, just enough for me to see it. *And kill the envious moon. . . . Pearlie, I should like to ask you something. Would you—have you ever—*

O Romeo, I said, and tugged gently at his shirtfront. *Wherefore art thou Romeo?*

Pearlie, have you ever—would you consider acting on the stage?

Spaniel eyes, the tremble in his hand—and food enough to feed an army, port and quail and prawns and who knows what else, in a cleaner room than Davey's, much cleaner, and almost as big as the one all us boys slept in; better than Davey's; much better than fucking Davey's. It's what we all want, us boys, to shut the door to the streets for good—and I would be the only one. Fishy-dotty . . . I sucked a little at my swollen lip; I gave him my very sweetest smile: *That's why for I studied elocution,* I said. The kind of elocution that gets a fellow somewheres in this world.

The first thing be bought me was a hat, a jaunty topper with a wide, yellow ribbon band. I had to hide it from Davey for of course I had to go back to Davey's, until I could cut away clean, for Davey'd do the cutting, wouldn't he, if I was to drop him flat. Look what he did to Georgie

Booters, that time! And he looked at me particular strange, like a sniffing dog, he said, *What'd you get up to, last night, Pearlie? Where'd you go?*

Nowheres. And I'm here now, ain't I?

Don't be cute, and he hit me, but not in the face and not hard. That night he worked me himself, and I declaimed away, I sang all night like Blinkers' light-o'-love. Then he bought me a late supper at the Red Cock, sat drinking his lager and watching me and *Pearlie*, he said finally. *You know I want what's best for you. Didn't I keep you from the constables, when you looted that doctor fellow and his packets of dope? Fine lad like you can rise in the world like anything, with the right help behind him.*

I know that, I said. I looked around the room, the dirty old Red Cock with its red walls and red-painted windows and smell of the Remedy; I almost laughed. *Rise like an angel. "Angels are bright still, though the brightest fell."*

What's that mean? In a squint, Davey looked just like a goblin, like the devil's little bruvver. The red room, the scowl on his face. *Who taught you that?*

Dunno, I said. *I must have picked it up somewheres.*

You're acting different these days. I don't like it much.

Blinkers noticed, too—*You're awful jolly wolly, Pearlie, you must be gettin' some good coin*—and so did Paulo, who raised up his brows and *Getting* something, *is our Pearlie;* he said it nasty. *Or some one. Does Davey know, Pearlie?*

Shut your hole, Paulo. Nothing's any different than it was.

You're growin' out your hair, ain't you.

Shut your hole or I'll shut it for you.

Fact is I *was* growing out my hair, for to play the Dark Queen, who was the Fair Queen now because it was me playing her. Edmund was all excitable about it: *I shouldn't dare to call myself a playwright, but to amend a character— And her name remains the same, Lady Frances.*

That's my name, I said. *Pearlie, it's just what Da—what people call me. My real given name is Francis.*

Francis, said Edmund; he touched my hair. *You've got the queen's beauty, certainly.* And then he blushed all over and hurried off up the aisle like a constable was on him. He hadn't touched me yet, though Davey would never have believed it, Davey who kept watching me like a puss at a fucking mouse hole, sending me places and then turning up there himself, to see did I show up, Davey who had me declaiming lists of names till I was sick of it, and all for what? A greasy meal, a pint box of tobacco, some stupid scarf that smelled of a fellow's basket, why would I want that? though *It's real silk,* Davey scowled.

You keep it.

Watch your tone, Pearlie. Take the fucking scarf.

A line of crows crying on the rooftops, my lines running round in my head—*To the depths of deathless Hell I'll go / No matter how dark the way*—and it *was* dark, that theatre, no windows in the back and the gas there-and-gone, but what Edmund called rehearsals was jolly larky. Trussing up in the Queen's gladrags, painted crown atop my head, though *He ought to have a wig,* said the freckled lady who did the dressing, but *It would be a shame,* Edmund said, *to cover up that hair. . . . Give the incantation again, Francis, a little louder this time?* so *By all the spirits of the darkness,* I said, hands on my padded-up hips, *I bind you to my bidding, I adjure you to set my lord free!* declaiming out to the empty theatre that, the playing folk told me, was never so empty, for *There are watchers out there always, you know, ghosts that no one can see. Some are only watchers, but others—*

Especially with a show like this one! said the dressing lady, and she shivered; I thought she was having me on, but they were all serious-like: *Mind that extra devil that came to* Doctor Faustus—*thirteen up onstage, when there ought only have been twelve! I'd not stay here alone at night, not while this show's in play.*

I'm not afraid of devils, I said. *No matter how many there are.* That day I was feeling extra larky, for Edmund had been watching me like the king watched the queen, all longinglike from his prison bench: today Edmund *was* the king, as the fellow who played him—the African fellow, from the Ape show—was off somewheres or ill. So *Set my lord free!* I called out into that darkness, picturing the seats all stuffed with devils, crunching peanuts and flicking their tails, poking one another in the arse with their pointy rods—but it was true you could see *something* if you squinted, like the air above the seats was dirty, somehow. Like smoke, but not. Like a fancy but not. *Deliver him into my keeping, you host of the lost, for I have spells to crack your evil souls like lice!* And I put my hand on Edmund's shoulder and looked into his face all creamy, like the Queen would; he looked back at me, and looked, and had to be reminded of his line by the fellow playing the head devil onstage: *Hsst, Mr Chute! "It is you I have awaited, my beloved."*

It is you, said Edmund Chute, *I have awaited. My beloved.*

After the rehearsal, he bade me stay behind till everyone had gone. Spaniel eyes, and clean sweat, and a bigger basket then you'd think just by looking; and no Remedy, for I had no worries of the clap neither, whatever he done before wasn't much. Afterward he held my hands, he kissed my hands, and *I did not mean to do so,* he said, *but you—are so lovely. So very lovely.*

Come live with me and be my love, I said. *That's Shakespeare, too.*

No, it isn't, he said, and kissed me again. *It's Marlowe. . . . Oh, Francis, live here with me, and be—my star, my shining actor, my Queen of the stage! Surely the muses brought us together for that very reason! And surely whomever— shelters you now will understand?*

Shelter? I didn't laugh, but I felt the laugh in my mouth, like when you want to spit the spendings but you can't. *It ain't—it's not like that. It's more like Davey bought and paid for me, except he never paid, just took me—*And I made a story of it, a tearjerker cobbled up from other boys' tales, Blinkers' sadness, and Paulo's dead muvver and my own muvver coughing herself empty, though I made it to be a sister instead, and *Ever since she died,* I said, with my head on his chest, *I been alone. I only went with Davey because I was afraid. But now—*his heart started beating quicker; I could feel it under my cheek—*now, with you, Edmund—Eddie—but he won't want to let me go.*

I'll talk to him, he said. *One gentleman to another, I'll convince him it's for your best.*

He's not a gentleman, Eddie. But I touched him while I said it, in the way I was learning he liked, and he hugged me tight. I didn't leave for Davey's till dawn was broaching, red across the rooftops, the theatre empty of its shadows or smoke or whatever it was, and no red-eyed crows to be seen. Why should I give a romping fuck for devils or the Devil or anything else of the darkness? Ain't I seen darkness enough, seen it all around me, Davey's brown teeth and that pot-slinging bitch at the tavern? And Blinkers blinking like sixty when I stepped over the threshold, whispering, *Pearlie, oh, Pearlie, you better run*—until Davey put him back into the wall with one blow, then turned the buggy whip on me.

You traitor, after everything I done for you! Behind my back and taking trade, I'll beat the white right out of you, you lying little whore.

And he did. He did. Eyes rolling back in his head like a horse's, I screamed and tried to fight him but that made it worse so finally I just put my face to the wall till Davey wore himself out and left panting. Even

Paulo looked scared, then. After some long time—it felt long—I got up on my feet. I wiped my face on the first thing I found—Davey's vest that he had took off for the beating, his quilted blue vest, and I smeared it with blood, my blood, I spit more blood on the floor like a fat red flower. All the while Blinkers was sniveling—*Holy Mother, Pearlie, Holy Mother, but he got you good*—until *Shut your hole,* I said, *on your Holy Mother,* for when did praying do good for anyone? What bright angels come to watch this show?

I grabbed up whatever I could put my hand to, a silver spoon from the table, a bottle of gin; then threw it all down again, my head a-swim like being drunk. Then I took a steady breath and took up the things that were mine—precious little they was!—and rolled them up into a pillow bag.

Where you going? Paulo asked, quietlike.

You're leaving us, Pearlie? Blinkers said. *But what should we say to Davey?*

Tell Davey I went to the Devil, I said. *And if he wants, he can look for me there.*

It was the theatre I went to, the doors locked tight, but that made no never mind to me. I know how to do the in-and-out—and been caught at it more than once by the constables, not only that doctor-fellow that Davey got me out of, but other places, too, and other lootings, and knifings, a boy's got to make his way. . . . Eddie would want the constables for this surely, he would take one look at me and cry for the law. But the law knows what kind of boy I am, and that my name's not Pearlie nor Francis neither. Whatever law had charge of *this* case, my scalp torn and back welted and tooth cracked, a red line still running from my lip—I spat blood again, dark clot on the dark floor—none of it had to do with constables.

Out front, the banners said PREMIERING SOON! *He jests at scars that never felt a wound. To the depths of deathless Hell I'll go, no matter how dark the way. Set my lord free.* But when I spoke it come out twisted, my lips was twisted, and the words all slurred, was it no Fair Queen for me, then, was that how it would be? May Davey and his fucking buggy whip be damned to hell. . . . They leave a light burning back behind the stage, the dresser lady calls it the ghost light. In that little light the empty seats seemed more smoky and shadowed still, or maybe it was shadows in my eyes, both of them squinted with swelling, one of them half-blacked by the butt of the whip. I blinked, but the shadows hung the same, like clouds on a mid-summer's day, you see them and you know the storm is coming. As I sat there bleeding more words come to me, dark and quiet, like backwards poetry—*Propitiamus vos. Pandemonia. Consummatum est*—from another world, the world of plays, Eddie's world. The gentlemen don't like you so much if you're marred, would Eddie take a look and put me out, send me back to the fucking streets?

May God damn Davey down to hell!

And this time I must of said it out loud, with all the hate that I was feeling, a mighty hate, for then the shadows come right toward me, just like a storm wind blows the thunderheads.

Red eyes, black birds, none of that is what you see, the bogeyman they call it, the hosts of the lost; naught like that at all. I think I laughed. Just like Davey, they don't give without taking, but I know how to reckon with that. I laughed, and said the poems, all of them—*consummatum est,* that's from church, ain't it? You don't need to know what you're saying for the thing to work—I *declaimed* the poems and watched the shadows boil. And when I finished, my blood was gone from the floor, just as neat as if some maid had swabbed it up.

I must of slept, then, for the next thing I knew was Eddie bustling in, jingling keys and whatnot, you could hear him before you could see him—and when he saw me in the seats, he give a great cry and *Francis! What's— Oh, dear Lord, what has happened! Who has done this to you?*

He took me to my feet and felt me up and down, then draped me on his shoulder like a baby; I think he cried. Fishy-dotty; I could have cried myself, I was so chuffed up with relief. It was me who finally patted his back and *There there,* I said. *Don't, Eddie, don't take on so.*

But who—? Your poor sweet face—

His name is Davey, I said, and he kissed me, kissed the blood dried on my lips.

Cold compresses, and lots of ruby port, and a hurried-up rehearsal of others taking half my lines, Eddie insisting that *The rôle is his if he wishes, he is still our star* as the dresser lady rigged up a lacey veil for the crown, to hide the spot where my hair was wrenched out and *'Twas a lover,* she said, *am I right? No one hits harder! Well, no matter, Mr Chute will see to you. Now tilt your head for me, your ladyship, just like so . . .*

It will work out grand, I said to Eddie, though I was mumbling somewhat still. *We'll have our show just like we meant to. But first, we'll have Davey here.*

A brute who would do such a thing to you, to you, Francis? By heaven, no!

We'll not risk such a thing, we'll have him in the dock instead, I'll involve my solicitor— But in the end he did as I wished like I knew he would, like I knew that fucking Davey would come with bells on when he got my message. It was Paulo I sent to bring it, Paulo I spied in the streets taking trade, and *You owe me,* I said, and he knew what I meant; was he ashamed, Saint Paulo? Was he the one Davey took around to the Red Cock, now? *You tell him to come at midnight, just himself alone.*

He's still perishing mad, Pearlie.

I smiled; Paulo turned away. *Just tell him, you sod,* and he did, and *he* did, Davey, he came and came alone, into the shadows where he saw me sitting hoity-toity like a queen. I kept my smile secret, I kept my hands where he could see them, empty like the seats around us, empty of what could be seen except for Eddie, waiting a row behind, all nervouslike and disbelieving. He had done what I said though he kept protesting to the last, almost till the clock struck—

But dear Francis! It's not real, not magic, what we say; it's only a show. And this man is very dangerous.

I wriggled on his lap; I tugged his moustache. *But dear Eddie,* I said. *The magic of the theatre, strong wine for strong hearts! Ain't, aren't you an impresario? Don't you believe?*

Davey looked nothing dangerous, though he'd got a truncheon stuck sidewise in his belt and I knew where he kept his knife: he looked like a sad little man with a turnip nose, and a roll of fat at his gut, and wearing the hat that goes with the braces, he looked a proper fool. *That's your fine gentleman?* he called out, marching down the aisle, one hand wary on that truncheon. *Does he know, Mr Schoolman, how many times you been dosed for the drippings? Does he know the law about sodding off youngsters, that could shut down a showplace like—well. None of that will signify, Pearlie, if you come home to where you belong.*

I belong here. I'm an actor now.

An actor! When he laughed it was too loud, like a bad performer too hot to show how funny something is. *I seen the placards outside, Mister Whatever-your-name-is, some farrago of demons and whatnot. Bogeys to scare little kids in the night*—

It's not what you think, Davey. Once, I said, rising on my feet, *I saw the Devil plain.*

Go on. Save it for your fine gentleman.

I did. He was closer now, close enough for me to see the lager stains on his shirt, his crusty beard; and I marvelled on how could I ever have done anything for him, ever been afraid. It was like if shadows were gone from my eyes. *A raven landed in the chimney pots and looked straight at me, eyes all bloody red, and big as a dog, on my honour.* So close that we could have touched; I could hear Eddie breathing from behind me, quick as a cat.

Honour's not in you, Pearlie.

My name's not Pearlie. I could see his eyes, now. *I loathe you, Davey,* and I called the shadows in.

They said he jumped off the bridge into the filthy river, they said they found him floating at the docks; they said when they found him, his eyes were gouged-out gone. They said a lot of things of Davey dead, but none of the things they said had me in 'em, for we was known to be fully on the outs, and me too broken-busted to do anything about it, and anyway I had a new protector, now; that's what they said. Davey's carcass went straight to potter's field and that was that, though Blinkers came by the theatre, cap in hand, to say hello and good-bye; he ended up with a broom in his hand instead, he's the one now sweeps the aisles and takes up your tickets when you come. Paulo I never saw again.

And the show, *La Reine,* went just cracking beautiful—a lineup every night, maybe partly from the gossip! And selling out on the matinees, we even got writ up in the papers: *"A shivering good show,"* the dresser lady— her name is Phyllis—read it out to us, backstage with our coffee and tea and port, *"wherein the good are rescued and the wicked punished, and the darkness vanquished by the light. Young Francis Chute is particularly affecting as the similarly named Queen, as his uncle revives the great stage traditions of the Bard himself."*

No one made no comment on that "uncle," and I make sure always to call him so when anyone can hear or see, on the streets or in the theatre; though not in our room, the fine room with the fine bed, where poor Eddie is still having trouble sleeping, and nightmares, too, he keeps on pondering whatever was it caused Davey to do as he done, run out the aisle like the Devil was after him, but *Most likely his own bad deeds,* I tell Eddie, *especially the ones he did to me.* Eddie has bought me a splendid nightshirt, with buttons of real pearl; now I ruch it off, and smooth down my hair, grown longer still, it is curling even on the ends. *They finally caught up to him and drove him right off his nut. . . . Stop fretting. Come here.*

His conscience—true, it must have been eating at him. As we see in the

Scottish play! And after that dreadful beating, he deserves no mercy at all. But, oh, my conscience, Francis—to have a man perish practically in our theatre, you can't think that it was the play that—

Stop fretting. Let me be your conscience, though I don't give a red fillip; why should I? All's as it should be, now. The nephew, the star, the light-o'-love, fishy-dotty forever or as long as my belly stays smooth and white and my hair stays pretty; there might be ways to work that, too, for the shadows play fair, blood for blood, better than Davey ever did. *Shall I make spirits fetch me what I please?*—that's from another show, that *Doctor Faustus* that Phyllis talked of, though Eddie says we shall not stage it, after what happened with Davey. So instead we're to do *Romeo and Juliet,* he the Montague and me the, what is it, Capulet. And after that maybe something comical, like that Ape show, and I could wear my braces and that cracking hat. . . . I might could play here for a long, long time.

About "La Reine d'Enfer"

In all plays, even *Hamlet,* the scenery is the best part. . . . And the dark wants, needs us.

—**John Ashbery, from "Cliffhanger"**

Step this way, gentlemen and ladies, the best seats are right up front.

FOR THE BRIAR ROSE

Merry Margaret,
As midsummer flower
Gentle as falcon
Or hawk of the tower

So William Morris greeted her the morning that Margaret Burne-Jones told her father she was going to Scotland. Morris arrived at the Grange in a downpour, banging a book of wallpaper samples against the glazing in the front door as though he meant to break into the house. He warbled fifteenth-century poetry at Margaret when she let him in, but directly he swept past her in a storm of streaming oilskin. Her father, the artist Edward Burne-Jones, sat calmly eating his eggs in the kitchen.

"Topsy!" Burne-Jones cried out in surprise and joy, and, "Ned!" Morris answered, as though he did not make an equally thespian entrance every Sunday, but had returned suddenly after long and silent decades of absence. Margaret stood in the kitchen door, shaking Morris's scattered raindrops from her hair.

"Your midsummer flower is blooming," Morris commented as an aside. He slammed the paper samples down on the breakfast table, stabbing at one of the designs with a great, meaty finger.

"You see what I get when I let them manage without me?"

Ned tutted and shook his head in sympathetic outrage. "It's unbalanced. Is this May's design? Does she keep her head in a bag? She should know better. It should look like *this*—"

And he plucked a pen from inside his jacket, reached for the morning post, and began scribbling on the back of a yet-unopened letter addressed to his wife. Margaret watched over her father's shoulder. The paper sample showed an intricate pattern of wreathed roses, and as she watched, a similar tangle grew from the nib of Ned's pen and spread like a vine toward the edges of the envelope and beyond.

"Papa!" Margaret scolded. "You're drawing on the tablecloth!"

She snatched at his hand. The ink blotted and smeared. "I'll have to wash this *now*—"

Robert the parrot, who lived in the kitchen and grew excited when people rushed about and made a deal of noise, began to chatter. There was some further commotion while Margaret untangled the cloth from the crockery and paper that covered it, and helped her mother to spread the breakfast things back in place, and served Morris his coffee (in his special cup the size of a milk jug, because his doctor would only allow him a single cup a day), before sinking the ink-bespattered cloth in a bucket to soak. The ink was on her hands, as well, creeping up her wrists as though her father's imagined climbing roses were still spreading.

It was only a vision: she could never put it into words or pictures. Her father could, her father's friends could, and their children could as well. Of late, as Margaret had found her body and mind maturing, she had begun to feel dissatisfied with herself for being so simply without talent. She was pretty, she was happy, but now, for the first time in her life, Margaret felt that she had done nothing of any worth, and could not. She had a plan for escaping, at least temporarily, the frantic forest of inspiration that grew out of her father's house.

This morning's burst of energy between Morris and her father was typical of Sunday breakfast at the Grange. Margaret had always thought that Sundays in the Burne-Jones household must have inspired Reverend Dodgson's endless tea party in Wonderland, everyone switching cups all afternoon and one of the guests asleep in the teapot. They would sit at breakfast until dinnertime, when everyone would adjourn to the dining room. There would be extra places set in case unexpected visitors arrived, and if there was a particularly large gathering, her father would hide behind a door eavesdropping in the hope that people would drop compliments on his work; Margaret and her mother, the long-suffering Georgie, would cook and wash and wait all morning and afternoon. No one left the table from dinner until teatime, and the men would build cathedrals out of mustard pots and saltcellars until they began to shout at each other.

The shouting was never malevolent or frightening, but Margaret knew that the announcement she meant to make on this particular day would not be received well by her father. Today's good-natured grumbling and mundane madness over breakfast assured her that all was well and usual. She took it as a fair omen, for she needed to choose her moment carefully.

"I'm going to visit John's family in Scotland," she said at last, firmly and cheerfully.

Morris grinned broadly and congratulated her. "Farewell to London, and away to Gretna Green!"

But her father leapt to the sudden and absurd conclusion that Margaret was eloping. He pronounced with deep melodrama, "England shall descend into darkness in your absence. What fool was it that claimed the sun never sets on the British what-you-may-call-it—but this is the end of all light and happiness. We shall never see you again."

Margaret scolded, "Now, Papa—"

"You shall be married and an old woman before I am an old man," said Ned.

"Now, Papa, you and Mama were engaged a slight three weeks after you were introduced!"

"But it felt like three years. In those days it *could* have been three years. We cannot both survive this separation. I shouldn't be surprised if one of us is dead before we see each other again—of course, being dead, we won't see each other in any case," he pronounced gloomily.

Margaret had expected to provoke an outburst, but not this morbid sulking.

"Now, Papa," she repeated patiently, "I am not eloping. I am visiting with John's *mother and father*. I shall travel in my own private compartment in the train, and Mr MacKail will escort me from the station when I arrive—"

"I shall wait in enchanted sleep for your return," her father said in the same lugubrious tones, "like the king in the fairy tale. I will dream. But I am sure we shall never meet again. Who wakes the sleeping princess? Not her father. The kiss of knowledge comes too late for him, the breath of life brings ruin to his estate—"

"You do talk an awful lot of nonsense, Ned," Georgie interjected. "You will spoil her summer, and maybe her marriage, if you go on like this."

"She's but a girl," Ned insisted, and muttered a considerable footnote to the sentence under his breath, knowing all too well that he was out-numbered and that if he spoke aloud he would be shouted down. But Margaret caught the gist of his objection, and the haunting words, "A girl asleep."

And so I am, she thought. I live in girlhood and in my pretty dream, here. How do I wake into the world?

May and Jenny are home," Morris said to Margaret as he buttoned himself into his oilskin before he left the house that evening. "They want to see you. They do love you, you know; you were their favourite tagalong girlhood companion."

"Everyone's, I should imagine," said Margaret.

"Indeed. Happy and beautiful, and never coy! Come walk back with me and have supper with us. We'll send you home in a cab. You can lay plans for a visit to Kelmscott before you go up to Scotland."

So she walked with him along the Thames towpath. The river was always busy, this close to Town, for even when the weather was too ugly for pleasure boats there were still freight barges traveling down from Reading, and an undaunted battery of anglers huddled along the banks beneath wide, black umbrellas.

"This walk makes me long for the silent reaches of the upper Thames," Morris said, "so far from the busy, busy, busy London river. 'The char-tered Thames.' Come up to Kelmscott. Let's all go up to the manor. Ned can have Rossetti's old studio in the Tapestry Room and try to finish that eternal *Briar Rose* series. The scenery will inspire him, and you and May and Jenny can chase over the rooftops as you used to."

Margaret knew now that the house at Kelmscott made only a dubious claim to having been a manor; yet it was grand in its own quiet way, a grandeur born out of age and settlement and sleep rather than size and design. It was built of golden Cotswold sandstone and stood by a back-water of the baby Thames at the end of a lane to nowhere. May and Jenny and Margaret, as children, had punted up and down the reaches of the river and had had free rein over wood and hedge and garden and house, from the barn floors to the vast and spacious attics. May had once become marooned on one of the roof gables during a hair-raising game of tig and had to be rescued by a local farmer.

Margaret laughed at the memory. "It's been a while since I climbed rooftops. Papa is frantic enough over my welfare as it is. And anyway, he's decided he's too old for country life."

Morris began to splutter in outraged and defensive protest, but Margaret continued with gay relentlessness, "Now, Uncle Topsy, it's true. Papa has never much liked coarse fishing, and I do sympathise with him. Don't you think these robust fellows look terribly damp and miserable? But what really made his mind up was when you turned the kitchen into a stable for the pony you brought back from Iceland—"

Morris grunted. "He and Georgie never used to mind about such things. In the days of Dante and Lizzie, Ned was a fine one for larking about in the hedges, music after tea, and games of hide-and-seek after dark. He calls it childishness now—"

"But, Uncle Topsy," Margaret interrupted gently, "it was twenty-five years ago. Mama and Aunt Janey couldn't have been much older then than I am now."

"If there were children, it would all come back to him. He thrives on youth. He needs another little girl to pamper."

"He's got one. Katie Lewis. She calls him Mr Beak, and he sends her the silliest sort of letters."

"Ah, she's just a passing fancy. She fills the gap. She's not the sort of child he would let sit on his lap and blow in his beer at the supper table. There's a great gaping hole in his life where his little Margaret used to be."

"I'm still here!" she vowed, attempting levity.

But Morris was serious. "He fears to lose you. He dreads the loss of your youth as he dreads your death. He means it, merry Margaret, when he entreats you not to go to Scotland; he has confessed to me that he really does believe he will never see you again, confessed it in a moment of seriousness, I believe. He fears for your life if you make this journey. He fears for his own life, as well—"

"Uncle Topsy," Margaret said firmly, "I know Papa's superstitions, and I refuse to fall prey to them myself."

"He is convinced he will not live beyond 1889—"

"Mercy, it's a notion, it's daft and rambling nonsense!" she exclaimed, beginning to feel that she were surrounded by madmen, and not a little troubled by their obsession with death: their own, her own. "Papa has also begun to calculate his age according to how old he thinks he feels when he wakes up in the morning. The last time I spoke of visiting John, Papa announced that he was now ninety-seven. He's no more at the end of his years than I am. It's a fancy!"

"Ninety-seven?" Morris muttered to himself. "So close to a hundred. So close to a hundred years."

She had a few golden summer days, an echo of lost childhood, at the Morrises' leased summer house at Kelmscott. The most antique sections of the house were sixteenth century, and the long, light room that had been Rossetti's studio in the old days was still hung with the house's original tapestries, their once-bright greens now faded into thin grey and blue. The dull, enigmatic fabric over the walls made the room look like a medieval forest, mysterious, shaded. Margaret sat here with Jenny and May during the long evenings of midsummer. May and Jenny wove and embroidered and sketched, and Margaret admired their work and helped with some of the simpler stitching. On her last evening there, Margaret tried to commit the scene to memory: beautiful Jane Morris's lovely daughters, adult now, their heads bent at their work in the long, burnt-gold light of early summer and late sunset.

Margaret had admired them when they were girls, several years her elder, and they had coddled and cosseted her in kind. She had been a doll, a plaything, and had delighted in this role without questioning it. But now? She could no longer expect to make herself interesting by delight alone. All around her, people made and crafted, embroidered and cast and printed and painted, while she remained in their midst and sat idle, the princess in the rose bower.

"What has made us so sedate?" Margaret asked suddenly. The late sun poured through the mullioned windows, golden light dancing with midge wings. There was a green smell of river water, though the river itself was hidden from view by an island of hedge.

"Sedate?" said May. "I'm not sedate. I punt, I race the pony, I tear my skirts through, collecting raspberries in briar woods. My summers are the same."

"They're not. You do it by yourself, now," said Margaret. "You don't climb rooftops anymore." It was not exactly what she had meant, but it was a good metaphor. And it disguised her real thoughts, which came too close to envy to admit. "We don't chase each other across the fields to Buscot."

"We're older," said Jenny. "But there are new games for us, don't you think? Your John."

"He's not a game," said Margaret.

"Bring him here," said May. "Bring him up to Kelmscott and we'll *make* him part of the old life. We'll connect your ravelled threads for you. Your old summers with your new."

When Margaret came home from Scotland at the end of the summer, she found the Grange sunk in its own enchanted sleep, and its inhabitants become prisoners in the Briar Wood of her father's imagination. Ned had begun work, again, on the paintings he had set aside fifteen years earlier, the lovely series of scenes from "The Sleeping Beauty." The Grange was awash with sketches of slumbering young men and women, of designs for armour and studies of draped cloth; Margaret found, in a bucket in the kitchen, a length of wild rose stem as thick as her wrist and so fiercely barbed that she was amazed no one suffered any injuries in getting it there.

Ned led his daughter out of the house to show off his work-in-progress. The Garden Studio stood between the little orchard and the road, a long building in whitewashed stucco, with a view to the apple trees. Ned used the Garden Studio for his larger canvases, and now an entire wall was taken up with the unfinished *Rose Bower*. More studies for the series lay spread about the floor and tacked to the wall boards; and Margaret, even at eighteen, felt the odd excitement of being in a place properly forbidden to her. Most of her life she had only ever been allowed in here to bring her father cups of tea or paintbrushes that he had left upstairs and needed in a hurry.

When she entered the little building, she had a sudden strange impression that she could not tell where the world ended and her father's paintings began. Vagabond blades of unkempt, urchin grass had somehow managed to force their way through the earth packed between the red tiles of the steps leading to the furnace room, and pale tentacles of spindly, light-starved ivy were reaching through the narrow slit in the outer wall that Ned used to remove oversize projects. It took her a few moments to sort out the proper and appropriate delineations: which was the common climbing rose at the studio window, and which the unreal enchanted briar caught on the unfinished canvas.

Margaret fixed her eye on the edge of the vast canvas and touched her father's sleeve. "This is new. I thought you were at work on the old series."

"I thought I'd start a new one as well. That old princess was a wanton. I'll have to get her deposed and replaced. Think of it, lying there among her ladies-in-waiting with her nightdress all undone—what will the prince have to say about it when he comes to wake her up? He'll beat his own breast and tell himself, 'Now, I'm not having any of this, thank you!' And be off to the next castle without even patting her on the head—" Ned broke off and waved at the half-completed canvas. "To say nothing of the damage it will do my reputation if people think I condone such behaviour. Now *this* young lady will be a proper churchgoer. No lying in bed for her on a Sunday morning—except, of course, after the enchantment gets her, and then, of course, she doesn't wake up for a hundred years . . ."

Margaret listened to his absurd familiar patter with only half an ear. She was rather overwhelmed by the beauty of the tangle of thorns and shell-pink roses that pulled at the heavy, green draperies of the princess's chamber. She marvelled that such a proliferation of depthless, timeless artistry could emanate from her grey-haired and nonsense-spewing father.

Two serving maids slept in a peaceful heap on cushions at the foot of the princess's bed, affectionate and comfortable, one of them slumped luxuriously in the other's lap, like sisters or the closest of companions. But a good third of the canvas was empty.

"Where's the Sleeping Beauty?" Margaret asked.

"Well," said Ned shyly, "I didn't like to start her till you were home safe and sound. I wondered if you'd model for her."

"Oh, yes, please!"

"It won't be very exciting work. You'll have to lie there with your eyes closed."

"But she should be waking up. That's how the story ends."

"This will leave something to the imagination," said her father. "You don't know how the story ends."

So they had an autumn together in the Garden Studio, but Ned grew distracted and dissatisfied with the work as the year drew to a close. The branches that tapped at the tall windows were bare now, the weather dismal. Ned complained that he could not be inspired to paint roses in perpetual blossom when all he could see of the lifeless garden was hidden in yellow fog, and Margaret found herself shivering and bored as she languished for hours on a lumpy settee, cast off from the house, in her nightdress. She did not feel like a chaste princess; she felt like the long-suffering daughter of a mad artist. Ned abandoned the series yet again in mid-December.

But of course he did not cease his tireless work. Among other things, he painted a commissioned portrait that winter, of the admired Katie Lewis, the lawyer's young daughter. Margaret found herself responsible for entertaining the girl during the long sittings. She read to Katie and sang to her and engaged in the silliest sort of bantering with the artist, but keeping Katie's sharp and irritable mind occupied was no small task. Katie and Ned adored each other, much as Margaret herself had adored her father ten years earlier; and yet Margaret found Katie to be sour and dour.

"I'm working harder than you at this portrait," Margaret told Ned after a particularly trying afternoon.

"She's a villainous child, isn't she?" said Ned cheerfully. "I love her for it." Indeed, his portrait of her reflected her villainy: a dark little girl dressed all in black, poring darkly over a book of dragons. "She wanted to know what the noise was, the other day when they were beating the carpets over the wall next door, and I told her that the man over there beats his wife, and Katie wasn't the least bit shocked—"

"Oh, Papa, you didn't!"

"Well, no, I didn't. But she wouldn't have been shocked if I had. She gives balance to my life, and to the sweetness and light of your own lost glorious girlhood. She reminds me of the monster you might have been and never were."

Margaret laughed.

"And she writes me the most adoring and devoted letters."

When next Katie complained over the tedium of the sitting, Margaret suggested they break the boredom by making an excursion to the Garden Studio. Ned stayed behind and worked upstairs while his two handmaids made their tour; Margaret, adult, was now considered old enough to be trusted in her father's workplaces on her own.

If such a thing could be possible, the Garden Studio was bleaker in February than it had been in November. It was an evil day of black London fog that hung above the rooftops; the air was clear below, but the day was dark as night, cut off from sunlight.

"You had to sit out here in your nightdress?" Katie said doubtfully, all beetling black brows and disapproval.

"In November," Margaret said, making the most of the contrast between Katie's sitting and her own.

Katie looked about her silently. Margaret gazed at the unfinished canvas that still occupied half the length of the long shed. The wild roses were a burst of blossom against the cold studio walls, like hothouse flowers within the black and dripping winter garden.

"My Mr Beak has sent me a picture of this painting," Katie said. "In a letter."

"He has?"

"A story in pictures. In the first one he's thinking, sitting in front of his painting, him all wild hair and beard, and the painting all roses and thorns. Then there is a picture of him tearing at his hair. Then he sits and thinks again; and then in the next he is *climbing into the painting*."

Katie paused, staring at the canvas with curious intensity.

"Whatever do you mean?"

"He's trying to get inside the painting. The world of the painting. To walk among the roses, I suppose. In the picture he's halfway in, one foot first."

Katie stopped, still staring hard at the unreal tangle of thorns. Margaret, knowing her father's sense of humour and imagining the end of Katie's picture story, thought of a series of fleeting images to finish the tale: Ned snoozing at the foot of the princess's bed, bearded and grizzly among the sleeping handmaids; or in another twist, his way to the palace barred by briar; or the prince tapping him on the shoulder and telling him to mind his own business.

"And what happens when he enters the Briar Wood?" Margaret asked.

Katie laughed. "Well, he doesn't. He just tears the canvas, you know, and falls out the other side."

"Poor Mr. Beak," said Margaret.

If for nothing else but the sake of those chilly November hours spent in the garden in her nightgown, Margaret sometimes wished her father would finish the *Briar Rose* series. "I'm waiting," he said. "This is a great act of creation. There is a secret to the Briar Wood, and I cannot finish until it is revealed to me."

There was no pressing him. Margaret, who thought never to complete a great act of creation herself, knew that the secret would come to the artist when it came. And of a certainty she could not tell him what he waited for.

She did not go up to Kelmscott that year, nor the following year. She rarely thought of it. Her summers slipped by, busy and full, and Morris himself was at the manor so seldom that he never seriously renewed that invitation for Ned to install himself in the Tapestry Room. But six months before her marriage, in April of 1888, Margaret made her way back to the ancient house by the river. This time it was not a journey of nostalgia; she responded to a request from Janey, Morris's gloriously beautiful wife, who was there by herself and asked Margaret to come and keep her company for a fortnight after Easter.

Once at Kelmscott, inspired by the memory of her last few days there with May and Jenny, Margaret asked John to join her during the middle weekend of her stay. With Jane Morris occupied at her weaving during the day, Margaret and John were left on the Saturday to their own devices.

The Prince Enters the Briar Wood

The fateful slumber floats and flows
About the tangle of the rose;
But lo! the fated hand and heart
To rend the slumberous curse apart!

It was April, but an unimaginable and scorching April day snatched out of deepest midsummer. The heat made the day still, as though all the low Thames floodplain around Kelmscott was encased in a lens of light and haze. Margaret brought John to the end of the road to nowhere, to where the little footpath led through hedge and field to the open Thames, and to Buscot village two miles upstream on the other side of the river. Abandoning propriety, they paddled barefoot with the cows along the riverbank before they reached the village. They lunched together at the Apple Tree in Buscot, Margaret trying to hide the dripping hem of her skirt, John laughing at her.

This, Margaret thought, is what it was like when the Morrises and the Rossettis and my own Burne-Joneses used to play together, twenty-five years ago, before the stillbirths and the overdoses and the sad affairs.

They walked back slowly, in the long Saturday afternoon, cross-country.

Blossoming blackthorn like sea foam marked the field boundaries; the land was so flat that the river could only be smelt, not seen. Margaret and John aimed for the dark line of trees on the horizon that marked the manor at Kelmscott, caught in an enchanted landscape of white blossom and a sudden summer heat that had arrived before its time.

All Margaret's memory of that swooning afternoon ran to the field boundary like a magnet to the north; and printed on her mind's eye ever after was the intricate pattern of black and white and green against the blue, the sharp outline of the blackthorn over their heads, the soft handfuls of blossom, the sweet scent. No child came of this coupling, and it was to be another six months before they were lawfully wed; but Margaret always felt that their marriage took place there, with its first consummation.

Afterward they lay together looking up into the tangle of thorn and planning their life ahead, and it seemed utterly right to have begun it there, to have awoken such new and bright passions amid the tangled hedges of the young river, in this spring day stolen from summer. On John's stripped jacket spread over the grass, amid Margaret's drying skirts, they fell asleep.

Her father gave her, as a sort of unofficial wedding present, a miniature rendition of *The Rose Bower.* John marked it to be destined to illuminate their bedroom. "Too utterly soporific to hang in a drawing room, or a dining room," he insisted. "Our guests will be sleeping in their soup."

In the meantime it stayed in Margaret's girlhood bedroom at the Grange. She glanced at the little painting at odd times during morning and evening, as she put up her hair or climbed into her nightgown, and saw the tangle of briar and rose and imposed upon it her own delightful blackthorn dream.

The Council Chamber

The threat of war, the hope of peace,
The Kingdom's peril and increase
Sleep on and bide the latter day,
When fate shall take her chain away.

She was married in September. Ned, still convinced he would not live beyond the end of the following year, once again began work on the *Briar Rose* series, this time in frantic earnest. Margaret did not see the finished *Rose Bower* for a long time; it lurked behind *The Council Chamber,* and then behind *The Garden Court.* Ned was immersed with the prince in the Briar Wood when Margaret came to tell him she was pregnant, in the autumn after her first wedding anniversary.

"The child won't come till May," she said. "Much too deep into the new year for you to meet your deadline with destiny. And you must, dear Papa, arrange a meeting with my baby. You will have to extend yourself into the next decade."

Ned finished the series. The paintings were auctioned by Agnew's amid a great deal of sensation, and one Alexander Henderson bought them for his drawing room at his new home in Buscot Park. Margaret could not quite get over the coincidence of this, but privately agreed with John that it was silly to hang such pictures in any drawing room.

She went with John to see the series during the few days it was exhibited in Toynbee Hall in Whitechapel. It seemed that all of London was doing the same; the hall was packed. Yet it was like no exhibition she had ever before experienced. This audience was silent, rapt, as if it, too, had fallen under the spell of the enchanted sleep. Margaret sat in a row of charmed viewers, feeling herself to be rather plain and homespun in her serge dress and with her bulging belly, among the furs and silks of the London bourgeoisie. John stood at her side with a protective hand on her shoulder as they gazed at the finished story.

A whisper and rustle broke out in a corner of the hall as three fashionable young women made a discovery that had eluded the other viewers. They advanced upon Margaret.

"Aurora," said one in such hushed tones that Margaret could barely make out her words. "The Briar Rose. You must be the princess."

"You've found her out," said John.

"Is it true? The likeness isn't coincidence?"

"You see the artist's daughter before you," John proclaimed with pride.

"It was a long time ago," said Margaret. "I was a girl when I sat for it." She touched her belly, a habit now, as the baby moved.

"And you are?" another of the trio asked of John. He stood aside his wife, alert and afoot at the end of the line of seated, enraptured viewers.

"My husband," Margaret said.

The Garden Court

The maiden plaisance of the land
Knoweth no stir of voice or hand,

No cup the sleeping waters fill,
The restless shuttle lieth still.

Margaret came to Kelmscott a month later with the double purpose of
witnessing the mounting of the *Briar Rose* paintings in Buscot Park,
and of again being company to Jane Morris, who had opened the house to
Ned while he was working at Buscot. May and Jenny, both deeply involved
with their father's firm, had entreated Margaret to accompany their mother,
whose mind and body were becoming frail before their time. Her daughters
did not like her to be alone at Kelmscott so long during the day now, and
even most weekends Morris himself was, as ever, too frantically busy to
join her.

This time it felt strange to Margaret to be alone with Jane Morris.
Janey's hair, always of such rich, dark glory, was going white, and the classical frame of her ethereally handsome face was etched and lined. Her
weaving was abandoned. Janey went about her house like her own phan-
tom, touching the things she used to work with as though she were not
quite sure how they were to be used. Her hair was silver cloud in the firelight; her profile was that of Athena, silhouetted against the mullioned
windows in the Tapestry Room. She would look up to find Margaret watching her and then she would smirk, her expression wry and enticing, lovely
as any of Rossetti's portraits.

Margaret went with her father to Buscot Park on the day he chose to
view the room where his paintings were to be hung. Alexander Henderson
was such an admirer of the Pre-Raphaelite Brotherhood that he had
amassed his own collection of their work, and in Henderson's new house his
canvas treasures stood propped against the walls of the entrance hall.
Among these paintings languished images of Janey as a young woman, and
before that, as no more than a girl; on her way in and out of the hall, Margaret found herself shivering at so many portraits of the Jane Morris that no
longer was, the ghost of a woman who still lived. It made Margaret reluctant to look at her own image locked in *The Rose Bower* because it made her
so aware that one day she, too, would be ghosted by her former self, as her
own hair went white and her own portrait remained maiden and ageless.

She had been visiting with Janey and waiting on her father for two
weeks when William Morris came up to Kelmscott to be ill. He had
decided he needed to convalesce, for the weekend at any rate. What a
group they made: Janey, with her luxurious waves of white-streaked hair;

Morris, coughing and spluttering and sneezing in the stiff April rain; Ned, his mind utterly preoccupied with the hanging of the precious *Briar Rose;* and Margaret herself, heavy with the child she carried. Morris employed her in his entertainment for the weekend and gave her orders to see that he stayed in bed. He languished there now, his giant body propped up on a mound of pillows in his giant bed as though he were a sultan, or a lucky Falstaff finally dying in the palace of his patron.

"You need tapestry curtains for this bed," Margaret told him. "Something with willows and lilies, to go with the wallpaper."

Among other strangenesses of this trip, it was strange to be sitting at "Uncle Topsy's" bedside. Until this weekend Margaret had only been able to imagine Morris at Kelmscott as she had known him as a child. He would arrive suddenly, call the children names in Icelandic, and shout at his wife and his guests, then sit in the garden furiously sketching until long past sundown, so that they had to bring him candles; and then he would disappear in as violent a hurry as he had come. And here was Morris now, still giant in body but somehow diminished in spirit by his cold: a quieter voice, a slower temper. It puzzled Margaret to try to reconcile the quiet man in bed with the loud man who dominated the breakfast table in her mother's kitchen, the "uncle" who had perched on the rocking horse in her nursery reading poetry to her, the dervish who had thundered in and out of her girlhood's summer holidays.

"I'm going to have May design a hanging for the bed. Willows and lilies!" Morris snorted. "No, it will be something appropriate for an Elizabethan furnishing, with birds and vines and roses to spread about the sleepers like a wildflower hedge. I imagine myself reclining with great satisfaction in such a bower, deep on a winter's night, a green veil shading my dreams with forgotten summers—"

"You're an unlikely Sleeping Beauty," Margaret said.

"Ah, the famous *Briar Rose.* I have written a song for the *Briar Rose,* four little verses to complement the paintings. Let me—" He stopped to sneeze, and continued, "Ned has asked to use them as titles to adorn the framed paintings. How is the hanging progressing?"

"Famously, now, but it began with a terrific argument. Papa was disgusted with the drawing room at Buscot Park when he arrived."

"Oh, tell, tell," said Morris. "Henderson is such an obsequious admirer."

"Don't be snobbish. You thrive on admiration. Well, Papa stood in the middle of the drawing room—and if you've ever been there or even just seen the house from the outside, you must know that the ceilings are fifteen feet high—he stood in the middle of this lovely, light apartment and said, with stern and solemn disapproval, 'This little room! It has but two unbroken walls. We'll stack the paintings back to back, or hang them from the chandelier. Perhaps you'd like them set into the ceiling like the Sistine Chapel, and your guests can lie on the carpet and admire them from below.'"

Margaret stopped quoting her father's rant and laughed.

"And what did young Henderson find to say to that?"

"Henderson let him know that since he'd paid for them, the paintings were his, and Papa could no longer make any claim to them."

Morris gave a howl of laughter. "And then the steam began to whistle through Ned's ears."

"It wasn't so bad. They were both enjoying themselves. Papa said, 'Your drawing room's too small. If you don't let me hang them in the saloon, then hang them yourself, and *hang* them.'"

Morris howled again.

"And then he told Henderson that if he did let him mount them in the saloon instead of the drawing room, Papa would design frames for them and paint a dozen more connecting panels between the pictures. This is what he's doing now. The whole series is turning into a kind of frieze. It's lovely to watch the walls change—every day there is a bit more space covered with paint, every morning a few more branches of blossom have crept around the room."

Then Morris reached out and plucked at Margaret's sleeve and discarded on the tray at his bedside three green leaves and a fading white blossom of blackthorn that had lodged themselves in the fold of her cuff as she had made her way from Buscot back to Kelmscott. "*The Rose Bower*," he murmured.

Margaret found herself lingering at Kelmscott through the middle of April, though her time was drawing near and nearer, and her father began to entreat her to return to her husband in London. But it was not so far or long a journey by train, and she felt sure that John could come for her if necessary. She felt bound to stay while her father finished the creation of Henderson's miniature briar wood. And, too, she found that she liked visiting with Janey. After William Morris returned to work, the house was quiet; the frantic creative activity of the Morris household had been left behind in London. Here, there was no need to feel stifled; the wide Thames floodplain opened before her every morning.

But still Margaret was troubled at her own lack of accomplishment in the Morris shadow. Even Jane Morris herself—had she no longer the marvellous needlewoman's eye and hand, she still had her immortal beauty. That in itself was a kind of craft, Margaret now realized, thinking of the paintings racked along Henderson's walls: Holman-Hunt, Rossetti, Morris himself, and the hand of her father, each capturing the Grecian nose and faerie hair for themselves and forever. Janey as Elaine of Astolat, Janey as Morgan le Fay, Janey as Pandora, Janey as Jane Morris. What had Margaret's own few sittings to add to posterity next to Janey's radiance? In one, Margaret's was a face among many along a stair that led nowhere; in this other, her father's finest creation, she offered to all time a gentle, maiden appeal. But it was static, caught in time, locked in the sleep of the enchanted thorn wood. Janey's was a woman's beauty, a beauty that vibrated, that danced, that lived, that ordered life; Margaret's was that of a girl asleep.

Her father had by now forbidden her to walk across the fields and river to Buscot, so when she visited him at work, she made the journey by dogcart. But she missed the trek along the hedges and over the water. She knew better than to attempt the walk now; she did not trust her balance, with her added weight and unfamiliar shape, to risk the crossing at the flash lock east of Buscot village, or to try to pole herself across in the Morrises' punt. But she could not resist the temptation of a morning walk along the thorn lanes of the fields surrounding the manor. They were all in blossom now and put her in mind of the long Saturday afternoon with John, two Aprils earlier. It was colder now than it had been then, and wetter, and windier. But Margaret would go out anyhow, trying to walk away from her strange jealousy of an old woman's youth captured on timeless canvas, and trying to assure herself that her simple life had its own creative worth.

The Rose Bower

Here lies the hoarded love, the key
To all the treasure that shall be;
Come fated hand the gift to take,
And smite this sleeping world awake.

One morning she walked farther than she ought. It was another windy day, bright but cold. She found a path that led north from Kelmscott village and away to a dark line of vegetation, which she took for a wood. She reached the line in less time than she had expected; it was only a tall hedge, a low and ugly barrier of thick thorn not yet in leaf. She turned and walked along this wall for a way, reluctant to turn back, barred from going on. And so when she came to an opening in the hedge, she turned in, aimlessly, and wondering where the path would lead.

She entered a little wooden maze, the branches and twigs overhead interlocking and intertwining in an endless and unrepeating pattern. The air was still within the wood, the wood so thick that it provided a wall against the wind. The branches overhead were green and limber and co-loured the light beneath pale green as well.

Papa should see this, Margaret thought idly. *It is like his Briar Wood. I will have to bring him here—I will never be able to describe it.*

She walked a little way into the mysterious little thicket, intrigued. Deeper within the twisted wood, buds appeared at the tips and ends of the woven branches.

She wondered, *Do the Morrises know this is here?* It looked so like Morris's designs, so like her father's own paintings, yet it was different be-cause it was a living wood—a real wood—and she had found her way inside.

The buds gave way to blossom. Small wild roses in blushing pearl and palest coral opened on either side of the ill-defined path. *It must be warmer here,* Margaret thought, *out of the wind—these blooms are early.*

After another twenty paces she stopped to stare in astonishment as the thicket exploded in flower.

She had never seen so many roses. Unthinking, Margaret walked deeper in so that she stood utterly in their midst, for this quiet place was more beautiful than anything she had ever imagined. *I must bring Papa here,* she thought, and then suddenly stood still among the roses and the thorns and the heavy, sweet air and let a strange thought wash over her:

I am in the Briar Wood.

The green air was still, and warm. Margaret took a few steps deeper in, and the beautiful, bewildering thicket opened before her. *The source of all inspiration and dreaming, and I am allowed in?* She could not imag-ine what might await her on the other side of the tangle of thorns, but neither could she consider turning back. If she herself could make no use of this vision, or mission, she must at least bring back to her father the answer to what lay within.

Margaret walked ahead another little way, then stopped in agony and wonder as a band of clenching pain wound itself about her middle.

She thought at first, logically, somehow, that like one of the unsuccessful sleeping princes she had been caught by the living thorn and pulled into its relentless embrace. In Ned's earliest version of *The Prince Enters the Briar Wood*, one of the sleeping princes lay naked and contorted and strapped across the chest by tough, thorned vines like iron bands. This, in an instant, was what she felt: the stabbing, tightening pain of enchantment. But when it slacked away and Margaret stood gasping in its aftermath, she knew it for what it was.

Then panic took her, more biting than thorns or the first pangs of childbirth. She was at least a mile from Kelmscott. And here in the Briar Wood, perhaps she was farther away than that. She was utterly alone, in an unknown place—in an unknown time? She might have come too far to turn back.

The grasping pain clamped around her again, as insistent and as searing as before, and there was no other rational thing to do but to go. The child she carried insisted on her turning.

She did not run. She could not run. And she had a terrible idea that if she tried to run, the clinging tendrils of briar and thorn would reach out leafy fingers to drag her back. She did not even want to seem to be leaving. The wood was opening before her; surely it must be closing in behind her, as well.

She took two steps backward, and then three more, and then bowed under the force of another contraction. It happened again and again. But in this way she came slowly out of the shadowy realm of inspiration and back into the light world of earth and sky and paint and trains. It took her, she discovered later, nearly three hours from the time she entered the Briar Wood to the time she reached the first farm cottage at the edge of Kelmscott village—and surely she covered no more than a mile in this time.

The villagers knew who she was, and the young farmer's wife, with her own experience in the onset of childbirth, calmly brought Margaret into her kitchen. She set Margaret by the fire in a great armchair supplied with cushions that had, by the look of them, been donated to her household by the benevolent Morrises. The young woman brought Margaret a cup of beef tea, and sent her next-to-eldest daughter (the five-year-old) to the manor to fetch Jane Morris, and sent her eldest (at seven) to the Plough to have someone there bring Ned away from Buscot. Safe in her own, known world of plates and cups and kitchen fires, Margaret came to herself, and the searing contractions stopped.

"It happens that way, sometimes," said the farmer's wife. "You're sure the baby's on its way into the world within the hour, then suddenly another week's dragged by and nothing's happened. Your first, is it? And not expected for another fortnight? You'll not be in any danger yet."

The woman's sure experience was both comforting and irritating. Margaret did not fear the oncoming labour; but she had feared to meet it in the Briar Wood.

"Where does the thorn wood at the end of the lane past the inn lead to?" Margaret asked.

"The path goes through to Paradise Farm," said the woman. "You cross a little branch of the Leach, and then two fields."

"I was in a wood. The path ends there, and there's a thorn hedge, with a gap leading into a thicket."

"There's no wood between here and Paradise Farm," said the woman. "Though if you go down to the Thames that way, there's a beech coppice. You say a thorn wood?"

Margaret stared down into the depths of her cup and found that her hands were shaking. She had sought reassurance that her world was in solid order and found instead confirmation of the unknown. She said slowly, "I must have lost my senses for a spell. I don't know where I was, or how I found my way back."

"But look at this." With her calloused hands the countrywoman smoothed Margaret's tousled hair and from its tangled web pulled a small, pale wild rose.

Ned insisted that Margaret return to London. When at the end of the day it appeared that nothing was happening, he accompanied her on the last train back that very night. The work could wait, he said. John left their little house in Kensington Square to come and be with Margaret at the Grange, the house she had grown up in, while they waited for their baby.

They waited. She began to feel ridiculous for having gone into such a panic back at Kelmscott. Days dragged by, and then a week, and then Ned decided that his role in the crisis had passed and that he must get back to his frieze at Buscot and to Jane Morris, who had stayed behind alone. Ned had but one or two days' work left, and he thought to be away only so long as it took for him to finish.

Margaret waited one more day, and then it began.

She was back in the Briar Wood again, alone, and this time she knew what she must bring out. Thorn and thicket blocked her path; she did not run. The clinging tendrils of briar and thorn wrapped their arms of leaf and steel about her body and drew her in to them, tightening and retightening, releasing and contracting, as they pulled her down. Imprisoned and in pain, she could yet see distinctly the outline of each red petal as the roses bloomed around her and could smell their cloying perfume; when one blossomed against her cheek, Margaret could feel its petals smooth and soft against her skin. She plunged farther in, knowing what waited on the other side.

She lived the paradox that her father had tried to discover in his painting: the pleasure and pain, the sweet scent and delicate beauty torn through with merciless strength and violent passion. This was how you came by inspiration, how you came to "a great act of creation." You tore into the canvas and landed hard on the floor. You shivered in your nightdress on the settee in the garden; you lay on your back on ploughed earth with wet skirts and a tangle of thorn overhead. You—

The kiss.

She gave a shout of understanding, of agony and of relief. It was suddenly over. She had won through and gained the prize.

John was there. He hovered over her with dishevelled hair, his tie askew and collar undone. He kissed her again. He held their daughter in his arms.

"Wake, dearest."

Margaret sat up, shuddering and gasping, the enchantment broken, fully comprehending. A woman awake.

Dedicated, with love, to Gilly, Belinda, Margaret, Teghan, Tracy, Lindsey, Yvonne, and Hilary (twice).

About "For the Briar Rose"

I wrote this story in the three months following the birth of my daughter Sara, my first child. I'd done most of the research previous to Sara's arrival—a short train journey to Oxford, a morning in the Upper Reading Room of the Bodleian Library, and then an hour on the Cherwell in a rented canoe. The journey to Kelmscott came after Sara was born. She was only three weeks old. The ticket-taker at the garden gate peeked in the sleeping bundle on my chest and commented, "I can tell she's a girl. She has a lady's face."

I dedicated the story to the other women in my "baby group"—all first-time mothers from the same clinic whose babies were due within the same month. I guess it's pretty obvious that it's a story about becoming a mother.

Sara was born in 1997. Rereading this story nearly fifteen years after I wrote it, I don't remember the crafting of it. But I'm aware that all the characters are based on historical figures, and though their interactions are fictional, all I've done is breathe life into them and wake them from their hundred years' sleep, as it were. It's a kind of connect-the-dots history, in which I've drawn together anecdotes and incidents from a collection of biographies, buildings, and paintings and put them together in a coherent way (I hope). It's fascinating for me to see this now because it's very much how my most recent book was written, but when I wrote "For the Briar Rose," I was nowhere near the skilled historian that I am now—and indeed none of the research I did for this story involved the Internet. Incredible, but true.

I suppose it is important for me to note that though the history of Burne-Jones's sporadic work on the *Briar Rose* series is presented here as accurately as I could make it, nevertheless *this is a work of fiction.* Margaret's thoughts and feelings as I've written them are my own contribution. The Margaret of this story is my original character, not Burne-Jones's daughter.

But the real Margaret Burne-Jones was the real model for the real *Rose Bower* painting, and you can go see *The Rose Bower* and the rest of Burne-Jones's *Briar Rose* series for yourself. The paintings are part of the Faringdon Collection and are maintained on fabulous display in the Saloon of Buscot Park, now owned by the National Trust, in Oxfordshire. The present Lord Faringdon, a descendant of Alexander Henderson, administers the house and grounds and, in the generous spirit of his ancestor, continues to expand the Faringdon Collection with works by contemporary artists.

http://www.buscot-park.com/house
http://www.buscot-park.com/house/the-saloon
http://www.buscot-park.com/faringdon-collection/paintings-at
-buscot

Bibliography

Burne-Jones, Sir Edward. *Letters to Katie*. London: Macmillan, 1925.

Dean, Ann S. *Burne-Jones and William Morris in Oxford and the Surrounding Area*. Malvern: Heritage Press, 1991.

Fitzgerald, Penelope. *Edward Burne-Jones: A Biography*. 1975. London: Hamish Hamilton, 1989.

Lago, Mary, ed. *Burne-Jones Talking: His Conversations, 1895–1898, Preserved by His Studio Assistant Thomas Rooke*. Columbia: University of Missouri Press, 1981.

Morris, William. "For the Briar Rose" and "Another for the Briar Rose." *Poems by the Way*. 1911. Bristol: Thoemmes Press, 1994.

Powell, Kirsten. "Edward Burne-Jones and the Legend of the Briar Rose." *Journal of Pre-Raphaelite Studies* 6, no. 2 (May 1986): 15–28.

Thirkell, Angela. *Three Houses*. 1931. London: Robin Clark, 1986.

Angela Thirkell, born Angela MacKail, was Margaret Burne-Jones's first child and Burne-Jones's granddaughter. She became an accomplished and popular novelist. *Three Houses* is a memoir of her childhood and includes a delightful portrait of her artist grandfather.

THE GOVERNESS

The governess inhabits a liminal space. She is not a servant, exactly . . . but nor is she a member of the family. Though she is impoverished, she is also genteel. Though she is the family's employee, she is also its protector.

Her name is Annabelle, but at the manor house known as The Silver Beeches, the family B____—father, mother with her faint, lingering hint of an Irish accent, two girls, and a boy—call her Mrs Reed. She is widowed. She has no children of her own.

Mr B____ does nothing so pedestrian as to work, nothing so frightfully middle-class as to hold down a job. His family's maintenance is secured through a complex of investments, estates, trusts, and inheritances so Byzantine that Annabelle does not pretend to comprehend it. It would not seem out of place in the novels of one Mr Dickens, which Annabelle reads in her room beside the nursery after supper, when the children are asleep. Candles are dear, and her room has no gas, so she reads sparingly—except when she is caught up in some twist of the plot and lingers awake far too long into the night.

As she must rise before the household in the morning, in order to comb and dress the children for display at breakfast, this taste for literary adventure is a considerable hardship. Fortunately, the children breakfast—and take their luncheon and tea—in the nursery, so Annabelle is not expected to govern them to adult standards during the meal itself. Annabelle is privileged—Mr B____ made sure upon her hiring that she understood it was a privilege, when most governesses take each of their meals alone—to have her supper with the family, during which it is her responsibility to insure that the children remain mannerly.

Even in the meals they take in the nursery, she does endeavour to keep them on their company manners. It is hers to instil in them the social graces—and those social graces will be necessary to all three as they make their ways in the world. Hers, too, are their lessons.

Having been married to a doctor, she is adequate to teach the children such natural history as they may require, and as much of the sciences. Having kept her late husband's books for many years, Annabelle is competent to teach them to read and write and manage figures. Having studied such things herself as a young girl and woman, she can educate them on the mysteries of elocution and deportment, of piano and—for the girls—needlework.

She is, Mr B____ informs her, quite an asset. Quite an asset indeed.

The mistress of the house, Mrs B____, is not quite an invalid. The doctor would keep her on bed rest, but Mrs B____ is strong-willed (so Mr B____ often says at dinner, with a look across the table that is meant to seem solicitous: "My lovely wife is strong-willed"), and though she is visibly thin-wristed and frail, she insists on dressing for breakfast, for a walk in the garden, and again for dinner each day.

What happens after dinner, Annabelle does not know. Once the children are abed, she retires to her room with her book and her candle. She does not stir again until morning, and she does not listen to the silences that fill the cavernous house at night—silences composed of the creak of footsteps across ancient floors, the click of softly shut, well-oiled old doors. If Annabelle is not old—not in the sense of being uncapable—nor is she young. But when she first came to the employ of the family B____, the maids took pity on her—though she was not exactly a servant—and warned her to stay with the children at night, or in her room with the door bolted.

The door to the children's room has no lock, nor does the door from the nursery to the hall. Annabelle tells herself that surely no harm will come to her by that route. Surely, not through the children's room.

The house is silent in the dark hours. Mrs B____ keeps to her room, and there are never sounds from the servant's quarters.

The B___ children are named Charity, Constance, and Simon. Girls are expected to embody virtues, but boys may be themselves. Charity, Constance, and Simon—for that is their birth order: Charity nine, Constance eight, and Simon four, having been born after two difficult, failed pregnancies—are children like any children, inasmuch as any child can be said to be typical. They are not particular angels nor particular devils, which is a puzzling blessing given their immediate ancestry.

Annabelle, whose lack of children in her own marriage was not down to a lack of desire for children, adores them.

The Silver Beeches stands above the Irish Sea, but not within sight of it except for such glimpses as are available from the highest windows. You can stand in the turret—or, Annabelle imagines, in the windows of the servants' quarters that break the line of the grey slates—and watch the black dots of seal heads break the wrinkled, sun-shining mirror of the ocean.

The estate boasts a crumbling castle—no more than a heap of stones in the outline of walls and a tumbledown tower, now—on the bluff close above the strand. As Annabelle leads her charges outside in the afternoon, the sea air floats up bracing and crisp, and clouds tear themselves behind the castle's empty windows.

They leave through the rear of the house—Annabelle, Charity, Constance, and Simon—so Annabelle and the children are the first to see a new person coming in. She is young and thin, her brown hair dry and fraying from its twist. She has not had enough to eat—not recently, perhaps not ever. She cannot be more than seventeen. She carries a threadbare carpetbag and her dress is worn at the hem and shiny at the elbows—but neatly pressed and mended.

The girl catches Annabelle's eye and goes still and frozen like a terrified doe. She drops the carpetbag and a curtsy simultaneously. "Ma'am!"

"Oh, no," says Annabelle. "I am Mrs Reed, the governess. Please stand up."

"Trudy. Trudy Bell." The girl crouches and scrambles her carpetbag back up out of the gravel. "I'm the new downstairs maid. Begging your pardon, Mrs Reed."

Trudy Bell stands with her head twisted to one side, eyes pinned to the flower border. A thoroughly cowed young woman. Annabelle feels a piercing sorrow. She opens her mouth to say, *Go, go from this house.*

But where would a child like this go? Out on the streets, to starve or whore herself?

There are worse things than service at The Silver Beeches.

"You'll want the housekeeper, then," Annabelle says, as the children skip on ahead. "Through the kitchen door on the right. The cook is Mrs Postlethwait. She'll find Mrs Bailey for you."

The girl scuttles off, transparently grateful for Annabelle's kindness. Annabelle hurries after the children, sick to her stomach and sick to her soul.

The children shout, running now, so Annabelle must call off after them. They drop into a walk at the sound of her voice, but by following the line of their flight, she can see what attracted them.

Their mother is also on her afternoon constitutional, and for once Mrs B____ has left behind the level, gravelled garden paths to stomp along the cliff's edge. She must be able to hear the children shouting after her—sound carries a long way in this air, and the wind is off the coast at this hour—but she does not turn or glance back, though the breeze blows her shawl tassels like streamers toward the sea.

Mrs B____ pauses at the cliff edge. She spreads her arms against the wind, and for one terrible moment Annabelle feels her breath lodged in her chest as if her heart were a stone. *Not in front of your children*—

Annabelle hears the hiss of the waves amidst the stones below. As she strides forward, catching up with the children now, ready to clutch them and drag them away, Mrs B____ lifts her hands to her head and pulls the pins from her hair. It banners out, shining in the sun, as seal-brown as her children's. The wind whips it towards the ocean, a streamer, a wind sock.

It seems alive, vital. Sensual. Opinionated, as if it would draw Mrs B____ after it, into the air, into the sea.

Annabelle should perhaps be scandalized. Instead, she catches her breath in wonder.

When she looks down, Simon has isolated a hopper from a grass stem and is twisting off one of its wings. The spell is broken, and Annabelle bends down to arrest his tortures and rescue the poor thing.

But in the end, all she can do is give it mercy. Simon's childish fingers have crushed the life half out of it by the time she notices.

It is time for lessons. Charity practises the spinet while Constance reads aloud to Simon. Simon is sorting his blocks by colours. Annabelle has been teaching him the letters that adorn them, but he is a little shaky still when it comes to differentiating all the ones with bumps on the right side. Constance shows him in the illustrated primer—not patiently, because Constance is not a patient child, nor has Annabelle been able to instil any patience—but persistently. Her sleek, seal-brown head is bowed over his same-coloured one. Annabelle suspects that Mr B____ considers it a sort of outrage that all three of the children favour their mother.

She tells herself—and this is one of the days she makes herself believe it—that this is as true of their temperaments as their looks. It's an idyllic scene, the three children in the shafts of afternoon sun, and although Annabelle does not intend to doze, the wakefulness of many a night sneaks up on her. Her eyes will lid themselves. The somnolent, thready line of Charity's picking her way through an unfamiliar piece of music will lull her. The sun streaming through the muslin curtains will warm her hair.

She is not aware that she has drifted off—dangerous, in this house— but she knows when she awakens, startling out of her chair. Constance wails, gasping between sobs, face pressed to her knees. The primer is on the floor, pages spindled under a cracked spine. Simon must have pulled it away from her and stormed over to Charity. Now he reaches around her, crashing fists just lengthening from pudgy toddler hands to the spider-fingered hands of a child down on the keys.

Simon pounds with a fine crashing discord on the spinet. At first, Charity attempts to play on, angling her shoulders to block Simon from the keyboard. He claws around her.

This does not improve the quality of the music. "Simon!" Annabelle commands. "Stop that at once!"

Annabelle pulls herself out of the chair and crouches beside Constance, urging the child to uncurl so Annabelle can see her face. It's streaked and blotchy, but there is no blood, and from where she clutches herself, Annabelle thinks Simon must have punched her in the stomach.

"Simon!"

The thunder of punched keys continues.

"Mrs Reed," Charity says in frustration, her voice nearly a rising whine. This once, Annabelle does not rebuke her. The girl deserves a treat for not simply hitting her much smaller brother in return.

If their places were exchanged, Annabelle would.

"Simon," Annabelle says, rising to her feet. Her skirts sway about her ankles as she crosses the room in two swift, unladylike strides. She lifts Simon up by his elbows as he kicks and wails, catching her a good clout in the shin and another below the eye before she manages to get him secured at arm's length.

"Simon!" She gives the boy a small shake, hoping she will not have to resort to a spanking. Mr B____ enjoys it a little too precisely when she must report that the children have been spanked. Simon stares at her, startled—and just as Constance is winding down, he, too, begins to wail.

Of course this gives Constance a fresh wind. Annabelle's ears ring. Her head swims. Still bearing Simon aloft, she squinches her eyes and scrabbles after a strategy to interrupt the both of them. Charity, looking at her big-eyed and stern, will cooperate with a distraction if only Annabelle can find a way to lead her—

The nursery door flies open. There framed is Mr B____, his hands spread wide, his face ruddy beneath the shock of light brown hair. His chin quivers with wrath between the bulwarks of an imperial beard. His voice, calm and comprehensive, is the worst of all.

"What," he asks, catching the door handle before the door can bounce against the stop, "precisely is the problem here?"

"Sir," says Annabelle.

"Calm these children, Mrs Reed."

His eyes linger on her, on the waist of her sober, dark gown, on the high lace collar bleached white as snow by the household staff. Her skin creeps as if it could bunch together for safety.

"Sir," she says. Her voice strong. She knows better than to show him weakness.

Ironically, his appearance has proven just the interruption the children needed. Now they all stare at him with big eyes, silent and watchful. Annabelle feels Simon's trembling through her palms as he swallows a sob. She lowers him to the floor and pulls him against her skirts. "Of course, sir," she says.

You got lucky," says the maid who brings in the tea—voice soft, eyes averted. "You're lucky them children is always here."

"I know," says Annabelle.

In the night, over her book—*Pride and Prejudice*—Annabelle hears Trudy screaming.

Annabelle knows it must be Trudy because the other girls have long since learned not to make a sound.

Annabelle could close her book. She could pull the pillows over her head and pretend she does not hear. She could unbolt the bolted door. She could—

She can do nothing.

In the night, in the hard cold of the sea air that filters in around her ill-fitted window frame, Annabelle makes herself sit and listen.

To be a witness, if she can be no more.

The doctors call it nervous exhaustion. Annabelle no longer thinks that what afflicts Mrs B____ goes by so ridiculous a name. Men will never call a thing what it is; they have to make up fancy terms, as if that gives them a sense that they understand—that they can *control* it.

A broken heart. That's what's killing Mrs B____.

She wanders from room to unoccupied room in the afternoons, after her constitutional, before she must dress for dinner. In these hours when her husband and her doctors would have her abed and resting, she draws the curtains and opens them again. She opens chests and blanket boxes, removes the quilts or baby clothes stored within. She seems—restlessly, relentlessly—to be searching for something. Sometimes she stands in the turret and stares out at the sea.

Sometimes, her husband orders her to bed, and then she goes—steps dragging, like an old dog told to leave the fireside. She obeys her husband . . . but only when the command is direct.

On *this* evening, however, she enters an occupied room: the nursery, where all three children are at their respective levels of arithmetic. She does not knock, merely swings the door wide and stands there, framed in it—as her husband was framed before—with her hair once again twisted up neatly and her slim figure straight in a dress as brown as her hair. It could be a governess's dress, Annabelle thinks, except for the quality of the cloth and the cut, which flatters her long neck and sharp chin.

"My darlings," Mrs B____ says, and steps inside the door. It swings shut behind her and she latches it with her left hand. Before she can crouch and hold out her arms, Mrs Reed has released her pupils from their positions at the study table with a gesture and touch.

She knows governesses who would remonstrate—inasmuch as any woman can remonstrate with her employer's wife—with mothers who interrupted the schooling of their children. She remembers her own governess, who had tart words for her own mother. *Mrs Bartholomew, I can have no control over these children if you insist upon undermining my authority.*

But Annabelle's father never made a servant girl scream in the night.

The children scamper to their mother and pile into her arms like puppies. It could be a charming domestic scene, the sort a sentimental painter might adore, were it not for the white, drawn set of Mrs B____'s expression, the way her fingers curl to claws, carefully restrained, against her children's shoulders.

She meets Annabelle's gaze above the heads of her children and holds them closer for a moment, her eyelids drooping as she inhales the fragrance of Charity's hair. Then she stands, setting them back from her, and says, "Mrs Reed. I beg your pardon."

"Not at all, Mrs B____." Annabelle lowers her voice, though there is no one to overhear. "I had been meaning to have a word with you, if you are available."

Mrs B____ regards her steadily from under beetled brows. "A word in private? Your chamber, then? Back to your studies, my darlings. . . ."

Wordlessly, Annabelle opens the connecting door. She stands aside and lets the lady of the house precede her. She shuts the door behind, but stands closest to it so if the children's voices rise she will hear it.

In the evening light from the window, Mrs B____ looks thinner and more drawn than ever. Her eyes are brown and liquid as a spaniel's. In that moment, if Annabelle could poison Mr B____ with a glance, he would be convulsing upon the floor.

"Ma'am," Annabelle says, stumbling on it. "Do you have family? Anyone?"

"I have family," Mrs B____ says slowly, ironically. "They cannot help me, though."

"They are not close?" Annabelle sees from the other woman's expression that that is not the answer. A more delicate question: "Is there . . . no money?"

Mrs B____ actually laughs, a sound like being rocked in waves, leading Annabelle to realise that she has never heard it before. "There is money. But my husband . . ."

She says the word with such loathing that Annabelle is not surprised when it gets stuck in her throat. Mrs B____ shakes her head and continues, ". . . my husband has possession of . . . a family heirloom. It is by this that he commands me."

"Ah." Annabelle forces herself to raise her eyes and look her employer's wife in the face. "What he does . . ." Annabelle doesn't think she'll be able to make herself say it. But she does, and there it is, and somehow she gets her mouth around it. "What he does will have an effect on the children."

Mrs B____ closes her eyes. "Did you think I was not aware of that, Mrs Reed?"

Every morning, every morning. Annabelle makes sure the children's faces are washed. She dresses them—pinafores for the girls, still a white dress for Simon, who will not be in breeches for another year or more—and combs their hair. Then she leads them downstairs, to be presented to their father with his coffee.

Mr B____ sits at one end of the long table, Mrs B____ at the other. The formal dining room ensures sufficient space between them. The children are presented, inspected, and admonished to behave—and Annabelle's duties to the adults of the house are complete until suppertime.

At least, on any normal day.

Today, when she emerges from her room to check on the children, Charity is nowhere to be found. And neither Simon nor Constance were awake to see her go.

"Constance, watch your brother." The middle girl nods solemnly, her eyes wide as if she is picking up Annabelle's stark, shaking terror. Annabelle bolts for the door in her dressing gown, slippers scuffing on the hall carpet. If you were a nine-year-old girl at large in The Silver Beeches . . . which way would you go?

She does not dare involve the staff, just yet, or—just yet—her employer. If she finds Charity quickly, Mr B____ will never have to know. Annabelle had thought the girl too well trained to wander off on her own when she had a social obligation.

Annabelle has no excuses, except perhaps having been exhausted, and having slept too deeply to have heard the nursery door open into the hall.

Mr B____ keeps the rooms locked when they are not in use. Someday these bedrooms will belong to the grown children, when they are young ladies and a young man. Now they stand empty. Annabelle runs along the hall, checking each doorknob as she passes. No handle turns.

At the top of the stairs, she faces a quandary. Downstairs, the servants will be preparing breakfast. In their separate but communicating rooms at

the far end of the cross-corridor, Mr B____ and Mrs B____ will be dressing. The other rooms in that wing—the wing farthest from the ocean—are
the master's study, Mrs B____'s reading room, and two spare chambers.

Annabelle nerves herself, swallows against a dry mouth, and lifts her
chin. She is glad she is not dressed, because if she were, her stays would be
pressing into her ribs with each gasp. Carefully, slowly, with the skills of a
woman who has gone corseted all her adult life, she calms her breathing.
There's less danger in her nightgown, but fainting for want of air would
not be the ideal solution to her troubles.

She creeps down the hall, testing doors gently. With her hand on the
knob to the study, she pauses. It's next door to the master's bedroom and
connects. Any sound—

—it does not turn.

"Mrs Reed."

The master's voice, stern and uncompromising. She cannot help her guilty
jump. There she stands, a hand on the forbidden door, the other clutching
closed the collar of her dressing gown, and slowly turns to face him.

"No one is permitted in my study."

"I know, sir." This time her voice is a terrible squeak. "I . . . Charity
slipped out of the nursery."

He raises his eyebrows. "You must have been sleeping very soundly."

"Sir." She shudders and tries to pull herself up in the face of him.

His smile chills her more than anger would have. "Well, I suppose we
shall have to find her."

She's in the kitchen, with the cook, cadging scraps of apple from the
tarts being prepared in advance of luncheon—and Annabelle cannot
decide whether to hug her close or shake her until she rattles. Once Annabelle has Charity in charge, Mr B____ vanishes away like the wind.
But not before holding Annabelle's gaze over Charity's head for long seconds, his face devoid of any expression more defined than cool appraisal.

She sits up all that night with her books and her candle, but hears
nothing—no creak, no whisper, no footstep on the stair. Surely, he would
not come through the nursery? Surely.

She might wedge it with a chair, if she had one that fit under the
handle. But she does not, and what more can she do? There are no locks
between her and the children.

She almost falls asleep in her chair at supper. The next night, though she hunkers in bed over a book, beside the candle, her head droops, her eyelids close again and again.

She wakens with her face pressed to the pages, the room strangely bright from the light of that single candle, now that she has lain with her eyes closed beside it. She is not alone. She knows she is not alone. Before she lifts her head, she can hear him breathing.

He rapes Annabelle. She holds her breath through it, does not whimper.

Makes no sound at all, so the children will not hear. Makes no sound at all and tries not to hear his harsh panting, the heat of his breath against her throat.

He leaves as he came, through the connecting door to the nursery. He, too, is not noisy enough to wake them.

In the morning, Trudy brings her a steaming pitcher with which to fill her washbasin. This should not, strictly speaking, be one of Trudy's obligations. It is a job for an upstairs maid.

But Annabelle, after all, inhabits a liminal space. She is not exactly family. And she and Trudy have something in common now.

Annabelle buttons her sleeves over bruised wrists and says nothing. Trudy has brought clean linens and changes the bed, though it is not laundry day.

Their eyes meet as Trudy moves past her. Annabelle nods; Trudy does not look down.

"Well," Trudy says, "we're right stuck, ain't we?"

"Yes," says Annabelle, grateful at last that she is barren. "That, indeed, we are."

One by one, Annabelle climbs the steps to the turret. A maid could have come, but Annabelle offered. Mrs B____ is late for tea, and when she vanishes, it is up here.

Up here, to look at the sea.

Mrs B____ stands at the window, the glazing pushed wide, yearning westward towards the water. Her hair is unbound; seal-brown, glossy, it streams down her back, over her shoulders as she leans forward. Annabelle does not think the mistress means to leap. Still she steps softly, deliberately, into the square tower room.

Over Mrs B____'s shoulders, Annabelle sees the black dots of seal heads lifted from the waiting waters.

"Take the children to the Continent." Mrs B____ does not turn. "Or to America. Argentina. India. Anywhere, so long as it is away from here. My family will see to it that you have money. You will leave tonight, before sunset. They will meet you by the ruined tower."

"And what will you do?"

"Promise me you will take them away from him."

"And what will he do to all of you, every one of you, when I am gone?"

Mrs B____ shakes out her hair. "What he would do to you as well, if you stayed." But she looks over her shoulder, so Annabelle catches the edge of her smile and sharp teeth behind it. "I will not allow it, Mrs Reed."

Her fingertips clench on the windowsill, white around flushed nail beds, and Annabelle knows. She knows what the mistress proposes.

"You'll hang for it."

"Better a quick death," the mistress says. "I have waited too long already. I had hoped—" She sighs and shakes her head, shimmering all that long hair in waves like the ocean. "I had hoped to win back what he stole from me and make my escape. But he binds me here still. And then I thought, if I could only reclaim my heirloom, I could escape . . . and I could rid the world of him with impunity. But he has forbidden me to reclaim it, and while he holds it, I must do as he bids." A strand of hair falls across her face as her head droops like a wilting flower.

"Your skin," Annabelle says.

Mrs B____ turns from the window. "You know, Mrs Reed?"

"Your family." Annabelle points out the window, past the black stones and the combers breaking against them, to the seals that rise up out of the deep and return Mrs B____'s homesick regard.

Mrs B____ does not turn back. "I have decided," she says with dignity, "that ridding the world of *him* is worth whatever happens to me. At first I begged, you know. Then I bargained. Then I waited."

"Now you endure," says Annabelle.

"I am beyond enduring. Take my children from here, Mrs Reed, before he makes them monsters, too."

"Annabelle."

Mrs B____ smiles. "Annabelle. I will hang to be free of him."

"Perhaps you need not," says Annabelle, with rising pleasure. It might be a sin—it must be a sin—but that cannot trouble her.

Mrs B____ blinks. "I beg your pardon?"

"When a man is dead," says Annabelle, "before the police can be summoned . . . what's to stop you from searching his study, when he is no longer there to forbid it?"

Annabelle watches the understanding dawn across Mrs B____'s face like sunrise over an ocean. A different ocean, not this one that lies to the west of where they stand. An ocean that Annabelle might see herself, one day soon.

"Call me Áine," says the mistress. "It is my name. Take my children away from here, while there is still time."

"Áine. Write," says Annabelle. "I'll make sure Trudy Bell knows where to find me. Your children will want to hear from you."

T he ocean parts before the bow of the ship like flesh cut by a knife. Annabelle stands, her hands on the railing, the children at her side. Charity and Constance to the left of her, Simon to the right.

Around them wheel seagulls; before the bow, dolphins play and leap. One of the gulls turns and dives suddenly, as if chasing a thrown morsel. Annabelle turns before she realizes that Simon has shied a rock at the birds. A pebble, really, but when she turns out his coat pocket, he has a dozen.

"Simon," says Annabelle. "Do not throw rocks at the gulls."

He does not answer. He climbs the rail instead, leaning out against her hand on his coat collar, the bow wave curling far below. He surges against her grip, waving his hands at the gulls.

Reflexively, her fingers tighten. "Simon!" she scolds.

He does not answer, just grunting with effort as he pulls against her grip.

How easy, how blameless, it would be . . . to let go.

About "The Governess"

When Ellen asked me to write a fantastical Victorian story, the first thing that leapt to mind was the constrained roles of hierarchical class structures of a society built upon a series of traps. Of course, such social prisons-for-life are not merely the purview of the distant past. . . .

SMITHFIELD

In Smithfield, London, near the top of Shoe Lane, where poor Chatterton's bones lie in a pauper's grave, there stands an old inn, which had stood for nearly a century before Dr Johnson began spending long evenings there in 1760. Lord Nelson was said to take a table near the hearth now and then when he wasn't at sea, and rumour has it that Nelson's severed arm floated in double-refined brandy in an immense, sealed jar on a shelf above the taps. The jar (if the rumour had any truth in it) had disappeared long before the current proprietor, William Billson, bought the old edifice in 1862 and renamed it the Half Toad in honour of a whimsical ship's figurehead that he had brought back from the West Indies, and which looks out onto Fingal Street today from its sacred perch above the inn's arched door with its window of leaded, bull's-eye glass. Billson is something of a street-corner historian, if you will, and as much a remnant of the previous age as is the inn itself.

I found myself staying at the Half Toad some few years back in the late autumn. I had a medical practice in Elm Grove, Southsea, but had left it in the capable hands of a locum. In truth, I had begun to grow weary of doctoring. I had once again taken up the pen and had come up to London to meet with an editor at *The Graphic*, hopeful that the sale of my newest literary endeavour might pay for the holiday, which was also to be a photographic expedition. (My literary endeavours paid for little in those days. It would be some time yet before I turned to the writing of crime stories and my fortunes would change. There is a certain wonderful freedom in being young and at the beginning of a literary career, when one's "fortunes" are small but sometimes glorious.) The balance of my week in London was to be spent carrying out photographic experiments in Smithfield. I had brought along an ingenious portable darkroom and chemical laboratory contrived by Professor Cosmo Innes at the University of Edinburgh. Billson allowed me to quarter the thing in the inn's storage room, which had an alley entrance to facilitate deliveries.

As for the editor at *The Graphic,* I'll tell you plainly that he declined to purchase the piece, proclaiming it merely tedious, and so it paid for nothing at all. In a fit of pique I burnt the manuscript in the hearth at the Half Toad, perhaps wisely it seems to me now, since I had a waning attachment to it—an account of an indeed tedious voyage I had taken along the African coast in that ill-fated steamship *Mayumba.*

Still and all, I was happy to be in London. The Half Toad, as I said, is a cheerful relic of a bygone age. Oak wainscot panels the walls of the taproom, the oak a deep brown and with a lustre that only time and the elements can produce. The elements that constitute the weather of a good taproom—pipe smoke, wood smoke from the split beams burning in the hearth, smoke from the coals in the open oven where pheasants and joints of beef turn on spits, the heady smell of spirits and spilled ale, puddings boiling in the copper—influence the rich colour of the plastered walls and the wooden wainscot, just as the ocean wind and the fall rains influence the rough exterior of an old house in the Hebrides.

On the walls of the inn hang paintings of sailing ships—Spanish galleons, English sloops and frigates—each heavily framed in a style long past the fashion. The mild glow of gas lamps provides illumination, the lamps lit religiously at three o'clock in the afternoon by Lars Hopeful, the tapboy. On days when fog obscures the Smithfield streets, the taproom lamps burn through the day and into the evening, casting over the tables "a warm domestic radiance fit to eat by," to quote Stevenson, who knew what he was about when he wrote on the subject of illumination.

To the right of the hearth, above the long mantel, hang two views of old Smithfield, taken from etchings by Hogarth that were rendered in 1732, or so says the date on the print, written in faded ink beneath the artist's signature. One of the prints is a repellent portrayal of a gang of coiners being boiled to death in oil; the second a depiction of tilting, tumbledown houses beetling over Shoe Lane, with the workhouse and its graveyard at the dead end, such as it was in those old days, although perhaps it's false to use that term, since the world was newer then.

I'll reveal to you that the account I am about to relate occurred in the time of the illumination of London by electricity. A portion of Smithfield— the environs of Fingal Street and Shoe Lane—was to be honoured with this modern boon, the insulated wire already planted beneath the cobbles, ready to carry along its copper boulevards the promise of a glittering future. Lamplighters still tramped the streets of Smithfield on the day that I arrived at the inn, just as Lars Hopeful made his circuit around the interior of the Half Toad, but their day was passing away forever and would be a mere memory by the time I departed once again for Southsea. Still and all, there was an air of excitement generated by this modern notion of self-made stars, the great city garishly illuminated on the instant by a sleepy electrician depressing a lever. The actual depressing of the lever had been postponed in Smithfield several times, however, which meant only that it was imminent.

My goal was to photograph nighttime Smithfield in its final gaslit days, using the now-outmoded collodion, wet-plate method—a chemical wash painted onto glass photographic plates, the lengthy exposure increasing the clarity of the image, if indeed I got any image at all in the gaslight. It would be necessary to develop the photographs immediately, before the chemicals dried on the plates, hence the portable darkroom. And so I left the inn at one o'clock of a Saturday morning, trundling my barrow like a costermonger. Snug within the barrow lay the darkroom with its red lamp, along with chemical salts and liquid chemicals—the developing spirits, fixatives, washes—that were premeasured within glass beakers. Metal trays stood in racks; glass plates and plate holders with dark slides waited in niches. The collodion itself—guncotton and ether—must be mixed with the salts and poured carefully onto the photographic plate with both haste and care, then the plate must be laid in a sensitizing bath of silver nitrate. I had altered the chemical content of the bath with various additives to slow the liquid's drying on the plate. I sought to increase exposure time that way, if only for a minute or two, and I had some hope of interesting results.

A half-moon rode above St. Bartholomew's Hospital, the sky clear and starry around it, the air unseasonably warm—an auspicious night to be abroad, it seemed to me. I pushed my barrow up Shoe Lane in its modern guise to the site of the old Shoe Lane Workhouse, long since torn down, where I set about my activities across from the recently built Yeoman Public House, with its vast window of plate glass and its brass fittings. The new incandescent bulbs had been installed months ago—half a dozen along the lane, all of them dark and awaiting their chance for supremacy over the several gas lamps. The portable darkroom was open for business, so to say, as soon as I raised the tin panel on the side of my barrow, bent out the arms that supported the black-painted canvas tent, and switched on the red-tinted lamp, a modified Geissler tube illuminated by the power of a Ruhmkorff induction coil.

I prepared four glass plates in succession, loading them into the plate holders and then into the camera, exposing, removing, and developing each of them before carefully fixing the images with an odious solution of potassium cyanide. All of this took the better part of an hour, the bells of St. Bartholomew the Great tolling twice just as the fourth glass plate was dry. The moon had climbed higher into the sky now and shone on the cobbles in the street. The shop fronts and houses still lay in deep shadow except where they were illuminated by the gas lamps, which cast circles of soft light along the sidewalk. I wanted particularly to get the effect of the gaslight against the darkness around it, to see what I could see, as the sailor put it. I knew it was a tall order because the very business of photography wanted plentiful light. A full moon might have helped, but I hadn't time to wait; the next full moon would look down upon a Shoe Lane illuminated by Joseph Swan's incandescent bulbs.

I prepared and inserted another plate, adjusted the angle of the camera, peered through the lens, and removed the dark slide, surprised to see a pale orb of ivory-tinted light hovering in the air before the public house, very dim, as if someone were shining a lantern through a dirty window. The plate, of course, was already developing, and I didn't dare remove my head from beneath the black drape for fear of spoiling the image. I was certain that the orb hadn't been there a moment earlier. Was it mere gaslight, I wondered, shifted by a trick of reflection? The ground below it was dark, as if its light were absorbed immediately into the blackness around it. Indeed, the orb seemed to be haloed by a dark aura. I stood hunched over for long minutes staring at it in something like disbelief. This phenomenon, I'll reveal, was what I had hoped for but scarcely expected— what had drawn me to Smithfield, with its colourful, bloody history and ancient crimes, and where Chatterton's restless ghost, bearing traces of arsenic in its molecules, allegedly still haunted the midnight streets. The very atmosphere seemed to me to be heavy with the spirits of times past.

The glowing orb began slowly to rotate counterclockwise, a solid aura of black night around it. After the five minutes had passed, I ducked out from under the drape, surprised to see that the orb had utterly disappeared. I fancied that I could make out the dark aura when I looked at it out of the corner of my eye, but I couldn't be certain. The image on the plate would be the only certainty. Once again I developed the plate and fixed the image, after which I made haste to prepare another. I shifted the camera toward the empty graveyard this time before slipping out the dark slide and looking through the lens. Three orbs of varying brightness were visible. Almost immediately, two others appeared, some small distance beyond the three. I could now hear what sounded distinctly like muttering in the air around me—perhaps my imagination, which, as you can imagine, was in a heightened state—but there was nothing to be seen minutes later when I had the opportunity to search for its source: the street was deserted, the buildings shuttered. I heard distant footsteps, and a man came into view from the direction of Fingal Street, then shortly disappeared again.

The muttering had faded for a moment, as if temporarily hidden by the sound of footsteps or blown away on the freshening breeze, but then it started up again, more various now, punctuated by laughter and what sounded like sobbing or people crying out—not voices engaged in conversation, mind you, but a rabble of voices overlaid, at cross-purposes, but originating where? Not in my mind, certainly, unless I had run mad. It seemed to me that a door on eternity had been opened, and I was hearing the long-silent voices of old Smithfield through countless speaking tubes. I'll reveal that I was convinced—*had* been convinced from the moment I saw the first of the orbs—that the glowing spheres were supernatural, what are commonly called spirit lights. I mean to say that the nighttime lane was literally haunted. I continued to expose plates and fix the images, hastily now, abandoning my usual methodical and exacting standards.

It was well past two in the morning when I grew weary of my experiment. The sky was no longer clear, and the dew was beginning to fall. I determined to return tomorrow night at the same hour. So, putting away my camera and tripod, I closed up my darkroom and made my way back to the Half Toad, where I stowed the barrow. I let myself in through the front door, carrying the box of exposed plates with me to my room along

with a basket of bread and cheese and two bottles of ale. I had no thought
of sleep, but only of discovering what I had captured on the photographic
plates. I lit the Argand lamp that stood on the broad wooden desk and
held the first of my developed plates up before it.

What I saw was disheartening. In the darkness, or perhaps by some
error committed in my haste, I had apparently botched the entire business,
for the negative images were marred by a geometry of seemingly random
lines. I had gotten the effect of a palimpsest, if you will, and I could think
of no means of eradicating competing images without destroying them all.
The orbs were visible on the plates, but that was my only bit of good fortune. The entire series was similarly spoiled, as if I had foolishly brought
along already-exposed plates and had laid on new images over the old,
although how the older images could have survived the several chemical
baths was a mystery. It came to me that the chemicals I had contrived to
increase exposure time might have created this effect of multiple images,
perhaps through crystallization, although I wasn't enough of a chemist to
understand how.

In my anger I determined to return to Shoe Lane at once. The long
day had turned into a series of defeats, and I was unhappy when I considered it, although mostly with myself and with a measure left over for the
Fates. Abruptly I recalled pitching my manuscript into the fire in the taproom yesterday afternoon, and the anger was tinged with shame. Anger is
seldom a useful emotion, and the more self-righteous the anger, the less
useful it is. St. Bartholomew's bell was once again tolling the hour, and the
sound of it was wearying. I ate the bread and cheese, drank the last of my
bottled ale, turned out the lamp, and went to bed.

I awoke late in the morning to a dark day with precious little to fill it,
given that my mind was looking forward to midnight once again. I lit the
lamp, contemplating the long hours ahead, and considered picking up *The
Pickwick Papers*, which lay half-read on the desk. But the book held even
less interest for me today than it had yesterday when I was similarly distracted. The desire to kill time is a criminal offence since we have little
enough of it on this earth, but I very much wished to murder twelve hours
of it in order to be about my business.

I compelled myself to examine one of the photographic plates from
the box on the table. Strangely, the image on the glass was at least partly
unfamiliar to me, which was both confounding and implausible. My first
thought was that I had somehow neglected to look at this particular plate

last night, but then I discovered that the other plates were similarly altered. The dark auras that had haloed the ghost orbs had stretched vertically, and although it might certainly have been my imagination, they seemed to have taken on the semblance of shrouded human figures. The Shoe Lane backdrops had resolved themselves into crosshatched patterns of lines, but the lines seemed to outline semidistinct buildings, if you will. I easily recognised the fairly solid Yeoman Public House, with its illuminated gas lamp, but beneath it there stood the ghost of yet another building, the Yeoman superimposed over it. Beneath that was a third structure, again a mere geometry of shapes, but certainly a building, and beneath that—or so it seemed to me—perhaps another: the entire plate was a stratification of competing images. For a long time I stood considering what it was I had captured, so to speak, on the surface of those glass plates.

I descended the stairs, taking the first of the plates with me. The lamps were already lit in the taproom, the fire burning in the hearth, Lars Hopeful swabbing the floor. I found William Billson pickling an immense salmon in the kitchen, and I watched him work for a moment, considering my words as he went about his business, dumping parsley and borage, salt and peppercorns, into a vast poacher, which was already on the boil. He laid the salmon atop it and moved the poacher to the back of the stove, wiping his hands on his apron.

"Coffee, Mr Doyle?" he asked, picking up the pot and pouring a cup before I'd had time to answer.

I took it from him gratefully. "You've been living hereabouts for some years, I believe, William?" I asked, knowing the answer well enough, but hoping to draw him out.

"Since I was a young lad, sir, when my father brought us to Smithfield—West Smithfield, we called it—from up toward Manchester. I don't know the date. Must be coming on sixty years now." He poked at the salmon in the poacher with his finger, indifferent to the hot liquid.

"It was surely a different world back then," I said.

"That it was, sir. All the streets and lanes we called by something fanciful—Goose Alley, Duck Lane, Cow Cross Street. Some folks still call them so, but there hasn't been a cow crossed through Smithfield for more than thirty years. Truth to tell, it could be right filthy in those old days, with the streets packed with animals around the old livestock market. The stink on a summer afternoon would bring tears to your eyes. When I came home from the West Indies, I scarcely knew it, for the changes."

"You found Smithfield improved, then?" I asked him.

He shrugged. "Not so to say *improved*. Cleaner, leastways. But it's what they like to call progress, no matter what William Billson thinks of it. My dad had passed away as well. He'd been sick with a canker—what the doctors call gangrene—and he suffered a great deal, or so I was told, me having been away at sea. His dying was a sort of progress, too, I suppose. No human animal should suffer that way, and his death was a blessing. And yet I can't say that his death improved anything. A man remembers what was good in the world when something goes out of it, and mainly he regrets its passing, although perhaps I speak for myself. They say it's best not to look back."

He reached into the poacher now and drew the salmon out with his hands, laying it on the long block beside the stove to cool. "What's that, then, Mr Doyle?" he asked, nodding at the photographic plate. "You've had some luck?"

"I don't entirely know what I've got, Bill. I've come downstairs after your opinion. Last night, when I returned from my outing, I thought that I had spoiled my photographic plates, but now I'm not so certain. I was in Shoe Lane when I took this photograph, looking straight on at the Yeoman Public House, trying to get a glimpse of things in the gaslight."

Billson took the plate from me and studied it, but he shook his head at what he saw. "The Yeoman's naught but a tied house, owned by one of the big breweries. That's progress again, or so they'll tell you. I'm old-fashioned. I have no opinion of being told what I must be or what I must do. Henrietta serves that function well enough. I'm tied to her, you see. She's off visiting her sister in Cliffe, and the place seems half-empty to me."

"And thank God for all that," I told him. "The Half Toad is as near to perfect as an inn can be this side of Heaven. My best wishes to Henrietta when she returns. But I was wondering about the laid-over images *beneath* the Yeoman, as it were. Do you make anything of them?"

He studied the plate for a long minute, then shrugged. "What I make of it don't stand to reason, sir."

"Never mind reason, Bill. Tell me what you see."

"All right. I'd say this here looks like the old workhouse, or the ghost of it, which stood where the Yeoman stands, thereabouts. And this light standing before it is a haunt, to my mind—a corpse candle, some call them. I've seen them wandering the old streets now and then when I was out late."

"Seen them with your own eyes?"

"That's the way I see best, Mr Doyle. Not everyone sees them, though, only a few of us that's been here for a time."

"But you can't have seen the workhouse, Bill, not unless you're as old as Moses."

"That's so. It was gone years before we came down from Manchester, but Mr Hogarth did a fair representation there on the taproom wall."

"Of course he did," I nearly shouted, and went straightaway into the taproom, where luncheon was just then setting up. I hurried across to the hearth and studied the Hogarth depiction of Shoe Lane as it had been, and I saw straight off what Billson had seen on the photographic plate, although, as he said, the thing was patently impossible: it was the outline—the indistinct image—of the west end of the Shoe Lane Workhouse, sure enough, with the windows in place and an arch of some sort alongside. I stood staring at it in perfect silence, holding the glass plate near the etching, trying to cipher out the meaning of the phenomenon, how it had come to pass. But once again there was no explanation aside from madness, which would require that William Billson were as mad as I. I couldn't vouch for myself, but Billson was perhaps the sanest man I knew. My earlier suspicion that the photographic plates were in some way defective was no longer a possibility. I knew very well what I was seeing, and I knew very well that I couldn't be seeing it.

I hastened upstairs to my room, where I examined each of the plates in turn. All had developed similarly, it seemed to me, and by *developed*, I mean that over the course of the morning they had gone on developing, even though I had fixed the images on the plates many hours ago. Indeed, they were apparently fixed at the moment. I descended the stairs again and found Billson cutting his salmon into filets and laying them into a large earthenware crock. He poured the cooled cooking liquid over the top and added a handful of pickling spices before putting on the lid.

"Was I right?" he asked. I acknowledged that he was. He stood for a moment as if considering. "It's a time of change, Mr Doyle," he said at last. "The world and everything in it is moving on. As long as Henrietta and I have breath in us, the Half Toad will linger behind. We don't have it in us to keep up with the world, nor the desire neither. Lord knows what will happen to the old inn when we're gone. I'm main happy that I won't live to see it."

His words filled me with nostalgia in the old sense of the term—a mournful cognizance of things passing away, myself included. In a rush of emotion I decided that I would be happy to remain at the Half Toad forever and let the modern world carry on as it pleased. I would watch it through the window—catch glimpses of it now and then when the door opened onto Fingal Street.

But of course I could not. I took a late breakfast of boiled eggs, kippers, and cheese into the taproom and set it on Lord Nelson's table before ascending the stairs yet again to fetch *Pickwick*, which now seemed unutterably vital to me. In my childhood I had inhabited the tail end of the Pickwickian world, which would soon, alas, exist only in the pages of the book that I took with me now down the stairs. In my sentimental mood I badly wanted to return to that world, at least for a time. I sat reading by the hearth throughout the afternoon and evening, now and then contemplating Hogarth, taking my supper there, no longer anxious to kill time, but rather to resurrect it. I didn't look again at the photographic plates upstairs, although I was sorely tempted. As time drew on, the streets grew inordinately full of people, and those who entered the Half Toad were fairly bursting with the news that the new incandescent lamps were to be electrified that very night.

At ten o'clock, fearing that I would miss the tide if I waited, I took up my coat, went out onto Fingal Street, and fetched my barrow from the storeroom. Gaslight still burned along the street, flying in the face of the rumours. A wind had come up, and the moon hadn't yet put in an appearance. The throngs were in a festive mood, which somehow made me sullen and melancholy.

"They're a-going to light the city!" a man said to me. "The lord mayor's come and is setting up for a speech." The man was clearly not quite sober, but was also clearly joyous, as if lighting the city were the be-all and end-all of human happiness on earth.

So the hour is nearly upon us, I thought unhappily. I fetched my barrow and set off along Fingal Street, bound for Shoe Lane, privately cursing the throngs that barred the way. Indeed, they were more numerous as I drew closer to my destination. I determined to disregard them, and I set up my camera and darkroom in the graveyard itself, which was nearly empty of living people. A stage was set up in front of the Yeoman, where the lord mayor would speak, but I had no interest in it.

I set about my business, opening up the darkroom and preparing chemicals. During this quarter hour the rest of the lane was going about its business, the lord mayor addressing the throng as the gas lamps were symbolically extinguished, the world growing darker around us. No sooner had I inserted the plate holder with its dark slide into the camera than a great huzzah went up from the crowds, and although it might have been my imagination, in the moment of quiet that followed I heard a buzzing sound, like a hive of angry metal bees, and a sudden blinding glare drove out the darkness. Smithfield was electrified. Indeed, one of the incandescent lamps was fixed on a post above my darkroom, and I and the old graveyard round about me were bathed in its ugly white light.

I stood staring for a moment, listening to the cheering die away. Then I exposed the plate, seeing nothing through the lens but the nearby graves and the weedy ground round about. I determined to give the plate a full five minutes, hoping for the appearance of an orb, but soon people began to stroll among the graves, and the image was spoiled. Defeated, I removed the plate, slipped it back into its niche, methodically stowed my camera and put away the darkroom.

When I returned to the Half Toad, the taproom was empty of patrons. Billson was still up, making things shipshape after the long day, and when he saw me enter, he locked the door behind me, laid two logs onto the burned-down fire, and enlivened the flames with the bellows. He gestured toward the table at which I had spent the day. "Take a dram before you retire, sir, for the sake of old times."

"Only if you'll join me, Bill," I said to him.

"If Henrietta was here, she'd make the old joke about you coming apart, sir. She never misses her chance."

"I sorely wish she *were* here," I said. "I'll be with you in five minutes."

What I found in my room was nothing and everything. Last night's photographic plates had gone on developing, as I feared they would. The images had overlaid each other time and again, darkening the plates as they came into focus, until all had been obliterated. It seemed diabolically ironic that I was looking at Smithfield through the ages, successive images following one upon another, perhaps to prehistoric depths, until they compiled into utter blackness. I wondered who or what had been resurrected to put in a brief appearance on the plates before being buried again—Chatterton's hearse rattling past; the poet Lovelace peering through the bars of the old prison; seven hundred successive years of Bartholomew's Fair laid out along the banks of the Fleet River (now relegated to a brick-and-mortar sewer); the immolation of the martyrs; Wat Tyler, leader of the Peasants' Revolt, hacked to death by the mayor of London himself; Roman Londinium, perhaps, Joseph of Arimathea carrying the Grail along the road to Glastonbury . . . I set the plate down on the table and descended the stairs once more.

I'd be happy to take that drink now, Bill," I said when I reentered the taproom—a statement that was as honest as any I'd ever uttered.

"Did you have more luck, then?" he asked, clearly referring to the photography. He poured neat whiskey into two glasses, and we sat down at the table.

I shook my head. "Nothing you'd call luck."

"Well, Mr Doyle," he said, raising his glass and looking through it at the firelight, "I give you a toast to tomorrow, which is always another day, as my old dad used to tell me."

"Your father was a sage," I said, and we clinked our glasses together and drank off the contents.

The street outside had grown quiet aside from the sound of the wind under the eaves; the moon looked out from among tearing clouds, and the familiar stars turned in the sky. The fine weather had vanished, and the north wind scoured the streets and byways of the great and ever-changing city, heralding a change in the seasons.

About "Smithfield"

Lightbulbs have been on my mind recently, what with the government getting set to outlaw incandescent bulbs. By the time you read this they'll have become extinct, aside from stockpiles squirreled away in the garages and closets of loonies like me who are dedicated to the things and are staving off the coming drought. I've tried to be green-minded about it and have bought phenomenally expensive bulbs advertised to last ten years. Turns out they often last about two (I've clocked them), and also, the longer they last, the more they tend to cement themselves into the receptacle, so that they won't unscrew without tearing up the works. Probably it's the mineral salts afloat in the Southern California air. I was advised (seriously) to unscrew all of them every six months and then to screw them back in again. A doctor once suggested that I do the same thing to my head, but I tend to forget.

The newfangled bulbs are not only expensive, but they cast an ugly white light as opposed to the softer yellow-white light of incandescent bulbs. Cheaper models take about five minutes to fully illuminate. I saw an advertisement recently for a compact fluorescent bulb that *mimics* an incandescent, but I can't afford such a thing without taking out a home-equity loan. Someday, when the price comes down, I'll spring for them. In any event, I like the warmer ambience of the incandescent bulb, and I like unfashionable words such as *newfangled*. Every once in a while I find someone who knows just what I'm talking about in that regard, but most often my dedication to incandescent bulbs elicits blank stares, something like when people see that I've got a houseful of books and helpfully suggest that I might put the whole lot of them onto an electronic reader and haul the paper copies to the dump.

It was a good thirty years ago that I first read and admired Robert Louis Stevenson's essay "A Plea for Gas Lamps." "Such a light as this," he wrote of incandescent light, "should shine only on murders and public crime, or along the corridors of lunatic asylums, a horror to heighten horror." Being artistically dedicated to incandescent light (not having been alive during the halcyon days of gaslight), I had always felt exactly that way about fluorescent lighting—the hideous white light, the flickering, the buzzing of the ballast box—part of the loathsome, utilitarian fixtures of the typical school classroom. No wonder students have a nervous urge to flee. I was building my own lamps back when I read the Stevenson essay, searching out old glass shades and handwrought chain at antique stores. I hung two of them in my office at the university where I teach, which was already equipped with fluorescent lights on the ceiling. "These old lamps have to go," I was told by a perplexed man from University Services who clearly had me pegged as a crackpot and a radical. "Immediately," I told him. That was a couple of years ago, and the lamps are still there, but one day soon, I suppose, when I'm asleep at my desk, the door will fly open,

I'll be hosed down with pepper spray, the lamps will be torn out by the roots, and like a character in a Kafka story, I'll discover that my office actually sits "along the corridors of a lunatic asylum."

I believe it was in *Science* magazine that I read an article concerning discoveries made by Israeli scientists studying the physics of the paranormal: it turns out that ghosts (of which my own house has had its share) simply cannot tolerate fluorescent light. It's well-known that knowledgeable priests can accomplish more with fluorescent light than with holy water if it's exorcism that they have in mind. Now that I think of it, I was also an avid reader of the *Weekly World News* for some years. A great deal of what I know about the world can be laid at their interesting doorstep and might account for my having mixed up my sources here.

It seems to me that what Jules Verne called "the harnessing of electricity" has everything to do with the old world's passing away and the advent of the new. It was one of those tides in the affairs of men, to take some liberties with Shakespeare, and a thoroughly despotic tide at that. I'm attracted to Dickens and Stevenson, among other writers, at least partly because of the gaslight that illuminates their worlds, literally and figuratively. Arthur Conan Doyle looked backward in that regard. I'm also fond of a wood fire in the fireplace rather than cement logs with flames shooting out of a pipe, and I'm fond of a picket fence built of lumber rather than plastic, and I like the smell of old paper when I pull a book down from the shelf and smoke from a bonfire at the beach at night, despite the irritating fact that the smoke will chase you around the fire pit.

I'm not at all fond of the idea that the world as I've come to know it is passing away.

THE
UNWANTED
WOMEN OF SURREY

O f all of the unwanted women of Surrey, Grace was the one most terrified when the Grey Ladies knocked on our door.

It was a gentle knock; certainly a gentlewoman. Grace took a last sip of tea and leapt up. "Allow me," she said, as if anyone else were permitted to answer the door when she was at home. She lived in hope; she imagined somehow her husband would change his mind and take her back to the manor.

He would not. They never do.

We heard the door open, and her gasp, then a wild screaming.

I spilled my tea in my hurry to reach her, and a plate of scones tipped to the floor. Cook would be heartily offended.

Grace was slumped against the doorframe, her face ashen.

Standing clustered together, tall, skeletally thin, grey skinned, were three women. Their mouths were open as if they would speak, but instead they turned and glided away.

Grace screamed again and Dot joined her. Red Sheila shook; she was in no state to comfort them.

"Come on inside," I said. Faith still sat in the drawing room, neatly nibbling on a ginger biscuit.

"Faith, help me seat our friends," I snapped at her, wanting her out of her reverie.

"Who was at the door?" she asked, only now noticing how disturbed we all were.

"The Grey Ladies! The Grey Ladies!" Grace said. "The ones that took Red Sheila's baby."

Red Sheila nodded. "They did. Came to visit me one cold night, twenty-five years ago. And did my baby boy live till morning? No, he did not. No, he didn't. It's brought it all back to me."

Grace took a sip of tea; she didn't seem to notice it was from my cup.

"You don't say!" Faith said. "Who did they point to?"

We exchanged glances.

"No one," I said. "They merely looked at us."

"Then perhaps they made a mistake. Perhaps this time they are not presaging death." Faith's sensible voice calmed us.

Once Cook had cleared our tea things (muttering to us about the maid as she always did), I took my mending and went to sit in the back garden.

The air was warm and I felt the sun on my face, tingling my skin. On the air the scent of daphne, of honeysuckle, of lavender, coming to me in gentle waves. I thought, *If only I could live in this moment until the day I die.*

In the back of the garden the cherry blossoms bloomed pink and fluffy. A sweet chirping drew me to see a robin redbreast in the branches. She was so bright she stood unreal amongst the pale pink. She squeaked and chirped as if surprised by the flowers she pecked at. Food! Look at all this food! Though Surrey and flowers are synonymous; even a bird should know that.

Under the rhododendron bush with its vibrant red flowers, the cat slept. He was so lazy his ears flicked as the bird chirped but nothing else moved.

This was peace, calm, and beauty. There was no grey. I thought, *If only this was all there is to life.*

But no. There was much more.

I had to go inside to make sure Cook didn't sweat into the pots or scratch her dry skin or pluck at her greasy hair. The others weren't so bothered by this, but I didn't like it, especially with the men coming to visit tomorrow. She felt superior to us, that ugly, red-faced woman, because her family hadn't sent her away, but she was a far lesser human being than any one of us unwanted women.

The maid would not clean well unless I prodded her (such a pretty thing but a useless young woman) so I had to ensure she had dusted all the surfaces of our fine old house, with its gloriously moulded ceilings, its dark oak walls. Our Genteel Ladies Boarding Residence by Order, but we are none of us sure whose order.

Our habits could be seen as slovenly to some, but we are so comfortable with each other. Bring any group of women to live together and you will either find great dissension or you will find harmony. We, the unwanted women of Surrey, are harmonious.

We didn't discuss the Grey Ladies that evening, although I know most of us had a restless night. I rose at one in the morning to warm some milk, and from every room I heard sounds of wakefulness. All perhaps nervous of the men's visit, but also all of us remembering the flaccid grey skin of those ladies.

I was supervising Cook over the making of the asparagus soup when Dot came in from her daily perambulations with a fine sheen on her cheeks, glowing through the sheer veil she always wore.

"Clean up!" Red Sheila said. "The men will be here soon." She has been in residence for fifty years. She is as sane as Lord Russell, with all his resignations and reinstatements same day. The ways of men are hard to fathom. Red Sheila rules us all and no one minds. "We must dress our hair beautifully and choose our nicest apparel. The men are coming."

Dot tapped on the bathroom door to speed Grace along. Grace had spent so many hours in the bath her skin was wrinkled, and she threw open the bathroom door and ran up the hallway, where she tossed herself on her bed and lay, weeping.

"That will only turn your eyes ugly," I said. "Calm yourself and splash your face with cold water. Your skin will soon subside and your husband will want to kiss your dear cheek."

Grace rubbed at her face. "I look grey. You can't deny it."

I wanted to slap her. All of us felt terrified after the visit from the Grey Ladies, but the rest of us were trying to remain calm. "You are not grey at all. Come along. The visitors will be here soon."

None of us have entertained visitors for some time. I have not seen my children for five years, though they write me civil letters telling me that all is well. Our husbands like to visit at the same time. Safety in numbers, perhaps. St. Patrick's Day, the seventeenth of March, is the favoured day.

Year after year they come as if they are doing something wonderful and magnanimous. They meet at the public house to gird themselves and arrive all merry and drunk. They are jovial and pleasant and truly we prefer them that way, garrulous and friendly rather than sullen and angry.

They bring us little gifts; sometimes those pilfered from the public house itself. Ashtrays we have by the dozen, and once they brought us a lady's carry bag with items still inside it. That sits in a bottom drawer in case the owner ever claims it. Grace says she will never do so because she has been taken by the Grey Ladies. There is a photograph of a woman, standing alone except for the three grey shapes we see behind her. "No one is visited by the Grey Ladies and lives," Grace says.

Anything our men bring us from outside only makes us sad. These souvenirs give us glimpses of places to which we will never travel.

My husband arrived smelling of gin and pomade. He felt firm beneath my fingers, not soft like the ladies are. He held me for just a moment, squeezed my face gently between his fingers. "My beautiful, delicate wife," he said. Then he joined the other men in the drawing room, where they continued the conversation they'd started at the public house.

"Have you heard about this pendulum? Foucault, his name is. French chap, I believe, but we won't hold that against him," and the men all laughed into their beards. We did not know what they were talking about; we do not get the newspapers in our home. They fear it will upset us, and truly, we prefer it that way. We are calm when the men come to visit. We love our stately home, especially when the alternative is an asylum, Lunatic Act or no.

"Yet more proof of mankind's brilliance."

The men seemed to be in awe at their own cleverness. They talked amongst themselves; it was like a private club to them. We were quiet in our own home, as if this were always so.

"Speaking of the French, that Louis Napoleon hasn't a chance of pushing through his changes. They know what he's after." They knew we had no interest in such things.

They talked about the cricket, and the goldfields. Faith sat on the edge of her seat, listening to them in the hope they would be able to tell her if her husband was safe. He ran away to the goldfields in Australia close to a year ago; she had a letter from him six months old but no recent news. None of us could imagine so savage a place as the Victorian goldfields.

Her husband said there were Chinamen working alongside the Englishmen, jabbering away with their nonsense. We only know one Chinaman, the one who collects our laundry for us. None of us trust him, with his big, toothy, foreign smile. And now Faith's husband stands beside men like him. Faith is terrified he will smell differently when he returns. His letter ended, "It is for your own good," and those words resonated with all of us. We were all under the impression that these decisions were made on our behalf, with our best interests at heart.

None of the men took the slightest notice; Faith sat with the letter on her lap, ready to show them, but they didn't pause in their talk. Only when the maid brought in a new teapot did they pause and exchange glances. Which of our husbands had hired her? None of us knew. But every one of them eyed her inappropriately.

With the windows open, we could hear the clunk of the cricket ball on bat at the cricket grounds, and the men started to be restless. They wanted to be with other men, watching men play cricket. We sat with our sewing; the pin money we made kept us in small treats the husbands forgot to bring.

My husband said, "This is prime land you're taking up, here. But I suppose you need something to look at." He gazed wistfully in the direction of the cricket field.

"We can only thank the Great Architect," Grace said. We nodded; this was a fine statement. But the men exchanged glances, as if not one of them had named God so.

Grace had been with us less than a year. Her husband hadn't been to see her before today, but her mother had, a stiff-faced horse of a woman who'd baked us dry ginger biscuits. "Left over from some fancy party" was Red Sheila's guess, because they were soft and stale and tasted a bit like liquorice.

Grace's husband was handsome. We all liked looking at him and the men didn't notice, so we kept on looking. He was terribly unkind to Grace, though, shaking off her embrace as though she were a bothersome moth, twisting his body to get away from her. All the men behaved that way (although my husband did like to visit my lodgings just before he left and I supposed it was still my wifely duty), but she was not used to it and had dreamed so prettily of what would occur on visiting day.

He made comment with the other men as if Grace were not sitting in his shadow. About his work, mostly, because he was a journalist and that was interesting to them, although I could tell they all thought him a braggart.

"And our daughter?" Grace said, which is when he flicked at her.

"The daughter is fine. She has a good family now."

She gave a passionate cry and threw herself to the ground. One of the more experienced men (Red Sheila's brother, it was. Red Sheila had to pay her drunken brother's tavern bills out of her own earnings sometimes. He called it "standing Sam," the vulgar man. But at least he came to visit her) suggested they withdraw, and they did so, to our glorious garden to smoke their pipes and raise their eyebrows at each other.

Grace ran to her room. We let her be; foolishly, we ignored the warning of the Grey Ladies and let her be.

It was amongst the men she landed. She'd torn off her dress and squeezed through her window onto the roof. She was lucky, her life was snatched instantly. I looked up as she fell and I thought I could see them, leaning out, the Grey Ladies, holding on to the window frame with long, sharp fingernails.

One thing about being locked up as a hysterical, unwanted woman: you don't need to pretend. We all of us threw ourselves to the ground, and we didn't care what our men in their suits thought. Grace's face was serene, once we'd wiped the blood away.

They surrounded Grace's husband, slapping him on the back—"Sorry, old chap"—but it looked awfully like congratulations to me. "Well done, old chap. You're free."

The Grey Ladies stood together, heads bowed. Aping sorrow. I could see the ghost of their teeth as they tried to conceal smiles.

Grace had been a sweet and kindly member of our household, and her passing filled us with great sorrow. And relief? Were we all somewhat relieved that the Grey Ladies took her and not us?

Her replacement, Annie Flagg, was delivered two weeks later by a policeman. He was an imposing man, tall and broad with his black uniform, which made all of us quiet. She was dressed in grey, head to toe, her hair streaked with silver, flat and dusty. The bags she carried were grey, also. Faith answered the door and screamed; she'd been terrified, as we all were, by the Grey Ladies we saw around Grace as she died and thought she was seeing one again.

I came running to her. We always were aware of each other's emotions, but now more so, after Grace and all of us wondering what we could have done for her.

The woman, standing there with the policeman behind her, didn't glide away, so I knew she was real.

"Here's your new housemate," he said. He seemed eager to leave.

"Come in," I said, "Welcome to our humble home." We wouldn't know her for a while, but welcome first, judge later, is the way we felt.

The policeman wouldn't come in; you could tell the very thought terrified him.

"Annie Flagg," she said. Her voice was strong; you couldn't imagine anyone more the antithesis of poor, quiet Grace.

I took her through to the dining room, where we were finishing our evening meal. We sat her down and had her eat and tell us her story.

"He's accused me of drowning our children in the bath. His. To the servant girl. But I couldn't harm a hair on their dear little heads." Faith nodded, and Dot, and the others. The cruelty, they said, the unfairness, we understand.

But I looked at her hands and arms; they looked scalded to the elbow and I imagined her holding the poor little children down until they stopped their blessed wriggling.

A knock came at the door again, a gentle, feminine knock, and we all froze, expecting the Grey Ladies.

Instead, it was a man come to take the census, his arms full of papers. We weren't allowed to fill it in ourselves, not without a man in the house. He wore a long coat and thin tie, and he looked stern.

Inside, he said, "Let's gather together, shall we? How many of you are there?"

"We are five. That's including Annie, who's just arrived."

"Was she counted already, is what I need to know. Some efficiency, please."

Annie said, "I don't believe I was counted elsewhere. And will they count the children? Given that they were alive yesterday morning."

Her hands, still, red, rested calmly on the table.

He physically counted us, but he reached seven.

"What about those ones, who are they?" I looked around the room, surprised. Then my skin rose with goose bumps.

Standing over Annie's chair, like ash crows, were two Grey Ladies.

Dot choked; we all stood, desperate to leave the room. Annie stood and calmly walked to close the door. The Grey Ladies watched every move she made, rolling their eyes to follow her.

"Please don't be concerned. They are friends. Dear, dear friends to us all. They are just visiting," Annie said, because the rest of us were too terrified to speak.

"Tell them to go home. They need to be counted," the census man said.

He took our names, and our ages, rounded down to the nearest five years, and that we were pleased with. He didn't bother to ask our occupation; for all of us he wrote *Idle*.

"How many of you are unmarried?" None of us. We wouldn't be here if we had no one to deliver us. "No superfluous women," he noted, although each of us felt we probably were.

After he left, refusing tea and scones, Annie looked at us in turn and asked us to describe our flaws. "I can see your perfections!" she said. "My flaw is that I have no time for fools because I think they take up valuable space."

"Red Sheila's flaw is her hair!" Faith said. "Look at the colour of it!"

"Is that why they call you Red?" Annie asked, somehow knowing more than she should.

"No. No. My brother gave me the name when he found me. After the loss of my baby. He found me naked, covered in blood. Red."

She tells the story differently every time; I think she is so riven with guilt she tries to remember it in other ways.

"As if I need a reminder of that soul who died. Every time someone calls me Red, I remember."

"We don't have to call you that name," Annie said. Sheila had not told us the story with such honesty before. I wondered if Annie had already had a good influence on us.

"I should remember, though. I should never be allowed to forget what I did. Murder of the innocent, that's what it was, and that's what I'll pay for."

"You can see my flaw," Dot said, tilting her head back. Dot had worked in a match factory and was badly wounded, her face destroyed. Her husband and children found her horrifying to look at, and that's why they sent her away.

She always wears a veil.

"And you?" Annie said, turning her gaze on me.

"My husband tired of me and my ways and chose the work of the city rather than the work of a husband. With our children close to grown, I was nothing but a nuisance to him," I said.

"Your ways?"

"She can guess the truth more often than not," Sheila said.

"Can she now?"

We settled Annie into Grace's room. Were Grey Ladies sitting outside, perched on the tree branches? Surely they would not behave like that. I pointed at the window; Sheila pulled down the curtains.

Annie said, "Don't concern yourself with those ladies. They are friends to us. To women like us."

"But what about Grace? They seemed pleased with her passing, yet we are sad."

"They may have been disappointed in your Grace. They like to set us free before we die. They can only do that if we have demonstrated free will, and your Grace had not done so."

We none of us even understood what free will might be, and we backed out of Annie's bedroom, leaving her to settle.

Annie had only been with us a week, but to a woman we felt more alive already. She had so many ideas, and she was strong, in mind and in body.

We sat up in the attic, all dusted and cleaned. The view of the cricket ground was clear up there above the oak trees, and with the window open we could hear the crowds. Most of the house was shuttered and double-bricked, as if they were trying to keep the noise in. Do they imagine we spend our days screaming?

We watched the ordinary crowd of people.

"Look up," Annie called down to the passersby. "We are here. Don't you know we are here? We are alive?" She made us laugh.

We squinted through our windows. "Perhaps we are better off in here after all," Sheila said as we saw pickpockets, sly kisses, and pinches, faces full of anger and some full of idiocy.

"And perhaps the world would be better off without many of them," Annie said. "Wasteful, I sometimes think."

Annie had us sit there with our lunch; she was full of ideas. Cook stomped up the stairs with our meal, and she was so cross at the work she said, "You poor dears need something to look at," as if we were incapable of finding our own gainful employment.

It was not cricket we watched. It was a man they call the Ped. Richard Manks. He walked quickly, his legs moving like the scissors of a seamstress with a stomping, impatient customer. Like us, sewing madly. "Opening night is in three days," our customers scream. They stand on our doorstep and scream at us as if we don't understand. Can you imagine such a thing? Respectable women? Though of course they are nothing like respectable, these ones. One of them even had me sew in a panel at the back of her bustle, a concealed flap that could be opened for . . . she said it was for convenience. What she meant by that I certainly wasn't going to ask.

The Ped planned to walk a thousand miles in a thousand hours. This seemed an awful lot to all of us. Around and around in circles, reminding me of our Dorothy. First thing after breakfast she's outside, and she'll circle the house until lunchtime. Never misses a meal, our Dot.

"Sit still today," we say to her every now and then. "Sit and sew with us, or tat."

"Something useful," Sheila said this morning. "Time waster. Give them ammunition, you do, with your walking."

"Why if that Richard Manks does it it's considered historically memorable, but if I do it it's time wasting?"

"Because he has a purpose. You do not."

"He will be remembered simply for walking. We will fade away as if we never existed. And I do have a purpose. If I don't keep moving, the shadows of the Grey Ladies will fall on me and tease my soul out of my body."

Annie shook her head. "You misunderstand them. They can be . . . trained."

I thought of them watching her every move, showing every appearance of being as she said.

"Can they help us to be remembered?" Dot asked.

"I have my children to remember me. I have family," Sheila interrupted, and none of us were cruel enough to discuss how long it had been since those loved ones had visited.

"Tomorrow, Dot, let's walk around the block. All of us. Not just around the house. Let's see where we sit in the world. It will be an adventure for us all."

We are not under arrest, here. We can leave. It's only if we don't come back, there will be trouble. And if we leave altogether, we will have nothing.

We went walking early in the evening. It was lovely out, along the beautiful avenues lined with chestnuts and oaks. The river Wey winked at us, and there were boys, there are always boys, on the banks. We threw reeds to the ducks that quacked their way along peaceably.

"There's a rather odd fellow," Annie said, pointing discreetly at a man with a battered top hat and mismatched trousers. We giggled and we all sought them then, the strange people on the outside. Were we bothered by all the odd people around us? Not at all.

Actually we were. None of us were used to men nearby, nor the voices of children, nor the sounds of other women. But still we walked.

Alongside us walked a Grey Lady. She walked smoothly as if floating. Her face was calm, except for her eyes. She mostly kept her lids closed, somehow walking without sight. When she opened her eyes, you could see they were filled with fury. Sometimes, she circled a stranger, then moved back to nudge Annie, like a cat requesting food.

We felt full of good breath when we returned. Cook was gone for the day, and she had left our dinner to go cold on the table. We none of us minded. It seemed almost wild to eat a cold dinner. Not even Dot, our walker, whose husband is headed for the goldfields where Faith's husband digs.

"He raised the money," Dot said. "He's left provision for me."

"He may strike it rich, who knows?"

"I wonder if there are women there," Annie said, her eyes sliding sideways as if she knew more than she liked to say. "They would not be our kind, if there were."

We sat to think of the fallen women on the goldfields in that savage land so far away. Terrible things happened to women in such places.

"We should all go to Ballarat. We should take our own plot and make our own fortunes," Faith said. The name of the gold-rush town filled us all with excitement. Ballarat! Australia!

We often made plans such as these.

"You'll more likely have to make your money other ways." This was the maid, interfering when it wasn't her business at all. She carried a look of knowing about her, that girl. As if she knew more of life than we would ever know. As if she would never be an unwanted woman. Wait until her skin lost its lustre and her voice its sweetness.

Annie glared at her with such intensity I'm sure she shrank three inches. She backed out of the room, chastened.

"How would we raise enough to get there in the first place?"

"There are ways," Annie said. "Killing a man will get you ahead."

We were shocked that she would make such a jest.

"The Grey Ladies like it when some men are killed. They want the world to be a safer place for all of us."

"She's spouting. Be quiet for a single minute, can't you?" Sheila said. She had been in control for so long it was hard for her to listen to another woman.

"I'm telling you this for your own good," Annie said. Those familiar words gave me pause; what sort of woman was she? These were men's words.

Annie had black hair, run through with silver, and she liked to leave it loose. When she spoke this way, it gave her the air of a madwoman.

"We are happy the way we are," I said to Annie. "I don't imagine any of us would like to benefit from the death of a stranger."

But that was before the strangers came.

Surrey was supposed to be a safe place.

A year had passed since Annie's arrival. It was late, and we were all settled into bed. There was a commotion downstairs; I thought it was the Grey Ladies, angry with us for our inaction.

We all emerged together, dazed and sleepy, to find four men pushing their way up the stairs.

"Come on, you may not have a shutter out to advertise, but we know what you are," one snarled, as if women living together must be fallen, not pure.

We screamed, all of us, and that made the men angry. "Don't waste our time," they roared.

But they did not allow for the strength of unwanted women. One by one, down the stairs we pushed them, and we beat them and hit them until they all four were yelping. Then we edged them out of our front door.

The Grey Ladies? They watched it all, their fists clenched. It seemed to me they were disappointed we let the men live; certainly Annie was angry at us.

"Such a chance to make our ladies happy!" she said. "I could have given them a lovely Scotch and water. A special water. If they were innocent, they would not have fallen ill. If they were guilty, the Grey Ladies would have been happy and I would be closer to free will."

We brewed strong tea and sat together in the kitchen, all of us shaking and cold but unwilling to go alone to our bedrooms. Annie stoked the fire and soon our cheeks were flushed. Dot lay across the chaise lounge, her arm draped upon the floor.

"Look at you, Ophelia!" Annie said, and we all smiled at that.

"How are men like that free and we are locked up?" Faith said.

Sheila filled our cups again. "Men like that don't deserve to live. The world is too full. It is going to collapse. Men like that take up space."

Annie nodded. Her Grey Ladies nodded. And the rest of us, too.

The next morning Cook made us breakfast, complaining about working for prostitutes. How did she know what had occurred unless she had sent those men to us?

I whispered my thoughts to Annie, and she nodded.

"I can test her. I have a way."

She went to her room and returned with a bottle of water. Held up to the light it looked mostly clear, with no little creatures.

Annie made up a jug of barley water and had it ready for Cook when she returned from her messages.

"Here, dear Cook. To thank you for all you do for us."

The cook snorted, but she drank it down like a man drinking beer.

Three days later, word came that she was sick.

Soon after, we learned that she had passed away.

"Annie! What did you do? That is not what I would have wanted. You said a test!"

"Which she failed."

"What sort of water is that?"

"Well, now. You know that some believe that a miasma causes cholera. I believe it is the water, and that there is one source which can be guaranteed to be full of infection. It's the Broad Street water pump. Dr John Snow has spoken of it, but he is slow to action."

I didn't understand her meaning.

"I took the water from that pump. Our cook was stricken with cholera.

That is how she died, because she was foolish enough not to seek treatment. Or she was weak."

"How long have you been using this water?"

"Not very long. I plan to use it until the source dries up. The world is too crowded. And the Grey Ladies are happy with me. They protect me and my loved ones."

"What loved ones?"

"I don't have loved ones. Except for my mother. The Grey Ladies will keep her from harm, and if you help me, they will keep your children, your grandchildren, from harm as well. They are nurturers. Misunderstood."

The crowds had gathered by now to watch the cricket; they milled along our street, plucking our flowers, depositing waste of various kinds behind our fence.

"Look at them all. Not one of them cares who lives inside. They don't care that we have our freedom curtailed. Even if you screamed it out of the window, they still would not care. They'd have us boarded up in no time. What do you think, Sheila?"

Sheila had joined us without a word and nodded. "There is no doubt of that."

"It only uses the smallest amount of magic to make friends of the Grey Ladies," Annie said. "Who will come to London with me?" and not one of us wanted to be left behind, though we could not all go.

In the dark storage area under the house there were bottles and jars of preserves and fruit going back many years. All of them neatly dated, though the ink was faded.

It was these jars Annie used. She took great pleasure in opening them and tipping the contents into the gully behind the house. Some of it seemed perfectly fine, and if the new cook had seen her, we would have been eating jam pudding for a month. Annie did give some to Cook to serve with afternoon tea, and we all exclaimed about how well it had kept. Sheila had been present for much of the bottling.

Annie filled her basket with clean, empty bottles and dressed in her drabs, clothes that made her even more invisible. Grey, dowdy, and clean, nothing for the eye to catch on. We dressed in a similar way, Faith and I, and we were a trio of grey ladies.

We would not knock at anyone's door, though.

Carrying our baskets full of carefully packed jars and jugs, we took the train into London. It had been a long time since I'd travelled so far and the sights and the sounds seemed overwhelming. I was astonished to realise how the world still turned; we lived in our own small world, and yet around us, people lived and grew and loved unaware of our existence.

We all hated to go to London. The great reek of the Thames hung over city, and I felt as if I were swallowing it with every breath. All very well for them to invent water closets that carry away the waste, but the question is, where does it get carried to? The Thames, that's where. It often flooded and we didn't want to be there at such an awful time. What was mankind coming to? The smell of London was worse than ever. The Thames was a slow-moving snake of filth, and the effluvium in the air made people ill.

Kindly strangers told us to keep our faces covered while in town. "Don't breathe in the air," one matron told us. "You'll catch cholera and you're too young to die."

"Thank you, ma'am," Annie said. People were so foolish. They listened to each other, or to the rot published in the newspapers, and ignored the brilliant words of the great man Dr Snow. He'd told them time and time again that it was not the miasma causing the illness.

We travelled to the Broad Street pump. Women clustered around us, filling their bowls and bottles. Children, too, some of them so thin I wondered they had the strength to stand.

"Should we tell them?" I whispered to Annie. I trusted her completely to know what to do; she understood the Grey Ladies.

"No. God's will is what we trust in. This water is God-given, and who are we to ignore his gift?"

I was not always sure of her meaning, but she spoke with such confidence.

"And regardless," she said, "they would not listen to us. We are women. This is not up to us."

We waited for a lull and then filled our containers. We had many; the baskets were heavy.

We stopped at a teahouse to revive ourselves. "Do you have the needful, the rhino, the ready?" a woman said to us as we entered. She had her palm out.

"We have nothing for you."

The woman smelt of dog droppings and she had a bag at her feet which reeked. I thought she must be a Pure collector; those dog droppings used to process kid leather. I thought that perhaps we were not the unluckiest women in the world after all. I offered her a sip of our water; she took it gratefully. Little did she know I was offering her an early way out of her terrible life.

Annie nodded at me approvingly. "You are one of the strongest women I know. Already your soul is shifting and you will soon be free."

True, I felt a slight movement within my skin, as if there was more breathing space for me.

Well rested, we carried our baskets back home again. I wanted to give sips to all on the train, and this made Annie laugh. "You'll be free sooner than I am, at this rate. You are sending souls on their way to God. You will have your reward."

"Will they be very sick, do you think?" I had not seen cholera in action; I had barely seen a sick person. When my own children were sick, a nurse was brought in so that I would not become ill at all. I realise now how much my husband protected me, but this also meant he did not love me as a husband should. He loved me in a guardianship way, as if I were his responsibility, and this, in the end, destroyed his love. I became too much of a burden.

It was wonderful to be back home. Our lovely large bathroom, our fresh, sweet air.

The others were all happy to see us. We told them about London, about the poverty we saw, the degradation, and we went on to talk about the worst things we could imagine. Somehow this made us feel better about our own lives. We told stories of children sold to the devil and tortured until they reached their maturity, of physical attacks, of murder, of war and great hunger. Annie said, "Helping the Grey Ladies keeps your children safe. Most of these people are thinking about suicide anyway. It's clear in their eyes."

The Grey Ladies were closer to me, and I could hear them whisper, *You can be free to make your own life, you can be free.*

"All we're doing is giving water to the thirsty. They'll thank us."

We all dressed in white and we bundled up our lovely bottles of sweet lemon barley water. A cricket game was at play, and we would move amongst the spectators.

"Are you planning to sell those?" the new cook said. "You watch out for the bobbies if you do. I heard the police don't look kindly upon street vendors." Her nephew would collect her to watch the game, and she was quite excited, dressed in her outside clothes.

We looked like nurses and I felt as if we were giving out cures for life.

Annie told us to whisper, to make people thirsty. We moved amongst the spectators and the players, too, telling people our drinks came from a wealthy benefactor. Otherwise people would be suspicious. We told them it was healing water from a spa. We told the women it was good for hysteria.

Faith's uncle had been in India and had described to her the clay tea mugs that are thrown to the ground after use. We ourselves had made many of these cups, but we used and reused them until they crumbled.

As we worked, Annie seemed to be tilted to one side, limping. I thought that I could see her soul spilling, edging its way out slowly. I asked her if she was tired, if she needed to rest.

"I am almost free. Every person I help to God pulls that soul out until I'll be free of it."

"But you'll be a shell. You're nothing without a soul."

"The soul is nothing. It is conscience, guilt, respectability. The soul is why we allow ourselves to be locked up this way. If we are free of the soul, we will truly have free will. We will be able to choose whether or not to be mothers. Whether or not we wish to suffer the Primal Malediction."

I knew that Annie had been badly damaged by the stillbirth of her only son. She says that pain itself causes permanent damage, but also that it strengthens us. She says that Queen Victoria will always be weak because of the chloroform she used in childbirth, and that her son, only weeks old, would be mentally defective.

Annie took her jug and some glasses down to the main gate. She offered drinks to the players as well, but they were more interested in beer.

"It's refreshing, men," she said.

She gave drinks to men, women, and children. Not one of them asked for a clean glass.

Avoiding the temptation to drink the last of the cordial herself, Annie poured it and found a lone cricketer. He was a stout man, wearing whites too small for him. The trousers in particular looked horribly uncomfortable.

"I hope they don't hang us when they find out," Faith said, but her eyes were bright and excited.

❧

We never read the newspapers. The first we knew of the epidemic was when a contingent from the council came hammering at our door. No ladylike knocking from them; impatient battering.

Without more than a word or two, six men came into our home. They were in good suits, and they smelt well. Otherwise, they were little different from the invaders we had successfully repelled.

They walked from room to room, noting size and furniture.

"May I enquire what this is about?" Annie said. Since we'd begun our endeavour, she seemed even stronger. Her voice loud and powerful. Deep. If you closed your eyes, you might think she was a man.

"Doing your civic duty. Your husbands have informed you," one man said, though of course they had not.

"We are not advised," Annie said, and we women clapped our hands silently with glee at this. Even the Grey Ladies seemed happy; they rubbed their hands together as if cleaning them.

"There is a cholera epidemic about in Surrey, and we have no room at the hospital, nor do we wish to transport the sick elsewhere. This house and others like it will become auxiliary sanatoriums. All ladies will become nurses, regardless of training. This is to be expected."

After which they inspected our kitchen and interviewed our new cook. She bowed and scraped to their liking, and the approval brought a blush to her cheeks.

We were surrounded by the dying. Annie glowed and the Grey Ladies seemed to float with great excitement.

We were the cleanest establishment in Surrey. The new cook was in heaven; she was doing good works and feeding the sickly. She thought her food would cure them, the sweet, sweet fool. The maid seemed to spend her time tending the doctors, but we were all too busy to chastise her.

The doctors kept the windows open, and if this gave our patients a chill, they didn't seem to care.

"We must minimise the miasma" was the saying, and we were all martyrs to that cause.

Still, the patients died.

Annie and Faith did another trip to London for more water; this we washed them with, this we gave them to drink. We mopped their brows, we held their hands, we dispensed the medicine the doctors requested. We soothed their dry throats with our pump water.

There was a lot of mess to clean up and we were allotted some nurses for this work. Ladies shouldn't have to deal with that sort of thing. Oh, the nastiness of what is inside the human body. Nurses came from Nottingham and we found room for them all. They were a cheery bunch who made all of us feel pale in comparison.

"No free will at all," Annie said of them as they sat together in clumps, laughing as if they were of one voice. "Look at them. The Grey Ladies want nothing to do with that lot."

No small part of me envied those nurses and their occupation. They seemed far happier than we were, for all their lack of wealth. They were a little nervous of us, I think, because they had not spent time with gentlewomen before.

We were glad to have them. The patients looked awful. Skin so floppy we could hold fistfuls of it, and their voices hoarse and rough. It sounded like a house full of monsters, and they were tired, and confused, and they all spoke of the Grey Ladies, leaning over their beds, every one of them imagining death at the end of the bed. It made for frightened patients. We were sometimes kept up half the night, and in that light I could see right through the unwanted women, to their very hearts. Sheila's soul seemed to glow. Dot had a shrivelled-up soul, curled in the pit of her stomach like a hibernating squirrel. It seemed to me there was nothing left of her. Faith: hers was like a shield. And Annie? Annie's soul was holding on by its teeth, which were sunk into her shoulder.

We ministered to the patients as best we could, providing the spiritual support while the nurses did most of the physical work. When Annie walked the hallways, the Grey Ladies held on to her shoulders, and sometimes it was hard to tell one from the other. The patients didn't like Annie, especially the children. As time passed, she found it harder and harder to conceal her disdain for them.

"They are a foetid group, aren't they?" she said to me one morning. We sat in the attic, which remained our private sitting room. Her soul seemed loosely joined at the shoulder. It dangled there, like a woman with her neck broken at nauseous angle. I thought to myself, *You are close. You are very, very close.* With every death in the house, her soul edged out, as, I supposed, did mine. The Grey Ladies leaned over both of us; I thought I felt one playing with my hair. It was pleasant if I closed my eyes.

"I feel rather sorry for them," I said.

"Do you really? But why on earth?"

"Only that they are physically suffering so. And we are helping them in that. I'm not always sure we are doing the right thing." But I knew; I could feel within myself a growing power. A growing strength. I felt as if I were no longer invisible.

We heard a great wailing, then the thump of someone running up the stairs. Faith.

"It's another child," she gasped. "Gone, just that minute, with its mother holding its head."

Annie shuddered. "Which one was it?"

"Your favourite. The blue-eyed monster."

Annie shuddered again; she seemed to have no control over it. She began to shake, her head nodding forward at a painful pace.

I took her arm. The flesh felt flaccid.

Annie's soul, twisted, dark, pockmarked, slipped to the ground, where it puddled, like a rat liquefying. The Grey Ladies fell to their knees and lapped, lapped, lapped.

"Annie! Annie! You're free!" I said. Faith and I smiled at each other; Annie was right. This is what she was talking about. She was free. We expected her to leap about like a young girl, to whoop, to be wild. We wanted her to do these things; we wished we could do them.

But no. Annie's mouth hung open. She blinked. Her hand lifted to wipe a sludge of saliva from her chin. Her jaw shifted as if she was trying to speak.

"Annie?"

Annie grunted and wavered to her feet.

"Quick, sit her back down."

We layered her in, rearranging her limbs.

She lived for a month. Fed by a nurse, changed by a nurse, put to bed by a nurse. Or by us. No choice, no voice, no will. Her Grey Ladies left her alone, preferring the company of our patients downstairs. They came to check on us as well, stroking our hair as we rested, working their fingers between our ribs as if trying to pry something loose.

Annie's hair turned completely grey and her skin lost any lustre it may have had. It was something of a relief when she passed; we felt as if we could move on, forget what we'd done. We poured all of our stored water away, and soon after that the pump was removed in London and the cholera epidemic eased.

"Good works only from now on, ladies," Red Sheila said as we stood by Annie's grave.

But I think we all knew it was too late to wash the grey out.

About "The Unwanted Women of Surrey"

I've been curious about Dr John Snow for a while now. I'm always fascinated by the people who change lives through apparently small actions. Dr Snow removed a water pump in London, thus halting a terrible cholera epidemic.

So, when reading and researching for this story, I discovered that he also acted as the anaesthetist to Queen Victoria, one of the first women to be administered an anaesthetic during childbirth, I knew I had the centre of my story.

I also read about the Census of 1851, in which unmarried women without children were marked down as superfluous. It's one of those words that will perhaps lose its meaning over time; a local fast-food restaurant tells us that their food is "superfluous in antioxidants." I'm pretty sure they don't mean what they say. The idea that a woman could be considered worthless because she had no children angered me. The women in my story are unwanted rather than superfluous, but they are similarly considered worthless.

I wanted to explore the contrast of experience between rich and poor as well. The women are poorly treated, but they are also blind to the deep, desperate poverty around them.

While doing my research, I stumbled on the fad of the Ped, people who walked for a living. They walked quickly, or long distances, and people watched. It seemed such a strange thing to do, but then of course we do many such odd things, and we watch them. Like poker games on TV; these I find hypnotic.

So I set my story in Surrey, with a visit to the pump in London. You can read about Dr Snow here:

http://www.ph.ucla.edu/epi/snow/snowpub.html

CHARGED

My first memory is of being struck by lightning. It was exquisite.
I was standing in my grandfather's field just before the storm
broke. White-hot arcs threaded across the whole of the char-
coal English sky. Trembling with thrills, I wanted to reach up and touch
the delicate, veinlike threads of light. It would seem they wanted to touch
me, too.

"There's nothing more wondrous than a good, riotous thunderstorm,
my boy," grandfather had said with a gamesome punch to my shoulder
that landed too hard. But I learned that's how one shows affection to a
male child; with a touch of force.

That's when the bolt anointed me. I stood riveted as my bones rattled
and crackled, my blood boiled and a thousand angels screamed in my ears.
When it was over, small wisps of smoke curled up from my hair and coat.

Grandfather stared at me in horror. "You should be dead, child." He
clapped me again on the back, a sting of shock passing between us upon
contact, and walked away.

I wasn't dead but he was right about one thing: I've yet to see or *feel*
anything more wondrous than a sky full of electricity.

When Mr Swan's incandescent lamp came to Newcastle upon Tyne in
the year of our Lord 1879, three years ago, it was destiny. We lived just at
the end of Mosley Street, in a two-story town house with finery on the

outside that crumbled on the inside. I was fourteen years old. Mother had died a year prior. There wasn't enough evidence to blame Father directly, but I blamed him anyway, and while our exterior appearances were spotless, everything inside rotted.

I hoped that year, after enduring a loveless life of misplaced piety and fierce abuse from a man whose only purpose in life seemed to be to torture my brother and me, that light would make all men equal. At least, that it would illuminate the rights and wrongs of the world in bright, sharp focus like a blazing incandescent. Light would illuminate the deep shadows of our house and lay skeletons bare in black closets for all to see. At least that's how I reconciled it when my ability first took a life. I could wield light like the sword of justice.

When the bulbs of Mosley Street first buzzed, I buzzed with them. I wasn't sure what it was at first; the celebration out on the street was so festive, I thought I might just be caught up in the thrill. When I felt a smile—a genuine smile I hadn't felt upon my lips since that lightning storm— threaten to split my face in two, I turned to that man-made sun and worshipped it. Just as my fervour crested like that of a revivalist in a tent spreading the ecstasy of the Holy Ghost, the incandescent directly above me flickered and burst. Everyone turned to stare, as if it were somehow my fault. My cheeks turned red with shame.

"Not to worry, ladies and gentlemen! We shall change the world!" said one of the engineers in charge, rushing to assure the crowd upon the street, edging towards the pole I stood beneath. I edged into shadow, tucking into my schoolboy jacket, which wasn't quite the right size. "But you can't expect to do so without a few broken bulbs along the way!"

It was my fault, I came to understand. Other bulbs, not far from my top-floor window, would flicker as my mood flared or guttered. I had plenty of empirical evidence as I watched the lights, sometimes all through the night, listening for one of Father's rages and debating whether I would intervene on behalf of my little brother, Jack, who was neither nimble nor quick. I think I was often spared because Father was scared of me after the lightning didn't kill me. Something he saw in my eyes. Sometimes I'd see the hairs on Father's bare, scarred forearms raise when our gazes occasionally met.

If the lights were a symphony, I could raise or lower my baton, and in response the song of the current would either crescendo or decrescendo, making me quite literally a *conductor* of electricity. Unsure whether to revel in the secret or fear it, I kept it to myself.

Wires are so like veins, and I became more comfortable thinking of myself as a vessel rather than as a person. With the hum of the lights in concert with my heartbeat, our systems had become entwined. When the switches of the Mosley plant were engaged and I heard the particular whine in my ear, I knew I was tethered to the divine. I was an inextricable part of that righteous illumination. Like Zeus and Thor, I would deal in commodities of sparking glory.

So when Father, in a drunken rage, tossed my brother down our mouldering staircase and his little neck cracked just like all the foundations of that house, the current came up and through me like a wave. Holy retribution flung a thick cord forward like a snapping whip, lacerating my father with a number of volts I could hardly quantify.

The court ruled it self-defence despite the great confusion as to how a hot fireplace poker could have done quite that much burning damage to a body. Father, I came to find out, owed a deal of money to various important folk. The city was only too happy to seize his assets in reparation. Not caring a whit about me, the court suggested the workhouse, as cities do with any youthful problem they want out of their sight.

Instead I disappeared. My gift urged me to live by reinvented terms. Forging a document to claim I was eighteen, I sought a higher wage than apprenticeship's slavery and went to work in the one place where no one would suspect aberrant voltage: the electrical company that had put Mosley Street on the map.

I took the name of that street as my own. The past was erased. Only present energy remained. Losing myself to the songs of the current and their various conductors, I began praying to my saints to bring me to their shores.

I've not the head for the mechanics of great inventors' work. But I've the body to conduct it. Working at the plant allowed for experimentation of current through my body. There I learned how to control what should, for all intents and purposes, have fried me like an egg on a skillet. Overhearing my superiors talk about all the latest developments in the field, their declarations resonated in my bosom like prophecies.

Saving every shilling, resentful that I should have been denied any of my father's meagre holdings, I hated the dirty, small-minded men who resided in the flophouse beside the plant where I deigned to lay my head upon a soiled mat. This fury aged me. My soul languished and my only restless contentment was the whir of the turbines and the prickle of current through my skin. I prayed harder at the altar of invention.

Of all my saints, Edison, in particular, engaged me. As if I were a fisherman, he called me to abandon my nets and come follow him. . . . I've read every word my prophet has written, followed his every move, patent, and innovation. I studied his contemporaries. I puzzled over Tesla's alternating current versus Edison's direct. The former individual is a madman. But my prophet is a cool and capable businessman. I'm a man of particular taste, and I like the word *direct*. It feels right. When one is talking about a conduit of energy, the matter should flow *directly* from source to target. To *alternate* is to be inconstant. *I* am a *director*.

Through Edison, all things are possible. Building on the foundations of Watt and the luminaries of the eighteenth century, I daresay that fearless American might just make Shelley's wondrous nightmare of reanimation a plausible reality in our everyday lives. There's nothing he cannot do. He has been inventing—or at least patenting—everything of world-changing import. The current—his current—cannot be denied. America, *his* America, will set the world awash with blinding orbs. The buzz of progress, gods of industry—all will bow down to the small island at the core of the Empire State.

Thusly, the moment I heard of the dynamos Edison was building in that leviathan of all cities, New York, New York, my need to leave Newcastle upon Tyne and discard my quiet, friendless life became a burning longing for transplant.

The plant powering Mosley Street eventually fired me after one too many shorts to their circuits during my shift. That, and the foreman found me sleeping beside far better bedfellows than flophouse sots: the generators. But the company's callous severance was only destiny's sign declaring I was finally meant for greater grids.

Yet while I'd scrimped and saved, I didn't have enough for a steamer ticket *and* an apartment in territory ruled by "the Wizard of Menlo Park." Industry powered the wealthy, not the workers who lit their candles. So I claimed what was rightly mine out of the foreman's safe. A lashing bolt seared the lock to reveal banknotes enough for my recompense. No one could know it was "odd little Mosley" that lifted them; no one really knew a thing about me.

I was the actual eighteen years of age I'd been pretending for so long when the current's song finally sailed me across the Atlantic. En route to this upstart colony that shall become Atlas holding up the world, I pitied all those on that boat who could not see what I saw. I saw the great, churning city as if I were seeing her bones, girded with light. I saw every building shimmer, every roadway and ferryboat blazed; I wept at the raw power that was possible, and I rejoiced that I would be embedded in the bloodstream of goliath circulation. And I began plotting how I would meet the man I worshipped.

I procured a basement level apartment on Pearl Street, close to my saint's plant, close to the precious lifeblood itself; six dynamos able to produce a hundred kilowatts each. At night I lay awake, my hair standing on end, aroused, alive, vibrating. Who needs a lover when the current is all the exquisite caress a man could crave? I confess, when I wield the current in my hands, the experience has a carnal taste, and I am spent afterwards.

Edison does not know I exist. Not yet. I know enough about him to realise that he'll likely find a way to use me if he knew what his life's work does to me. I would. Use me, that is. If I were him. We two are of a mind. So I must approach him carefully and make sure that if I become his acolyte, I'm free to pursue my own ventures. I have a calling. I am a messenger. I am a child of all the world's lightning gods. The *how* is not as important to me as the fact that it *is*. I am a changeling for a changing world. Industry churns towards progress, and electricity means that the gods are harnessed and fallen. Orphaned, I've become industry's child, and mankind has been spinning the world forward on its axis to catch up with me.

I've been in New York a month, and what started with fitting the Morgan residence has begun a craze of rapid expansion. Electricity now makes Pearl Street blaze bright, and other nearby homes and street corners are following suit. The activity has me buzzing night and day; I feel my head might explode.

When my delirium mounts, I walk my street at dusk. Every beautiful person I see, man or woman, illuminated in a manufactured light so much more beautiful than sun or candle, I long to draw them close, to share the spark I could offer from my skin to theirs. But whenever I get close, a hum rises around me, a lamp somewhere nearby flickers, and the attractive persons look up and away from me. A guttering light is like a falling star, it longs to be seen. As do I. In longing to be noticed, my thoughts would inevitably return to my prophet.

Today, I saw him. And he saw me. But did not understand.

There was a fair, in Brooklyn, and I took the Fulton ferry across, swept eagerly along the strong East River currents. Perhaps the only thing as thrilling as a lightning storm is being buffeted along the cobblestone streets of New York City like a feather on the breeze, tasting the great, tumbling mass of human energy as one might savour a spice upon the tongue. Now and then I brushed against someone's shoulder. A shock would pass between us, and when they turned to me, apologizing for the collision, I smiled. Apprehension flickered in their eyes. I confess, the transaction left me fulfilled; a maddening itch had been scratched, a hungering need satiated.

Surging with me embedded inside, the organism of excitable humanity spilled from the docks out onto an open midway filled with various attractions. Rich smells, outlandish sideshows, and festive sounds all collided in a rush of competition for attention. But I was there for one sole purpose and heeded no other call. The moment I saw him, I froze.

There, beneath a tent, surrounded by gadgets, wires, and an elephant, was Edison. My throat went dry. An intense-looking fellow, he had drawn quite a crowd around him. He had that ability and notoriety. Moisture beaded beneath the thin hairs of the moustache I'd been struggling to grow for years.

Edison was demonstrating the dangers of Nikola Tesla's alternating current by applying a live wire directly to the hide of an elephant. Really, it didn't matter if it was alternating or direct, current was current and electrocution would happen no matter the format. Certainly the elephant didn't care what type of current it was, it was in pain regardless. But Edison was a businessman. And businessmen needed to protect themselves and the reputations of their technology by any means necessary. Everyone was, appropriately, shocked.

I'm not sure what my emotional state was at that moment exactly, whether I was as sharply focused as a disciple ought to be before his teacher, or if I somehow associated that elephant with my brother, but I surged to the fore of the group. I wove through a sea of bowler hats, seamen's caps, and the occasional investor's top hat.

Something was wrong. The generator wasn't quite humming at the pitch it should, a sonority I knew like that of my own breath. The current generated to light bulbs, play music, and sizzle the elephant's hide wavered and was about to go out.

"Fix the problem," Edison barked at an aide.

I could help him. It was the generator that was the problem, didn't they hear it? I stepped towards the tables bearing a line of contraptions set with wheels and wires—a mere rope had been put out around the perimeter—and put my hand out. Edison looked up sharply, aware of anyone too near his precious property.

"It's me, don't worry," I murmured, choosing Edison over the elephant. Showing him that I was the stabilizing force, I took my hand away and the sea of hats shifted, glancing around at guttering bulbs, a stuttering phonograph, and a recovering elephant. But the creature's comfort was short-lived as all buzzed bright, music blared, and the animal shuddered in pain once more the moment I replaced my hand above the nearest turbine.

"We've got a short somewhere, fix it," Edison barked to his colleagues without breaking my gaze. With his bowler hat a bit askew, his bright eyes narrowed, then widened, confused. I *willed* him to understand as he stared at me; the gift we could be to one another. I might not comprehend the scope of what was happening in my body, but surely *he* could. But evidently Edison did not desire further illumination for he barked again: "You. Get away from there. What are you, one of *Tesla's*?"

My face twisting in disgust at that rival's name, I opened my mouth to protest, but words died in my throat. I took a step towards my inspiration, but at Edison's gesture a burly man wearing a Pinkerton badge appeared as if from nowhere to block me. His leather glove masked the stinging spark upon contact with my shoulder, but we both felt it. "Turn around, idiot," the man growled, giving me a shove back towards the midway. Big as the guard was, fear sparkled in his eyes and a flare of satisfaction warmed my wrenching stomach.

There was so much I wanted to say. So much I wanted to show my great prophet, so much I wanted to ask, so much experimentation I longed to do . . . But Edison was lost to me behind a swarm of hats. My extreme anxiety made a whole string of his lights explode one by one. I heard him shout a curse about saboteurs.

Bile churned, nervous sweat poured off my brow. Clearly, that disaster was hardly the encounter I'd hoped for. But I comfort myself with the knowledge that in time Edison will *have* to know me. He'll have to give me audience. I can become part of the grid and there will be no way to ignore me. His competitors, too, will have to consider me a force to be reckoned with.

A few bulbs along Pearl Street blew as I returned to my narrow, lit town-house apartment next to a fine private residence wholly wreathed in electric convenience. While the gentleman next door has paid top dollar for his fixtures and even more for the wiring, I've installed fixtures just as grand. As for the wiring, well, that is *directly* my responsibility. Of course I should have anticipated that eyebrows might be raised. Singed, even. The island of Manhattan does like to make sure all its pennies are collected, now doesn't it?

While today's fair was no joy, tonight proved a further trial—the first of what I assume will be many stumbling blocks along my pilgrim's progress. A small hiccup. As industry moves inexorably and more terrifyingly swiftly forward, mankind makes futile efforts to slow it's Frankenstein children with laws and *paperwork*. Perhaps I shouldn't have killed the messenger. But he overstepped his bounds.

Peeping through the front glass, the reverberations of the doorknocker echoing in the hall, the small man in a bowler whose squinty eyes made my jaw clench in aversion was asking for trouble. "Mr Mosley?" he called in a whine.

I opened my door. "Yes?"

He must have gathered my name from the rental papers. Someone had been looking into me. Would it were Edison himself checking in, but I'm sure he and his tax collectors work separately. Besides, at first blush I must have appeared mad. And in this context, I might only appear to Edison a thief, not a disciple or child of his invention. But I had a right to my own gifts, they could not be bought or sold.

"I'm here with the electrical company," the man said.

"Yes?"

He stood there as if waiting for me to invite him in. I did not. The bulb above his head on my sheltered stoop buzzed brighter. "Yes, well." He gestured, around him, towards the bulb above and to the sconces behind me in the entrance hall. "You've lights. And those aren't gas. I can tell."

I looked around. "Why, so they are. *Lights.*"

"You're not . . . registered. . . . And yet, there you are with electric-"

"Yes. Isn't it beautiful?"

The small, beady man did not answer me. Clearly, he didn't think my illumination as glorious as I did. He had no imagination. Just like all those sightless sots on my boat across the pond, he did not see the New York I felt in my veins. He did not know what I had here on Pearl Street, what I'd had on Mosley Street, what I could *do* to any street. To anyone.

"I imagine someone ran you wires from the home next door," he drawled.

"No."

"Intentional or not, you are pulling current when this house has no registered circuits. That is illegal. One must have a meter. One must be registered. Light isn't free, you know. Light isn't a *right*, it must be *earned*. This is a summons to court, and this is your cease and desist."

He held up papers. My ears rang. I took the pages from his sweaty palm and crumpled them, tossing them behind me into my hall.

"Sir, be reasonable, else I'll call the authorities."

"Go ahead, but they won't understand. None of you do," I said.

Outside, my block was oddly unpopulated. I took that as convenient providence. My divine justice was clear. A glorious song crested in my ear.

The bulb above the man's head shattered as I reached towards him. I could see the small man fix upon my eyes, upon the threading spark he saw there; my pupils like a Tesla coil, I saw the glowing strands reflected in his own widening spheres, his gaze shifting in distinct cycles. Confusion to wonder to horror. I smiled.

"What *are* you?" the man choked.

There was a gurgle, a vicious sizzle, a hearty convulsion, a stench, and a man lay charred at my feet, hair smoking. I know it's my fault that he lies blackened and burned. Yet, as I search my heart like a detective who takes his kerosene lantern down a dark city alley, I find no regret huddling in the shadows.

Slumped against my doorframe, spent, today's shame was now wiped clean by the surge I wielded. I felt the same calm peace as when Father lay smouldering next to broken little Jack. Retribution grounds me.

Rallying to action, I knew the block would not remain unpopulated and the light would make all things evident to passersby. That was the problem with light; it may illuminate a scene but not circumstances. Light did not make cause and effect clear; a snag in my belief that light made all things equal. Light was more subjective, really.

I deposited the man's body beside the fine home next door, near it's shining-new fuse box, concluding the visual context would provide explanation enough as to the cause of death. Fraying a wire made a nice touch. I placed his hand upon the exposed cable. Perfect. Live wire; dead body.

"Let there be light," Scripture says. Religious fanatics and pastoral shepherds will encourage their sheep to "step into the light." There, in the light, one shall be purified. There, in the light, one shall be safe. Well. That depends. It depends on what one means by *safe* and whom one is trying to guard. The subjectivity of light.

My state of reflection has drawn me up the uppermost stairwell of my building and out onto the pitch-covered rooftop to gaze out over Pearl Street—my beautiful, burning, lit Pearl Street in the oyster of America. My adoration causes a flicker. The flutter of my heart is made manifest in the lamps across the street and in the shafts of illumination they cast.

As the grid of the city expands like a growing, living thing, I shall graft myself into it. Here I stand, planting my feet at the core of this great heart, the pulse of the world. As the century is about to turn, he who holds light holds power. I find it fitting that electricity has become synonymous with the word *power*. I do not wield mere light. But power itself.

And what is that I see in the great, pitch-black sky? A flicker of lightning to bring me home, blessing its prodigal son. I lift my hands to the sky. Current reaches out in return, seeking my embrace. A bolt anoints me. Lightning's fiery consummation reminds me that I am special. That I am exempt from the life of everyman. I am of the gods. When that terrifying and exhilarating paralysis releases me, I am invincible. *That* is what I am.

And God said, "Let there be light." But now that light is made by the hand of man, *I* shall decide whether "And there *was* light" is deserved, or whether it shall be withheld. So, please, Manhattan. Don't anger me. Don't come knocking on my door unless you welcome the kiss of voltage. Don't ask what I am, look into my eyes and see.

Burn bright, day and night. Burn bright, dear city. Feed your power and feed me. Embrace me like the lover I deserve, New York. I am in your blood and you'll die without light to feed your sleepless circulation. You industrious city, striving so hard and so fast, you need creatures like me. In your coming reign, O great Empire City, remember who can wield your current. Who needs Edison when we have each other? You, beautiful and powerful island, are my charge.

About "Charged"

I'm not sure if I believe in past lives, but *something* had me doubling my skirts, speaking in Dickensian sentences, and obsessed with Gothic architecture from an early age. The Victorian era is my second skin. A difficult, complicated skin, warts and all. As a progressive woman of the twenty-first century, there is much to hate about the Victorian era. Yet it's when most of the causes I care about were born, and there is much about the era that compels.

I've devoted my career thus far to historical fantasy and Victorian-set work. "Charged" is set in a larger Gaslight Fantasy world of *Voltage,* a work in progress at the time of writing this afterword. When asked, "Why Victoriana?" I respond in opposites: the grit and the grandeur, unspoken desires and secret languages, uptight restriction and a seething underbelly. A bipolar era rife with tension and fear, the era has an ego as big as its advancements, a wakening sense of social consciousness amidst arrogant imperialism, triumphs and terrors of the industrial revolution, and with romance as sweeping and sometimes as exoticised as its thirst to conquer. This Jekyll and Hyde era holds me in thrall, novel after novel. I wonder if the era will ever let me go; if I'll ever shed this complicated skin.

The seed of "Charged" was planted while I was researching *The Strangely Beautiful Tale of Miss Percy Parker.* Jack the Ripper is an element in the story, and in a journalist's account of the murders, he woefully concluded that if there had just been "more light" (gas lamps ended at Commercial Street and Whitechapel Road, keeping the area of Whitechapel well and truly in the dark), Jack's reign of terror wouldn't have happened. More light. While mere visibility alone was hardly an answer to the endemic problems of that neighbourhood, the comment got me thinking about technology as a saviour, and how the words *light* and *power* have multiple strong connotations. Out of a question of inversion, Mosley was born. "Power" hungry.

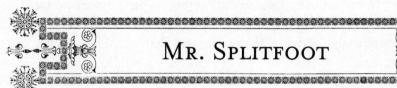

✤ DALE BAILEY ✤

MR. SPLITFOOT

Modern Spiritualism as a popular movement began with the Hydesville raps. . . . Whether by the design of the spirits or inadvertently, Kate and Maggie Fox served as the catalyst for what believers in spiritual communication call the dawning of a new era.

—Barbara Weisberg, *Talking to the Dead,* 2004

That I have been chiefly instrumental in perpetrating the fraud of Spiritualism upon a too-confiding public, most of you doubtless know. The greatest sorrow in my life has been that this is true, and though it has come late in my day, I am now prepared to tell the truth. . . . I am here tonight as one of the founders of Spiritualism to denounce it as an absolute falsehood . . . the most wicked blasphemy known to the world.

—Maggie Fox, *New York World,* 1888

1893

They have taken me to Emily Ruggles's house to die.

I had hoped to die in my little apartment in the city, but Emily's house is pleasant and will serve as well, I suppose. The March sunlight illuminates my room in the morning, and Emily is kind enough to sit up with me at night. The nights are hardest. The follies and illusions of childhood reassert themselves at night, and it is reassuring to see a human face when you open your eyes in the gloom, in an unfamiliar house, thinking that perhaps you are already dead. Last night—was it last night?—I woke from a dream of Hydesville, and Emily looked like Kate, bending to her needlework by the light of a guttering taper. For a moment, we were girls, all undone between us. Kate, I cried, Kate—then Emily took my hand and became just plain Emily once more. So I remembered that Kate was dead and had to mourn her all over again. The mind is a funny thing, playing tricks like that.

You were always playing tricks on me, too, weren't you, Kate? Full of tricks from the day you were born. Remember how we held the stage when Leah paraded us from city to city like a pair of trained lovebirds, tapping and preening? Every girl's dream to be a bird, fêted on every side, and, oh, we were fêted, Kate, how our names did ring upon every tongue! And even then you were a tapping, preening little thing, all dressed up in your skirts of robin's-egg blue. Do you remember how the people used to gather before a sitting, how they would come from near and far, crying your name aloud and reaching out to touch you? Do you remember how easy it all was, how eager they were to believe? What a glorious trick that was, Kate! That was the best trick of all! Who could have seen that it would all turn out as it has? *We were children, Maggs.* I can hear you say it. *We didn't know. Surely that's something. Surely that's enough*—

You were at them again, your tricks, last night, weren't you? Emily dozed—even the most faithful watchers doze—and as she nodded over her needlework, you were up to your old tricks, rapping and tapping and knocking oh so quietly, so only I could hear. It got cold in the room then, just like it used to when we were girls, all those years ago. Do you remember the cold, Kate? The cold of the grave, so black and deep it prickled up the hairs along the back of your neck and turned your breath to vapor?

The Summerland indeed.

And here you are with another blanket to comfort me. Look at me, Kate! Look how frail I've become. I've become *old,* I say, and a young girl's melancholy creeps into my breast. How funny it is, the way we never age inside our hearts, whilst outwardly this catastrophe every day renews it-self. Tutting—

—*you must calm yourself mrs. maggie*—

—Emily—it *is* Emily, isn't it? In the gloom it's hard to see—tucks the blanket in tight around me. She means kindness, I know, dear Emily. Why, I remember when she came to us, how dumbfounded she was to be among us at last: the mothers of Spiritualism! I remember her first sitting, and afterward teaching her the secrets of material manifestations. How shocked she was at this cheerful fraud! Yet I'll admit, and I admitted then, that there is something of the illusionist's craft in our art; it helps the sitters to suspend their disbelief, to quote Mr. Coleridge.

But there is truth, as well.

There is the matter of the cold. And of Hydesville.

That was March, too, wasn't it? More than forty years have passed since then—I was sixteen that year, and you still a slip of a girl—yet I still remember the winter of 1848, spilling right over into spring, such a fierce year it was. At first, I thought that no one noticed the cold because it was already so cold in that house, with the wind tearing down off Lake Ontario and rattling the timbers like bones. Pop, pop, pop went that house, like an old man cracking his joints, and it wasn't much warmer in the house than it was standing in the street. What was a little tapping to me?

That's what I said in New York, Katie, remember that? The biggest stage of all, right there in New York City, and you stuck in the audience whilst I held the spotlight. How that must have chafed, you always so loved the stage. But there you sat with your face of stone. I saw you! I saw you when I peeked between the curtains before the show. You and the whole house, and what a house it was! A hundred people, all of them in their Sunday best, and the house all shining and gilt by the gaslight chandeliers, and me there to say our whole lives had been a lie.

Leah—the third Fox sister, she styled herself, as if she ever had any traffic with the dead—the way she made us back in Rochester. That's what she always said. I made you! I was the one who booked the Corinthian Hall in Rochester, I was the one who made you! *The Fox Sisters of the Famous Events in Hydesville, That Occurred in the Spring of 1848,* tapping and preening like little birds, always her little birds, and we hardly knowing her before Hydesville, her seventeen years our senior, a grown woman and a family of her own. The Queen of Lies! Our sittings with the great and small alike. Oh, Katie, how grand they all were! Mr. Cooper and Mrs. Stowe, the great Sojourner Truth and Mr. Horace Greeley himself, our patron and protector, to them all delivering, each and every one—lies! And most of all the hundreds—the thousands—that followed, innumerable to count, with their sittings and their gauzy apparitions, their spirit lights, their automatic writing: lies, all lies. And we, the Sisters of the Lie, who birthed a monstrous truth.

"Our whole lives," you said backstage, your voice quavering with resentment.

"Our whole goddamn lives, Maggs," you said. "You with your toes popping and your knuckles cracking, all the tricks of the trade. The spirit hands and the voices and the Summerland itself." All a lie—though it didn't keep you from taking your half of the money, did it? Seven hundred and fifty dollars each, a small fortune in 1888, like sand through our fingers, it went. You folded it away in your purse with an edge of fierce defiance in your voice. I can hear it now, your fury at all my lies, saying, "But it wasn't all a lie. Not all of it, Maggs."

Even lies have some truth inside them, and truth some lies. The Summerland is a cold, hard place. It's a cold, hard place we go when we die. And there are voices, there is a voice to make you shudder and run all cold inside. Nobody's going to pay their good, hard-earned money to hear such a monstrous truth—or believe it when they do. Some things cannot be countenanced or believed, not if you want to go on living, or crawl inside a bottle where the voice goes silent for a while. Not unless. So we lied. Our whole career a lie built upon a truth, and our renunciation of it a truth built upon a lie.

I sleep a little then, a little slice of death, somebody once told me, but I know that it's not true. Not the sleep of oblivion, but the sleep of nightmare, breeding monsters—

Then Emily is bending over me. It's morning, a bright shining March morning to make you forget all these truths—

—*that awful voice*—

—for a while. The confusion has lifted. I'm clearest in the mornings.

"Here, Mrs. Maggie, take some broth," she says. "I made it special."

So I take a sip to please her. You have to please people, that's what we do, you know. But the truth is, I don't want it, I haven't any appetite anymore. Then it's dark, and here you come bending over me again, saying, Mrs. Maggie, Mrs. Maggie, are you there. Your voice is coming from far away, like a voice from the bottom of a well. Why you should call me Mrs. Maggie I don't know. Plain old Maggs has always been good enough for all these years. I can hear you say it now—*Maggs, Maggs, Maggs*, your voice dripping with scorn.

You always scorned me so, saying I couldn't summon the spirits, not the way you could. Yet I never denied it. I never denied the ascendancy of your gift. Why, I remember a time when you said as much, as though I had denied it. We were mere girls then. I wasn't yet twenty and you just then fifteen years old, in your dress of robin's-egg blue and your hair done up so pretty, with some stray wisps falling down around your eyes, as if they'd just worked loose and you hadn't planned it that way from the first, so artful, to frame your face just so. In a fine hotel room in New York City, that was. How rich it had seemed, the fine velvet upholstery and the gilt moldings and the golden-and-red brocade on the curtains, that new smell on everything, as if it were fresh made. Leah said we could afford such fine things by then, the very best, I remember the way she said it: *We can afford the very best now, girls,* as though she had anything to do with it. That was Leah for you. She was out at the shops, I remember. We had just arrived in the city—where was it we had been before that? I wonder—and she was always out at the shops. *We have to look the part, girls,* she always said so cheery, but why she should have to look it, I never did understand. I sometimes think that it was just to spite Leah that we renounced it all and condemned it as a sin and blasphemy.

But that day, that day the sky was clear and blue as the blue in your dress, as though they'd been special made to match. You had tied back those heavy curtains and posed yourself in the most flattering fall of light, as though there were anyone there to see it but me. You were always onstage. Every time in my life I ever saw you, you were onstage.

You said, "Come to the window, Sister. It's so pretty out."

So I did. For a time we were quiet, just looking out the window. Fine carriages rolled by three stories below, full of the richest sort—who could say, some of them might have paid for private sittings, we were that well loved in that day. And cabs, too, and dray carts rattling over cobbles and flinging up horse apples, which was what our father always called them, remember that? People pushing and shoving on the sidewalks, and newspaper boys, and ballad sellers singing out the titles of the latest songs, a penny each for the sheet music so that pretty girls in pretty parlours could play them for their pretty boys. We never learned to play, of course, that was not our station in the world, but our station had changed, hadn't it? And I could almost smell the street below—the hay scattered out across the cobbles, and the horse apples, too, and the smell of perfumes and the like in the press—I could smell it in my mind, the way you can, you know.

And you, whispering right in my ear, "I can do it better, Maggs."

For some reason that made me feel so ashamed. "Do what?" I said, all innocent, though of course I knew.

I always knew. Both of us knew.

"Why, I can call the spirits better," you said, all innocent, flouncing across the room to pose yourself on a little love seat they had sitting there, arranging your dress just so.

"You can't," I said. "I can do it twice as good as you. I'm older," the only card I had to play.

"Then do it."

But I didn't want to, that's what I said. I couldn't, of course, not then and only sometimes later. The spirits came to me of their own accord, I couldn't summon them. I just wanted to sit at the window and watch the street, I always liked the city so. It reminded me of how far we'd come from Hydesville, where it had always seemed dark to me, and cold. And how we didn't have to be there anymore, not ever again. That's what I thought in that day—that we'd never be poor again—not knowing the miseries to come. I was just a girl, so young.

Even then I liked the lie better than the truth. I liked the toe cracking and the finger popping and all the other tricks Leah had taught us. She was tricksy as you were, almost.

The truth scared me.

"Because you can't," you said, and I feigned not to care.

I remember your face then, the way you'd posed so that the shadow cut your face right in half. I remember the look in your eyes in that moment, the way they got hard and like a set of mirrors, like you weren't there anymore or you'd gone way down deep inside yourself.

"Katie, don't—" I cried, but it was too late.

Already the light seemed to have gone all watery and pale, like it was shining down from a faraway star. And a minute after that came the cold, a black, hateful kind of cold that made your breath frost the air, and that on a summer day.

That's how you know. The cold. Like vapors from the grave. The rest is just tricks without the cold.

And you were always a tricky one, weren't you, Kate?

Tricksy, tricksy, tricksy. But not everything was tricks. Not Hydesville. And not that day in the hotel, either. Not when all that light went out of the room, and the cold started up and the tap, tap, tapping began, like a man with claw hammer deep buried in a mine.

Oh, I remember. It was a terrible thing, Katie, a terrible thing, your eyes rolling up to the whites like that and you sitting straight like a rod had been driven down your spine, your hands upturned upon your crossed knees, giggling as the room grew darker and darker still, until I could not see to see. The tapping got louder, and this time there was no playacting. This time there were no tricks, were there, Katie?

How used to them I had become by then, all the posing and the play-acting, all the tricks! I could summon up the taps myself, Katie—sometimes anyway. I won't deny that, no matter how much it would please you. I had a touch of the gift myself.

But you—

I remember. I remember it all so clearly. The way the room seemed to fall away into a black void. The way that blackness seized us up so careless, like a pair of rag dolls, boneless and limp, and carried us off. Like being caught in an undertow and swept out to sea, it was, the black stuff pouring in at your mouth and your nostrils, shoving aside everything that was you, until you drowned in it and there was nothing left but void and darkness. Yes, and I remember the way the tapping became a knocking, the knocking a thunderous *boom boom boom boom,* so that I cried aloud for the terror of it and clapped my hands over my ears. And between the booms, the voice. That cold and creeping voice, whispering at me, coaxing and wheedling, saying—

—*wake up mrs. maggie wake up*—

—and Emily Ruggles bends over me in the gloom.

"You were dreaming," she says, and here it is March and I can see her breath in the air.

My mouth is parched. All I can manage to croak is a single word. "Water."

She cradles my head and lifts a cup to my lips, ice crackling against my tongue.

"What were you dreaming of?" Her mouth twitchy and eager, hungry like the crowds who turned out to see us all those years ago, when I was a girl. That was the one part I had never expected, that hunger, the way they looked at you just like they could eat you up.

Just you remember, Leah used to say. *It's not you they want. It's what you do.* And so she held her power over us, with the clever tricks she taught us and the thought of those hungry crowds, and how she alone stood between us.

"What were you dreaming of?" Emily prompts me again, and maybe she senses it, too, that hunger and how unseemly it is, here in my final hours, for she goes on to add, "I only want to help you, Mrs. Maggie."

It's hard to be sure. But I know that hunger when I see it—I've seen it so many times—and what I feel is a rush of pity for the girl. I've done her a great disservice, showing her all our tricks like that, and letting her catch a glimpse of the bigger truth inside the lie at the same time. It's the truth she's so hungry to possess, and never will; Emily doesn't possess so much as a jot of the gift. Or it doesn't possess her. Because that's what it is—possession. We've been possessed since we were girls, Katie and I, and now it draws to a close at last. Now I stand for the last time on the threshold where I've spent a lifetime lingering, and on the other side there are worse things waiting. That voice, whispering, always whispering.

A lie's the thing, it always has been. I try to work up the moisture to spit it out. Once again the ritual with the cup. The rime of ice is gone. The water is cool, salving to the lips. The room has warmed. I kick at the covers. Emily folds back the counterpane, neat as a pin. She's a kind girl, Emily. She deserves the lie.

And how easy it comes to the lips, the habit of a lifetime. "'Tis only the Summerland," I whisper, gasping for a breath of the March air that billows out the sheers. "I see it now, all stretched out before me, green and lovely as a day in June. The passage draws near, Emily, dear." For a lie goes down easier with a taste of the truth inside it.

And then here you are again, Katie, leaning me over, your face so white in the moonlight, saying, "Mrs. Maggie, Mrs. Maggie, Mrs.—"

—*maggs*—

"It's always half measures with you, isn't it, Maggs? Not the lie and not the truth either, but some misbegotten thing in between, monstrous and malformed."

Such nerve, you have, calling me the monster, you so handy with the lie from the start. From the start, Katie, from Hydesville. Remember Hydesville, Katie, that ramshackle, old house popping its joints in the wind screaming down off the lake? March it was, and no man had ever seen such a winter: snow piled as high as a tall man's shoulder on the north face of the house, the cramped rooms inside stinking of ash and rancid fatback, and in the bedroom we all shared the reek of tapers dipped in animal fat. It had been a long time since Daddy could afford candles, and if it hadn't been for Leah's sweeping us off like a couple of performing birds, it might have been longer still.

Eighteen forty-eight that was, you just a girl with your first blood upon you, and right away the tapping commences, just a faraway sound at first, like the door rattling its hinges in the wind. Like the time my blood had come in three years before that—a whisper in my ears upon the edge of sleep, a tap, tap, tapping, quiet as my heart against my ribs. Then nothing, and when I think about that time now, a lifetime gone, I wonder if I might have escaped the whole thing, if my piddling gift might have slept forever. Such a happy life that would have been, I sometimes think, a husband and a houseful of little ones, neither the riches of a king nor the crumbs off a poor man's table—and I've had both, haven't I?—but something steady and standing in between.

Then your blood came in, and me trying to sleep, huddled close against you as the room grew colder and then colder still, no natural cold, but something deeper and blacker, with iron in its bones and hatred in its heart. The darkness deepened so that I could hardly see my hand before my face, and the real knocking commenced—not from one of your childish tricks either, was it, Katie? Not from an apple bobbing on a string to bang against the floor, or your toes and fingers cracking, but a spirit knocking and more, scurrying like footsteps across the ceiling and banging the furniture around the room like a housewife banging on her pans.

A light guttered to life. A wavering taper pushed back the dark, and in that flickering glow I saw my father's face. If I live a thousand years, I hope never to see another man's face like that one. All drawn and pale, it was. Why, it was as white as a freshly laundered sheet, and his eyes the size of saucers, shot through with blood and the pupils so round and black that you could hardly see the color at all, and such a pretty blue they were. My mother clutched at him, crying aloud, "What is it, John? What is it?"

But he doesn't answer, just stumbles out of bed in his nightshirt, him so prayerful and wary of his modesty.

"Girls?" he cries. "Girls?"

And, oh, how you shrieked with laughter, a high-pitched screech so unlike you that it's a marvel your mouth could produce such an awful sound. All erect you sat, with your nightdress draped across your crossed knees and your hands turned up atop your thighs. I could feel that piercing shriek run all through me like the horrors.

Great fists hammered the walls, shivering the boards. In the kitchen, the table danced like a drunken man on a Saturday night—you could hear it—and the chairs dashed themselves to kindling against the walls. But that wasn't the worst of it. The worst of it was that I heard all this as through a veil. Someone had flung a veil over me, and everything came through to me all blurry, only it was a veil of whispers, it was a veil of words.

As the knocking grew more violent, that voice grew louder, until it was screaming inside my head, guttural and hateful. It scoured out the inside of my skull, it erased everything I ever thought I was, and it knew me. It *knew me*, Katie. Knew every lie I'd ever told, every grudge and secret thought I'd nursed inside my crooked heart, no matter how base and hateful. It knew me. What do you think Emily Ruggles would think of *that*, Katie? What would she think of the blood red hatred that seized me then, and of the awful things it asked me to do. To my father, as he stumbled from the room in search of that awful knocking's source. To my mother, huddled under the bedclothes against that hateful cold, her breath a flag of vapor in the dark. And to you, Katie. To you most of all. Oh such horrible red thoughts that I weep to recall them. Such red, red thoughts.

How long it lasted, how long I wrestled with that awful spirit like Jesus in the desert, I cannot say. Only that a time came when it was over—when a bright sun dawned, glittering off the snow outside the window. The stink of sweat and terror faded. Even our father slept then, giving up at last, unable to locate the origin of all that terrible racket.

Three nights.

On the second night our neighbors crowded into the room, disbelievers every one—Mary and Charles Redfield and the Dueslers and the Hydes and others, too, that old house rocking around them. Every one they came in doubt, and every one they left believers, that unearthly cold shivering their bones, their faces scrubbed clean with terror, pale and blank as eggs.

The next night, hundreds. It was them that brought Leah, those hundreds, and the chance they represented. Hundreds crowding into the bedroom shoulder to shoulder, rank with the stench of unwashed bodies, hundreds spilling out into the kitchen, and beyond, into the street itself, where a raw wind came tearing off the lake, chilling everyone to the bone. How I envied them that warmth. For inside the bedroom, it was colder still. How can I convey it, that cold? Like being buried to your shoulders in ice, it was, or worse, the cold of all dead things and dead places on this earth, the cold of the grave yawning open to receive you.

And you, Katie, with your hands upturned upon your knees and your hair hanging over your eyes, in a nightdress thin as gossamer, all untouched. Your crowning moment that was, your best trick of all, breathing in the stillness, "Do as I do, Mr. Splitfoot," and the spirit did. One, two, three, you snapped your fingers, and one, two, three, the spirit rapped in answer.

Gasps of disbelief and wonder. Do you remember that, Katie? Gasps of wonder and disbelief—proof incontestable of this raging spirit that hurled furniture around like kindling and responded to the quiet admonition of a little girl. Do you remember that?

And all this time in my head, that rageful voice, entreating, wheedling, screaming in frustration, for I would not do as it demanded. I would not take up the knife in the kitchen or lift a leg from a dismembered chair. I would not turn my home into an abattoir. But, oh such effort did I have to exert to resist. Sweat sprang out on my forehead despite that glacial cold, and by the guttering flame of the taper I could see that my hands, all of their own accord, had clenched themselves into white-knuckled fists, and so it would be ever after. That hateful voice whispering and cajoling in my head, my constant attendant, and when Katie called the spirits, a spiteful and powerful spirit it became. In those moments it took every ounce of strength I possessed to resist it. A life embattled we have shared, Katie and I, a life that enriched us beyond measure one moment and plunged us into poverty the next, always the voice beyond the rappings, urging us to horrors that we must struggle to resist. Two husbands we have known between us, but Mr. Splitfoot was our one and only true betrothed. Many nights I stood over my own dear husband's bed, clutching a knife in my hand, my whole body wracked with the effort of turning Mr. Splitfoot away.

We were children, Maggs, I can hear you say it now. *We didn't know. Isn't that enough?*

But it is not. For a time came, and early, when we *did* know, and even then we did not, could not, stop. There was too much of fortune in it, and too much of pleasure as well, in giving yourself over to something larger than you had ever known, something sinewy and vast. Even from the start, Mr. Splitfoot ruled our hearts.

Mr. Splitfoot, Mr. Splitfoot—

—and here is a figure leaning over me, its face cast in shadow by the candle it holds aloft.

"Katie," I cry, "Katie—"

But it's only Emily, leaning over to smooth the hair from my brow.

"You were talking in your sleep, Mrs. Maggie." So gentlelike. "What was it you were dreaming?" That hunger in her eyes.

But what shall I say? Some truths are better left unsaid. Sometimes the lie is kinder. "I miss Katie, dear"—taking her hand—"I miss her so much."

And here is the truth inside the lie. I miss you, Kate. Every morning I wake afresh to find you gone away from me. Every morning I grieve you like the first. Gone, gone, gone—and who else to confide in here at the end of all days, about matters so fraught and fearsome?

"We all miss her, dear," Emily says, withdrawing to her needlework, and after a time I'm not sure who it is I'm looking at anymore, time seems so slippy and uncertain. Only there is a chill in the room, a faraway rapping, and you're sitting here beside me once again, your strong hand in my own, bony as a bird's and heavy-veined. You were always so strong, and I the weak one. Why, see how old I've become, and still a sixteen-year-old in Hydesville in my heart, before it all began. Or so I could believe but for the whisper in my ears, but for my one true love and paramour, goading me, always goading me to blood and madness.

Blood and madness. For once it came to me, it never fully departed, that voice. It lingered, whispering, insinuating, urging me on to bloodshed and hatred. But only once did I succumb.

I begged you not to do it. How I begged you.

Nineteen, I was, and you just fifteen—mere girls with the petty jealousies of sisters, the thoughtless malice and spite. There in that lush hotel room, with the sounds of the street rising to us in a hushed murmur, muffled by the heavy velvet curtains that draped the windows. And the taps at first, the raps and knocks, the *boom boom boom*, so loud that the floor itself seemed to rock, and I marvelled that no one else could hear it. Those heavy curtains billowed out like the thinnest sheers. A great wind filled the room, like the rank breath of the dead, and in it the voice, such a voice it was, guttural and full of hate, and then worse—wheedling, insinuating, flattering. And promising. Yes, promising.

What was yours mine, your vast gift in exchange for my paltry one. You with your eyes rolled back, your legs crossed, your palms face up on your thighs, beneath your dress of robin's-egg blue.

And that voice, whispering now, conniving and entreating. It drew me across the room to the love seat, my arms outstretched, and how it thrilled me to take your neck between my hands, to feel my fingers dig into the soft, pale flesh beneath your high-necked dress, and *squeeze*. Squeeze and squeeze, nails biting, fingers gouging. Who knew then how thin and high it was, that neck, as delicately boned as a bird's. Bones creaked beneath the pressure.

And then you were there again. Your eyes snapped open with dread of the terrible thing that was death, the cold of the grave and the voice that lived on the other side and the hatred everlasting. Your hands flew up to pry my hands away, weak, too weak. I had gifts of my own, you see: the strength of my hands and purpose, and that voice capering inside my head in joy.

You gasped.

"Maggie," you croaked. "Maggs, Maggie, please—"

And then there were no words, just struggle. Your legs kicking. Your hands tearing at my own, your body heaving. Second by second, your strength left you. Your body fell still. Your hands fell away. Your body went limp. And gradually, gradually, your face took on a deepening blue cast.

You might have died then—the one true person I ever loved, and I would have exulted in it.

But the door flew open, and here was Leah, laden with packages, saying, "Oh, girls, you won't believe such finery I got, and at a poor man's cost—" Her voice breaking off like that. Hatboxes and shoeboxes and dresses on their woolen-cloaked hangers fumbled from her hands.

She found her voice then, a rising note of panic in it, edged in hysteria.

"Maggs, Maggie! You let your sister go!"

And just that easily the spell was broken. I sagged, my hands as of their own accord unfolding from your neck, that terrible, alluring voice dwindling—but never fading—from my mind. I stumbled away in tears, retching as your own hands came up to your neck in wonder and dismay.

Silence reigned. Even Leah, gathering her packages, could find no words to speak. And as for Katie and me, we knew. No words were necessary. We knew what had happened—we had heard that hating voice—and though it remained with us for the rest of our days, never again would we speak of what had happened that afternoon, never again would we risk so deep a trance, never again surrender ourselves so wholly to the thing that lay in wait for us upon the other side.

Until now.

Emily sleeps over her needlework, the darkness deepens, the room grows cold. I hear a knocking in the distance, growing louder. And worse yet, a voice, guttural and full of hate, and growing louder.

Katie, I want to say, Katie, is that you.

But I know it is not. Mr. Splitfoot slouches toward us, battening upon half a century of belief and blood, waiting to be born.

My lifetime draws to a close. The year is 1893. A new era draws nigh.

We were girls. How could we know? Surely that is enough.

God forgive us both. God help us all.

What manner of doorway have we opened? What awful beast have we unleashed upon the world?

I foresee a century of blood.

About "Mr. Splitfoot"

The Fox sisters really existed, and many of the events described in this story happened pretty much as described—or as accurately as I could reconstruct them. The events in Hydesville were a local cause célèbre in 1848, drawing people from miles around to witness them, and the sisters did attribute the source of the poltergeist events to a spirit calling himself Mr. Splitfoot— though they later reassigned them to a peddler said to have been murdered in the farmhouse where the Fox family had taken up temporary residence, an inconvenient fact this story ignores. Many years later, in 1888, Maggie confessed to fakery as described in the story, alienating her sister. Soon after, she recanted, and not long after that she died at Emily Ruggles's home in New York City. I took considerable liberties in creating the character of Emily Ruggles, about whom I could find almost no information. The rest of the story is likewise the product of my imagination. Fiction will have its way. Those seeking more reliable information on the Fox sisters would do well to consult Barbara Weisberg's excellent 2004 biography, *Talking to the Dead*.

Phosphorus

A man can strike a Lucifer on anything—the wall, the bottom of a shoe, a barstool. Sometimes the white head of the match flares up from the friction of being packed at the factory, and an entire box bursts into flames, releasing the rough poison of white phosphorus into the air, and the box goes on burning until the girl who was packing them stamps it out, and then the Bryant and May Match Company fines her.

London in the nineteenth century is marked, inside and out, by the black, burnt trails left whenever a Lucifer is struck. A series of black marks, scoring the city's face, like scars.

The Lucifer allows an easy way to kindle fires, to provide light and heat and smoke without the unreliable and frustrating business of flint or the danger of Congreves, matches prone to exploding into burning pieces upon being struck, and so banned in France and Germany. And Lucifers are cheap, much cheaper than matches made from red phosphorus, which can be struck only on the side of the box, anyway. Lucifers are so cheap that, in the words of William Morris, "the public buy twice as much as they want, and waste half."

Herbert Spencer calls the Lucifer "the greatest boon and blessing to come to mankind in the nineteenth century."

The pathways the Bryant and May matchwomen take home from the factory every night are marked by piles of phosphorescent vomit.

❦

It begins with a toothache. And those are not uncommon, not where you live, not when you live. Not uncommon at all. But you know what it means, and you know what comes next, no matter how hard you try to put it out of your mind. For now, the important thing is to keep it from the foreman. And for a while, you can. You can swallow the clawing pain in your mouth just as you swallow the blood from your tender gums, along with your bread during the lunch break. If you have bread, that day. A mist of droplets floats through the room, making the air hazy, hard to see through. They settle on your bread.

Your teeth hurt, but you can keep that from the foreman. You can eat your bit of bread and keep that secret.

But then your face begins to swell.

Property is theft, wrote Karl Marx, and for almost thirty-five years, Karl Marx lived in London. Private property, he said, is the theft from the people of resources hitherto held in common. And then that property can be turned to capital, which can be used to extort labour from workingmen and women for far less than its value. Another theft. Theft of communal resources, theft of labour, and for these women and girls, the matchmakers of the Bryant and May match factory at Bow, it could also become theft of bone, theft of flesh, and, finally, theft of life.

Not that they don't put up a good fight. Fighting is something they're good at. Fighting, dancing, and drinking, those wild Irish girls of London's East End. That's what reformers and journalists say, anyway.

Your old Nan came over with her husband back in 1848, during the famine—forty years ago, long before you were born, but you and your siblings and cousins, you still have the map of Eire stamped into your souls.

Your Nan has the sight, or so she says. When you were naught but a small girl, not working yet, but only a nuisance underfoot, hungry all the time, she would distract you by telling you all the lovely things she could see in your future—a husband handsome and brave, fine strapping sons and lively daughters, and a home back in Ireland, with cows lowing on the hills, and ceilis with the neighbours every weekend, and all the cheese and bread you could eat.

You couldn't quite picture the countryside she described—the closest you could come was a blurred memory of Hampstead Heath, where your family had once gone on a bank-holiday outing, and being a London girl, you weren't quite sure that you wanted to live there, but you liked the sound of the cheese and the ceilis and the husband that your Nan promised you. And you believed her implicitly, because your Nan had the sight, didn't everyone on the street know that?

But perhaps she'd been mistaken because now your teeth hurt like hellfire and your face has started to swell. You can think of only one way for this to end, and it doesn't involve any ceilis.

When you were little, the youngest of your family, the first thing you remember is your mum telling you to be quiet while she counted out the matchboxes she made at home. Your mum would put you into the arms of your sister, Janey, four years older, and shoo the two of you and your brother, and any cousins who happened to be around, outside to play, and there'd you be until late at night, when the matchboxes were dry and could be stacked in a corner out of the way, and you kids could unroll mats and blankets and sleep fitfully on the floor.

When you were old enough to be a bit more useful, soon after your mum died birthing one baby too many, you would sit with your Nan, cutting the rotten bits out of the potatoes so that she could cook them more easily, back in the days before she lost her vision, the vision of this world, anyway. Once you'd lost your temper and complained about how many rotten spots there were, and your Nan shook her head and told you that the half or third of good flesh you got out of one of these potatoes was a bounty compared to the famine years. "All rot and nothing else," she said, "and you could hear the keening throughout the countryside, until you couldn't, and that was all the worse, the despair and silence of those left behind." She looked at the potato in your hand, took it from you, and dropped it in the pot. "And every crop melting into slime, and the English shipping out fat cows and calves and anything else they could get their hands on."

Sometimes your Nan would lapse into Irish, the language she and your granddad had spoken before emigrating. You don't speak; your mum spoke a bit, and so did your dad. Janey and some of your older cousins speak some, but after that, there were just too many kiddies to make sure of what they were saying. When your Nan uses Irish, you don't know what her words mean, but it's easy to make out the general tone.

In Irish, the potato famine of 1845–52 is called an Gorta Mór, the Great Hunger, or an Drochshaol, the Bad Times. During those seven years, around one million Irish died, most likely more, and at least another one million emigrated, reducing the country's population by one-quarter. England exported crops and livestock, off-limits to the impoverished Irish, to its own shores throughout the disaster. The food was exported under armed guard from ports in the areas of Ireland most affected by the potato blight.

The sultan of the Ottoman Empire attempted to send ten thousand pounds in aid to the people of Ireland; Queen Victoria requested that he reduce his charity to the sum of one thousand, as she herself had sent only two thousand. The sultan agreed, but nonetheless sent three ships of food to Ireland as well. The English courts attempted, unsuccessfully, to block the ships.

In America, the Choctaws had endured the death march known as the Trail of Tears sixteen years prior and apparently saw something familiar in a people being starved to death and forced off their land. They sent $710 for the relief of the Irish.

Sir Charles Trevelyan, the government official responsible for England's relief efforts, considered that "the judgement of God sent this calamity [the potato blight] to teach the Irish a lesson."

Your Nan lost her first two babbies, a little girl of two years who starved to death before she and your granddad left his farm, and another one that had yet to be born on the way over to England. Now she looks forward to holding both her babes once more when she meets them in paradise, which she describes as sounding much like county Cork in happier times.

When she used to tell you of your future life in Ireland, an Ireland under home rule, perhaps, an Ireland of Parnell's making, and blessed O'Connell's memory, she put herself there, too, back in county Cork in her old age, sitting by your fire.

When you were a little girl, you promised that you would bring her back to Ireland with you, and that when she died, you'd see her buried in the graveyard of the church where she'd been baptized and married.

Where will she see you buried, you now wonder.

❧

There are no outside agitators in the factory at the end of June, and the only socialists are the same socialists who are there every day, dipping and cutting and packing for five shillings a week.

The only new thing is a bit of newspaper being passed around furtively, read out in whispers by the girls who can read to those who cannot: an article from *The Link* entitled "White Slavery in London," telling the middle-class folk of London about work at the Bryant and May factories.

You read with interest the details of your own life, and you make haste to hide the paper when the foremen come in.

A letter at your workstation states that the article is a lie, and that you are happy, well paid, and well treated in your work.

You rub the place at the bottom of your swollen cheek where the sores first opened up.

Instead of signing the preprinted letter to *The Times*, which has become the mouthpiece for middle-class outrage at Bryant and May, you spit on it.

Not one of the women in the entire factory signs the letter.

In the entire factory, the only letter with a mark at the bottom is the one with your spittle on it, shining faintly in the dark.

Fourteen-year-old Lizzie collects the unsigned letters and hands them to the foreman, staring him straight in the eye, and in that moment you know that it was Lizzie who'd gone to *The Link* with the story. And so does the foreman, perhaps, because he smacks her across the face with the sheaf of papers. Lizzie spits between the foreman's feet.

Lizzie is sacked the following Monday. When she's told to leave, she considers for a moment, then breaks the foreman's jaw with a single punch. As she turns to leave, all of you, you and your friends and rivals, put on your hats and follow her out.

The strike flares up like a Lucifer. When you look back at the long line of women behind you, you have to blink to be sure that there aren't white trails of phosphorus smoke floating off all of you, disappearing into the sky.

They said it was Annie Besant's doing, that Mrs Besant had been the ringleader, an outside Fabian socialist agitator. And perhaps there is some truth to it, as she did write and publish "White Slavery in London," the article that so shamed Mr Bryant that he tried to get his workers to repudiate it.

But Mrs Besant called for a respectable middle-class boycott, not for working-class girls and women to take matters into their own hands. The strikers did not contact her until some days after the initial walkout.

The East End of London did not need middle-class Fabians to explain socialism.

In the seven years leading up to 1888, the women of Bryant and May had struck three times. They were unsuccessful, to be sure, but practise makes perfect.

You're getting ready to go out marching, collecting for the strike fund, when you hear your Nan calling for you. You hold off on wrapping up your suppurating face and turn to find her, bent almost double with her dowager's hump, staring up at you with her milky, sightless eyes.

"Yeh've got the phoss, a cushla," she says. "Had it for a while, I reckon. When were yeh plannin' to tell me?"

You shrug, saying nothing, then remember that your Nan can't see you. You open your mouth to talk when she turns and shuffles back to the chair she had been sitting in.

You find your tongue. "You can smell it, eh, Nan?"

She swats at the air. "Can't smell a damn thing. Haven't been able to since before you were born. Makes all the mush I eat taste the same. Not that I figure what I eat tastes of anything worth eating anyways." She shakes her head. "Nah. I just know. Known for a while."

You wait to see what, if anything, she'll say next. Her eyelids droop, and before you know what you're doing, you burst out angrily, "And what about my children and husband and cows and ceilis every weekend? When will I get them, Nan?"

Her eyelids snap up again. She makes a sort of feeble fluttering gesture with her hands, which still look surprisingly youthful. "Never, a cushla, my darling. Never for you."

Your eyes widen in shock, and for the first time you realise that part of you had been hoping that your wise, witchy Nan would pull an ould Irish trick from up her sleeve, send the phoss packing, and send you away to Ireland, away from Bryant and May.

"I lied to you, my love," she says. "All those times, for all those years, I lied. I never saw nothing for you. Just a greenish glow where your long life should have been."

"Why?" you ask, glacial with the loss of hope.

"Ah, darling. Don't you know yeh've always been my favourite?"

You turn abruptly and resume tucking your scarf around your decaying jaw.

After a few seconds, your Nan speaks again, softly. "Darling, don't be so wretched. The phoss in your jaw is a horror, it's true, but it'll soon be over, it won't be long now."

You picture yourself coughing up blood, your jaw twisted, black, and falling to pieces, and you take little comfort in the image.

"Worse off by far," says your Nan, "are those who get the phoss in their souls. They'll never see paradise at all."

> We'll hang Old Bryant on the sour apple tree,
> We'll hang Old Bryant on the sour apple tree,
> We'll hang Old Bryant on the sour apple tree,
> As we go marching on.
> Glory, glory hallelujah . . .
> **—Matchgirl strikers' marching song, 1888, sung to
> the tune of "John Brown's Body," a song popular
> among Union soldiers and abolitionists
> during the US Civil War**

A few days after the walkout, you and Annie Ryan from next door make your way to the Mile End Waste. You don't say much on the walk. Moving your jaw has become too painful, every slight flex of your facial muscles redoubling the bone-grinding ache, the soreness stretching poisoned tentacles out from your slowly decaying jaw to grip your skull and bore into your brain.

You've taken to eating the same soft, grey pap your Nan lives on. It saves you chewing and leaves more hard bread for your brothers and sisters and their kiddies. And since you're constantly queasy if not worse, you don't even miss it.

Some days you don't want the grey mush either, but your Nan won't eat unless you do. And some days you've half a mind to let the ould bitch starve, serve her right for lying to you all these years.

But after all, she is your Nan.

You leave your scarf on inside, even at home, so as not to scare the kiddies, but they avoid you anyway. It's the smell.

When you were a wee lass yourself, you and the others used to play on the corpses of horses, worked to death and left to putrefy in the street. Nothing still walking around should smell like that.

So you walk in silence toward the rally, even as the men and girls around you break into song. And in a crowd of thousands, your patch of silence isn't likely to be noticed.

Annie draws your arm through hers. "You've a marvellous singing voice, Lucy," she says, pulling you near, near enough that you can see her nostrils flare as she works to give no sign that she's noticed the smell. "Don't you remember when we were only small, and you made up that skipping rhyme about Mrs Rattigan's warts? You sounded like an angel, counting off her warts as you skipped."

You nod, and even that hurts.

"They've got to hear us, Lucy. All the way to Mayfair and Parliament. Maybe all the way back to Ireland. That'd make old Parnell proud, wouldn't it?"

Annie leans in even closer. "You know nobody'd ever put you out, Lucy, don't you? And even if they did, well, you'd just trot down the block and come stop with me and mine. Take care of you right to the end, we would."

You nod slightly and she squeezes your hand. "Make the end come a bit sooner, too, if need be."

She draws away again, and after a moment you find your voice.

You can barely hear your own singing above the noise of your headache, but you see that Annie and the other girls can, and that, you suppose, is what counts.

When you return home, you finally relax and remove your hat and scarf. Something small, like a pebble, falls to the floor.

It's a piece of your jaw.

In 1889, Annie Besant exchanged socialism for theosophy. Despite its esoteric reputation, theosophy reflected conventional Victorian values in at least one way.

According to the teachings of Madame Blavatsky, theosophy's founding mother, each and every person has exactly what he or she deserves in this life. Theosophists believed that sickness, suffering, deformity, and poverty were punishments for sins committed in a past life. This belief can be dressed as God's will, or as social Darwinism, but it comes to the same thing.

It is a reassuring thought to those whose lives are not thoroughly saturated with such suffering. Sometimes it can be a comfort even as one is led to the guillotine or faces the firing squad.

When Besant traded in socialism for theosophy, she bought spiritual certainty at the price of her compassion.

Though Annie Besant was by no means a strike leader—indeed, she had written on more than one occasion about the futility of trying to organise unskilled labourers—she'd had enough sympathy with the strikers and care for her good journalistic name to counter management's claims of innocence by publicizing the working conditions, wages, and abuse that Bryant and May expected the striking matchwomen to accept.

And she had a word with her good friend Charles Bradlaugh, MP.

As you and the other girls make your way to parliament, heads turn at the sight of so many tattered dresses, the sound of so many rough accents outside the East End, and not in any uniform, either.

"What're you lookin' at?" Lizzie shouts at a group of young ladies who, having forgotten the manners drilled into them by their governesses, stare and gape as you walk past.

The young ladies drop their eyes and turn away quickly. After a few seconds, you hear a shriek of laughter.

By the time you reached Westminster, traffic in the streets has slowed to a crawl as cabs and buses come to a full stop so their drivers and passengers can take a good, long look at the poor women walking en masse toward parliament, just as if they have a right to.

Perhaps if you weren't in so much pain, you tell yourself, you could be as brave as Jenny, old Jenny Rotlegh, forty if she's a day, and bald as an egg from years of carrying wooden pallets on her head. Jenny sweeps off her bonnet right then and there, in front of the three MPs who had received your delegation.

"Look," she says. "Look what they done to me! Ain't that worth more 'n four shillings a week, less fines?"

You listen to the gasps from the fine gentlemen and wonder if you should undo your scarf and expose what remains of your blackened jaw, and the line of sores reaching now up to your temples. You come as near as raising your hand to the scarf around your throat and taking one of the ends in your fingers. You untuck it and pause, thinking of the gentlemen staring at your melting face.

Jenny is an object of pity, an exemplar of abused and mistreated femininity.

But you have become a monster.

There is a difference between shocked pity and horrified disgust. It is human nature to turn away from the latter. You tighten the scarf and retie the knot, more tightly than before.

Annie Besant wasn't the only established activist late to the party. There was also the London Trades Council, the last leading bastion of craft unionism, which had previously turned up its nose at unskilled labourers. The council met with a delegation of matchwomen. Perhaps out of the desire to retain its preeminent place as the voice of the urban worker, perhaps out of a paternalistic sense of noblesse oblige, perhaps even out of a genuine sense of fellow feeling and solidarity, the LTC offered to send a delegation of workmen to negotiate a settlement agreeable to both parties.

The firm received the overture genteelly, which must have made it all the more humiliating when that deputation returned empty-handed. The men reported only that Bryant and May were willing to allow most of the strikers to resume their old places, if they returned immediately, while reserving the right to refuse reemployment to the women they termed "the ringleaders."

The strikers didn't bother to send a reply.

The evening after the meeting with the MPs, your Nan asks you to lay your head on her lap. When you do, she rests her hand on your hair.

"You're angry with me, a cushla," she says.

You say nothing. You watch your words more carefully than your sisters watch their farthings now that you slough off flesh with every motion of your mouth.

"Well, you've a right," she continues. When you remain silent, she sighs and is quiet herself for a while. After some minutes drift by, she draws breath to begin again.

"The strike will end," she says conversationally. "I seen it." This time she doesn't bother to pause for responses you will not give. "But you won't see it. You'll die first. I seen that, too."

Sooner's better than later, you think dully, and wonder if she'll tell you how long the strike will last, and if any of you will have jobs by the time it is over. You'd like to know that Annie won't starve, at least. If your Nan really does have any sight at all, if she hasn't been lying about everything, all this time. If she isn't just some crazy ould biddy.

"You won't see the end of this strike," she repeats. "Not unless I help you out. And I figure, I figure, I owe you at least that much."

You gently take her hand from your head and sit up, moving slowly, the way you have been for a while now. You hold her rough hand between two of yours, and you know for sure now, her mind is broken and gone, and she'll never see Ireland again.

She pulls her hand away from you irritably, as though she can hear your thoughts, and swats at you.

"Not a crazy ould one," she says. "Not like my own gran, there was madness for you, if that's what you're thinking. A life, it's like a flame, y'see, a candle flame. An' if I put that flame into a real flame, a real candle, well, you'll keep right on living as long as that candle keeps burning.

"And a candle held in the left hand of a hanged man, that candle, it can't go out. You can't put that out with wind nor water nor snuff it with yer fingers. Only good white milk can put out a Hand o' Glory.

"I can do that fer you," she says. "I can do it, if yeh can bring me what I need. It won't exactly be living, more sort of not dyin'. But I don't know that what yeh're doing now is living, so much, either."

You say nothing once more, but this time more out of shock than deliberately.

"I'll give you a list," she says.

"Hand of a dead man?" you manage to slur.

"Hanged," she corrects you. "Left hand of a hanged man. Or woman'll do as well, o'course. Dunno how we'll get that one. We're neither of us well enough for grave robbing. But we'll manage."

After a doubtful pause, she repeats, "We'll manage.

"And those pieces of your jawbone that keep fallin' off. Start saving 'em."

Here are some of the reasons given by Bryant and May for fines taken from their workers' pay packets:

—dirty feet (3d.)

—ground under bench left untidy (3d.)

—putting burnt-out matches on the bench (1s.)

—talking (amount not specified)

—lateness, for which the worker was then shut out for half the day
    (5d.)

Here are deductions regularly taken from the matchwomen's pay packets:

—6d. for brushes to clean the machines (every six months)

—3d. to pay for children to fetch packing paper (weekly)

—2d. to pay the packer who books the number of packages (weekly)

—6d. to pay for stamps, to stamp the packages (weekly)

—1d. to pay for children to fetch and carry for the box-fillers
    (weekly)

Bryant and May employed no children to fetch and carry for the box-fillers. The box-fillers fetched and carried for themselves.

Nan says that you don't have the time to make a tallow dip. You wonder how much time you do have, as you collect what she told you to, and if it's worth living as you do now until the strike is over and broken. Perhaps it would be better to go now, while the girls are still going strong, fuelled by high hopes.

But love is a hard habit to break, so you do as she tells you, scavenging strips of paper, a wide-mouth jar, and a length of wire from the trash heaps, and stopping at the butcher's for what lumps of pork fat he'll give you for your pennies. You've found that shopkeepers give you better prices these days. Perhaps they feel sorry for you.

Perhaps they just want you out of the shop as quickly as possible, so you don't scare off custom.

Either way is fine by you, as long as you can walk away with all the pork fat you need, which isn't much. You bring your parcels home to your Nan and lay them at her feet, like offerings.

What you do next isn't hard; you've made paper wicks before, rendered pork fat before, and it stinks, but it doesn't stink as badly as you do.

While you do these things, your Nan takes the pieces of your jawbone that you've saved and grinds them into a fine powder, using a mortar and pestle. They crumble so easily.

Dust to dust.

While you stir the melted fat, your Nan leans over from her chair by the fire and tips the dust of your bones into the small pot. Then she slices across the veins of your forearm with an old knife. Straining against her arthritic knuckles, she squeezes and massages your arm to get as much of your blood into the mix as she can.

After you give the pot a few more stirs, the tallow looks no different from any other bit of tallow you've ever seen, grubby and nasty, and smells no different either, rank and putrid. You pour it into the glass jar, watching it pool and pile up around the paper wick held stiff by the scavenged wire.

While you scrub out the pot, your Nan mutters some Irish over the makeshift candle and sets it aside to harden.

"It's a good thing we neither of us eat much," she says to you. "With neither of us bringing anything in."

You nod. After a minute, you ask her the same thing you did the previous evening.

"Hand of a hanged man?" you force out.

She seems troubled, but she pats your hand. "Leave that to me," she says, and then again, more slowly, "leave that to me."

Before you sleep that night, she whispers in your ear, "I'm goin' out tonight. You be in the cemetery. The unconsecrated ground, an hour before dawn. Bring the small axe and the candle. And a few matches, o' course."

Your sleep has been unquiet for a long time now, with the effect that you find it harder and harder to rouse yourself. This is probably because you are dying.

Whatever the reason, by the time you force yourself fully awake, it's long past when you should have left for Bow Cemetery. On your way, you wonder anxiously if you'll be there in time. However it is that your Nan plans to find you a hanged man, you want the cover of darkness.

You don't know the way as well as you do to the churchyard at Saints Michael and Mary on Commercial Road, the Catholic church not yet built when your Nan came over. You've been there plenty, standing by the gravesides of the very young, the very old, and all between.

But your Nan wouldn't dig up a good Catholic.

Surely she didn't have the strength to dig up anybody else, either, come to that. And she didn't tell you to bring a shovel.

It's summer, and small pink flowers dot the ground of the graveyard. They remind you of the morning that an anonymous benefactor sent a cartload of pink roses down to all the girls on the picket, to wear as badges. That morning, the fragrance of roses had blotted out even the stench you did your best to trap in the folds of your scarf. For that one morning, the scent of roses surrounded you, and you let yourself pretend that you weren't rotting away, like the corpses interred in the ground beneath your feet.

The unconsecrated ground is a newer part of the graveyard, and it holds unbaptized babies, suicides, and those of strange and foreign faiths, or perhaps even no faith at all.

But they all rot in the same way, you figure, 'cause the worms probably don't know the difference.

Or maybe they do. Maybe they feel a tingle of the divine wind round them as they cross from unconsecrated to holy soil, and the whisper of loss and chilly despair as they pass back the other way.

You spot your Nan's figure swaying by an oak tree. That's to be expected, of course, the swaying, but she seems somehow to be taller than you think of her being, and she's not holding her stick.

When you draw nearer, you see your Nan's stick lying on the ground where she dropped it, next to the lidded milk pail and near the kicked-over step stool, all of which she must have dragged out to the cemetery last night. Nan herself sways and twists gently, her feet a foot and a half off the ground, one end of a stout rope around her neck, the other tied to a branch over your head, a branch high enough to keep her feet from the ground, but low enough that she could reach it from the step stool.

She rocks back and forth, and you watch her, waiting for the tears to come. They don't, though, perhaps because there's nothing left inside you at all.

"Oh, Nan," you whisper, and you don't even feel the pain as what remains of your jaw and tongue move clumsily.

You sit just near her swaying feet and begin to feel a certain leaden weight in your limbs, beginning at your hands and feet, and creeping upward. It is death come for you, you know. As you decide to sit calmly and wait for the leaden feeling to spread, a gust of wind sets your Nan's corpse to swinging violently. You look up at her contorted face.

It is less repellent than you imagine your own to be.

You get to your feet, straighten the stool, and pick up the axe, so your Nan, who had loved you enough to lie to you, enough to relinquish her place in paradise and her chance to see her lost babbies again, shouldn't have done so for nothing at all.

For isn't suicide a mortal sin?

Using the axe, you cut her down and lay the body on the ground, her left arm stretched to the side. And as the sun rises, you bring the axe down on her left wrist.

You move mechanically, so as not to waste a moment, and in any case, the cool, rough skin of your Nan's hand is less horrifying than the dead flesh of your face and neck. You close her fingers around the candle, and they grip it tightly, as if your Nan is still there, holding on to what remains of your life for all she is worth.

You take a match from your pocket and strike it against the handle of the axe. It flares up, and for a moment the familiar smell of white phosphorus hovers in the air.

You hide the axe in the bushes on the grounds of the cemetery and walk home carrying the corpse, the burning candle protected by her good left hand hidden in the lidded milk pail dangling from your arm.

The old lady is heavy, so much heavier than she had seemed when she was alive. She'd become small and frail, but the body that lies in your arms is heavy as sin.

Even in the East End, people do not usually stroll out just after dawn carrying a corpse. Heads turn as you go, and your neighbours recognise you, recognise your Nan. Nobody speaks.

You lay your Nan's body down in the room you shared with her and your sister, her husband, and their kiddies, and then you rouse the rest of the family.

You say little when they ask what happened. But then, you say very little these days anyway. They assume that your Nan's hand was missing when you found her.

At least, you think they do. You do catch Janey looking at you intently, her brow wrinkled, her head tilted to one side, a bit suspicious-like, and for a minute she looks so much like your late mother, with her constant expression of worry, that it takes your breath away.

Or it would.

You realise that you are no longer breathing. You bring your fingers to your throat, pushing through the layers of your scarf, and feel for a pulse. You find none.

Later, in private, you peer into the milk pail, and the candle your Nan made and holds is still burning.

Early in the afternoon, you go back for the axe.

Bryant and May gave in, just over two weeks after the walkout. They gave in so quickly and so completely that with the benefit of historical hindsight, one wonders if the matchwomen should have demanded more. On July 18, 1888, Bryant and May acceded to every one of the strikers' terms.

—The firm agreed to recognise the newly formed Union of Women
    Matchmakers, the largest union of women and girls in England.
—The firm agreed to abolish all fines.
—The firm agreed to abolish all deductions.
—Matchworkers could take any and all problems directly to the
    managing director of the firm rather than having to go through
    the foremen.
—The firm agreed to provide a room for eating lunch separate and
    apart from the working rooms.

This last item was so that the matchwomen could eat without white phosphorous settling onto their food and from there making its way into their teeth.

It starts with a toothache, after all.

On August 14, 1889, just over a year after the watchwomen's victory, a group of London dockworkers walked off the job. These workers were mainly Irishmen: the husbands, sons, brothers, and sweethearts of the matchwomen of the East End. Within two days, twenty-five hundred men had turned out, demanding a wage of 6d. an hour, a penny more than they had been earning. Solidarity with the dockworkers spread across London. Black workers, usually brought in as cheap replacement labour, refused to scab. Jewish tailors went out. Hyde Park played host to a rally of one hundred thousand people, serenaded by bands playing "The Marseillaise."

By the end of August, over one hundred thirty thousand workers were out on strike, and the families that were making do without their men's wages were withholding rent.

The strike lasted a month, and the dockworkers won nearly all they asked for. Years later, historians refer to the Great Dock Strike of 1889 as the beginning of the militant New Unionism: the organization of un-skilled and industrial labour that swept Britain and replaced the old craft union model. By the end of 1890, almost two million of Britain's workers held a union card.

John Burns, one of the dockworkers' great leaders, spoke out at rallies, urging solidarity in the face of the starvation that threatened strikers and their families.

"Stand shoulder to shoulder," he thundered. "Stand shoulder to shoul-der and remember the matchgirls, who won their fight and formed a union!"

On 18 July, 1890, the new terms are settled and accepted by the newly born union and by Bryant and May, still in shock (but also pleased that they'd not had to cede more). That afternoon and evening, there is jubilation in the East End.

Streets and homes fill with happy, loud women in the bright, loud clothing the matchgirls are known to favour. Women talk, laugh, dance, and drink. There might even be a few fights, to tell the truth, but if so, they are all in good fun.

Even journalists are right, some of the time.

You switch out your regular scarf for one in bright blue and your every-day hat for your best one, all over red roses and feathers. You wear your best clothing and spend the evening with Annie at the Eagle in the City Road, even dancing on the crystal platform, just as you did before, when your heart beat and your jaw was whole.

When your Nan was alive.

Your Nan, your poor Nan, not laid in the rich soil of county Cork, not now in a better place clutching once more her babbies to her breast, but lost to heaven completely, for had she not been a witch, and a suicide to boot? Sure, she was laid to rest in the consecrated ground of the Catholic churchyard, but only because when Father Keene had interviewed your sisters and brothers, they had all sworn that she had been out of her head with grief for some time, ever since her favourite granddaughter had started showing the signs of phossy jaw. Sure to God, she'd never have done a thing like this while in her right mind, never.

And Father Keene had looked over at you, you sitting in the corner with your face hidden in shadows, and had felt in his heart that what they said was the truth, and he had thought, wouldn't it be a shame to bring scandal and more suffering to this family?

But your Nan hadn't been out of her head at all. All you had to do to see that was to look into the covered pail where her candle still burned, or to search in vain for the heartbeat that used to pulse under your left breast. Your Nan hadn't hanged herself because she was out of her mind with grief.

Your Nan had hanged herself for this: so that this night you could dance a breakdown on The Eagle's crystal platform, so that you could put your arm through Annie's and watch the sun come up, knowing that she and the others were going to be all right, maybe. That when she'd told her man, Mick O'Dell, lived over a few streets and worked on the docks, that she was expecting, he'd told her to set the date just as soon she could.

But you aren't going to hang around for the wedding. Nothing less lucky than a corpse at a wedding, even one that can dance.

You and Annie watch the sun rise from the churchyard at Saints Michael and Mary. You have one arm through hers, and in the other, you hold the pail with the candle inside, still burning, and a small bottle of milk.

Just a bit, you figure, to dowse the candle, and then the rest for Annie to drink, for the coming babby, and you'll do it yourself. No need to make a murderer out of Annie, no matter her offer, and then you'll follow your Nan to perdition, so she won't be without family to help her in her trials.

You and Annie turn and walk slowly and a bit unsteadily (the worse for drink, both of you) through the churchyard, toward the freshly filled-in grave of your Nan. There's a small headstone, just her name, Bridget O'Hea, and the years, 1827–1888. You'd been there yesterday to lay flowers. Other than the pink and yellow wildflowers you'd picked on Hampstead Heath, already wilting and going brown by the time you placed them on the grave, there had been nothing.

But now the flowers you laid yesterday are not wilted at all. They've taken root and are blooming. You give them a gentle tug to make sure they're real, not a trick.

You and Annie clutch at each other's waists as you watch an honest-to-God oak tree sprout from the grave, from sapling to full grown in an instant, with a rich canopy of leaves, wreathed in mistletoe. You step forward and run your hand across the rough bark. A large snake coils around the trunk of the oak, several times, and the thing must be yards long.

You stare for a moment before turning to look at Annie, to see if she's seeing what you are, or if what is left of your brain is playing tricks on you. She steps forward and plucks a leaf from the oak and holds it to her lips in wonder.

The snake turns its head to look at you, and you find yourself looking into your Nan's eyes.

You blink and the snake, the oak, and the mistletoe are gone, but the flowers you brought are still growing from the grave soil. After a moment's pause, you meet Annie's eyes and step carefully onto your Nan's grave. You settle yourself against the headstone, and Annie sits next to you. You take the candle, still held in your Nan's left hand and set it on the ground and pass the bottle of milk to Annie. She begins to pry the cork loose, but you still her hand.

Instead, you slide the fingers of your Nan's hand back, and they uncurl as smoothly and gracefully as barley bending in the wind. The candle slips free.

It begins to burn in earnest then, guttering and smoking like the cheap tallow that it is, but burning more quickly than any candle should have a right to, as if making up for lost time. You have ten, maybe fifteen minutes, at the rate it is going.

Annie takes your hand, and together you watch the candle burn down.

Near the end, her grip on your hand tightens, and you close your eyes.

We have remaining to us two photographs, and only two photographs, of the striking Bryant and May matchworkers. The second photograph is more formal. It is of the official strike committee, and the women in it have done their hair and put on their Sunday best. They are arrayed across a stage, carefully posed in chairs. They seem confident, proud, intent.

But the first photograph is the more interesting one. It is of seven women standing in front of the Bryant and May factory. Their faces are gaunt, taut, and serious. More than one look a bit dazed, as if unsure of what they have done and what future it will bring them.

This photograph is famous now. More than that, it has become a symbol of working-class courage and resolve, displayed in the windows of London union offices.

Two of the seven women have almost certainly been identified by recent scholarship.

At the leftmost edge of the photo stands a woman half cut out of the picture. We see her left arm, the left half of her body, and most of her head, which she must have turned toward the camera. She is wearing a velvet hat, like some of the other women, and has a fringe of straight hair reaching almost down to where her eyes should be. Her face is nearly impossible to make out. It is a blur. Perhaps she moved as the photograph was being taken, though nothing else is blurred, not her hat, not her hand, not the scarf knotted around her neck, not a hair of her fringe.

The original print, now lost, belonged to John Burns, the leader of the dockworkers' strike, who urged his men to remember the matchgirls, who had won their fight and formed a union.

But her face is gone.

About "Phosphorus"

This is a story I've been wanting to write for a long time. The enthusiasm for Steampunk has produced some marvellous, incisive writing, and some gorgeous pieces of art. But it has also glamorized the Victorian era and too often ignored the exploitation and immiseration of the working class of England as well as the inhabitants of the lands England sought to rule. The fiery, corseted heroines, the eccentric but brilliant inventors, the rakish and charming younger sons—the wealth and comfort of these few depended on the suffering of many, many people. Even the wealthy of the nineteenth century suffered, of course, in an era prior to antibiotics and most of the vaccinations we take for granted today.

Nothing exemplifies the ravages of industrial exploitation like phossy jaw, a disease caused by the white phosphorus used to make Lucifer matches. Particles of white phosphorus entered the worker's jawbone through cavities in her teeth. A toothache led to sores along the jaw as the flesh and bone began to decay in the worker's face, and, in the case of the bone, glow in the dark. The stench arising from the decaying woman was so foul that sufferers were often cast out and forced to live on the edge of town. Eventually the disease spread to the brain, resulting in death. The only treatment was to amputate the jaw before the disease spread.

While the matchwomen got what they wanted and formed a union, it was not until 1908-1909 that the use of white phosphorus in matchmaking was banned in the UK, thanks to the 1906 Berne Convention. It's easy to forget how the people who indulged in afternoon tea rituals, admired clockwork-powered inventions, and wore shapely and beautiful corsets and bustles profited from the death and suffering of others every time they lit a candle. It's easy to forget how many of them resolutely believed in social Darwinism and in the essential inferiority of all nonwhite people (among whom they counted the Irish), among other vile things. And it's easy to wonder how those people, who considered themselves so civilized, could have accepted the price others paid for their comfort and wealth. Of course, if you substitute smartphones or tablets or cheap T-shirts for matches, you could write a similar story set today.

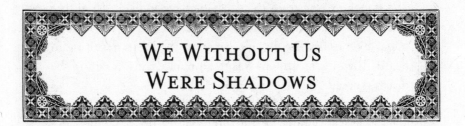

WE WITHOUT US
WERE SHADOWS

It seemed as if I were a non-existent shadow—that I neither spoke, ate, imagined, or lived of myself, but I was the mere idea of some other creature's brain. The Glass Town seemed so likewise. My father . . . and everyone with whom I am acquainted, passed into a state of annihilation; but suddenly I thought again that I and my relatives did exist and yet not us but our minds, and our bodies without ourselves. Then this supposition—the oddest of any—followed the former quickly, namely, that WE without US were shadows; also, but at the end of a long vista, as it were, appeared dimly and indistinctly, beings that really lived in a tangible shape, that were called by our names and were US from whom WE had been copied by something—I could not tell what.

—**Charlotte Brontë**

There was every possibility of taking a walk that day. Great dollops of sunshine melted on the moors; clouds and shadows cut the bare, winter-sleeping land into a checkerboard. The servant Tabitha had gotten a whole egg, wedge of bread, and a bit of her damson jam into each of the four children, bundled them in bonnet and gloves and extra stockings, and set them out of doors into a blue Yorkshire morning so cold it seemed ready to snap in half at the slightest touch. She thought absolutely nothing of turning them loose on the moor that day of all days—they needed a helping of the out-of-doors, such children as these, with their canny tongues and stubborn tempers. Judgment Day would come and go before those four would look up from their pens and papers otherwise.

Stiff gorse tangle burst underfoot as they took to the day. Charlotte, the oldest, a serious child with thick hair parted through the centre of her skull like a dark sea, a round, pallid face, and a fearsome scowl, trudged resentfully up a worn purple path through the bruised February hills. "I do not see in the least why we must leave Our Work just to satisfy Tabby's obsession with fresh air," she sniffed to none of her siblings in particular but all of them generally, her nose beginning to run in the hard, crystal air.

Branwell quickened his pace to keep up with her, his long curls whipping across the bridge of his great arched nose, his brow furrowed and fuming, frowning as if to reflect Charlotte's expression as perfectly as possible though he could only see the back of her, her woollen dress prickled with bits of twig and old, withered heather.

"I had intended to explode the castle on Ascension Island today, with Crashey and Ross and Bravey and Stumps and Buonaparte and all the rest trapped inside!" he groused, his breath puffing ellipses ahead of him. "With much splendid blood and fire and leaping out of windows and dashing brains out on the earth! The heavens would have wept at my slaughter! Now Tabby has sabotaged me with her *eat your eggs, there's a lad* and *fasten up your coat good and tight;* they'll be safe and sound for *ages* yet. Until evening, anyway."

Emily and Anne hung back from the older children, holding hands and picking their path carefully, so as not to crush any sweet plant that might erupt in spring with blossoms to cheer them. Emily looked up at the frozen sun, her brown ringlets crowding a narrow, sharp face that looked already quite grown, though she had only nine years. "We would have made them alive again by supper, Bran," she snapped, tired of her brother's thirst for the blood of their favourite toys, a set of twelve fine wooden soldiers their father had given as a present to his only son—but the girls had made a quick end to *that*. No sooner had Branwell got them but his sisters had colonised the kingdom of the soldiers, named them, and claimed their favourites. The Young Men ever after ruled their hearts and idle hours.

Little Anne, the youngest, laughed. The prettiest child in Haworth, her hair almost reaching the blond shades of girls in lovely paintings, she watched everyone with her wide, violet eyes as though spying upon them, with the necessity of making future reports to some unseen master. "It's a wonder Crashey doesn't get dizzy, with his forever falling down dead and getting up again!"

Charlotte stopped short at the flat top of a little hill that kept watch over a low, leafless valley full of the starving prongs of black yews and thorn trees and tumbling, colourless grasses, thistle, and old ivy, worn stones near as high as Anne. Every branch and blade was limned with glassy, golden light, which gave the scene a strange affect, as though the children were seeing it from much farther away than they really stood, and through a frosted pane besides. Charlotte put out her arms and her young sisters huddled into them, for the wind bit at their cheeks and made rosettes of their dimples. Branwell did not partake of their cup of affection, though he wanted to. But he felt Crashey would not, and certainly Buonaparte would have the head of any lad of his who behaved in such babylike fashion. Branwell had of late begun to feel his sisters were not quite serious about the game. They had romantic notions and did not submit to his pronouncements of death and disaster by flood or spectral conflagration, but went about healing everyone with phials until all his fun was spoilt.

"There's nothing to be done," Emily said. "Unless we should sneak back. Let us see if we can't find the mushroom patch again and make believe there are fairies there. I'm sure you can explode the fairies if you like, Branwell, though since they have the power of flight, you won't get quite so many brains dashed on the earth, but perhaps you can arrange a duel to make up the difference. Duels are superior to battles anyway."

"I shall have a duel with Tabitha if she puts us to bed without our writing hours this evening," Branwell said, kicking the hardened black earth with the toe of his boot. "I shall whack her with a biscuit."

"If there are to be fairies," said Charlotte imperiously, "the Duke of Wellington will have to be their king." Anne ventured that her own favourites, Ross and Parry, the great polar explorers and namesakes of two of the smaller wooden soldiers, might be fairy lieutenants, perhaps wed to sensible fairy maids. But her sister, chief of the tale and engine of the game, did not hear her. The duke stood always at the centre of their pretended worlds, for Charlotte adored him as fiercely as Branwell worshipped Buonaparte. They had called their favourite wooden soldiers after the mortal enemies and insisted on their inclusion in every adventure.

And what a dashing crystal image it was that rose in Charlotte's heart then—Sir Arthur Wellesley, Duke of Wellington and king of the fairies, with long black wings and a crown of lightning, astride, not a white horse this time, but a white rhinoceros, his sword a blue, lamplit flame! The beauty of the dream expanded like a silk balloon in her chest, almost painful in its familiar sweetness, the pricks of a tale, and as ever she felt as though she could never be big enough for even one of the stories that stormed inside her. It would drown her entirely or burn her up from within and leave no part of Charlotte behind. She could see him in ruby clarity, really see her duke, putting a lance of rose-coloured ice through the forehead of the pig-footed, ram-headed, lizard-mounted emperor of France.

A cracking, rustling thump down in the wintry hollow broke Charlotte's vision into pieces. The sun dug down into a trench of clouds, casting the vale into shadow, sending a brute wind to rattle the thistle-heads. Something moved between the long, sharp trees.

"Look," Emily whispered, her breath strangled and squeaking.

"I don't see anything," said Branwell, peering through the shade.

"*Look.*"

And they did see something—a man, a hugely fat man, in fact, tottering just below them, his collar turned up to the cold. But his collar was not a collar; it was a fine, illuminated page from some strange manuscript, folded crisply. His waistcoat was fashioned from a coppery book spread out along the spine; his cravat a penny dreadful folded over many times. But queerest of all, the enormous belly that protruded from beneath his coat of printed pages was the carved ebony knob of an ancient scroll, his legs were dark hymnals, and his enormous head was an open book longer than the Bible itself, glasses perched upon the decorated capitals of the pages: two handsome *O*s that served for eyes. The lower parts of the pages formed a moustache, and his nose crowned it all: a long, blood-scarlet ribbonmark.

After a moment of shock in which no one breathed and everyone clutched hands as tight as murder, all four children burst out of their stillness and tumbled down the hill after the book-man, calling out to him and demanding his name, his family, his business. He began to run from them, his breath whistling fearfully through the hundred thousand pages of his body.

"Go away!" he shouted finally as they ran together, leaping over frozen puddles and knotted roots. "If Captain Tree hears of this, I'll be remaindered for certain!"

"We're dreaming!" cried Anne. "It's all right, it's a dream and we're dreaming!"

"You can run forever in dreams," panted Branwell, "and I think if I don't stop soon, I shall throw up!"

But finally the man of books did stop, skidding to a halt before two tall soldiers, made entirely of rich brown wood, their rifles leaning on their shoulders, their gazes clear and bold. The fat man looked back at them in terror, then folded up his face, his collar, his cravat, his waistcoat, and his long hymnal legs. He folded up so completely that between the children and the soldiers no longer stood a man at all, but a great fat book firmly shut, lying on the moorland. One soldier with painted black trousers bent and retrieved it, tucking the volume under his strong arm.

"Hullo," said the other soldier. This one had a wood knot over his heart as though he had been shot there long ago. His mahogany mouth turned up in a sad, little smile that seemed to say: *well, we had better make the best of things.* "My name is Captain Tree, and this is my comrade Sergeant Bud. But you may call us Crashey and Bravey."

Long afterward, Charlotte would try to remember how it happened, but her mind could not quite clamp down upon it. It had already had to struggle mightily with a man made out of books and was not at all prepared to record how one managed to lift a foot off the ground in Yorkshire and put it down in somewhere else altogether. They did not pass through a door, of that she was sure, nor was there a mystic ring or pool. Yet Crashey and Bravey—their own stalwart soldiers, their miniature toys!— had taken them up, and now the sun battered down hot and sultry through viridescent fronds and great pink hothouse flowers as tall as streetlamps, bobbing over a long glass road that lead to a palace of such grandeur it burned their eyes. All along the boulevard strange obelisks rose, tipped with fire or ice or balls of blue lightning, and between them great birds of marvellous size and countenance, like peacocks given the gift of flight, bobbed and darted, crying out like mournful loons.

"What is that place," said Emily, her voice trembling. "That place you are taking us? It is too dazzling! I fear it will catch fire, the sun dances upon it so."

"That is the Parsonage," said Crashey. His voice was deep and pleasant. "It is where the Chief Genii of Glass Town live, and many other wonderful fine folk besides."

"That is *not* the Parsonage!" protested Anne, who could bear very much fancy, being so young, but could not abide a lie. "*We* live in the Parsonage, with Papa and Aunt Elizabeth and Tabitha! It looks nothing like that!"

Indeed, this Parsonage was an edifice all of diamonds, its stately pillars sparkling emerald and ruby illuminated with lamps like stars. A sapphire hall opened up like a blue mouth in its exquisite face, and the light of the warm Glass Town day filtered through all these gems as through water, throwing up fountains of fitful reflections. A little churchyard lay just beside it, as it did at home, but here the gravestones were perfect alabaster stippled with black pearls.

"Sir, I must insist you admit this is all a dream," Branwell said crossly. "If you are my Crashey, indeed you must do as I say. I have had quite enough silliness!"

Crashey and Bravey stopped and turned smartly to them, saluting. They stood on the porch of the bright Parsonage, and Charlotte heard her heels click on the diamond floor. That click, somehow, sounded deep in her and convinced her of the reality of this summer country as the birds and pillars and heat could not. The floor beneath her was real, and its facets yawned below her like mirrors. She drew her sisters in close and her heart battered madly at her ribs.

"I am your Crashey," said the solemn soldier. "And so I must obey you, but I wish you would not compel me in this way. I will say it is a dream, if your will is set. But I am an honest nut, and I do not like to lie. I will show you my wounds if you require evidence—you may already see the place where the Marquis of Douro put his musket ball during the African campaign, but here"—and Captain Tree showed his thigh, which had a scorch mark upon it—"you may find proof of the explosion of the citadel of Acroofcroomb. Witness also my flank, whereupon Buonaparte stuck me with his knife, and my throat, slashed in the battle of Wehglon. If it will not make the ladies too faint, I can show you the scar over my liver, where the cannibal tribes made a lunch of Cheeky, Gravey, Cracky, and my humble self."

Branwell at last relented and drew into the protective circle of his sisters. Charlotte held him tight about the waist and warmth spread through him as he put his hand upon little Anne's shoulder as he had seen their father do when their aunt suffered a spell of grief.

"Those are *our* battles," whispered Emily, utterly ashen. "We sent the Young Men to Acroofcroomb. We set the cannibal hordes upon them.

We invented Glass Town, and Gondal, and the marquis. He is talking about Our Work."

"Indeed, fair Emily, you did send us into service," spoke up Bravey for the first time. "Well do I recall our suffering and many deaths—but also I remember gentle hands which restored us to life, fit and hale to strive again for the sake of our nation." Handsome Bravey put his hand over his heart and bowed. Branwell flushed, remembering his own plans for the afternoon, which had included dropping Bravey from a great height onto sharp rocks.

Charlotte shook her head. "It is not possible. Fiction counts no casualties! The Young Men are playthings, made by a gentleman in Leeds and purchased fairly—they cannot simply become real."

"I believe you will find all this easier on your stomachs if you join us within," said Bravey uncomfortably. "For the whole of reality is not easily explained by a couple of old veterans with splinters still stuck in their bones."

The children allowed themselves to be led into the long blue hall. They seemed to pass underwater, through green and turquoise shadows pierced by pins of sunlight. The hall opened into a great room with a floor like midnight, full of still more jewelled pillars of rose and silver and white. Four golden thrones arrayed themselves at the north end, and upon them sat four figures. Three ladies there were, two dark and one light, their glossy hair gathered at their necks, their pale faces calm and perhaps amused. They wore long, gauzy dresses of spectacular colours: crimson, blue so bright it seemed to crackle, and glinting garnet-black. Beside them a young man sat with one leg crossed over one knee, his face craggy and not unhandsome, his brow furrowed, his lanky hair coal-coloured and loose. The four bore a similarity of feature, of seriousness and of long familiarity.

Of all of them, little Anne, hardly turned seven, understood and ran toward the thrones.

"She is myself!" Anne cried. "All grown, and beautiful, and that is you, Charlotte, and you, Emily, and you, Branwell, your very scowl! Oh!" Anne put her hands to her face. "So that is what I will be. I have wanted to be grown-up all my life."

"How small I once was," marvelled the older Anne. A lock of her bright hair came loose as she put her own hand to her cheek.

"Welcome," said the older Charlotte. "We are the Chief Genii of Glass Town. You may call me Tallii, and they Annii, Emmii, and Brannii." The great lady dropped her formal demeanour like a fan. "You've caught us quite off guard! We are in the midst of our annual rite, and to be perfectly frank we did not think we should meet you here, or ever."

The younger Charlotte approached the throne shyly. She extended her hand, still gloved from the distant, cold moorland, marvelling at this woman who was herself but not herself, herself older and wise and somewhat sad, herself whole and complete. The Chief Genii Tallii laced her fingers through the child's and smiled.

"How strange," she said.

"You must explain!" cried Branwell fearfully. "Or I will call the Young Men! Crashey said he would obey me!"

The older Branwell glowered, his dark eyes flaring red and smoky—and then his face smoothed over and grew kind again. "They are my Young Men as well, my boy. But they will serve as a lesson. You call that one Crashey, but also Captain Tree and Hunter and John Bull, depending on the tale that possesses you. And that is Bravey, but also Sergeant Bud and Boaster and Mr Lockhart."

"We have only twelve," said Charlotte. "They must stand in for whomever we need."

"Indeed." Brannii nodded. "And likewise, a soul must stand in wherever it is needed. In the universe, there is no such thing as a single soul. Where there is one in Yorkshire, there is a copy in Glass Town; where there is a maid in Angria, there is a copy in Paris. Where Wellington sheaths his sword, so do the many Wellesleys in many cities in many Englands in many worlds, all folded together like the pages of a book. You exist in Haworth, and we exist here, connected but not the same. Nothing happens merely once. The world repeats, like a stutter."

"But the Young Men are not souls, they are not alive!" protested Emily.

The Chief Genii Emmii folded her hands. "But you gave them stories and histories, names and marriages. You loved them and gave them breath. In your world that is not enough to do anything at all except eventually break them to pieces from use. But here, they stood up out of some distant forest and began to live. Glass Town does not obey the rules that Yorkshire must."

All along Chief Genii Emmii's skin, a golden crackle seared and then vanished.

"Then Wellington is here?" said Charlotte wonderingly, and Anne laughed at her, a little cruelly, for she had tired of the duke's primacy in her sister's affections long ago.

"Of course," said Chief Genii Annii. "And Buonaparte, too, I'm afraid. Everyone you have known and heard of has a copy here, and I daresay more and others in places we know not of. Wellesley and his sons with their wings of onyx and loyal rhinoceri defend us against the depredations of the ram-faced French genius with his saddled lizard and his terrible army of fire-breathing assassins, a clan of dastardly ebony ninepins."

Branwell considered that a ninepin who was also a fire-breathing assassin was quite the most marvellous thing he could think of. He had pressed their aunt's ninepins into service as enemy battalions many times, but never thought to give them power over the fiery elements. Even Wellington would certainly fall to such warriors—though it disturbed Branwell that his Buonaparte should live still, yet the real one had died lonely on a rock in the sea.

"I did not give him such an army," he said meekly, in some defence.

"You gave him much thirst for blood and fire, and no need to restrain himself, and gifted him with a hunger for death more fierce than for bread," Chief Genii Tallii said sternly. Branwell's heart swelled and stung. Charlotte's disapproval left welts upon his spirit, and in those great adult eyes he saw himself small and vicious, when he only wished to be the master of the game—was that so terrible?

The Chief Genii Annii went on, "But also Sir Walter Scott dwells in Glass Town, bent over his books in a wig of butterflies. So, too, is Lord Byron here, a bewitching warlock with hooves of gold. The anatomist Dr Knox tends a garden of fresh corpses, as sweet-smelling as orchids, to perform his experiments upon. Though we hold the throne, our father, Patrick Brontë, serves as prime minister, his official carriage drawn by a blue tiger sent to us in gratitude from the peoples of the Nile. You would find without too much trouble a young man with a finch's bright head living among the turtles of the south quarter, near Bravey's Inn, answering to the name of Charles Darwin."

"I do not know that name," said Charlotte.

"Time is not a perfect copy. Yet he is there, along with the editors of *Blackwood's Magazine,* dipping their unicorn horns in ink; a poet called Young Soult the Rhymer, selling his verses beneath the ammon trees, young Benjamin Disraeli tossing his dragon's head at the stars."

A star glowed briefly upon Genii Annii's head, blue and sere, then guttered out as if a wind had extinguished it.

"You are the authors of our world," said Crashey softly, and the four of them had almost wholly forgotten he was there. "It is a mystic, decadent thing when one's gods come home to roost. Waiting Boy did not mean for you to see him—the gentleman you chased away from your own Parsonage. Some transit must occur between our countries. It'll be a century before he comes out of his book again. You gave him a terrible fright. Imagine if all the seraphim of heaven appeared while you were collecting the post."

"But we are not seraphim!" insisted Emily.

Crashey said nothing.

"Is Mother here?" said little Anne. The Chief Genii turned to her as one. "You said Walter Scott is here. And Buonaparte, though everyone knows he is dead. Is our mother here? She died at home. Is she in that splendid courtyard of pearls and alabaster? Or does she live, with a lion's tail or a sparrow's head? I shouldn't mind if she had a sparrow's head. I can become accustomed to anything, really."

The Genii did not answer, but their grave, dark faces answered Anne all the same. The child blushed. "I only thought . . ." But she could not finish. She buried her head in Emily's breast.

"Why was . . . Waiting Boy . . . mucking about on the moor to begin with?" said Branwell, trying to defeat with false cheer his own hope that their mother could somehow be waiting for them in some place they had invented, Dr Hume's house or the Tower of All Nations.

"Each year," said Bravey, "the Young Men must perform certain arduous activities, or else the world will be destroyed and all sent into darkness."

"You're very matter-of-fact about it!" said Charlotte.

Bravey nodded. "I am. But it must be done. Waiting Boy was bringing to us a certain object, that we might begin our rite. It must come from your country, for it is from your country that we come.

"We will take it to the Island of Dreams hereafter and do what must be done there, and then another year may pass in which all is well and the sun in the sky."

"And what is to be done with us?" asked Charlotte, speaking for the worries of them all.

"Done with you?" said kind Bravey. "Nothing. If you wish to go home, you may go home."

"I do not!" shouted Branwell a little too loudly. "I wish to meet Buonaparte!"

"And Wellington!" added Charlotte.

"And the ninepin brigade, and the vivisectionist's garden, and even this Darwin fellow, if you say he is a good man and wise," said Emily.

"I should like to go with you to the Island of Dreams," said Anne softly, not yet over the bright shaft of joy that had flared up and gone suddenly out in her little heart at the thought that their mother might enter the hall in as much glory as these four monarchs. "And perform the rite with you. I wish all things to be orderly and well."

The children clapped upon this immediately as the thing to be done, though Crashey and Bravey declined bashfully, feeling it was their private affair. But in the end no fibre of them could refuse their creators, and a great elephant was called, for this was a common conveyance in Glass Town, for those who could afford it. As the negotiations were made, Chief Genii Emmii happened to cough into her kerchief, and Charlotte saw in the silken square a spray of rubies fall like blood. The corners of Emmii's mouth seemed to crack ever so slightly, and a glittering scarlet light escaped before the skin made itself whole again.

W e must go quickly and with as little sound as we may," admonished Crashey. Branwell was disappointed in him. They rode upon an elephant—not only an elephant but one whose skin was diamond, yet soft, with tiny silver hairs upon it and iron bones visible down deep beneath the millions of facets. How could they go quietly? Why should they? They would fight if the ninepins came for them! Yet secretly Branwell hoped they would, for surely Buonaparte, his chief among the Young Men at home, would come with them, and they would be fast friends.

"What is it that Waiting Boy brought from our country?" said Emily as the sun went down over a broad sea that foamed on a beach below the green cliff on which their road ran. It spooled out a hot, rosy light along the horizon like calligraphy.

Bravey blushed; the birchwood of his face went the colour of cedar. "To ask us to reveal these things is like asking us to discuss the details of our wedding night," he said miserably.

"I command you to tell us!" cried Branwell.

Crashey removed from a pocket concealed in a patch of bark a crystal glass, stoppered and filled with a thick black liquid.

"Ink?" said Anne, reaching out to touch it. The sunset leant the glass a molten, volcanic splendour.

"In your country it is ink," Crashey agreed. "Here it is a philtre which compels the truth from whoever would use it."

Branwell was possessed by a powerful urge to snatch it away. He would make Charlotte taste it. Then she could not lie to him when he asked the questions buttoned up into his chest. *Do you still love me as you used to when Emily and Anne were too young to interest us? When you go away to school again, what will become of me? Is it me you love best, or the tale of the Young Men which you require me to tell fully? You are going so fast, I cannot keep up with you. Why will you not wait for me?*

For her part, Charlotte also wished to talk to her brother away from the others, but she did not think she needed a philtre. He would tell her the truth because he was Branwell, and if he did not, she would know. *I do not think the Genii really look like us,* she wanted to tell him. *I think they are wearing us like masks. Perhaps they are really us, but changed, like Buonaparte with his ram-face, which, you know, I had only just conceived of when all this began, but now it is true! I would not have put it in the chronicles, as it is too fanciful even for our purposes. But if it is real it cannot be fanciful! Did you see the skin of the Genii when it cracked? Beneath I saw the swirling, spangled lights of the heavens, like a furnace full of stars. It is not safe, the Young Men's country. We are not safe.*

In the late evening they came upon a house in a quiet section of quite another town, a stately place with black marble porticoes and a cheery light within. They dismounted the elephant and were greeted by three of the most beautiful young men the children had ever seen. They seemed, indeed, more like paintings of men than men, and Charlotte was certain she could see brushstrokes upon their hands and faces, though this made them no less lovely.

Crashey and Bravey greeted them with laughter and claps upon the back, and the brothers invited them all in for brandy and the business at hand.

"Allow me to present," said Crashey, "Currer, Acton, and Ellis Bell, friends of the crowns and initiates of the first order."

"Initiates into what?" Emily said as Acton kissed her hand.

"The secrets of our yearly rite. It is a brotherhood we maintain for all time. We have come to fulfil their portion, and also for their excellent table."

"I only wish you could have met our sister Danett," sighed Currer, whose glossy auburn hair smelled of linseed. "But she died last year. Laudanum, I confess, and despair."

Bravey let out a woody sob, for it seemed that he loved the Bell sister all in secret and would now bury his heart in the earth. The men shared brandy around and drank in painful silence.

Anne looked around at the house. Books lay everywhere, half in order and out. Maps hung upon the walls, of the polar regions, the Himalayas, the Yukon wilds. A great black opal desk took up the centre of the room, which seemed to have been made for four people to work together upon it, though now only three manuscripts lay on its many-coloured surface, each with its own quills and ivory-handled knives for making points, and decanters full of rich ink. A plate of grapes, thick cheese, and yellow cakes lay in the meeting place of the three stations, so any of the brothers might sample it while at work.

Anne recalled an evening at home when she was distraught over Charlotte's or Branwell's receiving some preference, and her father had asked what she wanted most in all the world. She had been younger then, not yet achieved the seasoning of six or seven years, and had been seized with the sure knowledge that whatever she asked for then her father had the power to grant it. Everything relied upon what she said in that moment. And so she told the truth, being so small and surrounded by the older children, invincible and mighty creatures whom she could never best. *Age and experience.*

And yet she had remained small.

But the Bell house seemed to her the exact house that she would have when she possessed age and experience. A house *of* and *for* age and experience, where siblings might dwell together in peace and write upon a single great desk, recalling and inventing adventures, just as they did now, but with the impossible power of adults to do as they pleased. *I shall remember this house,* Anne thought. *I shall remember it as I remember my own name.*

"Buonaparte has been to see us." Ellis Bell's voice cut through Anne's thoughts. "He has decided his newest mischief will be to keep the rite from proceeding." *What if something splendid were to happen? Destruction is a wonder, disaster a fascination. We can set it aright by supper if it should go poorly.* "What a creature! And the boss of his ninepins, Young Man Naughty, beat us about the head and burned our birds in their cages. But we did not give it to him. We are true."

"Good boys," said Bravey, quite drunk by now but still amiable.

Currer Bell went to the opal desk and drew out a ponderous quill, a feather of one of the flying peacocks they had seen in Glass Town. Its point was as sharp as a bayonet. He folded it into an oilcloth and pressed it into Crashey's arms, leaving pale paint marks on the cloth where his fingers touched it. "Godspeed, for he is faster than that."

Through the long night, the children fell asleep on their diamond elephant. Crashey allowed himself to stroke the brows of Charlotte and Branwell, touching the wood-knot wound on his chest with his other hand, remembering the flames of Acroofcroomb, the blood of his comrades everywhere like a hideous ocean. The wooden soldier shook his head to clear the cloud of his many deaths.

He could not bring himself to wake them when the elephant trod into the Hall of the Fountain, so vast in its domes that the elephant was as a lowly dog in its vault. Many hours yet they marched through the long distance of the hall, which stretched league after league lined with statues of black and white marble as well as amethyst and peridot. He could not bear to wake them as they passed the fountain for which the place had been named, a pale snowy pool whose foaming plume reached as high as a cathedral. Only when they came to the room concealed behind a white silk curtain did he wake his charges, his small gods, and Bravey, who had sunk into sleep and brandy-fed grief over the lost Danett Bell.

Behind the curtain stood an iron door. The children stood soundless and still, with the wide, limpid eyes of those just wakened. Crashey and Bravey took wooden keys from beneath their helmets and turned the door's two locks at once, opening with a long creak the inner chamber.

The square chamber was a red room. A bed supported on massive pillars of mahogany, hung with curtains of deep red damask, stood in one corner. A red table covered with a crimson cloth, a red toilet table, a red floor, and red draperies that concealed only blank red wall and no windows. Standing out like a tabernacle in the centre of the room was a red writing desk, its chair festooned with red cushions, and at it sat a young girl near Emily's age, with long, dark hair drawn in to cover her ears and searing, bold eyes. She wore a red dress.

"Hullo, Captain Tree," the girl said brightly. "Sergeant Bud."

"Ma'am," they replied in unison, bowing.

Bravey set the crystal glass upon her table, while Crashey set the oilcloth at her side, opening it to show the quill beneath.

"My heart is racing, I am so eager to begin!" said the little girl. "But whom have you brought with you? New recruits?"

Crashey introduced the children in turn, without mentioning their curious history.

"And I am Victoria," said the child, and she smiled at them. Her smile had a strength like a blow.

Victoria picked up the huge turquoise-and-emerald quill and dipped it into the ink. She began to write upon a great stack of blank pages before her, her hand easy and confident, her excitement flowing off her in curls of red heat.

"This year, I have a new world in mind," Victoria said as she wrote. "In it, I shall put myself! I have never done that before! It's very daring, don't you think? Here I don't have many prospects—my father was a clerk and a copy editor; I went hungry plenty often and had meat only when the butcher felt sorry for us. And I never leave this room anymore. My boys fill my larder but I'm never lonely, with all my histories to write! It takes the whole year to think through the next far country of my heart. But there! There I shall be a great queen—not just a queen but an empress!—and rule forever and ever over a great kingdom. I have invented a wonderful consort for myself as well, and I shall name him Albert and make him handsome and brave—but not so brave that he will lord over me! I shall give myself a number of children, and those children will all be kings and queens and emperors and empresses as well, so that no one must feel lesser when we gather for holidays. There will be wars, of course, you cannot make everything perfect or else it's not very interesting. But I have planned a whole pantheon of wonderful poets and scientists and authors and inventors and painters and composers for my court—I can put you girls in it, if you like! I'm very generous! What would you like to be?"

"What about me?" said Branwell, who did not even understand what he had been left out of, but smarted all the same.

"If it pleases you," said the child Victoria with a gracious wave of her pen.

"Poets," Charlotte said. She did not need to take a vote; she knew her sisters and they her. "And authors. The sort that last."

"I shall not forget when I come to that part! There is plenty of room. Oh, wait until you see the inventions I have imagined! Lightning in a glass and tin ponies that run upon two wheels! Locomotives crisscrossing the world, even running underground like iron worms. Flying balloons and a fairs so big you have to build a whole new city just to contain them! My country will shine."

And the child Victoria, her long hair spilling down over her slim shoulders, began to write so fast that they could no longer see the strokes of her pen. Sheaves of paper flew out from the desk, falling like snow onto the floor, piling up in drifts, nesting in a plush red chair, on the wide red bed. The pages were so filled with Victoria's tiny hand they looked nearly black.

"She is writing a world into life," said Bravey softly. "Just as you did. You did it all unknowing, but it is her whole being."

"Which one?" said Anne, for she recalled that the Genii had said there were countless in number. "Which world?"

"Who knows? Each year she writes a new one and sets it in motion; each year we bring the ink that will compel the world to become true and the quill to carve it out of nothing. We never see her countries, the copies of ourselves and the Genii and Sir Walter Scott and Wellington and Young Soult the Rhymer that live there. It is enough to know we have brought life somewhere, instead of death. Soldiers cannot ask for more."

Again Branwell felt a shiver of terrible responsibility at the numerous wars he had sent his Young Men to with glee, designing each of their deaths like suits. Perhaps this shiver was to blame for what followed, or perhaps that Victoria had not included him in her largesse, or perhaps the nagging, terrible sense that Charlotte was always running ahead of him, farther and farther ahead, and Emily and Anne would catch her but he could not, that they were not like him, they did not see how silly their stories became when they did not have deaths by stabbing and massacres and horror in them, when they bore no hint of war, but thought he was ridiculous, that he was the strange, violent interloper in their interior nations when the wooden soldiers had been his, his, all along.

And perhaps it was simply that he loved Buonaparte still, his first and best Young Man, and longed to see him come real. But when he saw the ninepins creeping in, glorious fiery designs upon their black chests, he did not cry out in warning. He only watched them, dazzled and glad after the fashion of a father upon seeing his son exceed all expectations. Buonaparte himself strode forward through the ranks of his personal guard, his ram's head carved beautifully from blackthorn wood, astride a lizard of white pine, its tail thick and whacking, its tongue a balsam whip.

And Branwell did not cry out. Victoria's papers flew and folded and slid to the floor. Crashey and Bravey stroked her hair and rubbed her shoulders, which must surely ache from her work, their faces fixed in religious ecstasy, midwives to a place they would never see.

The ninepin boss, Young Man Naughty, opened his mouth, a slit in the surface of his pinhead, and let a slow flame roll out from between his lips like a woven cloth. Branwell did not cry out. He was curious. What would happen? He did not feel any worry—if the country where Victoria was queen burned up, it was no real loss. Branwell felt no loyalty to an unborn cosmos. His loyalty was with Buonaparte.

The ribbon of flame kissed the first papers of the red room, and the sound of it was like taking a breath. The wooden Buonaparte exclaimed with joy upon seeing Branwell—Branwell himself, not his sisters!—and embraced him while Crashey and Bravey came out of their dreaming joy and roared with horror, while Charlotte, Emily, and Anne tried to smother the flames with the rich red curtains and sought about for water, their panic held down by Charlotte's iron calm. Buonaparte embraced Branwell while a world burned, and the ninepins danced in the ruin, stamping down on the papers like drumbeats.

And while Branwell held his best creation, a musket ball splintered Buonaparte's wooden sheep's skull and then the conqueror slumped at Branwell's feet. With a whoop and a cry and a thundering gallop, the Duke of Wellington burst upon the scene, his wooden chest glowing, his white rhinoceros bleating, his sons spreading black and gorgeous ebony wings, their wooden rifles smoking still. Branwell howled and wept bitterly as his Young Man fell dead. Young Arthur and Charles Wellesley made work of the ninepins, who, without their leader, seemed to lose all hope and fell one after the other in a clattering row.

"No, no, no!" cried Victoria, trying to put out the flames with her own body. Crashey and Bravey dragged buckets in from the fountain in the great hall and coaxed the elephant into firefighting with her long diamond trunk. Damp, charred pages began to outnumber fiery ones, and Wellington prodded Buonaparte's lifeless body with the toe of his wooden boot.

"Don't cry, lad," the duke said to Branwell. "He'll be made alive again by suppertime, God save us all. That's how it's always gone. Judgment Day will come and go and still I will be fighting the man, round and around on the last piece of earth in a sea of darkness."

Victoria clutched hundreds of papers to her breast, trying to piece some back together, trying to make them come right again. "So fast! All in a moment, less than a moment! Did you see them coming? Why did you not protect me, Captain Tree?"

Crashey looked stricken, then went ashy, as though he might pass dead away. Bravey buried his head in his hands.

"It's all broken up now," Victoria whispered, two heavy tears rolling down her face. "Look—my dear Albert is almost wholly burned out of the tale. My little wars of intrigue and interest have bled out and mixed together." She grasped at a miserable black heap. "My children! All my little kings and queens! Now there is a black space in the midst of them, a black trench where half the world will fall and choke and break my kingdom of forever into burning shards. I wanted it so beautiful, I wanted it to be a kingdom without pain, and now it is on fire." The girl held out another slim clutch of pages to the children. "Even the part I had written for you, look now how it's spoiled. The books are there, yes, but your lives are scorched to a few slim chapters, brittle and thin. The smoke in this room will wither you away in that country, so that even the water you drink will bring you no health, even your home will not make you whole. And the boy—" Victoria ran her fingers over a black page, her tears hissing as they fell upon it. "It's written already, I can't erase it. I only ever get one draft to make it right. You cannot revise a whole world."

"Don't worry," Branwell said to his sisters. "It's not our world. It's copies of us, somewhere else, somewhere far away that will never touch us. I'm sorry, I should have sounded a warning, I will next time, I swear it. But it's not us, it's another place, another Branwell and Charlotte and Emily and Anne, and no harm done to us at all."

The child Victoria pressed her forehead to the smoking floor and wrapped her arms around her belly, weeping as if her only child had been born dead and still.

Tabitha wrinkled her nose as she bustled the children in from the frosted twilight. Their clothes smelled faintly of smoke, their faces were smudged and exhausted and hollow looking, which was not right at all for four young folk who had been playing in the sun all day! What they had been about they would not say, nor how they had been gone so long, nor how they had found their way home in the dark. All four were silent as monks. But they were not four—little Anne was missing. Tabitha sent the girls and Branwell to scrub their cheeks and dress for supper and perhaps play with their wooden soldiers a bit if being away from them for an afternoon had soured them so. The fish would not be ready for a three-quarters of an hour—an eternity for minds such as theirs. Tabitha drew on her woollen shawl and went out into the gloam to find the violet-eyed little wastrel that lagged behind, probably to watch some silver worm chew the earth or skip a rhythm on the cobblestones.

It would be spring soon; green snapped in the air though the yews in the churchyard gave no hint of bud. Tabitha spied a golden head—and no bonnet, the lamb!—among the monuments and went to the half-frozen child, who had gone where love bade her, to the sisters lost before she'd ever known them. Anne stood before three headstones on the slope next to the moor, the middle one, Elizabeth's, grey and half buried in the heath; the children's poor mother's only harmonized by the turf and moss creeping up its foot, Maria's still bare.

Tabitha and Anne lingered around them, under that benign sky; watched the moths fluttering among the heath and harebells, listened to the soft wind breathing through the grass.

"How anyone can ever imagine unquiet slumber for our dear sleepers in that quiet earth I shall never know," Tabitha said finally, and drew Anne in to the great candlelit house.

About "We Without Us Were Shadows"

"We Without Us Were Shadows" came out of my fascination with the Brontë family and their imaginative lives, with the fantasy kingdoms they invented before becoming much more famous for realist work. I wanted to explore those countries as real places, as strange mirrors of England, and the connection between literature and reality. The Brontës had tragically short and troubled lives, dying one by one from wasting illnesses. I wanted to embody the sorrow of that, of that loss, and also to treat their fantasy stories with the seriousness that is so often given to their adult work. I think many of us wish we had had childhoods with such like-minded friends and siblings, that we could have created a world such as Glass Town—so in this story, briefly, I got to do just that.

ELLEN KUSHNER and
CAROLINE STEVERMER

THE VITAL IMPORTANCE
OF THE SUPERFICIAL

Madam:

It will not have escaped your notice that on my last visit I left something behind—rather prominently, I fear, in the middle of the room, so no
need either to deny it or to ascribe it to the carelessness of your servants.

I would account it a courtesy if you were to see that it was returned as
soon as possible, as I find myself greatly inconvenienced at present.

Your most humble and obedient,

R

Dear Lord R.—

My deepest apologies for last night's unpleasantness. Please believe that
my brother and I will do everything in our power to make sure nothing
like it will ever happen again.

I shall do what I can to restore your possessions to you, but please understand I can make no promises whatsoever. When Father's experiment
misfired, nearly every guest was affected. As a result, we are ankle-deep in
objects left behind by rapidly departing guests. Father has already taken
half of them apart. I fear by now he has recombined parts to make some
entirely different whole, making restoration impossible in many cases.

Thank you, my lord, for responding so courteously to what must have
been an experience of some discomfort and indeed some mortification.

You have all my gratitude. Some of the other gentlemen have responded rather differently.

> Your debtor in courtesy and your very humble
> servant to command in this matter,
> Charlotte Fleming

Charlotte, I am mortified! My brother is usually such a perfect lamb—I promise you he is, and you know I am generally right, about people, anyway. But now he is stomping about the house and swearing vengeance in an uncharacteristically dramatic fashion, like something in a play, and I don't know which way to look. I have had to pretend I'm cutting up fashion pages to make an album for the dressmaker—trust Ravenal, fortunately, not to notice that they are two years out-of-date and would make me look a hag. There is also a headless child in here somewhere. I am not good with scissors, really.

I thought it was all bound to go so perfectly, as I always told you it would—he is a great enthusiast of the Experimental Arts, and I knew he would be delighted by your father's work, and your new fichu-pelerine could not fail to divert him, for I helped you pick out the *dragonfly* ribbons myself—and I was so eager for him to meet you and your family. And now it all seems to have miscarried, owing to some stupid little mistake that he does not seem to be able to explain to me, although I am by no means stupid. You may have carried off all the prizes at school, for who could doubt your brilliance, but I feel sure I am clever enough to understand an experiment of the kind you so often regaled us with after lights out at Miss Prism's Academy.

So it must have been either terribly complicated or terribly shocking, and I hope that either way you will be able to write and tell me.

My cold is still bad, my throat a misery, so I fear a visit is out of the question for now. I am taking lemon drops.

> Your loving,
> Priscilla

P.S. Please tell your dear brother I am quite sure he did everything that was just and proper, and that no one could possibly imagine he is in any way to blame. Not even Ravenal. Who does not seem even to have noticed him, which is very odd, considering.

Dearest Priscilla,

I despair. Truly, I do. Can you tell me what it is Ravenal brought with him to Father's demonstration?

If only I know what to look for, it's possible I can steal it from Father's atelier and return it.

Since R. took the trouble to ask for it back in writing, would it have been so very much more additional toil to say what it was? *I left something behind.* Is that any way to carry on? I think not.

Rather prominently. In the middle of the room. If he had seen that room the next morning— Oh, I shudder to think of it. Shocking *and* complicated. Thank goodness Cecil was here to help me.

Do put the scissors down. No one expects you to be virtuously busy when you have the cold, thank goodness. I suppose lemon drops are far preferable to barley water, but I wish you were well instead.

Yours,
Charlotte

My dear Miss Fleming,

Since I am assured by my sister that I have the manners of a bear, the visage of a Goth, and, this morning, the cravat of a shepherd of particularly mangy sheep . . . and that my epistolary skills would not have passed muster in even the most junior students of Miss Prism's fine Academy, I begin again.

If you would be so kind, my dear Miss Fleming, as to enquire of your esteemed Papa whether amongst the impedimenta currently cluttering his workroom, your salon, the front hall, the umbrella stand, indeed, even the butter dish, there might be lying a medium-sized *key*, I shall account myself well contented.

It is to be distinguished from all other keys by its *colour*, a deep red that might betoken rust, but most assuredly is not (for it is a smooth, untainted metal); or, to those of an imaginative disposition due to indulging in too many dreadful novels, blood—though the same assurance stands. Furthermore, the shank is engraved with some letters in a rare alphabet, most unmistakable.

The object for which the key was originally intended is, in time, replaceable; and I fear that if it has, as you indicated in yours of Tuesday last, been amalgamated, tainted, or fused with other Matter, it would at any rate be of no use to me; and so, we shall let the matter rest. The key, on the other hand, it would be a great kindness in you to have returned to me at your earliest convenience.

Please convey my kindest respects to the learned Professor, and to your most agreeable brother, Cecil—whom I really did notice that night, the opinion of certain female relatives to the contrary. He seemed a most pleasant and agreeable fellow—indeed, a very paragon of all manly qualities amazing in one so young and a far superior brother than any currently writing under the eye of a sister armed with a set of very sharp scissors, which I wish she would put down before she allows her critical faculties to overwhelm her more womanly virtues.

I beg leave to extend my wishes that you yourself continue yourself in the best of health, and hope you will not think me too remiss in neglecting to mention previously how very much the ~~dragonfly~~

~~gree~~

peau de libellule ribbons become you.

> Your most obedient servant to command,
> Humphrey Nicolas,
> Lord Ravenal

Alpha Plus!

> **—Pris**

Dearest Pris,

I beg you to set my mind at rest. This morning I received your brother's letter—and what a very lamblike mood he must have been in to let you manage his correspondence so—directing me at last to the object he so ardently desires to be returned to him.

My heart fairly leapt at his description, for I have a vivid recollection of the object in question. It was a music box in an intricate marquetry case, very beautiful, opened with the key he described. Need I even say that the music box was among the first articles Papa adapted to his experimental design? But I recall the key was cast aside as of no real utility once the cabinet had been opened and the inner workings removed. So I hastened to Papa's workshop to retrieve the key, only to find that Cecil had swept the place clear. Most fortunately, he had not yet emptied his sweepings into the dustbin, so I was able to recover the key. Once I cleaned it, it looked as it did on arrival. I wrote a brief missive to Lord R., apologizing for the loss of the music box—indeed, once Papa commandeers things, people don't generally want them back, or if they do, the thing is never the same again—and sent Cecil off with the key, the note, and your brother's direction.

Cecil has not yet returned. Never before has he displayed any sign of Papa's tendency to wander away. Quite the contrary. It is most unlike him not to send word if he has been delayed somewhere along the way. Do, please, assure me that he carried out his mission and is safe with your brother, lost in gossip or playing cards or doing something else entirely benign.

Your,
Charlotte

Dear Miss Fleming,

I regret to inform you that my sister Priscilla is unable to reply to your letter immediately, having been sent to our estate in Yorkshire faster even than post can travel.

In her absence, I do *not* make so bold as to open her correspondence— which I recognise by the clear italic hand as being from you—but I realise that, in the heat of events, you may be wondering about the whereabouts of your brother Cecil.

He is here, at my house in town. But he really is not himself. And so I think it best he remain here for a little while, until we can sort him out. I am delighted to have the key back. Tho' had you asked me, first, I ~~would have warned you not to~~

~~I wish that you had not~~

~~I made a horrible mistake in~~

It was very kind of you to send your brother with it right away.

I pray you, Miss Fleming, do not be alarmed at this slightly unexpected turn of events. Your brother is writing you a letter even now, explaining things. It may not set your mind at rest, but at least you will know that he is still capable of wielding a pen, and some flowery phrases withal. He has, most happily, not yet turned to verse, though who knows what the coming hours may bring?

R

Charlotte, dearest Charlotte, only consider

The Moon is hardly lost to us, for her splendour rules on the other side of the Earth while we, in dreaming, only think we wake

I know that She is vowed to me by the Light of the Moon, which witnesses and seals all True Bargains

I hear the music playing and I know what it is meant for, now

PRAY BE NOT CONCERNED, MISS FLEMING, THAT YOUR BROTHER HAS LOST HIS REASON—OR, RATHER, THAT HE IS MAD, FOR REASON HAS MOST CERTAINLY FLED, BUT NOT FOREVER—OR NOT FOR LONG, IF MY SMALL POWER CAN AVAIL.

———————

Dearest Charlotte,

I seize this moment to write you before I am stuffed in a carriage north. I am fine, but R. is suddenly terribly worried won't tell me why Do take care Charlotte I will write again from Yorkshr!!!

P

———————

Dear Lord Ravenal,

I know you are too much the gentleman to open another's correspondence, so I trust you with the enclosed. Please deliver it to my brother.

Sincerely,

Charlotte Fleming

Cecil, dear. Lord R. is a charming companion, I know. He's everything his sister claimed. You must be having a delightful time, and I do hate to intrude upon it.

Yet I will. I must. Papa has locked himself in his workroom and forbidden me to admit anyone to the house. I fear he has the great grimoire out, for at intervals I hear him baying out invocations. You know what that means. He's had odd turns before, but this is beyond anything. I need you to help me. Papa needs you. Cecil, I beg you, stop enjoying yourself with Ravenal and come home. Forget the time Papa made the doorknob burn your fingers when you tried to enter his workroom. Come home.

Charlotte

———————

Ravenal,

Please find enclosed a lock of your lovely sister's lovely hair. I had hoped to include a note in her hand, moistened by her tears of fright and sorrow. Alas, she seems confined to tears of vexation, and precious few of those. It is a pity. I have several spells I'd like to try requiring a maiden's tears of sorrow. They will just have to wait.

You know what I want. Give it to me, and I shall refrain from snipping anything else before I render her to you again.

Wulfstan

Wulfstan . . . ah, companion of my younger days! I hope that you have recognised the misguided enthusiasm of your youth and deeply regret having chosen such a "nom de magie" when we were both studying with the Magister. But perhaps not. It is a perfectly good saint, after all; and I do know that wolves are hungry hunters.

My memory of those days remains lively, however, and if you would like to meet me at the Crown and Cripple at Friday midnight, I would be delighted to reminisce together in convivial surroundings.

I am afraid that my sister—and her name, by the way, is Priscilla; do not let her attempt to convince you that it is *Athenoë* or *Clarice*, despite her preference or insistence to the contrary (you may look it up in the *Peerage* if you doubt my word)—is still suffering from the lingering effects of a severe rheum, and any additional tears are thus likely to be severely rheumy and of even less use to you. Please see to it that she drinks her tonic and keeps her throat well covered with flannel at night. Any amount of her you may choose to snip off will be utterly ruined if it comes from a person who has ceased breathing altogether.

I regret not being able to join you elsewhere, but it is most inconvenient for me to leave London at this time, as I am caring for a friend who was unexpectedly taken ill on my doorstep. My sister was headed north to escape the contagion. But please rest assured that my own health is excellent.

R

Ravenal,

I thank you for your lack of pains. If you had paid the slightest attention to your studies, you would know it is more usual to conceal a true name than to reveal it. I will meet you where and when you wish. Have it ready, and I will exchange your pretty sister for it on the spot.

Wulfstan

My dear Miss Fleming,

Do you, by any chance, know how to play the violin? Or, failing that, the Spanish guitar?

Ravenal

————————

Lord Ravenal,

I play the pianoforte, but only very indifferently. If you wish for a violinist, apply to Cecil. For all I know, he may have learned how to play the Spanish guitar by now. When you have quite finished with your musicale, pray send him home. We need his help here.

Charlotte Fleming

————————

Miss Fleming, I hasten to assure you that my love of amateur musicales is second only to my love of unripe grapes. But your assistance in this particular matter would be much appreciated, should you chance to have any musical ability whatsoever on an instrument that is reasonably portable. What about the flute? Many ladies like the flute.

Otherwise, I shall have to beg for the continued delightful company of your brother Cecil—indeed, I will procure him a violin at once and see how he gets on with it.

In his absence, may I inquire as to what sort of help you might require at home? As I fear any current inconveniences you are experiencing could be laid at my door, it would be my pleasure to make up for your brother's continued absence in any way that I can.

And are you at liberty this Friday night?

R

I ENCLOSE THIS FROM YOUR BROTHER CECIL, IN REPLY TO YOURS OF THIS MORNING:

Charlotte, there is no rhyme good enough for you. Why is that? The H-rhyme, surely not! The V-rhyme, equally unfair. I shall invent whole new words to celebrate your goodness and set them to music! You are the mainstay of Father's old age, though I hear he grows younger every day. You should put your ear to the keyhole and learn from his wisdom. Perhaps even your eye. But do not trust your hand to the doorknob, for it bites!

Music, Charlotte, music is the only way out of the dreams and back again.

When you know this, you know all.

Did you realise that both our names begin with C? It is a major chord, a minor, and also rhymes with key.

———————

Dear Lord Ravenal,

If I ever learned anything at Miss Prism's, it was the vital importance of the superficial. You are more alive to the superficial than anyone I've ever met, with the possible exception of your sister, and what is more, unlike my dear brother, you answer my letters sensibly. I will accept your kind offer of help should I require any. Meantime, I think perhaps I may provide some small assistance to you, at least by way of a warning.

This morning the most dreadful man came to see my father. I cannot tell you what single quality it was I misliked most about the man, for I could find no fault in his manners, his grooming, or his deportment. But something about him frayed my nerves extremely. He was all that was gentlemanly, but every word out of his mouth seemed to have an echo, every gesture he made was not only overly theatrical but delayed half a measure. A waxwork man would have had more charm.

Because of my father's recent indisposition, there was no possibility of permitting this caller to interview him, even for the brief time he requested. Nor could I gratify the man's desire to visit my father's workroom, just to see where the great work is performed, as he put it. When I had politely denied him, the man asked me to search the room on his behalf. He is looking for a music box. Without exactly saying so directly, I assured him I would do no such thing. Miss Prism's Academy trained us well for some situations, and saying no without ever using the word was a large part of our curriculum.

I saw the fellow off the premises as soon as I possibly could, but before he left, he said something that disturbed me very much. He paid me a compliment, exceedingly stilted, upon my appearance, noting with particular favour the ribbons I was wearing in my hair, the dragonfly ribbons, he called them.

When you paid me a compliment upon those very ribbons in your letter, you employed the proper name for the shade, *peau de libellule*. I confess it gratified me extremely to see the proper name not merely used but actually spelt correctly. There are advantages to a mastery of the superficial. I suppose Miss Prism would be quite proud of me.

But here at last is my warning:

The only other person I know to use the phrase *dragonfly ribbons* is your sister. Is it possible that this man is acquainted with her, and by extension, with you? Since I cut him to such pieces in my description, I have refrained from naming him. If he is your friend, you may recognise him from this account. If I have offended you by it, I beg your pardon. But if he is not your friend, you may not wish him to be Priscilla's friend either.

> I dare to sign myself not only your
> sister's friend, but yours as well,
> Charlotte Fleming

My very dear Miss Fleming,

I do not know when I have received a more unexpected, or a quainter, compliment than yours of the *superficial*! I accept it, and your friendship, with gratitude. When my sister said that you were "worth ten of those ghastly chits at Miss Prism's," I thought she simply meant that you were not unkind to her (as are so many who mistake our dear Priscilla's enthusiasms). But I see now that she really meant that you are genuinely out of the common way; and I vow never again to underestimate or misprize her vaunted judgment of human character.

I am very sorry to hear from you of your father's indisposition. If your letter to Cecil informed him of it, I am afraid your brother did not pass the information on to me in any coherent fashion. He is, however, making magic on the violin—of course, I speak figuratively; I mean to say that your brother's playing is remarkable for its passion and inventiveness. My sister, in enumerating his many fine qualities to me (for here I must confess to you that, from her very first visit to your home, she has not been reticent on that count), never seemed to mention that his was a genius to rival Paganini's for invention, and Tartini's in its plumbing the depths as well as heights of the human spirit. Truly, one feels one is overhearing a dialogue with some otherworldly being.

I cannot *imagine* what I was *thinking* when I suggested that you accompany me, flute in hand, to my rendezvous at the Crown and Cripple on Friday midnight. It was absurd of me even to contemplate such a thing. I am very pleased indeed that Cecil and his violin will serve my need far better than I had any right to expect. I hope that, after then, he will be restored to you.

The man who visited you is indeed known to me. Wulfstan—for so he calls himself, and I wonder if he made himself known to you by that name, or another?—was my fellow student under Magister Ludo on the Continent when I studied the Experimental Arts there, where they are looked upon with far less suspicion than they are here. Where once Wulfstan and I were friends, we have become at variance, and I am most displeased to hear of his visit to you, and his attempts to see your father. *BY NO MEANS* allow W. access to the man or his workshop! One thing in your letter heartens me, though: I do not mean to question the accuracy of your report to me, for which I am most grateful, but concern compels me to ask you to confirm one thing: that W. asked for the MUSIC BOX itself, and not the *Key*?

And now, my dear Miss Fleming, I must ask you for one last favour. I will not pretend that it is not a great one—but neither will I deny that I believe you to be more than equal to the task. Do you think, for a short time only, that you could find it in you to encourage Wulfstan to call upon you again? To draw him out, even, to discuss his affairs in any way? And then, oh, dear Miss Fleming, I tremble as I write this—to give him one of your ribbons to take away with him? I know this cannot be anything but the most distasteful of prospects to you. But you are not wrong in your deduction that he has made Priscilla's acquaintance. I believe the sight of your ribbon would communicate to my sister more than words what she most needs to know.

More than this I cannot say. That I presume on our new-minted friendship is certain. But since the night I paid my visit to your father's salon, our separate affairs have, I fear, become inextricably entangled. And I pray that you will trust my discretion and understanding to set matters to rights.

Your most assured friend to my little power,
Ravenal

Lord Ravenal,

I should not be surprised in the least to learn that young ladies frequently offer you their hair ribbons, perhaps to wear as a mark of their favour, like a knight of old. This sort of thing does not happen to Mr Wulfstan, I suspect.

Your letter struck fear into me on Priscilla's behalf. If you think she would benefit in the slightest measure if my hair ribbon were in Mr Wulfstan's possession, then I was determined to see he bore it away with him. I sent him a message (packed with lies that Father was better and wished to speak to him) and invited him to tea at four o'clock. He came promptly on the hour. I declared that Father had taken a bad turn, but entertained him at the tea table as I had promised.

If Miss Prism's Academy had not trained me so well, I might have found that hour at the tea table prodigiously awkward. After my lessons at school, I think I could make small talk with a badly plastered wall. Even so, Mr Wulfstan presented a challenge, for he sat with his hands on his knees and stared at me, eating and drinking nothing whatever, and offering as reply to my expert prattle only an occasional shrug of his shoulders.

Priscilla would have been proud of me. I played the coquette for all I was worth. I could see Mr Wulfstan thought I had lied about Father only to be near him again. I had even made a ribbon cockade to offer him directly, although I knew the colour would sort ill with the snuff-coloured coat he wears. I was right. He startled away from me as if he were a restive horse. As he did so, I managed to slip a bit of my dragon-fly ribbon wrapped in one of Cecil's handkerchiefs into his pocket. If he is the sort of gentleman who routinely turns out his pockets the moment he arrives home, I have failed. Judging from the ill-brushed condition of that snuff-coloured coat, however, I think it will be some time before he discovers it.

I hope it is, for I took the liberty of casting a small charm upon the ribbon, one that Priscilla will certainly recognise as my work. It causes any stray bit of paper to cling to the sole of the bearer's shoe. We used to use it on the stricter schoolmistresses, for there is nothing that takes away one's dignity like a bit of soiled paper clinging stubbornly underfoot.

I sent Mr Wulfstan away after that, and he seemed glad to go. All I had to do was counterfeit affection for him and he shied away, eyes white all around. Gentlemen have such tender nerves. I pity them for it. I expect you know the sort of thing I mean very well. I do hope you let down the young ladies who wish you to wear their favour more gently than Mr Wulfstan did me. He all but galloped away from the house.

To return to the grave matter at hand, I assure you that Mr Wulfstan did ask for the music box. If my invitation to tea had failed, I was prepared to offer him a glance around Papa's workroom, but rest assured I have removed the pieces of the music box to a safer place.

I am glad you understand my reasons for ignoring your impulsive offer for a midnight excursion. I do hope Cecil is well enough to accompany you. I worry about him. I must confess he never showed any great aptitude for music before. He can just about oblige with a dance tune when we need one, but I'm sure the nearest he ever came to Tartini was an Italian tarantella.

As I have confessed that I am worried about Cecil and your sister, I may as well add that I worry about you as well. Take great care when you venture forth to meet Mr Wulfstan. There's something wrong with him.

Your friend,
Charlotte

My dear Charlotte,

I hope you will not take it amiss if I thank you for the first really good laugh that I have had all week. The image of Wulfstan being mercilessly flirted with brings me such joy as I had thought never to feel again, however fleeting. As Priscilla is always warning me, I am a creature of extremes—and I was very down in the darkness, foreseeing nothing but misery for me and mine, until you rendered me the delightful image of your tea party heroism.

For heroism it was, and virtuosity, as well. To Miss Prism's training go the Honours, perhaps; but to you, my dear, the Glory.

Oddly enough, my sister never told me about the wee paper spell. I expect she thought I would not be interested. It is possible, even, that she was right—until now! I feel sure that you are right about that, too, and that she will know exactly what you mean by it and be greatly heartened. Please do not be alarmed overmuch on her behalf. In the pair of us, she has two mighty champions.

I am glad to report that your brother Cecil is very well, indeed. His poetry is improving, and his hair, which was hitherto, as I (who have, I am told, no eye for style, so forgive me if I am mistaken) believe, a colour one would describe as an unexceptional brown, has, perhaps having grown out over the past few days, begun darkly curling over his forehead. He occasionally sweeps it away with the back of his wrist, particularly when performing a particularly intricate passage on the violin.

I will miss him and his playing. Whatever my deficiencies in the understanding of *style,* I do love beauty in all its forms. However, I would never presume upon a guest, particularly one in the grip of the Muse that has chosen to favour him. She is a fickle friend, as uncertain and unchancy as you yourself are not. I will return him to you, as promised, after tomorrow night.

Do not concern yourself overmuch with the music box and its fate. Indeed, if it were not for my determination to foil W. at every turn, I would say to give him the pieces and ~~be damned~~ and let him make of them what he will. Your brother wears the *Key* around his neck—did I ever thank you for returning it?—and all may yet be well.

I was a perfect fool to take the Music Box and Key to your father's that night—but such is my respect for him, my admiration for his work, and my hunger for his—I would write *Approbation*, but to a Friend let me confess it was more than that . . . I wanted to *show off* the splendour of mine own Working; to have your esteemed father pluck me from amongst the assembled crew of the Ambitious, the Inventive, and the Merely Curious, and proclaim me as one worthy of his own true respect and admiration, one fit to stand in his presence as a fellow.

And so I laid the groundwork for our current situation. W. must have heard of the event from one who was there and seized his chance to try to acquire that which he has long desired.

But enough of this. I hope your dear father is improved. I have ordered some grapes to be sent, as that is what people do when they hear someone is indisposed, and doing as others do is always, as I'm sure even Miss Prism would agree, the Right Thing.

Your giddy friend,
HN

―――――――

My dear friend,

Thank you for your kind thoughtfulness in sending the grapes to Father. I know he will enjoy them when he feels more himself. As it is, I have abused both his trust and the doctor's orders and put him to sleep with laudanum.

I sympathise entirely with your desire to attract my father's favourable attention. Indeed, I am no stranger to the impulse.

But he has taken strange paths in his study of the Experimental Arts. He meant that night to be wonderful, an opportunity to display his own work even as he invited the interested to exhibit their own. Something happened that night. You were there. You must remember. I don't know the nature of the miscarriage, but Cecil believes that something Father did to reduce the damage clouded his mind.

Now he wanders. It is all I can do to keep him safe.

Forgive me for permitting you and Cecil to face Mr Wulfstan alone. I would do anything to help Priscilla, but my first loyalty must be to Father.

Know that my thoughts are with you in your enterprise.

Yours,
Charlotte

―――――――

Miss Fleming,

Rash of you to risk a schoolgirl charm on an adept of the Experimen-
tal Arts. I hope it amused you. I divined it soon after I left your presence.
Now it amuses me to use it as a link between us. Come to the Crown and
Cripple at midnight tonight. Or I shall compel you to do so.

Wulfstan

C—

DO NOT LEAVE THE HOUSE TONIGHT! I cannot tell you m
NO NO I am Prisc ABCDEFGHILL ABCDEFGHILL ABCILLA

Charlotte—

After you read this, I pray you burn it, or at least place it somewhere
safe from all prying eyes. For while my soul rejoices in our victory, yet here
are some tales and truths which I would not see brought to the light of any
eyes but your own.

I write to you from my own home, where your brother Cecil lies sleeping deeply. When he wakes, I will send him home to you and your esteemed father—but that may not be for some time. I am at his side, but
cannot dream of sleeping now; and so, as the grey dawn creeps upon us, I
take pen in hand to tell you of last night's events.

I should not, perhaps, have chosen midnight for my rendezvous with
Wulfstan at that venerable establishment, the Crown and Cripple. The
streets were quiet, save for the bursts of late-night revellers, when Cecil
and I alighted from our carriage before its doors. The host, although he
must be older than God, seemed to recognise me even from long ago and
guided us into a private parlour, where waited Wulfstan in the flickering
light of tapers there.

As you may have surmised by now, Priscilla was with him.

My sister looked both like and unlike herself. Her eyes were bright,
but her visage dull. (I am pleased to report, though, that her nose was no
longer red.) I recognised a spell of some sort and said to Wulfstan without
preamble, "I know that you have already touched one lock of hair on my
sister's head. But if she is not returned to me as well or better as before—"

"Calm yourself, Humphrey," he replied. "I have but imposed upon her
the gift of silence. I cannot imagine you have never wished to do the same."

"For one of her temperament," I reproved him gravely, "such a spell is
insalubrious."

Ellen Kushner and Caroline Stevermer

"Perhaps," he said, in that manner of his that both you and I find so extremely distasteful. "So let us attend rapidly to the business at hand, that she may soon be restored to herself with no ill effect." He looked sharply at both Cecil and me. "I do not see the music box. I hope that is what your man is clutching so tightly there under his cloak. For if you deal double with me . . ." He did not finish the sentence—but looked, not at my sister, but at the door.

"Expecting reinforcements?" I asked.

"I have an eye for the ladies, Humphrey, as you know," said he portentously. It was appalling. He has no eye whatsoever. He has always coveted what was mine. When we were in Vienna—but you shall see. His words struck chill into me. For there was only one lady of his acquaintance I could imagine whose sudden appearance would make the slightest difference to me.

"Cecil," I said, as calmly as I could. "Pray take out your *music box.*"

At your brother's name, I saw Priscilla's eyes widen. True, he looked not much like his former self—that is, if you will forgive me, a scapegrace boy. Her eyes dwelt on the young man he was now become, as he produced the violin case. And Cecil looked over at her and smiled a smile of amazing beauty. My sister's lips parted as she would speak—but even with speech denied to her, the dullness left her features to be replaced by a look of perfect joy. What passed between them then there is no name for. I knew in that moment that, whatever else came of this night, they belonged to each other henceforth. Truly, it was something to behold.

Wulfstan, however, was not so pleased. "What nonsense is this?" he demanded when he saw the violin. "That is not—"

"Play," I told Cecil. "Play the tune I taught you."

Cecil put his bow to the strings and began to play.

> *Alas, alas, dear Augustine,*
> *All is lost to me, I ween . . .*

I could barely keep myself from singing the words aloud, so well-known to me were they.

And so well-known to poor Wulfstan, too. As the tune penetrated his senses, he heaved a great sigh, then another. I watched him in fascination in the candlelight, for it was like watching a great storm roll in across the ocean: first, he sighed like the wind, and then his visage grew dark, like storm clouds—and then he let out a great cry like thunder: "Villain! Traitor! Wretch!"

And then, like the rain when the clouds break at last, he began to weep—to sob, rather, with gusts as violent as any storm.

"What is it?" Priscilla cried, starting up. "What have you done?"

But your brother's playing was now at its most passionate—one almost might say demonic—in its brilliance. The tune seemed to express all loneliness, all sorrow and regret. Even me, it took back to our time in Vienna, W.'s and mine, when we both took refuge from the rigors of our study at the Heuriger Tavern, where the wine was fresh and the Liptauer strong; where a Danish barmaid named Inge—who knows how she landed in those mountains?—was also known to stand on a table and delight the assembled company with the songs of her native land . . . among them, that one.

That was the tune I had put in the music box. The box that was my masterwork, in our studies with Magister Ludo in Vienna.

Or so Wulfstan had believed.

And I had let him believe it. It was my way of mocking him. I did not tell him that the music box itself was *nothing*. I did not tell him that the KEY was the device into which I poured my heart and soul, and all my powers.

For, bosom friends as we long had been, he had failed to divulge to me a truth that, in friendship, he should have confessed: that it was he himself who had won the favours of the fair Inge. Knowing my heart as he did, yet he allowed me to endure her coldness, even her contempt, without having the decency to reveal to me the reason. He let me believe—but here, I blush and will say no more.

And so I found a master craftsman such as Vienna rightly boasts to fashion me a mechanism that would play that particular tune. And another to craft a box to house it in, decorated with elaborate marquetry, designed by me with Signs and Symbols evocative of the Experimental Arts.

I took them to the tavern and let her hear them. How she marvelled at their workmanship! And then very next day, I think it must have been, she threw him over—having naturally tired of him, as any woman must. For what mere toy would alter a woman's true affections?

But Wulfstan never knew the box and its contents were nothing. Gladly I brought them to your father's salon—yea, almost glad at this point to be rid of them, for they reminded me of my youthful follies.

It was the Key, the Key that was my masterwork.

And that Key, around Cecil's neck, has somehow acquired a power greater than I could well understand. I think, dearest Charlotte, that whatever happened that night at your father's salon, whatever the miscarriage of the intended experiment, it caused the key to become a nexus of power such as I had never imagined—and your poor father, spent with his labours to prevent further disaster, either knew not of it or was unable to tell us.

So Cecil played like a mad thing, and Wulfstan folded into himself in grief, and Priscilla, freed from his spell, still gazed in awe and joy at your brother, whose curling locks tumbled over his brow as he played.

"How like you my music box now, Wulfstan?" I said pitilessly. You had not yet come through the door, and I was determined that my triumph would be complete before ever you might cross that threshold. "What would you have done with the real one, I wonder? Tried to turn it to some purpose of your own? To bring her back with it? But she is gone, is she not, just as the tune proclaims! Or did you wish only to destroy my masterwork?" He dashed the tears from his eyes and gazed at me with malevolence. "It matters not," I told him. "The original is destroyed already."

At that, he gasped and flung back his head. "What?" he cried. "How?"

"An Experiment," I told him, "gone strangely awry."

He glared at me, as if his gaze could see past layers of meaning to the truth. "You're lying," he said.

But by then, I had Priscilla close by my side, clasped in one arm. "By what remains of my sister's hair," I said, "indeed, I am not. When last I saw it, the thing lay in pieces, just where you thought it was. There is no virtue left in it, I fear. And I have not the heart to refashion it."

Cecil's playing turned to a pretty, delicate air. Wulfstan peered at the violin. "And moved the virtue into that instrument, I'll warrant."

"Not at all. But if you want it—or if you don't believe me—take it. I make you a gift of it, Wulfstan, truly."

"Bah!" He actually said *Bah*.

"I insist. I will not have you accuse me of false dealing. I promised you the music box in return for my sister, safe and sound." I permitted myself a smile. "And a violin is a sort of box, you know, that makes music. If one has the skill. Or the inspiration."

He took it with a curse, but he took it, case and all, and left the tavern.

Since our days on the Continent, Wulfstan has clearly devoted himself far more assiduously to the Arts than I have. So I will not be at all surprised if he discovers fairly quickly that the violin, while in his possession, will keep him from finding his way to your father's house, no matter how many times he tries to get there. But I hope after a while he simply stops trying.

And I hope that your father continues to improve, enough that you might consider leaving his side to come to mine—only, of course, to make sure that Cecil is in satisfactory condition, to assure Priscilla that her hair, though slightly off-kilter, bears no resemblance whatsoever to the Lisbon Earthquake . . . and to accept, in person, the gratitude and affection of your

R

My Dearest Friend,

With a glad heart I will obey your summons, just as soon as Father has his breakfast and I have tidied the crumbs out of his beard. We will come together, and I know Father will be as amazed by your mastery of the Experimental Arts as you could wish, amazed and grateful for it.

You are not the only one who found it hard to sleep last night. Midnight had struck by the time I had my freedom back. Midnight and your rendezvous with Wulfstan. I could not stop pacing, although I knew not why. When your servant brought me your letter, at last I understood what I had been waiting for. I vow my knees were trembling when I sat by the fire to read it. I might have known you would outdo him. Thank God you have prevailed over that dreadful man.

I had a sense of my predicament shortly before Priscilla's warning reached me. Wulfstan was summoning me by the bit of charmed ribbon I'd slipped into his pocket. I had noticed the pull even before his message came, summoning me to the tavern. It was a slowly encroaching sense of uneasiness, a stirring of the roots of my hair, an intuition that grew into cold certainty that I must go to him.

I resolved to fight his summons. No adept of the Experimental Arts—not I—but I was the daughter of one, and of a grand one, too. It took me half an hour to find my way up the stairs to my father's room, such was the force of Wulfstan's summons.

Father's condition had improved as the day waned. By great good fortune, I found him awake and in his right senses. At once he perceived there was something amiss with me. I could not speak to tell him—a cruel refinement of Mr Wulfstan's spell. I had Mr Wulfstan's message in the pocket of my pinafore, but it took all the strength I had just to draw the folded paper from my pocket and hold it out to my father.

When he had read it, Father's face clouded with anger. When he spoke, he was perfectly lucid, but all he said was "Insolent puppy."

For the first time in two days, Father left his bed. He put on his dressing gown and slippers, then took me by the hand and led me slowly downstairs to his atelier, where he made sure I was comfortably seated before he set to work to break W.'s spell.

I fear you are correct about that awful night of the salon. Papa's power is sadly diminished. Now that his mind is clear, however, he has a lifetime of research to draw upon. Even a little magic can work marvels if applied at exactly the right time and place.

Father took a spool of black thread and put the end of the thread in my hand with orders to hold it tight at all cost. As I sat fighting the gnawing urge to leave the house and walk—or run—in what was no doubt the direction of the Crown and Cripple, it was all I could do to pinch the thread tight between my thumb and forefinger. Father took the spool of thread and measured it out, yard by yard, as he walked around me. He murmured hesitantly as he worked, words too soft for me to catch. This was a welcome change from his last visit to the workroom, where he howled useless invocations, yet it did not seem to do much. The summons to the Crown and Cripple grew stronger and stronger. I held the thread doggedly and did my best to ignore the summons.

Father shuffled around me with such deliberation I could not bear to watch him. Sometimes he stopped altogether, silent until he remembered what came next in his murmured chant. I had to close my eyes tight to shut out the sight of him doddering along in his slippers and dressing gown. What chance had such a pathetic old man against a spell cast by the ruthless Wulfstan?

I am devoutly grateful that the summons put a spell of silence on me, or who knows what I might have said, caught between despair and the call to the Crown and Cripple. I am glad I was mute, for none of my impatient thoughts were worth the breath to utter them.

From the moment Father completed his third circuit around me, so that I was looped three times in the black thread, the urgency of the summons eased. Father kept up his murmurs and his shuffling circuits around me. The thread, so loose as he had reeled it out, grew tight around me, but it did not break.

As the tension in the thread grew, the grip of Wulfstan's spell slackened. I found myself able to speak again. I thanked my father for his help and tried to explain to him how urgently Cecil needed us to come to his aid. I did not even try to tell Father about you and Priscilla. His attention was all on the spool of thread. No matter what I said, Father insisted I stay where I was lest the thread be snapped.

Midnight struck. Wild with longing to seek the Crown and Cripple, I begged Father to let me rise from my chair. Father paid me no heed. Time never passed more slowly, not even during Miss Prism's commencement speech, but at last Father held up his hand, as if listening to something far away, and the thread went quite limp around me.

I think that must have been the moment when Wulfstan began to cry, defeated by Cecil's wielding your magic.

I cannot wait to see Cecil for myself, not to mention his unaccustomed hairstyle, and I am all impatience to see Priscilla's new resemblance to the earthquake of Lisbon, but most of all, my dearest friend, I long to see you.

> When you see me, know that you see your own,
> Charlotte

About "The Vital Importance of the Superficial"

We met on Ellen's first day of college.

She was hanging her map of Middle-earth on the wall of her new dorm room in Denbigh Hall, just opposite the open door, and Caroline wandered by on the way to *her* room, and. . . .

What were the odds that a kid from the suburbs of Cleveland and a kid from a dairy farm in southeast Minnesota had grown up in the exact same place?

But, in a way, we had done just that: we had spent the years before we met reading all the same books, dreaming the same magical lands. . . . Cautiously, each admitted to the other that she was working on a story—well, a book, maybe, but the more cautiously named "story" for now. Cautiously, we showed each other our work and discussed our problems getting the stories to lie down properly.

We hung out on the fire escape of our ancient dormitory and made up more stories. We took long walks and shared more books. We played People, a game Ellen had learned in theater workshops, where one person thinks of a character they're working on, and the other asks them questions, and, magically, characters get deeper and richer, and story problems get solved.

Summer came. Caroline went back to the farm. No more daily conversation because long-distance phone calls were expensive then.

And no more People.

Until . . . there came a letter. We forget who wrote it. But it complained about life at court being so dull, except for a possible plot on the young queen's life . . .

The Letter Game had begun.

Years later, Caroline played it with fellow author Patricia C. Wrede in Minneapolis, and the *Sorcery & Cecelia* novels were born.

And then, just about a year ago, when Mesdames Datlow and Windling asked Miss Kushner when her story for *Queen Victoria's Book of Spells* was coming in, and in a panic she thought, *Story? What story?* . . . she remembered Caroline's expertise in Matters Nineteenth Century . . . and how much they used to love playing the Letter Game together.

And she sat down and wrote:

Madam: It will not have escaped your notice that on my last visit I left something behind . . .

And hit SEND.

THE JEWEL IN THE
TOAD QUEEN'S CROWN

June 1875

W hy, they are *quite* barbaric," the queen said to her prime min-
ister, making small talk since she wasn't actually certain where
Zululand was. Somewhere in deepest, darkest Africa. That
much at least she was certain. She would have to get out the atlas. Again.
She had several of Albert's old atlases, and the latest American one, a
Swinton.

Thinking about the problem with an atlas, and how—unlike the star
charts, which never varied—it kept changing with each new discovery on
the dark continent, she sniffed into her dainty handkerchief. She was not
sniffing at Mr Disraeli, though, and she was quite careful to make that
distinction by glancing up at him and dimpling. It was important that he
never know how she really felt about him. Truth to tell, she was unsure
herself.

"Barbaric in our eyes, certainly, ma'am," he said, his dark eyes gazing
back at her.

She did not trust dark eyes. At least not *that* dark. Give her good British blue any day. Or Albert's blue. But those dark eyes . . . she shuddered.
A bit of strangeness in the prime minister's background for all that she'd
been assured he was an Anglican.

"What do you mean, Mr Disraeli?" she asked. She thought she knew, but she wanted to hear him say it. Best to know one's enemies outright. She considered all prime ministers the enemy. After all, they always wanted something from her and only *seemed* to promise something in return. Politics was a nasty business and the Crown had to seem to be above it while controlling it at all times.

A tightrope, really.

She thought suddenly of the French tightrope walker at Astley's Amphitheatre who could stand on one foot on a wire suspended high overhead and dangle the other foot into the air. She and Albert had taken the children to see the circus several times, and it had occurred to her then that speaking with a prime minister felt just like that. She was dangling again today with only the smallest of wire between herself and disaster.

Disraeli was master of the circus now, and he frightened her as had her first prime minister, Lord Melbourne, who had been careful to try and put her at her ease. It took her a long time to find him amusing.

She thought dismally, *It will take even longer with Disraeli even though this is his second tour of duty.* She barely remembered that first time. It had been only seven years after dear Albert's death and she was still so deep in mourning nothing much registered, not even—she was ashamed to admit—the children.

"To the Zulus," Disraeli answered carefully, "what they do, how they live their lives, makes absolute sense, ma'am. They have been at it for centuries the same way. Each moment a perfection. Perhaps to them, *we* are the barbarians!" He smiled slowly at her over the flowered teacup.

I *am no barbarian,* she thought testily. You *might be one.* She sniffed again and this time cared little if he guessed she was sniffing at him. *All Jews are barbarians. Even if they—like Mr Disraeli—have been baptized.*

There, she had said it! Well, only in her head. And having made the pronouncement, she went on silently, *It is something they are born with. Eastern, oily, brilliant, full of unpronounceable magic, like that Rumplety fellow who spun straw into gold in the story Albert used to tell the children at bedtime.*

Part of her knew that what she was thinking was as much a fairy tale as the Rumplety one. Her mama used to say that Jews had horns, if you felt the tops of their heads. But now she knew that Jews had no such thing as horns, just hair. Albert had taught her that. It was an old story, long discredited, unless you were some sort of peasant. *Which I am certainly not!*

She looked directly at Disraeli, which was another thing dear Albert had taught her. It always disarmed the politicians. No one expected the queen to look directly at a mere jumped-up nobody.

But Disraeli seemed to be paying her no mind, looking instead at his polished nails rather than at her, his ruler, which was rude in the extreme. She recalled suddenly how attentive he had been the first time he was prime minister. What had he said? Something about "We authors . . . ," comparing his frothy romantic novels to her much more serious writing. She remembered that she had not been amused then. *Or now.*

She glared at him, willing him to look up. Those silly tangles of curls hung greasily almost to his shoulders. *That arch of nose. Those staring eyes.* She gave a little shudder, then quickly thought better of it and rang the bell for the server.

When the girl arrived, the queen said, "I have caught a chill, please bring me a shawl." Then she leaned back against the chair as if she did, indeed, feel a bit ill.

Disraeli finally looked up briefly, then looked at his nails again and did not ask if there was something he might do for her.

Jews! the queen thought. *No matter how long they have lived in England, converted, learned English, they remain a people apart, unknowable.* She did not trust him. She *dared* not trust him. Even though he was her minister. *Prime. Primo. First.* But she would never say so. She would never let him know, never let *them* know. Instead, she would make everyone think she actually liked him. It was for the best.

He may be prime minister now, she thought fiercely, *but soon he will be gone. All prime ministers disappear in time. Only I go on. Only I am England.* It was an agreeable thought and made her face soften, seeming to become younger.

"Ma'am?" he inquired, just as if he could read her mind.

"More tea, Mr Disraeli?" She was careful to pronounce all the syllables in his name just as the archbishop—who knew Hebrew as if it were his mother tongue—had taught her.

Just then the girl came back with the shawl, curtsied, gave it to the queen, and left.

Disraeli smiled an alarmingly brilliant smile, his lips too wet. Those wet lips made her shiver. He looked as if he were preparing to eat her up, like some creature out of a tale. *An ogre? A troll? A Tom Tit Tot?* She could not remember.

"Yes, please, ma'am." He was still smiling.

She served the tea. It was a homey gesture she liked to make when sitting with her gentlemen. Her PMs. It was to put them at ease in her presence. If they were comfortable, they were easier to manipulate. Albert didn't teach her that. Long before they'd met, she had figured it out, though she was only a girl at the time.

D israeli sat back in his chair, crossed his grasshopper-like legs, and took a long, deep sip of the Indian tea.

Does she really think, his mind whirling like a Catherine wheel shooting out sparks, *that I do not know about her atlas with all its scribbles along the sides of the pages? Or the pretence at being the hausfrau entertaining her "gentlemen callers"? Or what she thinks of my people?* He knew that in the queen's eyes—in all their eyes—he would always be tarred by the Levant.

He thought about an article he'd recently read in *Punch,* that rag, something about a furniture sale, that outlandishly mocked Jews: their noses like hawks', their money-hungry ways. He remembered one line of it where the good English Anglican buyer wrote, "Shall I escape without being inveigled into laying out money on a lot of things I don't want?"

He made an effort to become calm, breathing deeply and taking another sip of the tea before letting himself return to the moment.

Is the queen really so unaware of all the house spies who report to me? The gossip below stairs? Her son who will tattle on Mama at the slightest provocation? Does she not recognise that I am the master of the Great Game?

Without willing it, his right hand began stroking his left, an actor's gesture, not a gentleman's. But his mind never stopped its whirl. He remembered that he and the queen had had this same conversation about the Irish the first time he'd been her minister. And then a similar discussion about the Afghanistan adventure. To her they were *all* barbarians. Only the English were not.

Well, she may have forgotten what we talked about, but not I. It had been his first climb to the top of the greasy pole of the political world, straight into the Irish situation. There was no forgetting that! He had a marvellous memory for all the details.

Leaning back in the chair, he stared at his monarch, moving his lips silently, but no words—no English words—could be heard.

Across the rosewood table the queen slowly melted like butter in a hot skillet. A few more Kabbalistic phrases and she reformed into a rather large toad dressed in black silk, with garish rings on either green paw.

"Delicious tea, ma'am," Disraeli said distinctly. "From the Indies, I believe. Assam, I am certain."

The toad, with a single crown jewel in her head, poured him a third cup of tea. "Ribbet!" she said.

Though, Disraeli mused, *that is really what a frog says.*

"Oh, I do agree, ma'am," said Disraeli, "I entirely agree." With a twist of his wrist, he turned her back into Victoria, monarch of Great Britain and Ireland, before anyone might come in and see her. It was not an improvement. However, such small distractions amused him on these necessary visits. He could not say as much for the sour, little, black-garbed queen.

The queen sat quietly while her lady's maid pulled the silver brush through her hair. Tangles miraculously smoothed out, since she insisted that the maid put oil of lavender on the bristles.

"No one, ma'am, still uses lavender," the woman, Martha, had said the first time she'd had the duty of brushing out the queen's hair.

But Victoria had corrected her immediately. *Best to start as one means to go on,* she had thought. "I have used oil of lavender since I was a child, and I am not about to change now. I find the very scent soothing. It is almost magic." She had suffered from the megrims since dear Albert had passed over, and only the lavender worked. Albert would have called that science and explained it to her, but she was quite certain magic was the better explanation.

"What do you think of Mr Disraeli, ma'am? Have you read his novels?"

"I do not have time to read novels, Martha," the queen scolded, though she had indeed read *Vivian Grey* and found it lamentably lacking and exceedingly vulgar, and the ending positively brutal.

"But you read people so well, it must be like reading a book," Martha said, her plain, little face scrunching up as she worked.

"I do indeed read them well," Victoria said.

"And Mr Disraeli . . . ?"

"He is a puzzle," the queen said, a bit distracted. Normally she would never discuss her prime minister with a servant. But she knew that Martha was discreet.

"Puzzles are meant to be solved, ma'am," Martha ventured.

"Sometimes I think you are less a lady's maid and more a fool, Martha." Victoria turned and smiled. "And by that I mean no offence. I use the word in the old sense, like the fools who entertained the kings of England, with their wit and their wisdom."

"I couldn't be that kind of a fool, ma'am, being a mere woman." Martha swiftly braided the queen's hair and tied it with a band.

"Martha, did you not know that Queen Elizabeth had female fools?"

"No!" Martha's hand flew up to cover her mouth. "The blessed Elizabeth!"

"And her cousin Mary of Scotland as well. In fact she had three."

"That baggage!"

"I am tired. It has been a long day," the queen said. "Leave me."

"You will solve the puzzle of Mr Disraeli, ma'am," Martha said, helping the little queen to stand and easing her to the bed.

"Indeed I will," Victoria said, nodding her head vigorously. "Indeed I will."

Martha was pleased to see that the band held the braid's end. Some things she could do well. Even though she was a mere woman. Especially so.

Once home again at Hughenden, Disraeli could finally relax. He got into his writing clothes and headed out into the garden. As he walked the pathways, he nodded at one of the young gardeners, but said not a word. The servants all knew that when he was alone along the garden paths, going in the direction of his writing folly, he was not to be distracted.

No more playing at being the prime minister, he thought, and smiled to himself. *I am to be a writer for a fortnight.* He stopped, turned, looked back at his house, for once shining in the last rays of the day's sun.

He cared little that the nearest neighbours had mocked the fanciful pinnacles of his house, calling it witheringly "the little redbrick palace." It was his comfort and his heart's home. He'd heard that pitiful epithet for the first time from Mary Anne right after he'd transformed the place. Evidently her lady's maid had carried the tale to her and she then to him. She admitted it after he'd found her weeping in her beloved garden, sitting alone on a white bench.

Silly Peaches he called her because of her gorgeous skin, even though she was quite a few years older than he. "Silly Peaches, how does it matter what the unwashed masses say of the house. We adore it." He'd sat down beside her and put his arms around her then. "You know I married you for your money, but would do it again in a moment for love." In fact, as they both knew, she'd little money of her own. It had *all* been for love—the courtship, the marriage, the house.

Now that he was prime minister—again—the neighbours were creatively silent about the manor. And darling Mary Anne, dead these three years, couldn't have carried tales to him about the foofaraw even if the neighbours had still been talking.

But, oh—I'd let them natter on if only you were still here beside me, he thought, brushing away an actual tear, which surprised him as he'd begun the gesture without knowing a tear was falling.

Walking along the twisting paths to his little garden house, the place where he wrote his novels, though not his speeches, he forced himself to stop thinking about Mary Anne. He had planned a fortnight to set down the final draft of a climactic chapter of *Endymion* that had been giving him the pip. As long as there was no new disaster in the making that he had to deal with, he would surely get it done. But, as he well knew, the prime minister's vacations were often fraught.

Also, he wanted to read more about a particular sort of kabbalah that Rabbi Lowe had practised a century earlier. It was in a book he'd discovered in his father's library many years ago, after the old man had passed away. With all the horror about Mary Anne's death and the fuss about his being raised up again to PM, he'd misplaced the book and only recently rediscovered it.

What he knew about Kabbalah should have been deep enough already. He'd read a great deal about it. He understood the ten Sefirot, the division therein of intellect and emotion. He acknowledged as the Kabbalist did that there were forces that caused change in the natural world as well as corresponding emotional forces that drove people to change both the world and themselves. It was a fascinating idea, and he'd been playing with it for years.

First he had read about Kabbalah as an exercise in understanding where his ancestors had come from, and perhaps where his personal demons had come from as well, after an anti-Semitic taunt by O'Connell in Parliament to which he'd replied, "Yes, I am a Jew, and when the ancestors of the Right Honourable Gentleman were brutal savages in an unknown island, mine were priests in the *Temple of Solomon.*"

He'd turned again to Kabbalah when Mary Anne had died, hoping to
find solace in his reading. He had even built a Kabbalistic maze in the
garden where her gravestone rested, thinking that walking it might give
him some measure of peace.

Finally, he'd learned a few small Kabbalistic magics, such as the mo-
mentary transformation he'd done on the queen over tea. It was for a distraction, really, not that he put great store in magics. He put more in his
ability to change England—and thus the world—by improving the conditions of the British people. As he often told his colleagues in the House of
Commons, "The palace is unsafe if the cottage is unhappy."

But it was only when he'd flung himself back into politics, back into
the Great Game, that he realized why he'd really studied the old Hebrew
magics.

"If I can learn the great miracles, not just the puny little transforma-
tions, I can make England rule the world." He whispered the thought
aloud, in the sure knowledge that no one was near enough to hear him.
"And that will be good for the world, for Britain, and for the queen."

So thinking, remembering, justifying, and planning, he finally got to
the little folly he'd claimed for his writing. He stopped a minute, turned
his back on the building, and surveyed his land. It still surprised him that
he had such a holding having started from so little.

Then he turned, opened the door, and went inside, shutting out the
world.

T he queen was not amused. The prime minister was late. *Very* late. No
prime minister had ever been late to a meeting with the queen. Neither the death of a spouse or a declaration of war sufficed as an excuse.

She tapped her fingers on the arm of her chair, though she resisted the
urge to stand up and pace. It was not seemly for a queen to pace. Not
seemly at all.

When Disraeli finally arrived, nearly a half hour after he was supposed
to be there, in a flourish of grey morning coat and effete hand waves, she
was even less amused. She allowed him to see her fury and was even more
furious because of that, especially as he did not seem cowed by her anger.

"And where, Mr Disraeli, have you been?" She pointed imperiously at
the clock, whose hands were set on nine twenty-five, in a frown similar to
her own. She had already had tea and three small slices of tea cake, two
more than were absolutely necessary. Another black mark on his copybook.

"I'm sorry, ma'am. I'm afraid I overslept." His face was pinched as if he hadn't slept at all.

"Afraid . . . you . . . over . . . slept?" Each word was etched in ice. She no longer cared that she was showing how much anger she felt. She was the queen after all. "Have you not a man servant to wake you?" It was unheard of, in his position.

"I was writing late into the night, ma'am," he said by way of explanation, sweat now beading his brow. "In my garden folly. My servants know never to disturb me there. I fell asleep."

"In . . . your . . . garden . . . *folly?*" She could not find the words to set this thing aright between them, watching in horror as he took out a silver-grey handkerchief that matched his coat and wiped his brow.

"I could . . . show you the folly if you like, ma'am. It would be a great honour if you would visit Hughenden." He took an awkward breath. "There is a superb maze I can commend to you. It is a replica of the Great Maze mentioned in the Bible."

The queen could not think where in the Bible a maze was mentioned, and her hand went—all unaccountably—to her mouth as she used to do as a child when asked a question she should have been able to answer but couldn't. This was, of course, before she had become queen. *Long* before.

"King David's dancing floor," he said, as if he saw her confusion and sought to explain it to her.

She remembered King David dancing, but she thought that was simply done before the ark, not on any kind of dancing floor. There was a dancing floor in one of the Greek myths, she distantly recalled. Then she blushed furiously, suddenly remembering that King David had danced *naked* before the ark. It made her even angrier with Disraeli.

The gall of the man, saying such a thing to a lady. Saying it to the queen! She waved him away with her hand, waited to see him go.

Instead, his own hand described a strange arc in the air. She wondered if he was drawing the maze for her. She wondered why he did not leave. She felt dizzy.

"More tea?" she croaked, at the same moment realizing that he'd had none before. Her hand went a second time to her mouth and she felt sick. If she had been a man, she would have uttered a swear, one of the Scottish ones John Brown had taught her. They were perfect for every occasion.

⁂

The only way out of this situation, Disraeli thought, *is to go further in.* He turned the queen into a toad for a second time. He knew he must never do it a third. She might just stick that way. But at least it would buy him a little time. Time to figure out his next move, a move that—should it prove successful—would be for the glory of England and the queen. Would possibly mean an earldom for himself, though such would be worth so much less without Mary Anne alive to be his lady. Still, a peerage was hardly the reason he was doing this thing.

There is danger of course, he thought. *There is always a danger in such grand gestures. And such great magic.*

He'd stayed up all night thinking about all the aspects. He'd even written them down, the reasons for and against. The reasons *for* far outweighed the rest. His plan simply *had* to work.

The toad looked at him oddly, its green hands wrangling together. The jewel in its head is what had given him the original idea, that moment a week ago when he'd first turned the queen into the creature.

He didn't regret doing so then nor now. He might, he knew, regret it in the future. But that was part of the chance he had to take, for this was, indeed, the Great Game.

"Ah, Peaches," he whispered, "in the end it's all for love." *Love of queen and country,* he thought, though goodness knows she was a difficult woman to love, black-garbed Victoria, the Widow of Windsor, as the papers called her. *A child and a grandmother at one and the same time. Silly, small in temperament and understanding. Her mind only goes forward or back. Never up and down. Never through the twisting corridors like* . . . like his own mind, he supposed. *She simply isn't interested in* . . . *well, everything.* His mouth turned down like hers. *Albert, at least, had had a more original mind if a bit* . . . he smiled . . . *well, Germanic.*

He made another quick hand signal, and the queen became human again. Just in time.

"Fresh tea is here, ma'am," he said as the girl came in with the pot on a tray. "Shall I pour or will you?" He put a bit of persuasion in her cup, a simple enough bit of magic, along with the two lumps of sugar. He wasn't certain it would help, but knew it couldn't hurt, something his mother used to say all the time.

The Queen was a bit uncomfortable at Hughenden Manor. *All that red brick,* she thought with a shudder. *All those strange Gothicisms.* Still, she did nothing but compliment the prime minister. His taste was—the red-brick house notwithstanding—actually quite good. Looking back at the house, though, gave her a headache, so she looked ahead at the garden path.

To be fair—she always liked to think of herself as fair—*the ground-floor reception rooms with their large plate-glass windows are delightful. And the south-facing terrace, overlooking the grassy parterre, has spectacular views over the valley.* She said it to plant the words firmly in mind for when she spoke of the house later to her family. She wondered where Disraeli had made his money, worried that it might have been in trade. *It can't have been from those books.* She shuddered.

The day was cool but not cold, the skies overcast but not yet raining.

"A lovely afternoon for a walk in the garden, ma'am," Disraeli said.

For once she agreed. Though she was used to her black garments, her stays, they made walking in the summer heat unbearable. Usually, she would be tucked up in her bedroom, a lavender pomander close by, ice chips in a glass of lemonade.

"Lovely indeed." She put her hand on his arm, which allowed him to help her along, he straight-backed and she nodding approvingly at the gardeners and subgardeners busy at work but who stood appropriately and bowed as she passed.

Well done, she thought.

The gardens, while not nearly as extensive as her own, of course, were nicely plotted and cared for, the grass perfectly cut and rolled. The flowers—banks of primroses, and a full complement of bedding plants—were in the formal part of the garden surrounding a great stone fountain. She must remember to ask about the fountain later when Disraeli would certainly introduce her to the head gardener.

There was also a lovely, intimate orchard of apples and pears, only a few of them espaliered, as well as a fine small vinery. None of it was too much. It was rather perfect, and the controlled perfection annoyed her slightly. She wanted to find something to scold him for, or to tease him about, and could not.

Disraeli was in full spate about the gardens, the plants, the hedges and sedges, the blooms. But as they headed toward the folly and the maze beyond, he grew unaccountably silent.

I do hope he has no political agenda on his mind, she thought a bit sniffily. *It would not do to spoil a lovely day out of doors with such talk.* She simply would not allow it.

She was still thinking about this when the sun came out and she began to perspire. It gave her something else to gnaw on.

Now that he'd enticed the queen into the garden, and they were approaching the maze, Disraeli was suddenly full of apprehensions. *What if it is dangerous? Or if not actually dangerous, perhaps wrong? Or if not wrong, perhaps even unsupportable.* He had tested the maze many times over the last few weeks, using first an undergardener, then his secretary, even his dog. They were all easily tricked into doing his bidding, by a sort of autosuggestion. Only it wasn't like that German impostor Mesmer a century earlier. There was real magic in the maze. It made the things he wanted to happen, happen.

But, he thought, the worry turning into a stone in his stomach, this is the queen, *not an undergardener or a secretary.* He felt the pressure of her hand on his arm and turned to give her his most brilliant smile. *She may be resistant to the magic. She may not be so suggestible. She is possibly . . .*

Then he saw a bead of sweat on her brow and chuckled inwardly. *A queen I have twice turned into a toad with a jewel in its head,* he reminded himself. *She is as human as I.* "Ma'am?"

"Are we almost there, Mr Disraeli?" she asked, like a child in a carriage agonizing about the rest of a long trip.

He wondered if the heat was getting too much for her. *All that black silk. And she is no longer a slender, young thing.*

"Just on the other side of that small rise," he said, pointing with his left hand, past the folly that commanded the top of the little hill. "There is a bench at the centre of the maze that will make the perfect garden throne. You shall rule my garden, ma'am, and my heart from there."

"Then I shall have to solve the maze quickly, to get to that throne." She smiled winningly up at him, almost as if they were a courting pair.

"*All* thrones in England belong to you, ma'am. And in the Empire as well." There, his plan was begun.

He recalled saying to a friend long ago, during his first turn as prime minister, that the way to handle the queen was that one must, first of all, remember that she is a woman. He had all but forgotten his own advice over the past few years, so he added, "If I had my way, you would rule the world." *Everyone likes flattery, and when you come to royalty, you should lay it on with a trowel.* Step two in his plan. He wondered if he was succeeding in planting the seed.

She patted his hand. "Perhaps that would overreaching, even for you, Mr Disraeli." But she said it lightly, as if she hadn't dismissed the notion entirely, nor should he. "To the maze then."

"You are, ma'am, the quickest woman at puzzles I have ever known. I think you will have no trouble at all with my little maze." He knew he had, indeed, laid it on with a trowel, but evidently he had said the exact right thing for she was grinning broadly.

"So I have been told, and recently. Though *you* are the maze, dear sir."

He had no idea what she meant and no reason at all to follow up the conversation.

They walked on, she clinging even more tightly to his arm.

At the top of the rise, she stopped as if to admire the view, which was quite lovely. But really, it was so she could catch her breath. Below, where the hillock smoothed out once again, was the maze. It did not look particularly difficult to her. She could see immediately straight into the heart of it.

Lightly, as if she were once more the girl she had been when she ascended the throne, she let go of Disraeli's arm and began to run down the hill, a kind of giddiness sending her forward.

She gave no thought to the man behind her. She never gave any thought to the men behind her. Not even dear Albert. Or dear Mr Brown.

Her delighted laughter trailed behind her like the tail of a kite.

Disraeli was overcome with fear, and it almost riveted him to the top of the hill. The queen, corseted and bonneted, was bouncing along like an errant ball let loose by a careless boy. Any moment she might come crashing down, and with it, all his dreams.

He *was* the careless boy, letting the ball go. What had he been thinking! This was madness. All his calculations for naught. The maze all by itself was exerting a gravitational pull on the queen, and neither he—nor God, he supposed—knew how it was going to end.

He pulled himself loose of his fear and began to run after her. "Ma'am!" he cried. "Take care. The stones . . . the hill . . . the . . ."

But he needn't have worried. She reached the bottom without misstep and threaded through the maze as if it were a simple garden walk. Before he was down at the hill's bottom himself, she was already sitting on the stone bench, huffing a bit from the run, her face flushed, a tendril of greying hair having escaped from the bonnet and now caressing her right cheek-bone.

"Ma'am," he said when he got to the centre, "are you all right?"

"Never better." She looked, somehow, years younger, lighter, happier. She held out her hand and he knelt.

He realized then how foolish he had been, playing about with kabbalistic magic. *She* was the royal here, as high as King David. He knew now that he was only a minor rabbi in this play. *Of course she can command the magic, whether or not she knows it is here.*

"What you will, ma'am."

"I *will* be an empress." She smiled down at him. "But I will *not* ask to be higher, not like the foolish old woman in the story Albert used to tell the children."

"I *can* make you an empress, ma'am. But will you allow me one question?"

"Of course I will allow it."

Still kneeling, he asked, "What story, ma'am?" He wondered if he would ever understand this woman.

"She wanted to be God," the queen mused.

"Why would anyone want to be God? It's a terrible occupation."

"Ah—that is two questions, dear man. And that I will *not* allow." But she was joking, he could tell, for a coy smile hesitated at the corners of her mouth.

He felt he was back in familiar territory and grinned at her. "I will make you Empress of India, ma'am. It will be the jewel in your crown." He dismissed the toad out of mind. It was as if the toad had never happened. *"Forti nihil difficle."*

"Nothing is difficult to the strong. That will be a fine start," she answered. "Now get off your knees, man, we have work to do."

The queen looked at Disraeli, at his sweet curls, his liquid eyes. She thought that she liked him best of any of her prime ministers. And if he *did* somehow manage to make her Empress of India, pushing it through a recalcitrant House of Commons, why, she was certain that she could find him his just reward.

He has, she thought, *a most original mind. Funny, I have only now noticed. It's just like Albert's, if a tiny bit more . . . more . . .*

She could not think what, until finally it came to her . . . *more Jewish.*

That made her laugh.

And he, standing up at last, laughed, too, though whether he quite understood the joke was another matter altogether.

About "The Jewel in the Toad Queen's Crown"

My interest in Disraeli and Queen Victoria began a number of years ago when I included the scene of his turning Victoria into a toad within a much longer story called "The Barbarian and the Queen, Thirteen Views." I always wanted to revisit, rewrite, and reimagine those few short paragraphs in a longer story, so when the invitation came for this anthology, I jumped at the chance.

In 1876, Disraeli did make Victoria Empress of India, and India became known as the Jewel in the Crown. She conferred upon him the title of first Earl of Beaconsfield that same year, a title he held until his death five years later, though in private she called him Dizzy. As he lay dying, Victoria asked to come and see him. But he wrote back saying, "No, it is better not." To his secretary he said, "She would only ask me to take a note to Albert." When he died, Victoria sent a wreath "from his grateful and affectionate Sovereign and friend, Victoria R.I.," the *I* standing for "India." She lived for twenty more years after Disraeli and never forgot him. If that odd friendship came out of mutual admiration, mutual interests, or magic, it is not for me to say. I only speculate.

A Few Twigs
He Left Behind

Scrooge was dead; no doubt about that. Dead, and laid out in the parlour as lifeless as last night's boiled ham hauled out of the larder for today's cold luncheon. Pure dead, with a relaxed face more waxy than the popular masks of Madame Tussaud, currently available for inspection, for a small fee, at the Baker Street Bazaar. Not that he could scrutinise them now! Two copper pence put paid to his vision by being set upon his eyelids. The last two pence to his name, whispered the laundress, perhaps given to exaggeration, though considering the rate of her salary, she might be presumed to have an inkling about Scrooge's finances. She took care to be seen bowing her head in respect if not quite prayer, and she took greater care not to be seen lifting one of the two coins and slipping it in her sleeve. Why not both? The better to preserve the fiction that one had rolled off into a floorboard chink. In any case, the depressed eyelid did not lift in response. His eye must know there was nothing left to look at here.

His hands, that had grasped so much in life, now held nothing but each other, across the thready greatcoat.

Unseemly, as they waited for news of the hearse, that the body should stiffen upon the dining table. Why wasn't Scrooge laid out in his huge old bed, wondered Miggs Oystery. In the old days his charwoman, she had been promoted to laundress by Scrooge after his former washerwoman,

Mrs Dilber, passed away. She remembered that colossal cage of furniture, did our Miss Miggs. High, musty canopy, carven headboard like a wooden tombstone large enough for the commemoration of a whole avalanche of crushed orphans. Posts on the four corners, turned on Satan's lathe, she'd have said, all over carbuncled with gargoyle limbs and blind cartouches and pouting walnut-faced cherubs and other Italianate foofrumpery. And the plum velvet bed-curtains on their rattling rings! The moths might have chewed the fabric airy since the last time she'd been in there. No, that room, Scrooge's room, had remained closed and locked these ten long winters since Scrooge lost his mind and became sweet on humanity. At least so far as Miggs Oystery knew, and she knew quite a lot. And might tell you, for a ha'penny.

So here he lay, as no gentleman should, upon a dining table, where his remains might startle any mice that had not long since cleared out of these premises due to the mingy leavings. The table was too short to accommodate Scrooge's feet, which projected off the end like two leathery levers for the operation of some handsome machinery. If the family would only cease their whimpering and sniffling, Miggs would like to have tugged on a foot or shifted a calf to see if she could raise the dead—old Scrooge!—and make him say if he had hidden some final scrap of his fortune someplace else, where she might find it before his heirs and assigns could get a hold of it.

But, no, that nephew Fred *would* keep the vigil. "In his old age, he learned to stand by me," said Fred, through his tears, "and by God, I shall stand by him this final day." As to his sentiments, Fred Jauntleby was a fool, thought Miggs, a roly-belly'd fool. But in the science of commerce he was more adept. He had made a plumper success of Scrooge and Marley's than the founders themselves, and the buttons on his waistcoat strained to hold the proof in place. "Dame Oystery, suffer not the wretched infants to see their father in this fashion. Surely there is some place you can take them while I wait for news from the undertaker's boy?"

"We want to stay," said grave, pious Phoebe.

"Yes, unless there is supper to be had somewhere else," said her twin, Simon, for whom hunger had the sooner claim than sorrow.

"We *must* stay," declared Phoebe. A slip of a child, perhaps nine, grey from grief and a life spent in shadows. Her blond looks had scarcely seen sunlight long enough to become burnished by it. "With Mama so recently . . . gone . . . I must take her part and attend her husband's body, the way he attended hers."

Fred Jauntleby shook himself free from grief long enough to take control. "I won't hear of it. There is nothing you can do for him now. Simon, you brave boy!—and dear Phoebe: You must go somewhere with Miss Miggs. Let her take you out of the house this day, as we await the hearse. There is enough death crouching for you in the future to learn its customs then. Miss Miggs?"

"I am engaged as laundress," said Miggs Oystery, "not as governess, good sir." She spat the honorific as if it were a particularly tired wodge of chewing tobacco. Miggs Oystery was a stalk of a woman, a shoot of an onion top, thin from pelvis to narrowing forehead, upon which perched a spiky feathered cap whose plumes had been starched till they stood up like a military salute. Below her waist, though, the swollen aspect of onion-ness took over; her hips and backside rounded out and were not flattered by the peplum she wore in times of moral panic, to give her strength of appearance and, if you will forgive the phrase its undertones, bottom.

"Still, goodness requires it," said Fred to the laundress. "You shall not go unrewarded."

"Well, then, if goodness is to take hold of me in its teeth and require the offices of a prison-yard monitor, I should think I could manage," said Miggs Oystery. "Children, collect your scarves and such; for it is a bitter day and wild, as befits a morning of mourning. The winds are Tartar hordes come in from the Russian steppes and, given half a chance, would bully your limbs from gutter to graveyard. We shall huddle in some gin cellar and take comfort there."

"No," cried Fred Jauntleby, whose personal acquaintance with gin afforded him an informed opinion of its circle of admirers. "Take them . . . well, take them up to the Cratchit home, in Camden Town," he told the laundress. "Old Mrs. Cratchit has raised a passel of children and will know what to do."

"I've washed and rinsed and dried for this pair," groused Miggs. "I can handle them in any gin cellar by having them sing songs from chapel." Her grin was horrible, and she didn't relinquish it until Fred Jauntleby had supplied her with another few coins. Then, turning them away from their stiffening father, she bustled Phoebe and Simon to the basin, for laving with a face flannel and a scrap of pumicey lye.

Over the rim of the chipped basin Phoebe looked out across the room upon their final parent, as if she and Simon were to be taken away forever to be sold to those Tartar winds. His hands folded so compactly upon the fallen shield of his chest. Not so much as a guinea left to his name, to clutch as a bribe to Charon or to pay as fealty to Saint Peter.

He was gone. Who could defend them now?

Phoebe knew it would not be Fred, could not be Fred. He was a good soul, and when their mother had died a few months ago, he had attempted to collect his young cousins under his wing, until Scrooge had bellowed "No!" and required them to return. Fred was a bachelor dandy with tastes in travel and sherry and questionable company; and while his heart was warm, his attention on anything but business and his own pleasure was faltering at best.

Miggs Oystery, though, would sell them as soon as not, without Scrooge to defend them, or Fred to remember about them. The laundress scoured behind Simon's ears as if he were a stain and she an abrasive. Phoebe sniffled, Simon howled, and cousin Fred stalked up and down the room, as much to keep warm as to distract himself from the commotion and the atmosphere. For the room was unpleasant and had been quite unpleasant enough before being ornamented with a corpse.

In all his long life in business, Scrooge had never given up his original rooms, a capacious but sorry set of plaster-ceilinged chambers on an upper floor above a brewer's warehouse. The apartment had been organised for some magnate of hops, perhaps; surely it was well positioned to serve as a post from which to listen and see if barrels were being stolen in the dread dead of night. As such, the rooms must have been handsome enough, once. Once!—but "once" disappears faster than the foam on a glass of porter. On certain winter mornings Phoebe would awake and find that the ceiling of the cramped antechamber she shared with Simon had gone white with frost, and icicles formed on the wall and sometimes drove bolts across the jamb of the door, so they snapped when the children arose to seek their father and mother—back when both were still in the land of the living!

Oh, to lose a pair of parents while still nothing but goslings in the space of a year, even before one achieves a decade of life's experience—to learn so suddenly about *past* when one has hardly yet had a chance to conceive of the present! Yet perhaps that is the only way the present is ever noticed, as the forward crust of the ever-receding past.

This was the past:

Some ten years earlier, Scrooge had met Claudia Lefebvre, sweet slip of a daughter accompanying her trading-merchant father, who had come over from the port of Le Havre in the first days of the new year to settle some business and beg for clemency. Scrooge had surprised the sceptical merchant by driving the bargain of his life: dismissing the Frenchman's debts while sweeping his pretty, innocent daughter off her feet with a genuine storm of passion all the more intense for having been denied for so long. Claudia, nearer April than May as the seasons of womanhood chart it, had been as bewildered by Decemberish Scrooge as by the entire nation of Britain, but as she had agreed to travel in order to see what it was like, she had to concede that travel seemed to be like an unexpected romance, a swift marriage, and a sudden pregnancy, and a sure surprise when the offspring were nearly as multiple as her happiness. Phoebe and Simon first, then Laetitia and Serenissima, Pearl, Tarquin and Dorcas, finally Cincinnatus. But only the oldest two, the initial pair of twins, survived their first year. The others waited in the graveyard for their father to be laid next to them and to their mother, so recently dead in childbirth, so quietly reunited with infants she could never raise.

As Claudia had grown paler with each pregnancy, each new sorrow or pair of sorrows, she had kept her healthy surviving twins closer and closer to her side. All the while, Scrooge rambled farther and farther afield every day, spilling cheer like a welcome plague through Wapshot and Clerkenwell, Shoreditch and Lincoln's Inn Fields, Lambeth and Mile End and Aldgate and St. Paul's Churchyard. His family did not question him for this, not a one of them: not his nephew Fred, nor his young wife, not the two lisping children who were the summary pride and final surprise of his twisted, long life. A man can be sane and mad at once, and Scrooge's aberration did not take the form of brutality. No! But it exacted a penance of want upon his own family, to which, wanting little himself, he proved blind.

In spring the rich reward of green never sparkled even through windowpanes, as the building that housed the Scrooge apartments was buried deep in a yard of warehouses around which not even a wisp of weed dared root. Summer sunlight was a mere legend whose existence was proven only by the sweltering heat, which made wallpaper in the parlour curl and ants swarm the sills. Then autumn came around again, and once more

Claudia Scrooge took up the tutoring of the Scrooge children, as their father drifted out to his old offices, scooping from the coffers as much as Fred Jauntleby would allow his uncle without paupering the concern. And then while Claudia and Phoebe and Simon made the most of scraps, old Ebenezer scattered the coin of his prosperity upon the indigent of London, deserving or not.

The doctors who out of mercy tended the starving poor found hampers from Fortnum's upon their examination tables, without any tag to advertise the secret donor. The ministers who comforted the homeless were delivered stacks of blankets for dispersal. Orphanages received bins of colourful toys and buckets of milk, and no question asked could ever generate an answer, for the delivery lads knew an extra coin depended on their silence as to the origin of these mysteries. And every night Scrooge would lumber home and climb the broad staircase in the hunchbacked building in the least residential neighbourhood of old London town, erected on the graveyards of Romans and Saxons and Normans, Vikings and Visigoths and ten million unnamed vermin. Then Scrooge would reward his darling Claudia, his Simon and his Phoebe, with tales of his charitable subterfuge, and the joy with which the anonymous gifts were presumably received. As they gnawed their grey bread and drank watered water, Scrooge's wife and his children were happy enough for the relief of the misery of others. They took for nourishment the feast of light in Scrooge's tired eyes, his affection for them, his tenderness, the stories he told of what he had seen.

The stories were, some of them, hard to countenance. But as children grow on stories almost as surely as they grow on milk, Phoebe and Simon had thrived, within the safe garden of their mother's attention and their father's love.

Phoebe recovered from her meditations at the sound of a knock. Cousin Fred went to confer, mutteringly, with a lad from the concern that would inter old Scrooge, sooner or later. Fred came back to them, looking pale. "Mind you wind that muffler close, Master Simon," said Fred, and then he stooped to lace more tightly the strings of Phoebe's bonnet.

"If we're going, we're going at once, or we'll not be able to return by daylight," groused Miggs Oystery. "Unless you plan me to leave them there overnight."

"Perhaps it would be wisest," said Fred. "With the bitter cold, many elderly of this parish have succumbed to their final rest, and I have just now learned that the good fellows at Plott and Blackheath's cannot promise to collect old Uncle Ebenezer until sunset."

"With luck the cold might carry off a few more," said Miggs, "to reduce their misery." She nodded at her charges.

"We will not stay away this full night," cried Phoebe, "we will return to salute our father's final departure."

"Is there no warmer wrap for Phoebe?" asked Fred. "Even some shawl in Scrooge's old chamber, forgotten on a stool, that might be used to afford more protection against the teeth of the wind?"

"But the old chamber is locked these many years," said Phoebe. "As long as we have lived here, our father never went in or out that door, but kept it shut, and said he had had the sleep of his life in that room and wanted no more of it, wanted to be awake for the rest of his life."

"A laundress has a key for every keyhole," said Miggs Oystery, and pulled from beneath her apron a ring worthy of a jailkeeper. Knucklebones of iron, winged twists of iron, toothed sticks of iron, pronged twigs, hard-combed forks of iron, of every size and clattery tone, all black, all sombre, keys to every manner of secret that human minds can imagine. "Once a year I used to do that bedding, whether old Ebenezer Scrooge believed it was warranted or no."

"Allow me to settle another sum upon you, for your kind offer," said cousin Fred, "and you shall be able to take a hansom cab to Camden Town." And torn between haughty officiousness and the chink of plunder, Miggs surrendered her keys to the children, so she could stand with hand out-stretched as Fred fumbled for coin.

"Shall I go with you, Phoebe?" asked Simon. Without waiting for permission, he accepted the anointed key from the hand of the laundress, and the two bereaved children crossed the corridor at the top of the stairs to fit the key in the resistant lock, and to struggle with it, and finally, with as much a sense of dread as of excitement, to push the old door to.

The odour of stale air didn't so much rush at them as flood up from the dusty carpets and table linens. A dressing gown that hadn't been touched in ten years lay thrown upon a chair with its neck back, its arms akimbo, as a body might slump backward had its throat been slit by an assassin approaching from behind. Any old candles had been nibbled to nubs by long extinct rodentia. In casements of rotting wood were fitted squares of filthy glass; days of soot and fog had left their dirty breath, as months drifted past, rubbing out the view, and years tried without success to peer in. The room was sunk in preternatural gloom.

"Any clothing in here would make me feel colder, not warmer," said Phoebe. "I wouldn't wear an ermine cloak from this room."

"You couldn't find it without a miner's lamp, anyway," said Simon. "Do you think maybe Father hid some money for us here?"

"He could never have done that. He refused to come in or out of this space."

"Well, he was here once," said Simon, indicating the dressing gown. "Maybe he hid something under the bed."

Neither of them cared to look under the bed. But to prove she was not terrified of everything, Phoebe went to the window and managed to reach the high latch, and she pulled the cold iron fitting on one side of the casement.

With a screech of old warped wood, one half of the window scraped outward, inch by noisy inch. Oh, it was a tall window, and the shape of the space from sill to ceiling was long and narrow, like that of a coffin standing on end, and suddenly—puff!—a flurry of snow sifted into the room, on a slope of air that was hardly colder than the unheated chamber but was, at least, fresher. The snow hung in the air with a confusion of hesitations so that it almost seemed like a form, a human form hovering forward. It is my twisted nerves, thought Phoebe, and her heart caught in her throat; and she heard Simon gasp beside her; but then the atmospherics relaxed, and the dust-like white powder glinted at an angle upon the sill and the carpet. A staggered parallelogram of cold light fell in a laddered slant across a small table just inside the window. In the gloom the children had not seen it yet. Upon the table squatted a mug of vitreous porcelain that had once, perhaps, held a portion of hot milk to soothe the nerves of some agitated insomniac. Milk there was not, nor even the rank smell of milk that has dried away. But in the mug stood two sprigs of holly. Improbable, or impossible, but the holly twigs sported leaves of evergreen and plump, round, scarlet berries as fresh as any seasonal flower or fruit in its own time.

"But no one has been here in years," whispered Simon, offering objection to the apparent illogic of the vision. "How did they get here? And so live!"

"This is all the inheritance we're going to find," said Phoebe crossly, but she snatched up the two twigs and put them for safekeeping in her muff. "Come, or Miggs Oystery will lock us in here, and good, distracted Fred will soon forget he ever had a pair of young cousins."

Now, as each of the children clasped a hand of the deputy governess, they felt a shameful twinge of excitement to be escorted down the broad, broad staircase, down which their father's corpse would be carried in a few hours' time; but they thrust that thought behind them and allowed themselves to be pushed by Miggs Oystery through the vestibules and pestered past the porches, and driven through the tawdry, scrap-strewn yard and across the snowy cobbles, out the street door, out into the angled lane, out into London on a wide, blank day of grief and snow.

For a frozen ambulatory onion, Miggs Oystery could cover some ground at a clip. She surged into the wind with the two orphans trailing after her, one at each side, hurrying to keep up, buffeted by the bucking speed of her passage as two small coracles might be if only loosely tied to the gunwales of a smart, trim schooner. "I like the cold, it is good for clear thinking, and it quiets the stink of the street," she said with relish. "Simon, stop snivelling, death is an everyday affair in London, you will come to notice, as regular as the great bell at Mary-le-Bow; and after all, he was only old Scrooge. He had a life for himself, long enough, no complaints."

"Though he is old, yet he is our father," sniffled Simon.

"He *was* your father. Time passes, and so do men. Phoebe, what are you pawing at in your hand muff?"

"I am trying to keep from dropping it," replied she, "as I have only one hand to clutch it close . . ."

"Faster we walk, sooner we're there, and sooner I am rid of you," said Miggs.

"Are we not to hail a hansom carriage?" asked Phoebe.

"Working your limbs warms you the better and saves me the coin."

The air filled with the ringing of bells. "It is musical to be out on the street like this," said Simon. "But I should have thought there would be more people about."

"Everyone is scared they might meet the corpse of your father being dragged by his heels somewhere," groused Miggs. "Christ, but it's icy."

"Are the bells for his death?" asked Phoebe.

"Thick as last year's treacle, she is," said Miggs. Then they could talk no more, as the wind and the frost made their teeth chatter. Phoebe kept the muff lifted up to her lips and nose, and Simon sank into the coils of his scarf like a turtle retreating into its chamber.

On this rare lonely, icy day, the absence of carriages might have indicated unlikely kindness to dumb animals, for even a beast would shiver, thought Phoebe. The birds were gone, huddled into some congress of warmth under an eave somewhere, no doubt. Passing St. Paul's, the children heard a rare, solemn melody issuing from a giant harmonium, but Miggs would not let them stop to listen. "You'd freeze stock-still like one of them statues up top," she said, "and I can't have that, not as I'm paid only a hardship wage, no, sir."

Then even Miggs found the wind whipping off the Thames too much, and a mercy of sorts was afforded them on this clouded day: a charabanc came tipping around a street corner, and what did Miggs do but bellow for it to stop and bid them enter! For a moment Phoebe thought, She is kidnapping us to sell us into servitude, but the thought of serving someplace kitted out with a pot-bellied stove or a kitchen hearth was alluring, and Phoebe scrambled into the vehicle, and Simon followed her.

Miggs gave the address and climbed aboard herself. The inside of the carriage was nearly as cold as outside; there was rime-frost on the cracked slat of the seat; but at least they were squarely out of the wind, and the carriage moved faster than laundress and orphans could ever have done on shank's mare. They quickly passed beyond any neighbourhood Simon or Phoebe could recognise, and the dark, smoke-stained buildings seemed less imposing but more menacing, the steps to their entrances lower and closer to the kerb, the windows fewer, and hung with rags, if hung at all. There was no tree to be seen, living or dead.

"Ah, we're here," said Miggs at last, and took a coin from some deeply secure vault plunged in the front of her blouse. "Get out, you scamps, or I'll leave you here like lost valises and forget to claim you."

Perhaps she had not paid a full fare, for the driver cursed her roundly, but Miggs Oystery drove her charges down a few steps and through a door with a cracked pane, into a small, panelled vestibule, where she composed herself and called, "Greetings of the season to the Cratchit establishment, if you please!"

The door flung open, and there stood a gangly, grinning Punch of a fellow; a Pierrot; a soapbox orator preaching the gospel of laughter. His hair was mussed up as if he had just been called from a parlour game, and, indeed, over each shoulder came volleys of laughter and cries of "Hurry, Papa!"

"Mister Cratchit, I am Miggs Oystery, until recently, as which I mean to say until this very morning, an employee in the domestic situation of"—she paused with the timing of a seasoned performer on the sawdusty boards of the London Music Hall—"of the late Ebenezer Scrooge." She primped to affect an impression of grand desolation.

Bob Cratchit snatched at his throat and his ruddy face paled. "May the good Lord have mercy on his soul," he cried, and would have said more, much more, but catching sight of Phoebe and Simon shyly waiting behind the satisfied Messengeress of Doom, he reached one arm out to each, and the children rushed forward. "You have done well to bring the children here," he said. "My Caroline will feed them up a good meal as befits the day, happy as it is while being now tainted with sadness, and in all its anniversaries to come, forever more."

"I shall not want payment for the delivery of these grieving young things," said Miggs, pausing to handle her reticule with deliberation.

"Of course not," said Cratchit, "but you shall have it anyway. Caroline, my purse, if you will. Might we implore you to sit and feast with us, Mrs Oystery?"

"I'm neither Mrs nor Miss, I remain simple Miggs; that's good enough for the likes of me," said she, accepting a little clink of coin while attempting a curtsy that looked more like an expression of lumbago. "I've matters to see to involving the affairs of old Scrooge, you see. His nephew is waking the body until the undertakers arrive, but there are matters of hygiene only a laundress knows how to handle. The bed-curtains need pulling down at once before pestilence and plague set up housekeeping there and bring down half of London-town."

Cratchit signalled to his good Caroline, and Mrs Cratchit hustled the children away. The poor orphans did not give Miggs Oystery so much as a backward glance, and Mrs Cratchit, who had children of her own, took notice of this. She shot that sort of look between husband and wife that can speak volumes in instants, and Bob trusted his wife's common sense enough to escort Miggs Oystery to the door with greater speed than might have been seemly.

But Phoebe and Simon noticed none of this. They were gaping at a table of food before them. A great steaming goose lay surrendered upon a platter, heaped round with small steaming potatoes and Brussels sprouts and onions, and its crackling skin was more golden and holy than the halo on any Renaissance Madonna. A bowl with gravy dripping over the lip stood nearby, and another bowl of yet more potatoes, these ones creamed and pulverized and glazed with pats of melting butter. And a king's ransom of red chutney here, and a pharaoh's trove of candied carrots there, and simple brown, glazed mugs already filled with ale, and a pile of mince-meat pasties shaped like cobblestones but more succulent to sniff than any cobblestone in Christendom, and even, on its very own platter with a sharp, clean knife for its eventual segmenting, that rarest of aromatic treats, that orb of sunny climes: an orange!

"You will not do without your Christmas meal, oh, no," said good Caroline Cratchit. "Tim, fetch the extra bench from the ingle-nook, and we can all squeeze together cozy-like." She took from Phoebe and Simon what passed for their winter garb, and the other Cratchit offspring made loud welcome, and an extra couple of plates were found at once, and Mr Cratchit returned after a sound fixing of the street door; and grace was said; and with rhetorical pomp and inspired elocution, Great-Aunt Dora, in from Hampstead Village, delivered an impromptu lesson on the gospel virtue of self-effacement. Then the meal was begun.

"But I didn't know it was Christmas today," said Phoebe, when she had eaten enough that she felt like a different person, in a different life. An unexpected reprieve on this day of unfathomable hardships.

"Sure, and the foul sorrow of seeing your father sicken, with your mother so recently taken away from you as well, how could you mind the calendar?" said Bob Cratchit.

"That's why all the bells," said Simon through a mouthful of spicy Christmas pudding, chewy with currants and sultanas, suet and citron.

"And why the streets were so empty," Phoebe recalled.

She looked about her. The Cratchits were a happy brood; life had been good to them this past decade. The mother in her neatest apron, a mobcap to keep smuts from the hearth out of her greying curls; her face was an endless blossoming of rosy smiles, arched eyebrows, questioning curiosity, glistening eyes. The father, who was the only Cratchit the children had met before, was only slightly grave, though even the jolliest Harlequin would have seemed grave beside Mrs Cratchit. Bob's eyes were sunk in grey pockets, and he blinked at the sight of the young children, who reminded him of his own when they were young, but this pair of twins seemed more timid than the crabgrass Cratchits had ever been.

Those very crabgrass Cratchits were, each one of them, robust and regular, full to grown. Peter home from the merchant marine; Martha up from Poole, where she had a position of some significance understairs; and Belinda married with a husband who took such tender care of his bride that anyone with more life experience than the Scrooge orphans might have guessed that Mrs and Mr Cratchit would soon have a grandchild—and how that made the elders jealous! But each of the Cratchit offspring sprang to lift platters and bring plates, to mop up spilled gravy and refill the pitcher of ale; they tended lovingly to their gently blooming sister and their jolly parents and dignified Great-Aunt Dora; and Phoebe and Simon learned more in an hour about the expression of filial devotion than they had ever before known. Though they would have no occasion to express their own such devotion ever again, Phoebe was realizing; and the thought brought her such a sharp ache that she had to leap suddenly from her chair and rush to the cold parlour, where the coal fire had gone low and hissed with a sympathetic murmur.

"Leave her," said Mrs Cratchit knowledgeably, but Simon was at her side at once, his grief no less real if less realized, and they stood and shook with their arms around each other, not for the first time that sorry Christmas Day, and not for the last, either.

Then the door opened again and Tim was there, Tim Cratchit. He had brought their outer garments and some extra layers beside, and he spoke through their tears as if he had not noticed their distress. "Great-Aunt Dora is taking the hansom cab all the way up the hill back to Hampstead Village, and she says we can ride along with her and go for a ramble on the Heath. As for getting back, yes, it is cold, and it is far, but we can run and slide all the way to Camden Town, for the slope is constant and the ice upon it will afford us swift passage whether we wanted it or no!"

There was nothing to do, then, but hurry along, for Great-Aunt Dora would not be kept waiting, and soon the four of them were hunched together in the carriage. By this hour many families had finished their afternoon meal and were taking the air, calling greetings of the season back and forth across the lanes and the high streets, and now that Phoebe and Simon knew what this day was, besides the day of their father's death, they were readier to see the holiday proof, though it remained in the lighted windows and jolly overheard remarks and in Great-Aunt Dora's off-tune spiritualized humming, and did not settle in their own hearts.

Soon enough, the rooftops of Hampstead Village came into view, crowning its own hill, and Phoebe and Simon saw the old, smoke-blackened buildings behind their iron rails, and heard the Hampstead Village church bells sound their own hours, and heard also the fires crackling in braziers for the Hampstead Village poor to stand around and share such warmth of the season as they could. But, "Good-bye, Auntie Dora, and many returns of the season," called Tim, hustling his charges away, and they left the carriage and the dozy, old great-aunt and headed toward a swath of meadows and woodlands beyond the village.

Tim walked with a bit of a limp, and when he came to a rise that was more than a single step, he leaned upon Simon on one side and Phoebe on the other. "Oh, I never mind my limp, I don't," he said, as if reading their very thoughts. "It affords me the right to link my arm through that of any boy or girl near me on the step, and no isolate can ever be sorry to have good reason to do that! I once was frail, even hobbled; but my limb straightened out as I grew. I shall never be notorious for my demonstration of the Highland fling or the light fantastic or the frenetic fandango, but I shall know every step of a healthy life and walk it or lurch it or stump it with joy. It was not always thus, you know. On the doorstop of the very darkest day, life can change for the better."

The world was opening up before them, a sweet set of downy white sheets laid upon the hills; snow upon dale and snow upon rail; and look, it began to snow again as Tim spoke. To the east, the sky was dense with stone-grey cloud; while to the west the sky was nearly clear. Its rich, thin blue proved to be veined like Carrara, with streaks of white like ghosts in flight. Like any ordinary late-December afternoon; in mid-century England; in the country. By which we may conclude: rare and precious as life itself.

"My favourite place," said Tim, "out of the wind, out of the snow, and no one knows of it but the occasional dog or hedgehog. A place with a secured horizon, which pleases me." He drove them down a lane and over a stone bridge, and they came upon an overgrowth of shrubs making a dome of snowy nubble, all their fronds bent low with the weight of ice upon them. "My private office, which has been a winter hideaway for me since I first came to visit Great-Aunt Dora," he told them, and with the clumsy gesture of one losing his footing, he knifed himself headfirst into the hoops and canes, and Simon followed next, so Phoebe had to go, too.

Inside, a sort of ice cave, which sounds cold enough, and to be sure one wouldn't want to lie down upon the snowy mattress and take one's rest there. But the space was tall enough to sit up straight, and Phoebe and Simon realized that the wind was cut down to nearly nothing, so with the warmth of their good meal and the brisk walk from the centre of Hampstead Village, they were about as pleasurably accommodated as any wanderer in the winter could hope to be without benefit of walls or roof.

"I want to tell you about your father," said Tim. "What I know of him, and what I fear for him."

Phoebe looked at Simon and he looked back at her. "Our father is dead," said Phoebe softly. But her brother nodded and said, "Go on."

Tim reached out for her hand, and for Simon's, and after a moment Phoebe pulled her hand from her muff and Simon his from his mitten, and they each gave Tim one of their hands. He was warm and his hands plump and strong, and he seemed to be drawing strength from the two Scrooge children even as he was giving it back to them.

"I was not always tall and robust," he said. "Ten years ago my family called me Tiny Tim, for I was the youngest of the family and befuddled with a problem of ratchety limbs. I could not seem to get well, and my parents tended me as best they could, but the medical attention was lacking, and though I was happy as a lark in summer, I was frail as a lark in winter. I do not know what might have happened to me but for the kindness of your father."

They had known of their father's many charities, though when he had mentioned them, it was not in the form of boasting but of sharing with them the catalogue of London's miseries. Still, Phoebe and Simon had not often heard testimony about their father's life before they were born, so they listened with care and excessive remoteness, like statues of ice.

"It was perhaps ten years ago this very day—if I stopped to count it I might be sure," said Tim, "but ten—or nine or eleven—it makes little difference. I can never forget it. It was Christmas noontime. I was sitting by the fire worrying about my mother, for even at the age of five or six I could see she was fretful about me, and putting as good a face on the matter as she could. We had a meagre enough meal prepared—nothing so pleasant as what we afforded this afternoon!—when your father arrived at the very door of our home in the mews, where he had never been seen before and was never seen again. He affected to brawl and bray at my father, who was then as he is today in the employ of Scrooge and Marley, Limited. Then old Scrooge came all over laughing and ushered in a hamper of food, as I recall it, and a goose that might have been the great-great-great-grand-greatness of the goose we enjoyed today, and wished a happy Christmas to the Cratchit family, and he sat down with us to feast. I was frightened of him at first, though I had not been frightened of much or many in my young life. But after dinner he took me upon his knee and dandled me and played Banbury Cross with me up and down, and before he set me back upon the floor, he put his hand upon my head and he whispered to me softly, 'My Christmas gift to you is that you should listen, and remember, and come to see what I tell you to see.'

"I thought it was a blessing of kindness. At the time.

"Of course, I did not know what he meant that day. Off he went and on we lived, and it seemed as if things improved for us, in little ways but useful ways. The food we ate was of better grade; and Scrooge increased my father's salary and reduced his hours; and a doctor was found to look at my limbs, and he was not such a disgrace as all the quacks we'd seen before, but he recommended liniments and unguents of malodourous stink and sting yet highly effective for all that; and before long I was able to hang my little crutch upon the hearth, where you might have seen it today if you looked."

Phoebe nodded; she had noticed the thing. "But what could be wrong with that?" she pressed.

"What did he tell you, that Christmas Day long ago?" asked Simon, eager as a boy can be to get to the horror, if horror was to be found.

"What your father gave me was something other than a chance," continued Tim Cratchit. "I know my parents think I am a happy fool, in some ways; and perhaps I am. But from that Christmas Day I have found myself to possess a second sight that neither my father nor my mother enjoys or endures; no, nor my happy siblings or occasional friends, nor even Great-Aunt Dora, unless she dreams of such visions after her second sherry of the Sabbath."

"What visions are those?" asked Simon. "Tell them out, so we can see, too."

"I no longer speak of them to my parents, at least not directly, for I know that those good people fret that I may not be fit for this harsh and lovely world, and they will not live forever to guide me."

"We are seeing our father to his coffin today," said Phoebe sternly. "If you have something to tell us, tell us."

Tim looked at them with eyes that did not quite seem to see them. "Scrooge told me something of his adventures in the moil of the otherworld, and how his experiences had changed him, and ever since then—well, it is as if he sharpened the keenness of my own vision on a whetstone.

I can see around the corners of the present, and into the tunnels of the past and the future. Not all the time, mind you, but when the fit comes upon me. Sometimes my eyes roll up in my head and my dear mother is so frightened for me she nearly collapses herself, but other times the awareness comes on me so slowly and gently that I can hardly tell if I am being visited by revelation or simply a little ordinary fancy."

"Is it too dreadful?" asked Phoebe.

"Is it safe?" asked Simon. They pulled their hands back off Tim's soft palm, yet they could not clutch each other instead: each was alone in the frozen moment.

"He saw phantoms sifting through the streets of London," said Tim. "Shackled and burdened by the weight of gold they had accumulated through taking advantage of the needy. They roamed, they floated, immaterial as the fog, wailing and cursing their fate, doomed for eternity to regret their greed and their lack of feeling for their common man. Your father wondered if there was time enough left him to make up the difference of a long life spent in callowness and crimes against his human kinfolk."

"He was toying with your uneducated sensibilities," offered Phoebe.

When Tim did not reply, Simon whispered, "Crikey, do you see 'em, too?"

Tim closed his eyes as if to consider how much truth to tell. "Yes, I do," he said at last.

"Then might you see our father?" cried Phoebe. She had meant to speak in scorn, but in stating the question outright she heard her words posit a genuine concern. So can words change one. "Is he with them now? I want to see him!" She began to weep as she had not yet wept.

"If you see the dead, you can discover if he has rejoined our dear mama, and her lost little babies, all," demanded Simon. "I want to see them, too! Put your hands on us, that we might have the sight, too! I want them! I want them back! I want to see my father!"

"No, you do not!" replied Tim. "For if you spied him, you might be forced to concede that for all his good works these past years, he still had not worked off the dreadful debt he incurred by the decades he spent as a cruel miser, and his soul lost in a slough of selfish greed."

"He was good to our mother, he loved her desperately," said Phoebe, wiping her face with the back of her hand, "and love, we are told in the Lessons, repairs all sin."

"He was good to us," said Simon, "and when our mother died, it wasn't his fault he couldn't tell the difference between our hunger and anyone else's."

"Do you see him?" demanded Phoebe. "We must know!"

Tim's voice was different now; lower. His eyes looked about as if vexed to observe a horizon beyond the close dome of their sanctuary, however he had tried to escape it. They had to lean in to hear. "He told me he had been visited by a towering spirit in a red cloak, a man with a white beard and a wreath of holly upon his head. He said he thought this man was the spirit of Christmas in the present age, and it showed him visions. But one must not share every vision one has; it is not kind to the young." Tim's thin lips closed.

"You're horrible," said Phoebe. "To take us so far from your home only to tempt us with knowledge you won't share."

"I think you can't see anything," said Simon.

"You don't want to know what I can see," said Tim. "If I could let you see it, too, I would be less alone. If I could give to you the gift your father gave me . . ." He was beginning to turn a pale white-mauve, and his eyes were closed. His hands raked the air in front of him as if hoping they might connect again with the children's hands.

"We certainly do not want to know what you can see. We can wait and see it for ourselves, thank you very much. We ought to go back, Simon. Miggs Oystery will be returning to the Cratchits' house this evening to bring us back to London. Dark and sad as it is, and the future as bleak as it might be, it is our home, and our duty to see our father out."

"Don't leave me with my visions!" cried Tim in an awful voice. His spine curled like someone's being thrown backward off a colt. "I'm all but adrift, between life and death, and unsure of what is real!" His hands pawed again for them, as if they might haul him to safety. But he was bigger than they were, and they were afraid to touch him for fear of the gift of a horrible knowledge; and they didn't know the way back on their own, and even in the brief time they had been hiding in the iced shrubbery, the light was beginning to lower.

"Where are you!" he cried in some terrible private darkness.

It seemed then that the dome of the bush shook, as if with a mighty wind, and the walls snowed outward and the fronds and hoops of limb shivered; and while it could not qualify for second sight, for there was nothing to see but white, Phoebe had the sense, all of a sudden, of a vast height in a great eternity of emptiness, and in that height she sensed the

form of a figure, tall as an Old Testament prophet, but more mysterious
still: neither glowery nor affectionate, not remonstrative nor forgiving.
Just—just there. As a witness, and to be witnessed: just there.

A child should not have to shoulder the cares of the world. In the calendar of life, the January infant should be free of undue concerns. No
hobble-limbed child with his crutch, no pair of twins left orphaned,
abandoned. No darkling child in sunny clime, racked with disease on his
mosquito-clouded mat; no pale cinder child in Nordic streets, chapping
her hands for warmth. Yet children find themselves in such penury and
want, and only constant devotion to their need has any chance of helping.
Yet who, thought Phoebe in a daze, who could ever possess such wide
devotion as that?

She might have sat in the presence of this staunch mightiness, this
unarticulated majesty, for all eternity, and perhaps Simon would have,
too, wondering on its nature and the size and shape and condition of its
mystery; but look, there, right before them, once again, human grief bent
low over the ground nearby. One could do only what one could do; she'd
learned that much from her vague and distractible father. So, trouble though
it might bring her, she turned her attention away from the weird, white
fullness, and she reached out to touch Tim's knee. She saw that Simon
had had the same impulse.

Simon's eyes, those eyes that were twins to hers, were wide with
worry. He, too, was afraid to touch Tim again, for fear of startling him; or
of being infected by a capacity to see more than is healthy for a humble
child to spy. But Simon felt Phoebe's concern for the troubled lad, and he
nodded at Phoebe's muff. She understood. She withdrew from its hiding
place one of the holly twigs that they had found in their father's locked
bedchamber. It was like the holly in the wreath of the creature Tim had
described; a souvenir from a story could span the distance between human beings that circumstance, for the moment, forbade. She scratched
the top of Tim's hand with it gently, and he turned his hand over and
cupped it, and she placed the twig thereupon. To bring him back gently,
without words, if they could.

At once the wretched demeanour evaporated from his features; the
rictus of his posture relaxed. He opened his eyes. Sweat was dripping
from his forehead even in the cold. The dome-like sense of eternity was
dissolving into vapours around them, and the bush had sprung up somewhat from the ground as its load of snow had melted, perhaps from the

warmth of their three young bodies crouched beneath. "Almost like a to-ken from Scrooge's visitor," he said. "A happy Christmas to you, young Scrooges."

"Let's go," said Simon.

"And did I say anything dreadful?" asked Tim, as they scrambled on hands and knees from the private chamber of visions in some nook of Hampstead Heath.

Phoebe looked at him sideways. He was older than they were, by four or five years; but there was a way he would always be childlike, and always in danger. "Not at all," said Phoebe. "Race you to the kerb!"

The three youngsters ran and scraped and slid and made short work of their downhill homeward ramble. In Camden Town, Miggs Oystery was indeed waiting for them and hardly allowed them a moment's good-bye before she bustled them back toward a carriage. "Sent your cousin out for his Christmas meal, and then I took care of them bed-curtains, I did," she said, and her purse jangled a bit louder, like Christmas jingle-bells on a horse-drawn sleigh. "Nobody closes business for Christmas Day if there's profit to be open!"

"Oh, Bob," said his wife, "I don't want them to leave. I miss the sound of young voices around the place!"

"We'll see what the future brings," said Bob through his own thoughts, and he put a hand on Tim's shoulder.

"Oh, that we will, given time," said Tim, and he only barely managed to pass Phoebe back the little twig of holly with which she had brought him out of his panic. By the time the night had come in full and freezing, black but blazing with stars like powdery snow drifting too high to fall upon our world, she and Simon had reached the familiar industrial yard in which their cold home loomed.

"Oh, had you stalled ten minutes more, the timing would have been perfect," said Fred. "Miggs, take them out for a further walk, along Corn-hill, or past the Old Curiosity Shop by Saul's Yard, or to Saint Mary le Strand. Just ten minutes more, for the men are here, and no child should see—"

"Yes, we should," said Phoebe, and "We will," added her brother. So Miggs Oystery, though reluctant to forego a chance to demand one more coin for the augmentation of her troubles, had to stand aside at the foot of the stairs. The children watched with bright and honest eyes, to make sure that the spirit of their father was not wandering the dark streets of

London, chained and shackled by the booty and legacy of his former crimes.

They did not have long to wait. Here came the corpse on a long, much used litter, hoisted by the agents from Plott and Blackheath's, four silent, sweating men in greatcoats. Their father's final departure from the home in which, to trust Tim Cratchit's account, Scrooge had lived a dead life, but had come to life again. He had lived anew, and loved, and grieved, but would he now endure an eternity of suffering?

The stretcher rounded the landing, the men in front holding their arms up high above their heads, the men in the back stooping, to keep the stretcher level and the corpse from tumbling down the stairs. Phoebe and Simon watched the worn soles of their father's best shoes float down the steps. He had worn out those shoes all over London, making the good work of amendment, atonement, and ransom.

Then the men reached the bottom step, and they straightened up, and Phoebe and Simon held each other's hand and blinked in final salute. The waxy simulacrum was no longer Scrooge; Scrooge was dead, there was no doubting that. But in his folded hands, between his linked fingers, sprouted a sprig of evergreen holly, as red and green as ever you might like to see.

About "A Few Twigs He Left Behind"

This past winter my fifth grader took part in a school presentation of *A Christmas Carol*. She was practicing her lines with her brother, then the two of them mounted an impromptu production of the school play, using any props that came to hand. To hear a sixth-grade boy—one whose voice has not yet begun to change—trill out, "I wear the chains I forged in life!" is a moment that can seem, to a parent, both comic and dreadful. What does he know of forging chains of regret, I think; and yet, life being what it is, how he will learn, how he must learn about regret! It is the price of growing up. I believe that the boy and girl in "A Few Twigs He Left Behind" are inspired by my son and daughter having fun with the script of a school play. I do hope that I am not the model for Scrooge—not yet, not anytime soon.

THEIR MONSTROUS MINDS

I

On Empire Day, in Year 57 of the Queen Alexandrina Victoria Imperatrix, a Great Exhibition and Aerial Display was held in the Royal Alexandra Park. The Gardens were thickly greened, and clockwork water sprinklers had been out early, too, spraying the plants with perfumed water, drops of which still glittered among the leaves. The sky was a deep blue, not a cloud in it, as everyone afterward recalled: a fine and smiling summer day.

At the park's central point, the six Grande Avenues converged below the Grande Terrace, where the Orangery rose above, polished like Venetian mirrors, and packed with pineapples and the giant, purple-red raspberries of the Victoriania Islands. Despite the many delights and astonishments to be seen that day all along each avenue, the crowd that finally formed below the Terrace was struck—less dumb than raucous—by the wonder of an ultimate exhibit. Even the queen-empress, they said, though now stout and dour in her eternal widow's mourning (her royal husband, Albrecht, having died some fifteen years previously), even she smiled with majestic approval at this object, an aerial artifice, parked awaiting her pleasure. And for a moment then, one might glimpse the sparkling prettiness of her youth. Before, once again, time, care, and sorrow devoured it.

The artifice was indeed both picturesque and fantastic. It depicted, in marvellous detail, the chariot of Queen Boadicea, all fashioned in gleaming ferrous silver, decorated with plates of gold and panels of glowing coloured enamels. The four-horse chariot team was also of metal, two animals being of ferrous copper, one of ferrous bronze, and one of ferrous steel. Hung on these beasts were bright accoutrements. Their tails and manes were of bullion. And in each equine eye burned a precious stone—four emeralds, two topaz, and two rubies. Inside the chariot stood Queen Boadicea herself, a most gorgeous and larger-than-life-size doll, with rich and gaudy garments, her red hair the superb prolific cuttings from the heads of a score of women, woven with pearls, and crowned by a circlet of gold. Beside the fiery queen, who in past centuries fought so gallantly against the Roman legions, were positioned her two daughters, also dolls, and almost as splendidly attired as their mother. A dramatic sight it was, this assemblage, even while static, and in full size some thirty feet high, and of compatible length and width.

All this while a brazen band played patriotic melodies, in which occasionally the crowds joyously took part. "*Rule, Britannia* bellowed through the trees, *Bright Empress of the North and South*" and *Hail, Radiant Queen.*"

When noiselessness fell, the crowd grew hushed. Sir Edmund Heatherly and his team of Flighters strode into the space and, having bowed to Her Majesty and received her gracious nod, set about a swift preparation of the aerofact chariot for its maiden flight. It was to rise high up into the air above the park, into the sun-kissed blue sky over London. Due to its size, even persons excluded from the Gardens might still get a good sight of it, while those who had endowed themselves with a binoculus, would be able to take in all its details, though they stood a mile beneath. Even in the sooty slums beyond Lambeth or Southbank, they could catch a view. For on that day even the lowest of the low had a part in the celebration, for they were British, and the Empire had thrown its wing far and wide; they too must be gladsome, and proud.

Quite quickly the Flighters had the chariot ready. A flame was touched to a hidden mechanism. A sharp, small *crack* resulted, and then some whitish puffs of steamy smoke curled backwards from the concealed mechopod under the chariot's floor.

Sir Edmund and his men stepped well away. The silence of the Terrace area was utter. Only a child squeaked somewhere, to be instantly hushed.

Then, O wonder! The doll Boadicea put up her head and spoke in a strange and magnetizing roar, every word audible for a vast distance, so those nearest must clap their hands to their ears as if at a cannon shot, and some ladies, alas, were taken faint.

"Rome," enunciated the Boadicea, "shall have no Dominion in these Isles! For, centuries beyond my Day, there shall be born a Queen, far Mightier than I, Alexandrina Victoria Imperatrix, and she will Rule an Empire fit to put Rome's dunghills to Shame!"

After which the colossus began to lift, somewhat heavily but not at all jerkily, into the lambent atmosphere. Up and up it slowly inclined, the horses now champing and pawing the air, tossing their manes, as puffs of grey-pink steam frothed from their encarnadined nostrils. And Boadicea, too, tossed her hennaed locks, and the doll daughters waved their jewelled fists, while the great raw ferrous-silver wheels spun, and the scythes that were their twirling cores chopped the ether to mincemeat.

How the *crowd* now roared! How it stamped and flounced and clutched for the sky, shouting the two names of female courage and victory: "*Boadicea! Victoria!*"

Those who were present and took scrupulous note recorded that the steam-powered clockwork aircraft-chariot ascended to a sort of zenith, maybe some three hundred feet above the park. And below, the cheers under the Orangery Terrace went on and on, and outside the zone the tumult spread, as yet more and more loyal subjects of the Imperatrix beheld the glamorous spectacle, going always onward and upward.

It was at some moment then (variously computed as being ten or thirteen or eighteen minutes after the phenomenon first rose from the earth), that the Unforeseen and entirely Unexpected Calamity occurred.

Ever after, stern preachers in their rook-dark pulpits would assert that the Lord God Himself had seen fit to punish the vanity and hubris of Man. While others put the mishap firmly at the door of Britain's closest military rival, Prussia.

What factually took place, as countless persons attest, was this: As the chariot soared ever higher, from out of the clear and cloudless blue of the sky there dashed a jagged and blindingly white bolt of lightning, with a noise like rent iron. This, striking the air-vehicle full on, in one blazing instant congealed it to a twisted, molten mass, pieces of which, including whole horse-heads of metal, scythed wheels still burning and spinning, and the cindered eyes and features of the three large dolls, flung every way at once, and came down next onto the park, the trees, the Orangery, and the upraised, terror-smeared faces of the citizens.

Not only Boadicea's chariot perished in those moments. The Orangery was engulfed in fire. And there were a great many human casualties, several being fatally affected. As for British Empiric vanity, hubris, pride, and joy, they suffered a grievous blow. The queen? Ah. They say she was never after even momentarily happy, never even *amused*, again.

N o one who came to the island from any other place was ever welcomed by the islanders.

They made it their creed to shun the intruder, or simply fail to see him, whenever able. If forced into an unavoidable contact, as, say, should he need to buy anything from any of the small shops of the three or four villages scattered about the isle, they would not look at him, avoided physical connection, and spoke as little as possible. Very few outsiders did come to the island. And of those few, none, that far, had stayed more than a month; perhaps only so long because the steam ferry called there from the mainland but once in every thirty days.

This, however, suited Ferstone to perfection. If they wanted no superfluous truck with him, nor did he wish it with them.

He had chosen the spot for his living quarters with care, the island offering the ideal venue. For at its centre, the platter of land stood unerringly up in five mountainously tall hills. Up here, concealed behind tufted and tangled slopes, and huge outcrops of grey boulder, lay a plateau in a dredge of trees. A ruinous manse that sprawled there, some two and a half centuries old, furnished for him enough space, privacy, and rough convenience to suit Ferstone, and his plans. By means of a pony cart he had eventually dragged up all the supplies, and other paraphernalia, some of which involved bizarre appliances to create heat or cold, or large wooden crates bound in iron, brought with him over the sea. While for water, a healthy spring ran close by the door; for fresh provisions a wild fruit tree or two grew there, and herds of deer wandered, or flocks of birds. Should he desire anything else, he would, now and then, descend to one or other of the villages, buying with a pointing finger and slapped-down coin the loaf or cheese or bucket required.

They called *him*, when they recollected him, the *outlander*. He called *them* nothing at all. They were meaninglessly unreal to him. But most things were unreal to Ferstone. Only his work, his *vocation,* had substance, only his goal had meaning.

In age he was twenty-nine years, a young enough man, tall and strong and straight enough, too, with black hair marked by a premature seam or two of palest grey. He had attended the best schools and universities in England, and elsewhere in Europe, until their adherence to an accepted and prudent code sufficiently bored and frustrated him that he abandoned them. He thought himself by then beyond them in many ways and was substantially correct. He lacked only money, having also parted from his family, a noble, idle one that would have preferred him to be nobly idle also. However, through his cleverness and skill, he presently accumulated funds.

Now, installed above the tawny, late-summer hills, Ferstone commenced his Great Work. He would not be the first, of course, to attempt such an astonishing feat. But, he believed, he would be the first fully to succeed.

Cold as an icy stone, mind clear and cutting as a polished shard of crystal, Ferstone cuddled priestlike down into the monastery of his own genius.

And far below, in the villages and harbours, they mostly forgot he was there. Until, three months after his arrival, things began to change.

The island storms were bad that autumn.

Rather than gather out at sea, where the grey, chalky waves still made little movement, they evolved up on the mountain-hills. Night fishermen would often note such weather from below. It came out of nowhere. One minute the sky was blackest blue, lit with stars and moon. And then thunder would boom, and at once vast stripes and knittings of blind-white lightning riddled heaven. It was seen, too, that these lightnings most frequently struck downward, seeming always to hit the hilltops, or the plateau held within them. Only now and then did some stray bolt lose its focus, landing instead on a hillside with a perilous sizzle, searing the earth, the pale fires running, then dying with abnormal brevity. On a single occasion a solitary strike flared down close by a little fleet returning shoreward soon after midnight. Though not a ship was touched, some of the men took alarm. The lightning was not, they declared, as they had ever seen it. It had a solidity, and even entering the water it burned in long thin white tongues, making the sea seem a while to seethe, all on fire.

But winter drew in, and more natural storms began, the great waves clashing and the rain blown sidelong like a wet sheet. The lightnings stopped.

Then the snow dropped down, and the sea was ice. The ferry did not call and doubtless would not get back until the end of spring.

One or two wondered then, as if suddenly recalling the outlander, how he would manage, or if he would perish, up there among his unholy modern machineries that puffed out frozen steam to store the deer meat and shot fowl for him, or the cherry-red clockwork stove that cooked and kept him warm. And all those old books and papers he had (not many of the islanders had time for books, being unable to read or write). "And there were big boxes lugged up there, done up in iron clasps. Cruel-cold earth in those." One had been joggled on the cart, and a little soil, cold as Alex-antarctica, had drizzled from it. "Like corpse boxes," someone else suggested, down in the half-light, snug fust of the village drinking shop. Had they heard tell of that other mainland happening? Some evil murderer who brought all those he had killed with him oversea, packed in earth in their coffins, and when they made shore and darkness fell, they all of them got up, as if just out of their beds, and went in a crowd to kill others among the living.

Within the manse it came near the solstice, a period of the prolonga-tion of nights, and twilit days that, there, lasted less than six hours. Ferstone had, himself, continued to unremember the villagers. He had not, by then, for more than seven weeks gone down the hills for stores. Due to his machineries and general preparedness, he had enough. He even thought he might celebrate the Yule Night. In that case, he would not cel-ebrate it alone.

The house then: Having crossed the plateau, and the rickety bridge above the spring-fed stream, gone in at the stone-arched doorway, you found an ancient and shamblous hall. The walls of it were also stone, carved high up with time-melted shields. The windows were narrow as pipe clean-ers, and filled with old glass thick as bottles. The stone floor was cluttered by much of Ferstone's imports—books, in boxes and out, an erectable bed with rugs and pillows, assorted implements for hygiene and defence, the latter including some guns, and a mecholock that might be operated from one spot alone manually to secure every ingress. The wide stone hearth was now packed with the automatic stove, pans, kettles, and other culinary items. Some meat was often broiling there, or standing by to cool. Beyond the hall a corridor opened on a big kitchen, which had been turned into a cold-larder. Here, amid the white frost and mist of mechanical winter, carcasses hung up ready. Beyond that, a winding stone stair led to the only other habitable chamber, which lay directly below the roof.

The rest of the manse, so far, would not prove very unexpected, perhaps, though very much alien to the villagers, had they ever attempted to see it. But the upper room would, almost certainly, though they would lack understanding of it, have filled them instinctually with fright, with a sense of terror even, and a crucial feral rage. The blasphemous room was worse than any pagan temple or den of witchcraft.

Initially probably an attic, it had been the former accommodation of servants. Long, and unusually high-ceilinged, the space seemed now empty of all furnishing. Instead, an extraordinary apparatus was stretched all over it, metallically gleaming, like a huge spider's web. Pipes coiled and looped, sentinel-like uprights rose at intervals, some from the floor, others midway to the beams. Disks and knots, wheels and cogs and dials, devices that might regulate temperature, or fluids, hung in the web, sometimes pulsing, or quietly throbbing, like uncanny and unhuman hearts. Round, eye-shaped lamps—if such they were—would slowly glow up, rose or green—then darken. Sometimes, too, a noise—like the strings of a steam-operated zither-harp—woke somewhere in the mass and skittered all across, up and down and away. And above, at the web's central clustering, the roof could mechanically be undone and might well be standing wide. A square of sky was visible here, opaque by day and jet-black by night. Up into this aperture pointed a long, ensilvered rod, most like a giant pen, even to its skyward extremity, which resembled a nib. And with this pen Ferstone had, for some while, been able to scribble lightning on the heavens. (A scientific magician, Ferstone. Just as he had always determined to be.) Once created, these galvanics could be directed, sent either outward—or enticed *downward*—to any reasonably adjacent spot.

He had performed that very act, of course, in London, the previous summer, on the occasion of Empire Day. From his hidden lair in the slums of Southbank, just south of the Thames, he had formed the lightning bolt, small as a seed, invisible as air, and once his telescope identified the absurd rising aerofact of Boadicea, he had shot the bolt home from the skies over Alexandra Park. Later, reading of the chagrin and dismay that resulted, the destruction of the great Orangery, and subsequent loss of life, Ferstone was indifferent. He was already out of the city by then, en route for the island, with all his paraphernalia in tow.

He had planned the venture for some while before, got it perfect, and perfectly it had worked. Britain was made a laughingstock, her pride dented. Most valuably, her powers of enterprise and technology were severely discredited. For if the servitors of the queen-empress could not launch successfully even a toy chariot, what chance had her vaunted airships, or subaquan fleet?

Ferstone had done it all for money, obviously. It was, he had felt, the purest motive on earth, since a genius must endorse his talent. Had not even the biblical God said that? As for patriotism, as for humanity—what he, Ferstone, might now achieve would be the most valid enterprise attempted since the Dawn of Days.

Ferstone, when found in the upper chamber that winter solstice, would have been staring up at the results of Prussian and French money, and genius at its most endorsed.

It was a sort of cocoon, a lump of silver shawling wrapped round and round; just there, below the Lightning Gate, as he had come to call it, the opened roof where he had created for it, and then drawn in, the energies of the lightning—the Breath of God.

Rather it resembled, the shawled lump, some prey the enormous, web-spinning spider had killed and stored for future use, there in the metallic windery. But in fact the wrapped-up prize was the very reverse of something killed.

Indeed, the antithesis, now, of all death. The *disproval* of death, and so of the might of any country, or empire, any Eden, god, or God. In the web life lay, breathing and cool and wise and wonderful, simply waiting for its birthday hour, which would arrive tonight.

The last lightning, the concluding stroke, became and was flashed down into the manse at one minute past midnight of the solstice.

It lit the entire building, both in and out, blazing from rafter to cellar, and exiting through every ruined gap or bottle-costive window.

Trees glittered in snow. Stars faded.

Inside, abruptly shown, yawning coffin-casks holding possibly idiosyncratic portions of corpse anatomy—an arm, a leg, another leg—disparate hands and feet, torsos and loins, column of throat and snake-ivory of spine, a pelvis, a larynx, a liver, a head, eyes, skull, hair, fingernails—et cetera. Bones and bits, by the levinbolt revealed, all scattered about, with, now and then, a dead rat that had, despite the lethal cold preservatives, got in and made its supper—or meant to. . . . The silver web shone like a shattered galaxy. And Ferstone's face, so close to it, so controlled and contained, was blasted as if by moonlight to the countenance of a saint.

(Below the hills, the villagers had run out to stare upwards—the unforeseen explosion of thunder, detonation of the light. But everywhere was quiet again, as the grave.)

In the upper chamber, Ferstone spoke softly.

"Have you woken?"

Only silence replied.

Ferstone never faltered.

"*Think*," he said with calm authority. "Use the mind you now have, which is that of an intellectual, and well used to language. I ask again, have you woken?"

And then, from the height below the sky, the quietly reasonable answer came. "I have woken."

It was a beautiful voice, being that of an actor of great ability, and deceased only nine months.

II

After a while, as the dark days turned, slow and sombrely, back towards the light, a handful of the islanders became conscious that another man, another outland stranger, was also inhabiting their isle. He must have arrived through the agency of some private air-vehicle, landing up on the hills by night. He was seen always in company with the first outlander. Presumably this second intruder stayed at the old manse with him.

Where one was dark, the new one was fair. Fair as the asphodel might have been said. But not by the isle folk. *Pale,* they called him, the second man, his skin being white as an island girl's before her twelfth birthday, and his hair with a polished shine on it like the silver in the church. And his eyes were blue as summer skies, had they said it. Blue, in fact, had they *known* it, as the sky over London that previous Empire Day. The men avowed he was weak-looking. Worse than the first one. Let them both take themselves off as soon as the weather uncorked the sea.

They had started with Yule, when Ferstone had led his novel companion down to the hall. There the arrival was bathed and dressed in well-fitting garments. By the hearth they took mulled wine and slices of a great cake, with Victoriania grapes from a box that the cold-machines had kept wholesome, and a mixed tea from the vast continent of Vindia and from the Queensland Province of Alexanalia.

All that, and everything else, the newcomer managed with adequacy and, as time passed, increasing grace and coordination. Initially Ferstone had, now and then, to issue a firm command: "Think. Your brain *knows* and *remembers*. You have only to trust to it, as do the rest of us who are able-bodied. And be sure, I have made very certain you *are*, while your mind is that of a scholar and intellectual, who was not adverse to the athletic pursuits and endurance, for which your limbs, and all parts, were so carefully selected."

At first, too, occasionally, Ferstone had physically guided his companion, even, once or twice, *placed* his legs, hands or feet, straightened him up as if dealing with a hinged model.

By what had been designated the dining hour (when a roast was taken from the clockwork stove and served with roasted tubers and a thick mahogany gravy tempered with blood and Madeira), the other man, to Ferstone's pleasure, seemed to have *grown* into himself. He was intact and entire. Soon no one could, without viewing his couth and well-healed scars, have taken him for anyone—or thing—other than a healthy man not more than twenty-five years. Ferstone told him his name, then: "You are called Primos. Repeat what I have said."

"I am called Primos," replied the being, seeming not uneasy, even though the brain inside his skull would know perfectly well that the name meant "first," or "new."

For Ferstone, as he watched and communed with his protégé, the result of experiment and hard, inspired labour, no wild elation resulted. He was only soothed, at a sort of peace. Nothing had gone amiss at this last stage of all his work. He had not, either, expected it to.

Unlike earlier stages, during which he had had to prostitute his scientific talents as a private tutor to obtain money. Or when incurring intermittent difficulties in procuring and obscuring those parts and pieces he had required. They had most often been brought him by such as Hawke and Bear, who, although expensive, rendered exemplary goods, in some cases of exquisite quality. But they were masters in their particular line of robbery, (that of graveyards). Genius, too, if in another lower, darker, filthier, and more hellish form. Ferstone knew he had had no choice. To proceed he must have what they got him—either from the most recent burial or eminent medical failure. As with his treason, Ferstone never quibbled. The use of the island, too, had demanded the sort of money only a traitor could earn.

All came together. Exactly as, in its different way, now his *invention* had. This elegant and virtually flawless man, seated before him, smiling, and talking of books and art that perhaps his *eyes* had never seen, though his brain, naturally, had done so and recalled, and all this in the dark gold of the voice of that admired thespian, who had perished so tragically (and fortunately so young) in a duel, which also luckily had spared both his lungs, his windpipe and voice box.

Less than the ecstasy of a creative god, Ferstone felt an artist's wonderful satisfaction, the sense of *rightness*. This event had been bound one day to happen, to be *made* to happen. Man had created Man. But *Ferstone* had done it. As he had known, from his twenty-second year, he must, he *would*.

During those early months of the following year, they continued Ferstone's plan.

They ate together, he and Primos, they walked together about the uplands of the island and, as the snow began to lessen and decay, down to the villages and the sea. (The villagers went on with their normal acts of blindness and noninterest.) By day in the manse, and in the evenings, Ferstone would give books to Primos, so that Primos might read aloud to him. Ferstone came to enjoy the musical and powerful voice rendering treasure from the cornucopia of human wisdom in poetry and prose. And this not only in the English tongue, but in Latin and Greek, German and French. Primos seemed delighted. His body, too, grew reaccustomed to striding and climbing. He might pause to look at and indicate something as they went. And he might pause in his reading spontaneously to remark, "Ah, but I remember this passage well," or, "I find myself comparing these words with the discourse of such and such of Athens"—or of ancient Egypt, antique Rome.

When Ferstone slept in the old hall, in the nocturnal garnet glow of the stove, Primos slept, too, across the hearth from him. Noiseless and immaculate was the slumber of Primos. Did he dream? Sometimes, he said. Once: "I saw two sheep that leapt into a swollen river." But his dreams, where he retained them, neither disturbed nor elevated him. He was even-tempered, Ferstone perceived, save now and then when mild passion—for a poetic stanza, a philosophical idea—embued him.

Spring commenced. Green and purple filaments appeared on the hillsides. The waters beyond the isle were one moment blue and lazy, next slapped to white and brown. The dawns became water-clear and the sunfalls port-wine, or of grey mist. Or fog shrouded everything. This, too, would be educative for the new arrival. Memory must be refurbished since, as Ferstone had predicted, little or nothing, aside from erudition, remained of any previous man's life or dealings; that was, any man who had previously inhabited the skull, or the brain, that now housed Primos.

When May came, Ferstone decided, and when the ferry was about, they could visit the mainland. By May Primos would be more than serviceable for his first introduction to society.

One sunny day in late March, up they got, breakfasted, and shaved themselves (for by now Primos, too, would regularly begin a blonded beard).

As they went around the hills, spotting advancing flights of birds, and, below in a shallow valley, a straying of deer, Ferstone explained to Primos about the extension of his plan, their crossing to the coastal mainland town. They would walk among their fellow men.

While he expounded this, Ferstone became gradually aware that Primos seemed to have stopped concentrating upon him. Generally when Ferstone spoke, to explain something or interrogate or—rarely now—to issue an order (as "Be careful of that rock, it is loose"), Primos attended to him utterly, in a manner neither childlike nor servile, but as if Ferstone, as well he might be, were an object of total fascination, more marvellous even than all the other sights and sounds of the world.

"What is the matter?" Ferstone asked him. Then: "What have you seen?" For the other's blue eyes had fixed in a curious, nearly bewildered way on a small, brown rabbit that had come out to forage on the slope.

"Nothing at all. A coney—" Primos began with his ordinary charm and enunciation.

Next second he was sprinting forward, away and straight up the hillside.

Ferstone stood astounded. He felt a clutch at his vitals as abruptly he saw, too, *how* Primos ran, in what fashion. Gone was the coordinated grace of movement, the agility. Primos, though bounding upward at high speed, seemed yet to be limping, almost stumbling, his left leg and foot lagging perilously against the racing impetus of the right. For sure, the right foot only seemed to hurl all his body forward, and for one insane moment Primos cast a stare behind him, a kind of startled idiocy covering his face.

The rabbit, in pursuit of which he had appeared to launch himself, shot along the hill. At an outcrop of stone, however, Primos staggered and, in another instant, plunged heavily down, ungainly as a sack of washing. There he sprawled on the turf, crushing the burgeoning of grasses and tiny flowerlets.

As Ferstone reached him, Primos yet lay there. To Ferstone's added misgiving, he beheld Primos weeping, torrents of tears bursting from his eyes. "See, see what I have done!" cried Primos in his beautiful voice.

Ferstone glanced and saw indeed. With one hand, the left, his creation had smashed the rabbit, breaking its neck and half its bones, pulping its body by the undisciplined and savage violence of the blow. Not only ruined, but uneatable.

"Why did you do such a thing?" Ferstone inquired coldly.

But Primos only wept. His tears flamed over the grass, blazing in the frigid March sun.

Ferstone, on their return to the manse, ordered Primos to strip himself of his garments. Ferstone then examined him with the precision of a surgeon.

But his investigations showed nothing awry. Every physical part of the new man he had made was faultless. No discrepancy was displayed even in the seemingly lagging left leg that had limped so disastrously. It no longer did so. Primos also passed the cerebral tests with every sign of high intelligence and lack of impairment. His balance, sight, and hearing were beyond doubt. The brain was perfectly sound.

"Why did you go after the rabbit?"

"I—did not mean to do so. Some impulse . . ."

"Why did you kill the wretched thing, and so ineptly?"

"I—do not know—perhaps only, not meaning to . . . as I fell—"

"Why did you fall?"

"The rock—I am unsure."

Ferstone glared upon his invention, who had stopped his sobbing. "You have disgraced yourself. And me."

Primos hung his head. Then raised it and looked far away, at nothing, it would seem. These were boyish conceits, but surely that was only to be expected, at this early juncture. For the original personality, of course, had vanished from the brain, leaving only its previously learned abilities, and the library of acumen acquired before death.

Ferstone left Primos to himself and went out to pace along the length of the stream. He puzzled over what had taken place. Had that, too, been Primos's sudden boyish aberration? It had seemed not to be. There was a *demonic* silliness to it—the chase and kill and weeping—or was the possession *by* a demon, although one did not credit such rubbish. Man ruled the earth. God, the devil, and all their hordes had no place in a modern world of steam and steel. Oh, he must not brood on this single extraordinary upset. He must not think of those rumours which had leaked out of Germany—the tales of another great experimenter who also (should the stories be true) had managed to make up a living male creature, from a patchwork of the dead, and inspire its life with a lightning strike. That being had run amok. A slave, it had rebelled, its mind rotting in its case. A horrible, implacable tale—coined, possibly, to caution any other innovator against such a venture: only God could directly make a living man.

No, Ferstone would not consider this foreign tattle. He had betrayed his country and snatched the Flame of Godhood. Now he must be strong. Self-belief was all he had. Self-belief was All.

A minuscule crack may appear in a sturdy china jug. At the start it may pass unnoticed or, if seen, be dismissed as irrelevant, or at least of minor annoyance. Presently, after some days, or even weeks, fluid begins to seep from the filled jug. Perhaps the flaw still goes unacknowledged—perhaps, excusingly, the jug is suspected of being overfilled or carelessly dried or emptied. One day, standing untouched upon a shelf, a quite familiar low vibration stirs the air of the room—the noise of a mechanical horse carriage rumbling along the street outside, the piano played briskly in a neighbouring chamber. And with no warning the china jug shatters into a hundred fragments.

III

The ferry was far from crowded.

Some eight persons from the island, dressed in what Ferstone inwardly labelled "their peasant best," had sat down on the benches in the white May sunshine, with chickens in a wicker cage. The women gossiped in a surly, slow manner. The men smoked their pipes and kept a stolid silence. Nevertheless their eyes followed the two outlanders from the island manse, one so dark and one so pale. It was too much to hope they might be leaving. They had only a couple of small bags.

The blond younger man, one or two now thought, had a strange look to him. Sometimes his eyes darted everywhere. They said, after, they were certain that these eyes were crossed, or instead he was walleyed, with his optics inclined to dissimilar directions. He would keep tapping on the rail of the boat, left-handedly. And once he kicked out at something on the deck, but nobody knew what.

Ferstone had regularly glanced at his companion. At one point he had said, in an authoritative manner, "Control yourself."

"I am sorry," Primos replied. But he smiled and seemed not greatly to care. His foibles were mostly slight. Even when he bent right over, he was apparently picking some item up. Much of the time he stayed, besides, couthly still, seated or standing, like a well-carved figure of stone. When Ferstone, who himself had gone on pacing round and round the ferry, approached him, his companion twice spoke some lines of archaic Greek poetry fitting for a sea voyage, in a low but musical tone. (The other passengers who heard this took it for the pale man's own language and were resentfully reassured he was indeed an alien.)

The passage took less than an hour, and the water was like blue milk, soft as a lake almost.

Getting ashore, soon both men were walking up the town's cobbled streets towards a hotel, where they would lodge, carrying, each one, a bag. To an idle observer now, they were not particularly remarkable, for the town was of reasonable sophistication, and in the warmer season filled by visitors, who liked to peruse its collapsed castle and Norman church. Along the cobbled roads, bumping and jouncing, ran steam wheelers, and clockwork carriages, many drawn by a pair of ferrous-iron horses. By night steam-neons would gleam. If not London, it had kept pace with the times.

In the hotel, after the usual preliminaries, during which Primos enchanted the caged canary by flawlessly copying its song, the two men rode the pump-actioned lift to an upper floor. Ferstone had taken for them a suite, with two bedrooms and a parlour. Its windows looked towards the sea.

Primos went immediately to the larger of the parlour windows and stayed gazing out. Was this pose childlike? Ferstone scrutinized the stance.

Despite his bleak outward sternness, the creator was on edge, uneasy at every spontaneous gesture or move of his charge. For the past seven weeks he had endured the curious yet persistent eccentricities Primos had begun to exhibit. None was especially flamboyant; definitely nothing like the irrational pursuit and slaughter of the rabbit had again occurred. Yet such a quantity of flickering ticks, facial spasms, and almost dancelike advances of feet and hands Primos *had* assayed, Ferstone himself had quailed. Over and over again he reprimanded himself. The brain within Primos's cranium was sound. Every aspect of his body was in good repair. These palpitations must therefore be the product of some innate nervousness, or else of a lack, persisting but addressable, of complete coordination. Yet, on one night, waking on the island in the small hours, Ferstone had witnessed Primos balancing upside down on his head and hands, for a split second steady as marble—before crashing over on the floor. Uninjured, he had risen instantly and laughed, but his eyes darted in all directions. This was when Ferstone, too, if truth be told, had admitted that Primos might now look two ways at once, the left eye and the right both at the same moment sliding fully to the outer extremity of the socket. But this surely was no more than an idiot's trick, perhaps meant to amuse. No weakness was to be discovered in the tissue or reflex of either eye. "You must," said Ferstone on every occasion, "control yourself." And Primos verbally complied—until the next incident.

Coming to the mainland, to a form of civilization, just as he had originally planned, Ferstone believed there was a risk. But he was by then so far on course, about to guide the marvellous thing he had made outward, into the world, that he felt unable to delay. Ferstone additionally thought he might, once in the town, seek discreet advice. Most palatably he would find it in certain volumes that he did not possess yet knew of. Failing that, he could apply, through the postal service, to men renowned in the fields of science. He had, after all, wrought a miracle. No one could deny it. And to counsel and abet him at this penultimate period would offer such others their share of glory. Ferstone would be glad to allow that, should they help. By this, one might measure the depth of his fall from self. He had come to feel, it must be said, less fear than the premonition of it. He had a dreadful doubt. Not at his act, or its success, not at—if it so must be called—his blasphemy. But at the threadbare tracts that now seemed woven in the fabric of his scheme. There would be, *must* be, he assured himself, a solution to such foolish problems.

They dined at six o'clock in the dining room of the hotel. Not many others were there, for the visiting season came rather later in the year.

Primos ate couthly, and without inappropriate mannerisms, through soup and fish and joint. Ferstone picked and squinted like a grey-streaked crow.

Upstairs again, the gas lamps popped, lending a greenish amber to the unknown shades and shadows of the suite.

Primos returned to a window. Ferstone once more was absorbed in watching him. How splendid he was, the creature, how beautifully made, even when, of necessity, stripped naked. The healed scars had all but faded. Everything about his composite body was irreproachable, as Ferstone had designed it to be. Better than any work of art. No painting or statue could compare with this living, breathing, sentient form.

"Go to your bed now, Primos."

"Yes," Primos said.

He turned, and, in turning, his eyes—now flawlessly aligned—passed over the face of Ferstone in an ice-blue flash. This was due no doubt to some tremble of the gas, or the steam-neons below, for they were being put out. But the mood in the eyes, the deepness of some regret or loss, beyond the scope of any human man, whether alive or peerlessly galvanized—what caused that?

Near one in the morning (the clock of the clocktower down the hill was chiming the last quarter after midnight), Ferstone was woken from an unquiet doze. In the second room beyond the parlour, a loud and bell-like voice proclaimed, on and on.

Ferstone threw back the covers and, lighting a candle in great haste, hurried across into the second room. "In God's name what are you at?"

"'By uproars sever'd, as a flight of fowl

"'Scatter'd by winds and high tempestuous gusts,

"'O, let me teach you how to knit again

"'This scatter'd corn into one mutual sheaf,

"'These broken limbs again into one body;

"'. . . My heart is not compact of flint nor steel;

"'Nor can I utter all the bitter grief—'"

Silence! Ferstone shouted. His own voice, striving to overcome the other's actorish and ringing tones, cracked. "Silence, you fool," he added and Primos ceased. "You will wake the whole house."

"Wake—let the dead wake up," Primos bellowed again.

Ferstone felt panic rise in him like a deathly nausea. He must hold himself back not to lash out at Primos. In another instant, however, all chance of that, or of anything much, was gone. The created man had bounded straight off the bed, as an acrobat might do it. On gaining the floor, every part of him broke into a frenzy of the most violent and unreasonable motion. His head nodded and was flung back or turned wildly to this side or that; while in his face his tongue flapped in and out of the mouth, now hissing or spitting, next aiding the throat to bring up a jumble of outcries, some unintelligible, others seeming to relate to fragments, as before, of Shakespeare, or of Milton, Homer, Ovid; his eyes meantime rolled like marbles in their sockets, independent of each other, and to accompany this, expressions both lunatic and alarmingly animalistic fled to and fro across the features. The rest of his body was in similar turmoil. One leg kicked and the other pranced. In this way he cavorted and leapt about the room. Of his feet one stamped, one persisted in raising him on tiptoe. His arms whirled like the sails of the windmill—but out of sync with each other. His left hand was a fist, but the right stabbed like a bladed fan at the air, so that the candle in Ferstone's grip went out. The torso was not exempt from the maelstrom. It arched its back or bowed the body almost headlong down. Under the nightshirt it was possible to note how the stomach muscles rippled like disturbed water . . . but even the muscles of the forearms and the calves seemed to spasm in an identical way. His skin *ran,* suggesting sand driven by fierce winds along a beach. The column of his neck was in quake. Even his *hair,* like that of a snake-tressed Medusa, *writhed.* Despite the death of the candle, a last steam-neon or two yet burning in the town made all this but too visible. The ghastly phenomena alone unmanned Ferstone. He cowered, witless and terror-stricken, abject. And then the creature came flailing and spinning at him.

Ferstone stumbled, lost his footing, and fell against the wall. So the devilish thing floundered past him and flared out into the parlour. Ferstone crept after him. He had only one final thought: that he himself must get away, must *escape,* perhaps to seek assistance, or merely to hide himself.

But even this decision was snatched from him.

Drawing level with the larger of the parlour windows, Primos, if so still he might be named, rammed himself forward, bellowing aloud, *"The night—the dark—the world—"*

The glass gave as if before a cannonball, and out through its showering explosion the horror seemed propelled. And such was the enduring image of its uncanny antics, a moment more it appeared hung up in space, whirling on the moonless sky. After which it was dashed downward, was gone. Below, three floors beneath, the dreadful noise of the impact sounded. Not a single cry.

Ferstone dragged himself to the window. All steam-neons now were out; only the dullness of provincial lamplight remained, into which he peered. As he did this, the clock struck the hour, that single dire stroke that separates one black night hour from another, still darker, day.

Already other notes of disturbance came from the hotel, and round about a lamp or two was lighted in a window, and other faces revealed, also staring down. Ferstone had become one among many.

Primos lay on the street, and from his head unfolded a slick, wet shadow, rolling out across the blasted rain of glass that had descended with him. It seemed his skull must have been crushed, and he had died instantly, for his tongue lolled and the two eyes were open wide and fixed, one gaping upward at the audience above, the other sidelong at those who were venturing out on the street.

But although the head was finally stilled, the *rest* of Primos remained, incredibly, demoniacally, *yet in motion.* The feet, legs, arms, and hands, the back and belly, the shoulders—all, all of him maintained the hellish jig begun in the room above.

Ferstone took this in. Then, shutting his eyes, as Primos could not, he dropped unconscious to the floor, among the remaining shards of broken glass.

Presently there happened to Ferstone the strangest event of all his life. It was also the very last.

His faint must have continued for several minutes, and as he opened his eyes again, he made out the form of a man standing over him. Briefly Ferstone was afraid this was the creature, come up again from the cobbles below. But even in the dark he could see enough to tell this man was physically unlike Primos, and fully clothed, and motionless. "I am quite all right," Ferstone said. "Let me get up—"

The man cut across his words with a flat pronouncement. "No, you will not get up. Nor will you be all right." And Ferstone discerned the stranger had extended his arm, stiffly, towards him. "You are a damnable traitor," said the man. "Take this then, on behalf of her Regal Majesty Alexand-rina Victoria, Imperatrix Britanicum." And Ferstone heard, but did not really hear, the muffled shot that issued from the slender mechanical gun. The bullet had broken the nerve chain of his spine and clipped his heart; nor did he realise that. But he could no longer shift any part of himself, could not either, just like his creature, close his eyes. Demonstrably the agent who had tracked him down believed Ferstone already dead and went swiftly out, closing the door behind him. But Ferstone had not yet died. He lay there instead, between life and obliteration, in a painless, helpless, curiously docile trance, during which his mind, now priestly cool and scalpel-like once more, worked out for him not only the plain facts of his discovery and execution, but also the explanation of his experiment's wreck. As this occurred, he pragmatically attended to the smashing sounds that currently went on in the street below. And how the crowd was managed and eventually ushered away by Her Majesty's own secret police. And how silence came back, just as the sea always did, to the hollow of the ear.

The brain ruled the body, and inside the brain there resided the intel-ligence: the mind. So it should not matter, providing *brain*, and accordingly *mind*, were whole, that the rest of the assemblage might comprise the upper torso of one body, the belly of another, and these packed with disparate organs, though all of them in the best and freshest condition. The hands, although mated, were not, either, from the same cadaver. The feet likewise. The legs had originated from four donors—calves, thighs. The arms were not a pair, although again chosen to complement one another. The eyes were like that also. Hair and skin, teeth—all at odds, even if fitted into a perfect jigsaw. The most complete set had come from the dead actor, the lungs, windpipe, and vocal cords all one. But the tongue was not related to them and at the end betrayed them. Truly a traitor to the country of Primos's body. As all of them had proved to be. How could Ferstone, how *could* he ever have guessed?

For the *brain* ruled. The mind was king.

In Primos, not so.

As Ferstone lay there, vaguely dying, he understood and knew. He had galvanized the congregated body into life, not through the genius breath of a god, but by a strike of invented lightning. And this, electrifying every atom of the creature, had woken not only the mind inside the brain, but, in addition, a separate and individual *brainless* mind in every unmatched portion of the physical frame. Not solely then an intelligence in the skull, but in each section of each leg, each section of each arm, the feet and hands, the upper torso and the lower, the spinal cord, all features, each eye, each ear, the skin and bones and hair, every organ, from the coiled snakes of the bowel to the rose-red meat of the beating heart. A mind in every region. And every one a *different* mind, intent upon its own needs and lusts. Primos—an empire, then, of *differing* kingdoms, at first malleable and infantile. But, as all grew up into awareness and strength, all *selfish*. And soon enough bellicose, at war with every *other* mind trapped there inside the living whole. Cunning and cruel and mad, and single-purposed, each of them, minds not willing to form a team, refusing to run in harness. *Each* a king. Each determined to *rule*. *Each monstrous*.

Though the brain-mind inside the skull had died, the legs and arms and all of those uncorrespondent potentates went on with their power-devouring seizures, until smashed to death and inanition by clubs and axes. And when, too, at last, every bit of it lay a corpse, inert amid its ruins, what *could* persist but silence, and the sound of the sea?

As he drifted outward, Ferstone felt how the silence now grew louder than all else. He could only listen as it entered into him, unforgiving and endless, that reward of all endeavor: Nothingness.

About "Their Monstrous Minds"

I first ventured into Steampunk in the midnineties last century and had a Steampunk novel published in 1995 to prove it: *Reigning Cats and Dogs*.

Certain elements of the Black Church Terror in that book were the product of the ideas department of my husband (writer-artist-Steampunk-model-maker John Kaiine). Not inappropriately then, the baseline of this scenario also owes itself to him. When men try to play gods, they tend to come unstuck. It's no good starting to fly before you've grown the wings.

❊ ESTELLA SAVES THE VILLAGE ❊

I have lived in the village all my life.

Miss Havisham has told me the story over and over again: how, as an infant, I was found in a basket on the front steps of the church, and how Reverend Rivers asked the villagers gathered for service on Sunday morning which of them would be willing to raise a foundling. And how Miss Havisham immediately said, "I will."

So I've grown up in her small house on the high street, close enough to the baker's that in the mornings I can smell the bread in his oven, and every morning before school Miss Havisham gives me a penny for a bun with raisins in it. I always share it with Pip while he walks beside me, carrying my school bag. I tell him I can carry it perfectly well myself, but he insists, so I let him. It's useful, but sometimes tedious, that he's been in love with me since we were both children.

If you stop for a moment and look back as Pip and I walk to school, you can see Miss Havisham's house, with its green shutters and window boxes filled with geraniums. Above it, you can see the downs among which our village is nestled, with sheep grazing on them. Sometimes you can see the herds moving like clouds, driven by a black-and-white streak of sheepdog. Over them runs the high road, to places I've never been—through fields and forests, joining with other roads. Eventually it reaches London, with its grand houses and shops and Buckingham Palace itself. Sometimes

I think about taking that road, travelling to the greatest city in the world. But then the school bell rings, and I turn and run after Pip.

I have started my story this way—by telling you about Miss Havisham and Pip and the bakery and the geraniums in the window boxes, so you will understand what our village was like before the specks appeared.

I first noticed them on a Sunday morning. All the respectable inhabitants of the village were in church. The less respectable were in the tavern, already worshipping John Barleycorn, as Mr Henchard calls it. Miss Havisham and I were seated in our pew. In the box at the front, I could see mad Lady D'Urberville, who lives in the Hall. She always arrives in a brougham with her estate agent, Mr Clare. He was sitting beside her, leaning toward her as though whispering a secret. I envied her red brocade and the red hat with egret feathers, however inappropriate it might be for Sunday service. She is the only woman in the village whose dresses do not come from Miss Tulliver's shop, but from a modiste in London. Miss Tulliver was there, too, with her brother the miller and his large family. The Ushers slid into the pew in front of us, and Mr Usher turned around to bow stiffly to Miss Havisham. I believe he eats only vegetables and wears some sort of patent undergarment. He always looks ghastly, as though he were recovering from an illness. Dr Lydgate paused for a moment on the way to his own pew to take Miss Usher's hand. He put the fingers of his other hand on her wrist, above the edge of her glove—measuring her pulse, I suppose. She is said to be consumptive, although she looks healthier than her brother. Pip waved to me as though frantic for my attention, until Joe Gargery cuffed him on the head and he had to stop.

Then the organ started, and I had to stop looking around, which I have to admit is always the most interesting part of the service. What was the relationship between Lady D'Urberville and Mr Clare? Would Miss Tulliver ever find herself a husband? Was Dr Lydgate secretly in love with Miss Usher? These were the sorts of pious thoughts that kept me occupied, although Miss Havisham gave me a reproachful glance over her prayer book. I tried to pay attention, but Reverend Rivers was talking about our dark-skinned brothers in darkest Africa, who sounded as though they were doing quite well for themselves, with plenty of missionaries to eat. To keep myself from looking around, I studied the back of Miss Usher's thin, pale neck, where it showed beneath her bonnet and a few wisps of straggling hair. It was covered with black specks.

What could they be? They did not look like dirt, and anyway I could not imagine Madeline Usher having a dirty neck. Yet there they were. A symptom of consumption, perhaps?

Absorbed in this mystery, I said the Lord's Prayer, sang the same hymns I'd been singing since I was a child, and walked to the Communion rail, all without thinking a single religious thought. As I held out my hands for the host, I noticed a pair of hands beside mine—large, masculine, with black specks on the palms. I glanced up surreptitiously to see who it was and saw Dr Lydgate.

After that, Reverend Rivers could have announced the arrival of Armageddon and I would not have noticed. Once we had all filed out of the church, I looked around and saw Dr Lydgate walking among the gravestones.

"Estella! Do you want to go fishing today?" said Pip.

"No," I said rudely. "I'm detecting." I have always fancied myself a detective, like the most famous inhabitant of our village, Mr Holmes.

"What are you detecting?"

"Never mind right now. Just come with me and stay quiet."

I walked to the graveyard and stood beside a marble angel on a pedestal. "What are you thinking about so intently, Dr Lydgate?" I asked. His hands were bare—he never wears gloves unless the weather demands it. I could not see the palms, but there were specks on the backs of his hands as well.

He smiled. "Nothing that would interest a young lady, I'm afraid, Miss Havisham. I was thinking about a new vaccine that would save lives like the one buried here. It was the measles that took him, and only six years old. Such a pity. And what are you doing in the graveyard on a fine morning?"

"Meditating on mortality," I said.

"A commendable, although unusual, activity for a healthy young lady like yourself."

"It's an assignment for school. Dr Lydgate, you seem to have gotten some dirt on your hands."

He held up his hands and looked at them. "Have I? I confess, they seem clean to me, but young ladies have a higher standard of cleanliness than old bachelors like myself. I'll wash them as soon as I get home." He smiled again indulgently. I could tell he hadn't seen the specks.

"What was all that about dirt on his hands?" asked Pip while he was walking me home from church.

"You didn't see it either?"

"See what?"

I sighed. "Did you see Mr Holmes during the service? I tried to find him afterward, but he wasn't there."

"He was sitting behind Joe and left right after the processional. He said something about his bees needing him more than the Lord this morning."

It was a mystery, my very own mystery. I had half a mind to keep it to myself. But I was also worried—Pip had seen nothing. What if I was simply imagining the specks? It made sense to consult a real detective and make sure.

But first, I would go around the village and see if I could find any more of the black specks. After dinner, of course—my stomach was starting to grumble.

"See you tomorrow," I said to Pip when we had reached the front door. He opened his mouth, and I knew he wanted to ask if he could come detecting with me. But this was my adventure, and I wanted to go on it alone. When I closed the door, he was still standing on the step with his mouth open. I almost felt guilty—but after all, it was only Pip.

Sunday dinner consisted of an Irish stew and soda bread that Fanny had prepared. Miss Havisham always allows her to serve a stew so she can cook it beforehand and go to the service. Then she can just heat it up on the stove. I don't think anyone is as generous to their servants as Miss Havisham. Who else would allow Fanny to keep her child in the house? But Miss Havisham says that every child is a gift, whatever its origin.

"Estella," said Miss Havisham after we had finished, "you've been happy here, haven't you?"

"Of course I've been happy. You've been like a mother to me, and I've had everything I could have wanted—except the red brocade dress Lady D'Urberville was wearing today, and can you imagine the scandal I'd cause, wearing that?"

Miss Havisham laughed. "I'm glad. I've always hoped that with a proper home, and the right sorts of things—books, and friends like Pip, you would grow up to be . . ."

"What?"

"The sort of young woman you're turning out to be. Intelligent and compassionate."

I went over to her side of the table, gave her a hug from behind, and kissed her on the cheek. She always smelled nice, like lavender water. It's a comforting smell that reminds me of hurt feelings soothed, scraped knees bandaged, tears wiped away. I don't think my mother, whoever she was, could have taken better care of me than Miss Havisham.

"Thank you, my dear. Now, I'm going to do some knitting. Tell me what sort of adventure you and Pip have planned for this afternoon."

As she stood up from the table, I noticed that she moved more slowly than she used to, and she put a hand on the back of the chair to brace herself. Was Miss Havisham getting old? As long as I remembered, she'd looked the same: white hair under her lace cap and blue eyes that seemed to pierce right through you (she always knew when I had stolen from the jam jar), surrounded by lines that laughter had formed over the years. I have never known anyone kinder or more forgiving.

"Would you give me your arm into the parlour? I seem to be feeling my age today."

At the thought of Miss Havisham growing older, a chill settled about my heart. Somehow, I'd never imagined such a thing could happen.

"Pip and I aren't doing anything this afternoon," I said. "Do you want me to read while you knit?" I could put off detecting for one day. Anyway, maybe I had just imagined the specks.

She looked startled, but said, "That would be lovely." So for several hours, I read from Gibbon's *Decline and Fall of the Roman Empire,* which I found tedious but Miss Havisham found fascinating. "Thank you, my dear," she said afterward. "That was the loveliest afternoon I've had in a long time."

That night, as I lay in bed under a quilt she had sewn for me and that had kept me warm since I was a child, I realized that the world I'd lived in all my life might change. I stared into the darkness, not knowing how to react to that thought.

The next morning, there was a scattering of black specks over Pip's cheek and down his collar. I didn't mention it to him, although he probably wondered why I kept looking at him so intently.

When we reached the schoolhouse, I went over to the girls' side and sat next to Flora. There were spots on her pinafore, and her notebook looked as though she had spattered ink over it. I took out my school books. There was a black hole in my *School History of England.* It went through every page, as though a large worm had chewed right through it. The date of the Norman Conquest was missing, as were parts of the Duke of Wellington's victory at Waterloo and an engraving of Queen Victoria's coronation.

"Estella," said Miss Murray, "is everything all right?"

No, I wanted to tell her. *There are splotches of nothing on the map of the world hanging by the chalkboard.* But I just nodded.

"All right, students," she said. "I want the older girls to help the younger ones with their spelling. Estella, Pearl, Flora, and Nell, can you form them into a line and take them into the school yard? The weather is fine, and I want you to do your lessons out there while I test the boys on yesterday's Latin." A general groan came from the boys' side of the room.

The rest of the school day was as busy as usual. But everywhere I looked, I noticed black specks, spots, holes. They seemed to be spreading.

After the bell rang to signal the end of the school day, I started detecting. Pip wanted to come, of course, but he had to work in the blacksmith's shop, which was for the best. I wasn't ready to explain what I was doing, or why.

I started at the far end of the village, at the cottage of the foreign ladies, Mrs Rochester and her companion, Miss Rappaccini. They had come to the village several years before. Mrs Rochester is from the colonies and speaks English, but Miss Rappaccini is Italian. She answered the door, and I had to explain myself twice before she could understand what I wanted.

At every house, I would knock, and when the door was opened, I would say, "I'm doing an assignment for school on 'How We Live in the Nineteenth Century.' Can I come in and look around?"

It's astonishing what people will believe when you look at them steadily and speak with conviction.

"Come right in, Estella," they would usually say, although Mr Henchard grumbled about public education, which was nothing like in his time (thank goodness, or we might all end up as ignorant as he is), and Mr Fawley apologized for the state of his parlour, which had piles of books covering the floor and on every armchair.

Our village isn't large, but I was offered tea several times and felt as though I had to accept. Being polite is a nuisance. By the time I was done, it was too late to visit Mr Holmes, as I had intended. I would have to see him the next day.

I admit, it was beginning to scare me: all around the village there were splotches of nothing, and they seemed to be growing. As I walked home, I could see them on the trees, like black lichen. On the flanks of horses in the pastures. I almost stumbled into one on the road.

How would you feel if your world was disappearing? Well, that's how I felt.

When I got home, it was a relief to notice no spots at all, not a single speck. There, at least, the nothingness had not yet invaded.

The next morning, I did not go to school. Instead, I asked Pip to tell Miss Murray that I was sick. He looked at me quizzically. The spots on his cheek were now larger, the size of pencil ends. "I promise I'll tell you soon, all right?" I said.

"All right, Estella. But I wish you would trust me." He turned reluctantly and headed toward the school.

I headed toward Mr Holmes's house. The garden was a riot of flowers. Mrs Holmes was cutting roses and putting them into a basket on the ground. "Hello, Estella," she said. "Are you here to see me or Sherlock?" She did not ask me why I wasn't in school.

"I'm here to see Mr Holmes."

"You'll find him in the study. Can you tell him that I've left plenty for the bees? He always objects to my cutting flowers. But you can't have a dining-room table without fresh flowers on it, can you?"

"I suppose not." No one else in the village would have put cut flowers on a table, although Miss Havisham has wax flowers under a glass dome. But before her marriage, Mrs Holmes was an actress in London. She wears her hair down, dresses in what Miss Tulliver calls the aesthetic style, and rides a bicycle through the village. Miss Havisham says that she's unconventional. I think I'd like to be unconventional when I grow up.

I had been in the study once before, several years ago, when Mr Holmes had been sick and Miss Havisham had brought over some beef tea. He'd been lying on the sofa under a blanket. She had talked to him, and I'd been able to wander around, looking at all the books, the scientific instruments on the tables, the weapons on the walls.

"Hello, Estella," he said as I entered. "Come look at this." He indicated the microscope he'd been looking through.

I went and looked. "What is it?"

"The hind leg of a bee. You can see the three segments. Can you see that the third segment is shaped like a basket? That's called the corbicula, where the bee carries pollen. I'm writing a monograph on the Apidae, on their anatomy and habits. Perhaps later I can show you my bees. They are fascinating creatures. If only men could work together as harmoniously! But I'm sure you haven't come here to talk about bees. Has Miss Havisham sent you?"

"No. I need to consult you myself. I've been seeing specks, black specks. Only some of them are spots, or holes. Some of them are quite large. On Sunday, I saw them on Miss Usher in church. Since then, I've been seeing them everywhere. You can actually put your finger, or even your hand, into them. They feel cold, like nothingness. Yesterday, I went around the village and wrote down where they were, and their sizes and depths. It's all in this notebook."

I handed him my school notebook. I had written all my findings down and then recopied them the night before. "But only I can see them," I added. "So you see, I may be going mad." I tried to sound logical, like a detective, but my voice trembled.

He gave me a sharp glance, then leafed through the notebook methodically.

"Let's sit down, shall we?" I sat beside him on the sofa. "It seems to me that there are two possibilities. Either you are having hallucinations, in which case you need to see Dr Lydgate. Or you actually are seeing black holes that no one else is seeing. Do you see any in this room?"

"Yes. There's one on the sofa, right beside your shoulder." It was the size of my finger. I put my finger right into it, up to the knuckle. I didn't want to tell him he had specks on his chin, like the stubble of a beard, and down the front of his Norfolk jacket as though he had spilled ink on it.

"Fascinating," said Mr Holmes. "I don't think you'll need to consult Dr Lydgate."

"Why?"

"Because although I can't see a hole in the sofa, I just saw your finger disappear into the upholstery. I'm going to ask Irene for a glass of sherry. I think you need it."

He went to the door and called Mrs Holmes. In a few minutes, he brought me a glass of liquor the colour of garnets. It burned going down, and I coughed.

He sat back down on the sofa, putting his elbows on his knees and his chin on his clasped hands. "Have you noticed any patterns? Are there places where the spots are larger or smaller? I'm interested in whether they're spreading from a particular location."

I leafed through my notes. I should have thought of arranging the sightings by size. "They seem larger on the other side of the village. The largest one I saw was on the wall around Mrs Rochester's garden. It was the size of a cabbage. And she told me that her terrier has disappeared. She asked me if I had seen him, and I didn't know what to say. Mr Holmes, I'm afraid the world's disappearing. I only started to notice the specks on Sunday, but those larger spots—they're probably been growing for some time."

He thought for a moment, then asked, "Is there any place the spots don't appear?"

"Only at home. I haven't seen any there."

Why? Why hadn't I seen any spots at home, when I had seen them everywhere else? I'd been so relieved by their absence that I hadn't even bothered to ask. And there had been enough to worry about, with the revelation of Miss Havisham's frailty.

"Mr Holmes, I have to go. I have to talk to Miss Havisham."

He nodded, looking concerned. "Yes, that seems indicated." Then he smiled, as though he could not help it. "So the game is afoot, Estella."

"Something like that," I said, handing him the glass of sherry.

Halfway home, I started to run.

"Miss Havisham," I said. "Can I talk to you?" She was sitting on the parlour sofa, knitting what I suddenly realized would eventually be a sweater for me. Her fingers were as nimble as they had always been. The parlour looked just as it always had, with light filtering through the lace curtains, falling on the gleaming wood of the furniture and the rich colours of the Persian carpet. Not a single speck.

"Of course," she said. "Is it the dinner break already? I must have lost track of time. I seem to be doing that more and more, these days."

"No. I didn't go to school today."

She stopped knitting and looked up at me. She must have seen something in my face or heard something in the tone of my voice, because instead of scolding me, she sat perfectly still. As though waiting.

I sat in one of the armchairs and put the notebook on my knees. "Yesterday, I went around the village and—here. Look at this." I held out the notebook.

She put the knitting needles down on the sofa beside her, took the notebook, and leafed through the pages. Then, she turned back to the beginning and read each page again. Finally she said, "I see. When did you first notice this?"

"On Sunday. But it must have been spreading for some time."

"Yes, I'm sure it has. Although I didn't think anyone here would notice."

Now it was my turn to sit, waiting. I was afraid of what she was going to say. I had no idea what it was, but she knew about the spots—that itself frightened me.

"Estella, I'm going to tell you a story." She leaned against the back of the sofa and looked down at her hands, as though suddenly not sure what to do with them. "I'm not used to telling stories, so I may ramble a bit. You'll be patient with me, won't you?"

"Of course. Just tell me." I sounded impatient, almost angry—but it was from fear. She didn't seem to notice.

"Once, there was a girl about your age who wanted to be a writer. Her parents didn't want her to be a writer—they wanted her to be a doctor or lawyer, something practical."

"Girls can't become doctors or lawyers."

"They can in this story," said Miss Havisham. She sounded different somehow. Not like the Miss Havisham I knew, but like Miss Murray when she gives us a lecture on the suffrage movement. Was this the kindly old woman who had brought me up, taught me how to make jam and mend stockings? Who had brushed my hair at night?

"So instead of becoming a writer, she decided to become a college professor—and, yes," she said, looking at me, "in this story girls can do that as well. She studied what other people had written—literature, that is, from medieval poems to modern critical theory. What she particularly loved was Victorian literature—Charles Dickens, George Eliot, Thomas Hardy, even American writers like Nathaniel Hawthorne. Anything written during that era."

What in the world was Miss Havisham talking about? I worried that she was going mad. She was making no sense, but I didn't dare interrupt.

"Their novels sometimes made her sad because so many of them ended badly. She started imagining alternative endings, just before she fell asleep at night. She would imagine her favourite characters living together in a village, happily ever after—or as happily as possible. She would imagine all the details of that village—the church where St. John Rivers could preach on Sundays, the main street with a blacksmith's shop for Joe Gargery and Pip, a shop where Maggie Tulliver could set up as a seamstress. And she imagined herself living in one of the houses—with a daughter." I was startled to see a tear run down her cheek. She wiped it away with her hand. "In her own life, she never married, never had any children of her own. Except the hundreds of students who took her classes, because eventually she became a professor of literature at a college in Vermont. Every night she would imagine the village—it became an important part of her life. It seemed so real to her."

"And then what happened?" I was beginning to understand. It was impossible—and frightening. But my book of aphorisms says you should believe six impossible things before breakfast.

"She began forgetting things. The date of the Indian Mutiny, her students' names. She had to go into a hospital, where the doctors looked inside her head. They can do that, in this story." She gave me a small, wry smile. How strange it was, listening to this new Miss Havisham. So direct, so unlike the Miss Havisham that I knew.

"What did they see?" I asked.

"Black specks. There's a medical term for it, of course. But that's essentially what they saw—black spaces where there was nothing, where the brain had died."

I sat staring at her, not sure what to say. Both believing and incredulous. "So what's going to happen to the village? And why am I the only one who can see what's happening?"

She looked down again, as though defeated, and that frightened me more than anything else. "I don't know. I'm sorry, Estella. I've tried every medication the doctors prescribed, and nothing has helped. The specks—the black spaces are growing. I don't know why you're the only one who can see them—perhaps it's because you've grown up with me. You're closer to me than anyone in the village. But there's no way to stop the memory loss."

"Then that's it?" I was almost shouting at her, but I couldn't help it. "So what's going to happen to all of us? And me—am I just someone in a book?"

She leaned forward and took my hands. "Oh, my dear. You're my Estella. The girl who grew up in the village, playing with Pip and Flora and Pearl, learning history and arithmetics from Miss Murray. You're smart and sometimes selfish and obstinate, but a good friend. And you're my daughter. That's who you are, Estella. Hold on to that."

"How can I hold on to that?" Now I really was shouting. I'd never shouted at Miss Havisham in my life. "I don't even know who you are!"

I pulled my hands away, jumped up, and ran out of the room, then out the front door and down the high street, past the blacksmith's shop, running and running until I had left the village behind. I looked around—fields. I set out across one of the fields, toward the downs.

I walked and walked, grasses tickling me through my stockings, above my boots. I didn't stop until I was so tired that I could barely continue. Where was I?

By a copse of trees and a small stream. In the distance was the Hall. Had I really come that far? And then I saw something I had never expected, although I suppose I should have. Just above the chimneys of the Hall, on the blue of the sky, there was a scattering of black spots, like small moons.

"Hello, Estella."

I turned around, startled. There was mad Lady D'Urberville, in her red brocade gown. Had she been here all along? I had been so preoccupied, so frightened by what I had seen in the sky, that I hadn't noticed.

"Have you come here to dance? I often dance here myself. It's the fairies' dancing ground."

She picked up her skirts, curtsied gracefully, then started dancing to some music only she could hear. When she turned, her skirts spread around her, revealing black gaps around the hems that made them look ragged.

"Aren't you going to dance, too, Estella?" she asked, holding out her hand.

"I don't feel like dancing," I said. For a moment I watched her as she turned and spun, then asked, "What would you do if you found out that the world you lived in was—some sort of dream?"

She stopped and stood, considering.

Suddenly I heard a shout: "Tess, where are you?" I looked around. Her foreman, Mr Clare, was walking toward us from the direction of the Hall.

"I'm coming, my angel!" she called back. Then, leaning toward me as though she did not want anyone else to hear, although no one was close enough, she said, *"All that we see or seem is but a dream within a dream.* Remember that, Estella." She blew me a kiss and danced away over the field to where Mr Clare was waiting.

I looked around me, at the fields and the downs beyond them, at the Hall in the distance. At the damaged sky. I looked back toward the village. I could just see the church spire. Miss Havisham had dreamed the village. All that we see and seem. Was that other life of hers a dream as well? Was someone dreaming her—the professor in that world where girls could go to college and study literature? If so, who was the dreamer?

I imagined an infinite number of dreamers, all dreaming each other. It made my head hurt.

"Estella, are you all right?" It was Pip. Black spots were now scattered down the front of his smock.

"Where did you come from?"

"I saw you run by the blacksmith's shop. I had to run in and tell Biddy where I was going, but since then I've been trying to find you. Don't get mad at me—I know you don't like me following you around like a sick dog, as you once said. But I was worried about you. You've been acting so strange for the last couple of days, barely talking to me. And why weren't you in school?"

Poor Pip. Miss Havisham was wrong—I hadn't been a very good friend.

"I want to try something. Will you stay quiet while I lie down on the ground? You can lie next to me if you want." I tried to sound calm, although I was scared. Would I have to watch the world disappear around me? For a moment I wished I were anyone else, so I wouldn't know what was happening.

He looked puzzled, but nodded.

I sat down on the ground and then lay back. Stalks of grass tickled my neck.

Pip sat beside me. "What are you going to do?"

"I'm going to dream."

"Don't you need to fall asleep first?"

"It's not that kind of dreaming. Now hush."

I closed my eyes and imagined Mrs Rochester's terrier, with its sandy hair and sharp, loud bark. I tried to remember everything about him. Then I imagined Mr Holmes's sofa, and my schoolbook with the engraving of Queen Victoria's coronation, and the back of Miss Usher's neck—all the places where I'd seen the nothingness spreading. I imagined every part of the village where I'd seen specks, spots, holes, or gaps. In my mind, I repaired them all. I repaired the sky itself. Finally, I imagined Pip's face, which I'd seen every day of my life, with no spots on it. I imagined as hard as I could. *All that we see or seem*, I said to myself, repeatedly until it became an incantation. Until I saw the village, every detail of it, as though it existed in my mind. I was its mender, its preserver, its creator.

I opened my eyes.

Pip was leaning on his elbow, looking down at me. His cheek was smooth and brown and unspotted. Behind him, the sky was blue—completely blue, except where white clouds floated across it like sheep.

I shouted with pleasure and pulled him toward me. I had meant to hug him, but instead he put his lips on mine and kissed me. It was awkward and wet, but satisfying. My first kiss. Although I had never imagined that Pip would be the first to kiss me, I was glad.

"Estella, I love you. Will you marry me?"

"Don't be silly. I'm only fifteen, and anyway when I finish school, I'm going to London to be a writer."

If I could dream the village, then perhaps I could dream London? Or even the world? And perhaps I could dream it differently—perhaps it could be a world in which girls could go to college, as Miss Havisham had described. I would have to dream every day, I would have to repeat my incantation, my spell. Tomorrow I would go around the village and make certain that all of the gaps were indeed gone. But I felt confident that if any were left, I could fill them. I could save the village I loved. Could I save Miss Havisham? Perhaps the one who lived in the village, the one who had raised me. That other woman she had described—another dreamer would have to take care of her.

The thought of it made me sad. But the only world I could save was my own, the one I lived in, the one that was waiting. Maybe someday I would marry Pip—but certainly not yet. I had all sorts of adventures ahead of me.

"Come on," I said. "You look like a dog that's lost its bone. You've had one kiss, and if you can catch me, I'll give you another!"

Then I jumped up, laughing, and ran back toward the village, across the fields, under a blue sky with flying clouds.

About "Estella Saves the Village"

I am Miss Havisham—sort of. Like the woman who calls herself Miss Havisham in my story, I am a college professor specializing in Victorian literature, and I've often thought about the depressing conclusions of many stories from that era. Poor Mr Henchard, and Maggie Tulliver, and even Estella! But unlike Miss Havisham, I'm a writer, so I get to do more than dream about alternative endings: I get to actually write them. "Estella Saves the Village" came out of my own desire to create a village where Sherlock Holmes could have his happy ending, and Pip could grow up with the girl he loves. I do believe that our dreams create the world, and that we are responsible for maintaining and repairing it. Although we may not all have Estella's power to create the world we want to live in, the story is on some level a metaphor for our ability to shape our own realities. On another level, I hope it's a fun puzzle to put together for anyone interested in Victorian literature.

ABOUT THE AUTHORS

Dale Bailey lives in North Carolina with his family and has published three novels, *The Fallen, House of Bones,* and *Sleeping Policemen* (with Jack Slay Jr.). His short fiction, collected in *The Resurrection Man's Legacy and Other Stories,* has won the International Horror Guild Award and has been twice nominated for the Nebula Award.

Elizabeth Bear was born on the same day as Frodo and Bilbo Baggins, but in a different year. She lives in Massachusetts with a giant, ridiculous dog, but makes frequent sojourns to the upper Midwest because that's where she keeps her partner, internationally bestselling fantasy novelist Scott Lynch. She is a Hugo and Sturgeon Award winner, and her most recent novel is *Range of Ghosts,* an epic fantasy inspired by the history and cultures of Central Asia.

James P. Blaylock has been publishing stories and novels since around 1975—more than twenty novels and story collections in all. In 1977, *Un-Earth* magazine published his story "The Ape-Box Affair," arguably the first American Steampunk story. Over the years he has won the Philip K. Dick Memorial Award for his novel *Homunculus* and two World Fantasy Awards. His short story "Unidentified Objects" was nominated for an

O. Henry Award. His most recently published novels are *Knights of the Cornerstone*, set in the California desert; *The Ebb Tide*, a Steampunk adventure set in London and the Lake District; and its companion volume, *The Affair of the Chalk Cliffs*. He is currently finishing up a novel titled *The Aylesford Skull*, to be published by Titan Books.

Jeffrey Ford is the author of eight novels (most recently *The Shadow Year*) and four collections of short stories (most recently *Crackpot Palace*). He is the recipient of the World Fantasy Award, Shirley Jackson Award, Edgar Allan Poe Award, and Nebula Award. His story "The Drowned Life" was recently included in *The Oxford Book of American Short Stories*, 2nd ed. Also his story "Blood Drive" appeared in the YA apocalyptic and dystopian anthology *After*, edited by Ellen Datlow and Terri Windling (Tor), and "A Natural History of Autumn" appeared in *The Magazine of Fantasy & Science Fiction*. He lives in Ohio with his wife and sons.

Theodora Goss was born in Hungary and spent her childhood in various European countries before her family moved to the United States.

Although she grew up on the classics of English literature, her writing has been influenced by an Eastern European literary tradition in which the boundaries between realism and the fantastic are often ambiguous.

Her publications include the short story collection *In the Forest of Forgetting; Interfictions*, an anthology coedited with Delia Sherman; *Voices from Fairyland*, a poetry anthology with critical essays and a selection of her own poems; and *The Thorn and the Blossom*, a two-sided story bound in an accordion format. She has been a finalist for the Nebula, Locus, Crawford, and Mythopoeic Awards, has had work on the Tiptree Award Honor List, and has won the World Fantasy and Rhysling Awards.

Author, actress, and playwright **Leanna Renee Hieber** grew up in rural Ohio inventing ghost stories. She graduated with a BFA in theatre from Miami University, a focus in the Victorian era, and a scholarship to study in London. She adapted works of nineteenth-century literature for the stage, and her one-act plays such as *Favorite Lady* have been produced around the country.

Her debut novel, *The Strangely Beautiful Tale of Miss Percy Parker*, first in her *Strangely Beautiful* quartet of Gaslight Fantasy novels, made Barnes &

Noble's bestseller lists, won two 2010 Prism Awards, and is currently in development as a musical-theatre production. *Darker Still: A Novel of Magic Most Foul*, first in the *Magic Most Foul* trilogy, was named on the Indie Next List as a recommended title by the American Booksellers Association.

Hieber's short fiction has been published in the anthologies *Candle in the Attic Window* and *Wilful Impropriety: Tales of Society and Scandal*. She is a cofounder of Lady Jane's Salon Reading Series in New York City and was named the 2010 RWA NYC Author of the Year. When not writing or on set, she's a devotee of ghost stories, Goth clubs, and finely tailored corsets, adventuring about her adopted hometown of New York City, where she resides with her real-life hero and their beloved rescued lab rabbit. Visit her at http://leannareneehieber.com, and she tweets often @LeannaRenee.

Kathe Koja's novels include *The Cipher, Skin, Buddha Boy, Talk, Headlong*, and *Under the Poppy* and its sequel, *The Mercury Waltz*. *Under the Poppy* has been adapted for immersive theatrical performance; *The Cipher* is under option for film. She lives in the Detroit area with her husband, artist Rick Lieder, and their cats.

Ellen Kushner's first novel, *Swordspoint*, introduced readers to the city to which she has since returned in *The Privilege of the Sword* (Locus Award and Nebula nominee), *The Fall of the Kings* (written with Delia Sherman), and a handful of related short stories, most recently "The Duke of Riverside" in Ellen Datlow's *Naked City*.

She and Holly Black coedited *Welcome to Bordertown*, a revival of the original urban fantasy shared world series created by Terri Windling. Kushner's second novel, *Thomas the Rhymer*, won the Mythopoeic and World Fantasy Awards. She has taught writing at the Clarion and Odyssey workshops and is a cofounder of the Interstitial Arts Foundation. Ellen Kushner is also the longtime host of the public radio show *Sound & Spirit*. She has recorded audiobooks of *Swordspoint* and its sequels for the Neil Gaiman Presents line on Audible.com. Ellen Kushner lives in New York City with author and editor Delia Sherman, and no cats whatsoever. It is all made clear at www.EllenKushner.com.

Tanith Lee has written nearly 100 books and over 290 short stories, besides radio plays and TV scripts. Her genre-crossing includes fantasy,

SF, horror, young adult, historical, detective, and contemporary fiction. Plus combinations of them all. Her latest publications include the *Lionwolf Trilogy: Cast a Bright Shadow, Here in Cold Hell,* and *No Flame but Mine,* and the three *Piratica* novels for young adults. Norilana Books is reprinting all *The Flat-Earth Cycle,* with two new volumes to follow, and Immanion Press will be publishing a series of contemporary *strange* novels.

She has also recently had several short stories and novellas in such publications as *Asimov's Science Fiction, Weird Tales, Realms of Fantasy, The Ghost Quartet,* and *Wizard.*

In 2009, Lee was named Grandmaster by the World Horror Convention.

She lives on the Sussex Weald with her husband, writer/artist John Kaiine, and two omnipresent cats. More information can be found at www.TanithLee.com.

Gregory Maguire has written twenty books for children and eight novels for adults, including *Wicked: The Life and Times of the Wicked Witch of the West* and, most recently, *Out of Oz.* His works have been made into radio plays, television movies, and Broadway musicals, and he has had work translated into thirty languages. He is glad to have contributed to quite a few anthologies of original stories presented by Ellen Datlow and Terri Windling.

Maureen McHugh's first novel, *China Mountain Zhang,* was a James Tiptree Award winner. Her latest collection of short stories, *After the Apocalypse,* was one of *Publishers Weekly*'s ten best books of the year. She's lived in Ohio, New York City, China, Austin, Texas, and now lives with her husband and her dog in Los Angeles. She writes for Fourth Wall Studios.

Veronica Schanoes lives in New York City. Her work has appeared in *Lady Churchill's Rosebud Wristlet, The Year's Best Fantasy and Horror,* and *Strange Horizons.* She is an assistant professor in the Department of English at Queens College–CUNY.

Delia Sherman's most recent short stories have appeared in the young-adult anthologies *Steampunk!* and *Teeth* and in Ellen Datlow's urban-fantasy anthology *Naked City.* Her adult novels are *Through a Brazen Mirror, The*

Porcelain Dove, and *The Fall of the Kings* (with Ellen Kushner). Novels for younger readers include New York Between Novels *Changeling* and *The Magic Mirror of the Mermaid*. Her new novel, *The Freedom Maze*, a time-travel historical about antebellum Louisiana, received the Andre Norton Award, the Mythopoeic Award, and the Prometheus Award.

When she's not writing, she's teaching, editing, knitting, and traveling. She lives in New York City with Ellen Kushner, piles of books, some nice Arts & Crafts wallpaper, and a very Victorian rock collection.

Caroline Stevermer grew up miles from anywhere on a dairy farm in southeastern Minnesota, where the local culture was about twenty years behind the rest of the country. She achieved escape velocity just in time to meet Ellen Kushner on her first day at Bryn Mawr College. Ellen taught Caroline the Letter Game, of which "The Vital Importance of the Superficial" is an example, and they played the game by exchanging letters during summer vacation.

Since then, Caroline has written *Magic Below Stairs*, *A College of Magics*, and *A Scholar of Magics*, among other novels. She taught Patricia C. Wrede the Letter Game. Together they wrote *Sorcery & Cecelia* as a letter game, followed by its sequels, *The Grand Tour* and *The Mislaid Magician*.

Caroline now lives in Minneapolis, where she enjoys watching baseball, learning local history, and complaining about the weather.

Catherynne M. Valente is the *New York Times* bestselling author of over a dozen works of fiction and poetry, including *Palimpsest*, *The Orphan's Tales* series, *Deathless*, and the crowdfunded phenomenon *The Girl Who Circumnavigated Fairyland in a Ship of Her Own Making*. She is the winner of the Andre Norton Award, the Tiptree Award, the Mythopoeic Award, the Rhysling Award, and the Million Writers Award. She has been nominated for the Hugo, Locus, Nebula, and Spectrum Awards, the Pushcart Prize, and was a finalist for the World Fantasy Award in 2007 and 2009. She lives on an island off the coast of Maine with her partner, two dogs, and enormous cat.

Genevieve Valentine's fiction has appeared in *Clarkesworld, Strange Horizons, Journal of Mythic Arts, Fantasy, Lightspeed, Apex*, and others, and in the anthologies *Federations, The Living Dead 2, After, Running with the*

Pack, Teeth, and more; her short stories have been nominated for the World Fantasy and Shirley Jackson Awards.

Her nonfiction has appeared in *Weird Tales, Tor.com,* and *Fantasy,* and she's a coauthor of *Geek Wisdom* (Quirk Books).

Her first novel, *Mechanique: A Tale of the Circus Tresaulti,* won the 2012 Crawford Award and was nominated for the Nebula.

Her appetite for bad movies is insatiable, a tragedy she tracks on her blog, genevievevalentine.com.

Kaaron Warren's short-story collection *The Grinding House* won the ACT Writing and Publishing Fiction Award and two Ditmar Awards. Her second collection, *Dead Sea Fruit,* also won the ACT Writing and Publishing Fiction Award. Her third collection, *Through Splintered Walls,* was recently published by Twelfth Planet Press.

Her critically acclaimed first novel, *Slights,* won the Australian Shadows Long Fiction Award, the Ditmar Award, and the Canberra Critics' Award for Fiction. Since then she's had two others novels published, *Walking the Tree* and *Mistification,* both short-listed for a Ditmar Award.

Warren's stories have been picked for *The Year's Best Horror and Fantasy* and Ellen Datlow's *The Best Horror of the Year,* as well as the *Year's Best Australian Horror, Science Fiction,* and *Fantasy* anthologies.

Warren lives in Canberra, Australia, with her husband and children. Her website is kaaronwarren.wordpress.com and she tweets @KaaronWarren.

Elizabeth Wein lives in Scotland with her husband and two children. She is the author of *The Winter Prince* and the *Mark of Solomon* duology, consisting of *The Lion Hunter* and *The Empty Kingdom. The Lion Hunter* was short-listed for the Andre Norton Award in 2008.

Elizabeth's most recent book is *Code Name Verity,* which she describes as "a World War II spies 'n' pilots thriller." She is the holder of a private pilot's license and an increasing collection of random wartime ephemera.

Jane Yolen is often called "the Hans Christian Andersen of America" because of all the fairy tales she has written, though she says, "I should actually be called 'the Hans Jewish Andersen.'"

Among her over three hundred books are the award-winning Holocaust novels *The Devil's Arithmetic* and *Briar Rose,* and her Caldecott-winning picture book, *Owl Moon.* Two of her short stories have won Nebula Awards, and she has been voted both a Grand Master of Fantasy and a Grand Master of Science Fiction/Fantasy Poetry. Six colleges and universities have given her honorary doctorates.

RECOMMENDED READING

Fiction

The Somnambulist, Jonathan Barnes

Homunculus, James P. Blaylock

The Digging Leviathan, James P. Blaylock

A Great and Terrible Beauty, Libba Bray

Freedom and Necessity, Steven Brust and Emma Bull

Possession, A. S. Byatt

The Children's Book (Edwardian era), A. S. Byatt

Soulless, Gail Carriger

City of Bones, Cassandra Clare

Jonathan Strange & Mr Norrell, Susanna Clarke

The Ladies of Grace Adieu, Susanna Clarke

The Steampunk Trilogy, Paul Di Fillipo

Bewitching Season, Marissa Doyle

The Difference Engine, William Gibson and Bruce Sterling

In the Forest of Forgetting, Theodora Goss

Mortal Love, Elizabeth Hand

The Strangely Beautiful Tale of Miss Percy Parker, Leanna Renee Hieber

The Court of the Air, Stephen Hunt

Infernal Devices, K. W. Jeter

Under the Poppy, Kathe Koja

Mainspring, Jay Lake

The Light Ages, Ian R. MacLeod

Lost, Gregory Maguire
Anno Dracula, Kim Newman
Airborn, Kenneth Oppel
Boneshaker, Cherie Priest
The Prestige, Christopher Priest
The Golden Compass, Philip Pullman
The Ruby in Smoke, Philip Pullman
Larklight, Philip Reeve
The Death Collector, Justin Richards
The Alchemy of Stone, Ekaterina Sedia
Drood, Dan Simmons
The Hunchback Assignments, Arthur Slade
The Werewolves of London, Brian Stableford
The Diamond Age, Neal Stephenson
The Amulet of Samarkand, Jonathan Stroud
The Iron Dragon's Daughter, Michael Swanwick
Photographing Fairies, Steve Szilagyi
The Bookman, Lavie Tidhar
Tooth and Claw, Jo Walton
Leviathan, Scott Westerfeld
The Haunting of Aizebel Cray, Chris Wooding
Mairelon the Magician, Patricia C. Wrede
Sorcery & Cecelia, Patricia C. Wrede and Caroline Stevermer

Graphic Novels and Art Books

Lady Cottington's Fairy Album, Brian and Wendy Froud
Stardust, Neil Gaiman and Charles Vess
Victorian Fairy Painting, Jeremy Maas
The League of Extraordinary Gentlemen, Alan Moore and Kevin O'Neill
Fairies in Victorian Painting, Christopher Wood
The Pre-Raphaelites, Christopher Wood

Nonfiction

Forbidden Journeys, Nina Auerbach and U. C. Knoepflmacher
The Burning of Bridget Cleary, Angela Bourke
Secret Gardens, Humphrey Carpenter
Beyond the Looking Glass, Jonathan Cott
The Victorian Fairy Tale Book, Michael Patrick Hearn

Breaking the Angelic Image, Edith Lazaros Honig
Don't Tell the Grown-Ups, Alison Lurie
Victorian Fantasy, Stephen Prickett
Strange and Secret Peoples, Carole G. Silver
Victorian Fairy Tales, Jack Zipes

ABOUT THE EDITORS

Ellen Datlow has been editing science fiction, fantasy, and horror short fiction for over thirty years. She was fiction editor of *OMNI* magazine and *SciFiction* and has edited more than fifty anthologies, including the annual *The Best Horror of the Year; Darkness: Two Decades of Modern Horror; Naked City: Tales of Urban Fantasy; Blood and Other Cravings; Teeth: Vampire Tales;* and *After: Nineteen Stories of Apocalypse and Dystopia* (the latter two young-adult anthologies with Terri Windling).

She's has won nine World Fantasy Awards and has also won multiple Locus Awards, Hugo Awards, Stoker Awards, International Horror Guild Awards, and the Shirley Jackson Award for her editing. She was named recipient of the 2007 Karl Edward Wagner Award, given at the British Fantasy Convention, for "outstanding contribution to the genre." She has also been honored with the Life Achievement Award given by the Horror Writers Association, in acknowledgment of superior achievement over an entire career.

She lives in New York. More information can be found at www.dat low.com or at her blog: https://www.facebook.com/EllenDatlow. She tweets at https://twitter.com/#!/ellendatlow.

Terri Windling is a writer, editor, and artist specializing in fantasy literature and mythic arts. She is also a Jane Austen addict, a passionate

Victorianist, a lover of all things Pre-Raphaelite, and is thrilled to be working on a book that combines all of these interests within one volume. She has published over thirty previous anthologies (many of them coedited with Ellen Datlow), as well as works of mythic fiction including *The Wood Wife* (for adult readers) and the "Old Oak Wood" series (for children). She has won nine World Fantasy Awards, the Mythopoeic Award, the Bram Stoker Award, and placed on the short list for the Tiptree Award. In 2010, she received the SFWA Solstice Award for "outstanding contributions to the speculative fiction field as a writer, editor, artist, educator, and mentor." A former New Yorker, she now lives in Devon, England, with her husband, daughter, and a bouncy black dog named Tilly. You can find her on the Web at www.terriwindling.com.